THE FORGE OF BONDS

By Wendy Terrien

The Adventures of Jason Lex Series
Chronicle One
THE RAMPART GUARDS

Chronicle Two - Jason
THE LEAGUE OF GOVERNORS

Chronicle Two - Sadie
THE CLAN CALLING

Chronicle Three
THE FORGE OF BONDS

"The Fate Stone"
A short story originally published in the anthology
TICK TOCK: SEVEN TALES OF TIME

"Light"
A short story originally published in the anthology
OFF BEAT: NINE SPINS ON SONG

THE FORGE OF BONDS

CHRONICLE THREE
IN THE ADVENTURES OF JASON LEX

A NOVEL BY

WENDY TERRIEN

CAMASHEA
PRESS

CAMASHEA PRESS | DENVER, CO

THE FORGE OF BONDS
Chronicle Three in the Adventures of Jason Lex
Copyright © 2020 Wendy Terrien

Published by Camashea Press.
All rights reserved. All logos are owned by Camashea Press.

First printing, February 2020.

Hardcover ISBN: 978-0-9983369-4-7
Paperback ISBN: 978-0-9983369-5-4
Ebook ISBN: 978-0-9983369-6-1

Camashea Press
PO Box 631444
Littleton, CO 80163

Library of Congress Control Number: 2019913273
Printed in the United States of America

For Lisa
Who is the best parts of princess and warrior
united in one wonderful, powerful,
unstoppable woman

ONE

Together

Jason veered to his right, pinballing Colette into Sadie, and Sadie into another freshman walking down the hall of Salton High.

"Sorry," Sadie and Colette said simultaneously, Colette to Sadie, and Sadie to the student she'd knocked into the lockers.

Sadie turned to Jason as they continued along the corridor. "Skyfish?"

"Yeah."

"Ratty or regular?" Colette asked.

"Ratty?" Jason didn't always understand Colette's British English.

"Cranky or not cranky?" Colette clarified.

"Not, eh, ratty," he said. "This one was just passing through."

"Seriously," Sadie said. "Please stop dodging them. That's the third time in two days you've swerved into us. Just let them fly through you like the rest of us have to."

1

She opened the door to the cafeteria. Jason and Colette followed.

"But it's weird." Jason *thunked* his bag on a table in a mostly empty section of the lunchroom. "Obviously it doesn't feel like anything, but knowing something is inside of you, even for a second, is just weird. You're lucky you don't see them."

Colette halted mid-reach into her backpack, her injured arm no longer in a sling. "How often does this . . . do they . . . fly through us?"

"Not often," Jason said. "But there have been more Skyfish around here than usual. And have I mentioned how dumb it is we're even at school?" He set down his water bottle. "With New Year's Day on Wednesday they should have just given us the rest of this week off. Making us come to school for two days is stupid."

"Totally." Sadie smoothed a paper towel on the table in front of her, her silver charm bracelet tinkling.

Jason cocked his head. "You agree with me?" Sadie had always been a fan of going to school.

"Yes, I agree with you," she said. "Being in school this week has not been productive. Even the teachers act like they don't want to be here. But it's nice to see everyone."

The holidays had been hard for Sadie since losing her grandmother, Mamo, only a few months earlier. After Jason lost his mom, school had helped make things seem less painful, less in-his-face sad, less swallowed by misery. At least for a little while.

"It's nice to see *certain* people. If I never had to see Derek Goodman's face again, I'd be one hundred percent good with that." He stared at the back of Derek's head five tables away. "At least he's minding his own business and not in full-on-bully-mode."

"I doubt it will last," Sadie said. "He'll accuse me of casting an evil spell on him as soon as he has an upset stomach or something."

"Is he truly that bad?" Colette asked.

Jason's mouth gaped.

"Okay, dumb question," she said. "Carry on." She took a bite of an apple.

"As for your powers, the real ones anyway," Jason said to Sadie, "how's it going figuring out Yowie life and the powers coming from the Calling?"

"I'm reading a lot," she said, fingering the hawk's eye pendant from Mamo that always hung around her neck. "I'm studying the history of the Clan and learning about Garrison Devine."

"I guess that's good, learning about the guy who wants you dead," Jason said. "Uncle A goes on and on about knowing the enemy as well as you know yourself." He took a drink of water. "But what about being able to sense Yowie energy. Can you do that yet? And shapeshifting—have you tried anything besides your Yowie form? I think it would be cool for you to go all cheetah, and we could clock your speed."

Sadie opened a package of carrot sticks. "Yowie sensing ability hasn't shown up. And no, I haven't done any shapeshifting. Connor wants me to take things slow." She kept her gaze fixed at her veggies.

"Wait—your great-uncle, the only other Yowie you know, the same person who you said was practically begging you to accept the Calling, and the one person who can prepare you for a guy that wants to kill you and everyone related to you, wants you to take things slow?" Jason asked.

"I thought there was a sense of urgency," Colette said, "lest your nemesis finds you before you're prepared."

Jason smiled at Colette's use of words that made her seem older than fourteen, a side-effect of growing up under the old rules at League of Governors headquarters.

"What?" she asked Jason.

"Nothing. You're right." He turned back to Sadie. "You need to up your game. At least come do training with me at Uncle A's."

"I have Tae Kwon Do classes with Brandon."

"He just started. He's five belt levels behind you."

"So?"

"So, I don't think he's the best person to train with, not for you, anyway," Jason said. "It's great for him—he can learn tons from you. But you won't get any better."

"It helps maintain my fitness." She crunched a carrot.

Jason leaned forward. "Sadie, you can't waste time. I've been thinking about it, and I'm worried about you. When I got my powers—"

"Stop," Sadie said. "You don't need to worry about me. The cloak from the Calling is working, so no one can find me, or Connor, or Brandon, or you guys, or Shay and Finn, or any of us. We're all safe. We have plenty of time. I have everything under control."

"What about the invisibility?" Jason asked. "Is that under control?"

Sadie shifted her gaze and waved at someone behind him. "Nix the cryptid talk. Here comes Nessa."

"Best friends!" Nessa squeezed into a space between Sadie and Colette and pulled them both close until her cheeks smushed into each of theirs. "I love you adorable people." She released them and smiled at Jason. "I adore you too, especially since you brought this lovey back from England." She tipped her head toward Colette. "And you two are the cutest couple in school."

Jason gulped from his water bottle to cool the flush in his face.

"Though you know, if Brandon went to school in real life instead of online then Jolette would be second cutest," Nessa inclined her head toward Sadie, "and Sandon would be first cutest."

"Who?" Sadie added.

Nessa turned to Sadie. "You don't like Sandon as your couple name? How about Bradie instead?" She squealed. "Oh! Epiphany! You and Brandon should name your first kid Bradie. Naming perfection. Works for a boy or a girl. No way you disagree with me."

Sadie rolled her eyes. "You are getting waaaaaayyyy ahead of yourself."

"Or . . ." Nessa touched the tips of her thumbs to the tips of her pointer fingers and held them high. "I see the future." She smiled and dropped the pose. "Since Brandon is staying in our dear little town a while longer while his parents are off on their project thingy, is he going to join us at real-life Salton High?"

"I don't think so," Sadie said. "He doesn't want to switch in the middle of the year, and he likes his teach—"

Nessa smacked Sadie's knee. "Shh, shh." Her eyes focused on something across the room. "I think he's coming over here, oh my gosh, oh my gosh." Her voice faded to a whisper, and she tucked her hair behind her ears.

Kyle sat down next to Jason.

"You lost?" Jason asked.

"Shut up." Kyle light-punched Jason in the arm. "I feel like sitting here."

"Won't it drop your cool factor if you have lunch with your kid brother?" Jason smirked.

"What can I say? I missed you while you were away."

"I've been back for over two months." Jason bit into a sandwich. "What's really going on?"

"I just, ya' know, want to spend more time with you," Kyle looked across the table at Sadie, Colette, and Nessa. "All of you. It's like . . . a new year's resolution."

A half-smile ticked up the corner of Sadie's mouth. She'd told Jason about what Kyle did while Jason was in London, how much Kyle had stepped up and helped her with everything that happened with Mamo and the Calling, almost like a big brother. But Kyle didn't seem all that different or more helpful to Jason since he'd gotten back. To him, Kyle still acted like he was cooler than everyone. Until now.

Kyle turned to Sadie. "How's school going? Have you caught up?"

"Yeah, I did extra work over the break. Nessa is a great tutor."

"Oh, I just, ya' know, helped a little."

"That's cool," Kyle said to Nessa. "I know you helped Jason catch up after his little jaunt to London, too. If I ever need help in any of my classes, maybe I'll call you."

"That means he'll call you a lot," Jason said. "He needs help with everything."

Kyle grinned and punched Jason in the arm again. "Not everything. I get As in PE."

"Right, of course you do." Nessa giggled. "You could tutor me in physical education." The smile dropped from her face. "Uh, I mean, not like that. I mean, like in regular . . . uh . . ." She looked at her phone. "Oh my gosh I have to go." Nessa scooped up her lunch and scurried away.

"Call me later," Sadie yelled after her. Nessa waved her hand in the air with her back still to the group.

"Is she okay?" Kyle asked.

"She's fine," Sadie said. "She's just getting back into the school swing of things after the holidays."

"I get that." Kyle stretched and yawned. "I much prefer the no-school swing of things."

Jason ducked as two Skyfish zoomed overhead. No one else flinched.

"Skyfish again?" Sadie asked.

"Yeah," Jason said. "Have you noticed anything else weird happening?"

Sadie checked the apps on her phone she used to track all things cryptid. "Nothing unusual online."

"Good," Jason said. "I hope it stays that way. I like how calm it's been around here, with no Rampart attacks, no mind-controlled League-bots."

"And no Clan," Sadie said.

"Definitely," Kyle added. "We don't need any more Clan or Calling or bounty hunting for a long time."

"Or ever." Sadie sighed.

Between what had happened in London, the news and sadness he'd come back to in Salton, and the fact that Sadie wasn't focused on training, Jason didn't think anyone was ready to tackle anything freakish or abnormal right now.

Sadie needed time to adjust, to mourn, to connect with her great-uncle Connor. Colette needed time to figure out her new life in the United States, living with Sadie and Grandma Lena.

And Jason needed more time to rest, to recover, to train. And adapt to living with a new secret about his younger sister, Della.

He rubbed his fingers on the embossed surface of the Lex coin he now always carried his pocket.

They all needed a little more time.

✳ ✳ ✳

After school, Jason walked into the front door of his house. Shay, his almost-full-grown pit bull-mix puppy, zoomed her white-bullet-body toward him.

"No jumping." Jason used his serious voice. The pup skidded to a stop. "Sit." She dropped her haunches to the floor, her tongue lolling, her tail wagging.

"Good job." He dropped to Shay's level and scratched her behind the ears. She licked his cheek and pressed the top of her head into his neck, snuggling close.

"How about we get a snack, then go hang out with Finn and Uncle A?"

Shay's ears perked and she dashed off, heading to the kitchen. Jason followed.

Brandon sat at the kitchen table, his head face down on his folded arms, his laptop open in front of him. Jason bumped him with his backpack.

"I'm awake." Brandon startled to upright.

"Your day at school must have been as entertaining as mine." Jason hung his bag in the mudroom.

"Non-stop fun ride." Brandon shut his computer. "At least it's Friday. You going to train?"

"Yeah—wanna come?"

"Not this time. I'm going with Sadie to visit Connor." Brandon yawned. "And I gotta say, it's still weird calling him by his first name, even though he told us to."

"I know what you mean," Jason said.

"Anyway, Connor has info on her problem, or power, or whatever it ends up being."

Jason opened the refrigerator and scanned the contents. "The invisibility thing?"

"Yep. He says he's learned how she can control it before it gets too out of hand, which is good. You know how bugged she's been about it."

Jason removed a block of cheddar cheese. "Can't blame her. I'd be bugged too if random parts of my body turned invisible while I slept."

"Right?" Brandon stretched. "By the way, Della is staying at a friend's house tonight and your dad's out. Said he'd be back later, and we should do our own thing for dinner."

"Okay." For a moment, Jason considered biting into the block of cheese rather than bother with a knife but decided the wrath of Dad wasn't worth the convenience. He cut off a chunk for himself and tossed a smaller piece to Shay. She gulped it down whole.

"Please chew your food. I really don't want to do the Heimlich on you."

"Since you're serving, I'll take some," Brandon said. "And I promise to chew it before I swallow."

Jason chucked what remained of the cheese and Brandon snatched it out of the air. "Do you want the knife?" Jason asked.

"Nah." Brandon took a big bite.

"You know that's gross, right?" Jason filled a glass with water.

Brandon signaled thumbs-up while he chewed and then smacked his tongue over his top teeth. "Are you picking up Colette on your way to Uncle A's? I'll walk to their house with you."

"No, I'm going straight to his place."

"Colette's meeting you there?" Brandon asked.

"I don't think so." Jason drained the glass of water.

"You didn't talk to her about going with you?"

"No. I mean I just saw her at school. And we hung out over break," Jason said. "I don't want to push it."

Brandon's face scrunched. "Whatever."

"Whatever what?"

"I don't know," Brandon said. "You like her, she likes you, seems like you spend time together. I mean, I thought you were dating, but whatever."

"We are dating. Seriously. And we have spent time together. You were there. We all spent time together."

"And this afternoon you're not spending time together," Brandon said, "because . . ."

"Because we already did." Jason punched his glass into the trigger to dispense more filtered water.

Brandon stood. "Colette has a limit on how much time she'll spend with you?"

"No. I don't know." Jason blew out a breath. "Why are you asking me these questions?"

"Forget it." Brandon headed out of the kitchen. "I just figure you like a person, you spend time with them. That's all." He waved. "I'll catch you later."

Jason drained his second glass of water, Brandon's words replaying in his head.

✳ ✳ ✳

After Brandon had gone to meet Sadie, Jason pulled on his coat, clipped a leash onto Shay's harness and they headed out into the dwindling light of the wintry afternoon. Three times Skyfish zipped close and Jason dodged each one. Shay paid no attention to them.

Sadie's right. I need to ignore them, or they will drive me crazy.

He paused, refocused on his route, and asked Shay to heel.

They took the shorter path to Uncle A's house, traveling along the canal past thickets of chokecherry bushes and scrub oak, near the hidden cove where Jason and Sadie had first met, and where Jason had first encountered Skyfish.

As if triggered by the memory, a tingle crawled around the base of his skull. He scanned the sky but noticed nothing.

Shay froze and growled, her gaze fixed on a thick clutch of bramble on the other side of the canal.

Twigs snapped.

A shadow shifted.

"Who's in there?" Jason asked. He flexed his fist. Bolts of electricity zipped inside him.

Nothing moved.

Shay pulled to get closer to the bushes. Jason held firm. Steam pumped from Shay's nostrils as she sniffed and cleared her sinuses, scenting what seemed to be hidden in the waning light of day.

He tightened his grip on her leash. "Hey," Jason yelled, trying to trigger a reveal. Still, nothing moved. Shay sat but remained trained on the spot. He waited another moment, his senses still triggering, but saw nothing and presumed more Skyfish had caused the alarm. He called to Shay to continue along the path.

Seconds later, something crashed through the brush on the far bank behind them. Jason's powers flared his arms blue and he pivoted, Shay yanking him toward the sound. A brown figure, seemingly on all fours, barreled into the canal, and cannonballed water in its wake. It scrambled up the bank and stopped about forty feet away, facing Jason and Shay, fixated for a moment while water dripped from its fur.

Sparks flashed from Jason's raised arm.

The creature stepped closer.

His powers flared. *Don't do it . . . don't make me do it . . .*

Shay yipped and strained on her lead.

The creature sniffed the air once, twice, water gurgling in its nostrils, then turned and scrambled away.

Shay tugged to take chase. Jason countered her momentum with his and lowered his arm.

If that was a dog, it was the biggest, shaggiest dog I've ever seen . . .

Before using his power, he had to be sure a creature, a cryptid, was dangerous. He couldn't let himself hurt something or someone when they didn't deserve it, when they didn't mean it.

Farther down the path, the figure faded from sight.

Jason's arms still glowed a fiery blue.

TWO

Invisibilis

Ding-dong.

A flutter flit through Sadie. Even though she'd been hanging out with Brandon for a few months, and even after everything they'd been through together, seeing him still triggered a tiny tizzy of nerves.

She opened the door. "Hey."

"Hey." Brandon stepped inside and gave Sadie a hug. "Happy Friday. Ready to head to Connor's?"

"Yep. Let me just say goodbye to Lena and Colette."

Sadie and Brandon walked into the living room where Lena Fallon, Jason's grandmother, sat reading a book, a steaming cup of creamy tea sitting on a side table next to her. She removed her reading glasses and stood.

"It's always so nice to see you, Brandon." She hugged him. "Is it good to be back to school, virtual though it is?"

"Virtual or not, it's still school," he said.

"Very true," Lena said, "And how are you feeling now that your parents have returned to their travels?"

Brandon shrugged. "It was nice to see them over the holidays, but it's also nice that they're off doing their thing and I'm here doing mine." He shoved his hands in his pockets.

Lena nodded. "Did they say when they might visit again?"

"*Nada*. Just depends on the 'demands of the dig,' as they like to call it. But I'm good with extending my time in Salton while they're gone," he said. "It's fun staying at Jason's house, and hanging with you all."

"Your parents believe being settled in Salton is better for you, too. And we love having you here in town with us. I know Sadie agrees."

Warmth flushed Sadie's face. "Okay . . . we're going to Connor's for a while to talk about the not-joys of random invisibility." Sadie kissed Lena's cheek. "I'll be back for dinner."

"Invite Connor to dinner, too, would you?" Lena sat back down in her chair. "He eats nothing but microwaved food when left to his own devices."

"Sure," Sadie said.

"And one more thing." Lena reached for a stack of paper and a booklet. "Take these to him, please. It's the paperwork for the new furnace I just had installed over there. I doubt Connor will need it, but he should have it handy just in case. Far be it from me to leave my renter unprepared."

Sadie took the documents. "No problem."

"Thank you." Lena turned to Brandon "And you have a standing dinner invitation if you'd like to join us."

"Like I'd turn down that offer," he said. "I'm in. Thanks."

"Where's Colette?" Sadie asked.

"Upstairs in her room." Lena opened her book and set aside her bookmark. "She's got something on her mind."

"Is she okay? Should I go talk to her?" Colette had moved into Sadie's home the same time Lena did, just after Mamo died. Sadie had connected with Colette as if they were long-lost sisters.

"I think she's fine, but I'll ask her about it later. You two go have fun." Lena put on her reading glasses.

"We will." Sadie's phone pinged and she stopped to check the message. "Snow's coming. I should double-check the insulation on the beehives. Okay with you if we do that before going to Connor's?" she asked Brandon.

"Sure thing," Brandon said. "I dig the beehives."

They went out to the backyard, examined each of the hives to ensure the winter insulation was in place and secure, then headed to Connor's.

Brandon took Sadie's hand in his as they walked down the street. He lifted her arm.

"What?" she asked as he studied their joined hands.

"Just seeing if you're all here."

"Hilarious." She pretended to yank her hand out of his. Brandon held tight.

"I still think the invisibility is just Calling stuff," he said. "More of your super-duper powers coming in."

"Probably, but it would be nice to have control over it. Turning invisible while I'm walking around school could be a problem."

"Derek would love that," Brandon said.

"Oh my gosh, he'd call for the town to burn me at the stake. He couldn't even handle me healing his hand."

"Except that," Brandon held up his index finger, "one, no one would listen to him since lying is one of his things. And two, no one in town could ever find you."

"Another upside of invisibility," Sadie said. "Easy to avoid angry mobs."

A couple of minutes later they walked up the path to Connor's home.

Sadie opened the front door and poked her head inside. "Connor?"

"In the kitchen."

Sadie and Brandon stepped into the foyer, the dry scent of dust mingling with the cool fresh air that followed them in. They passed the living room where laundry covered the couch, some of it piled, some of it folded, none of it neat. A plate sat on the coffee table, ketchup crusting its edges, and a crumpled napkin anchoring the center. They continued into the kitchen.

Connor smoothed his white hair while stuffing dishes into the dishwasher. One bowl *popped* as he unstuck it from the countertop. He rinsed the bowl, rinsed his hands, and dried them on a kitchen towel with scorch marks on its trim.

"Sadie, my dear." Connor hugged her. "I'm delighted you were both able to come by. Alexander and I had a eureka moment regarding the invisibility."

"So, invisibility is for sure a power I'm getting?" Sadie asked.

Connor and Brandon gave her a look like the question confused them.

"Well, of course it is, my dear," Connor said. "You didn't think you were fading away, did you?"

"Maybe?"

"Seriously?" Brandon asked.

"Your grandmother...she..." Connor sputtered. He looked heavenward. "Willy, I blame you for wild thoughts like this from my great-niece. No doubt you're responsible for encouraging her to be more...more...creative in her thinking than she need be."

Sadie chuckled. "Don't blame Mamo. I came up with the idea all on my own." A calm soothed her as she realized she'd smiled at Mamo's memory rather than feeling only a hard clutch on her heart, a first in the dark months since Mamo died.

"I know this is all still new to you, Sadie—the Clan, the Calling, what's coming . . ." Connor cleared his throat. "But you must know you're well-protected in Salton, cloaked from Garrison Devine until you're ready. And the powers that come from the Calling will never harm you, only help you."

"I understand that," she said. "I told Jason the same thing today. But I could still, poof," she magicianed her hands in the air, "turn invisible when I least expect it and scare the crap out of people."

Connor dismissed the comment with a wave. "That would never happen."

She crossed her arms. "I shifted into Yowie when I didn't expect it."

It was a day Sadie would never forget. The day they'd stopped Merinda. The day Sadie had shifted to Yowie without even realizing. And the day everyone there—Connor, Brandon, Lena, and Kyle—had seen Sadie naked after she shifted back, her clothes shredded on the floor. A small sliver of embarrassment wriggled through her memory.

"That doesn't count," Connor said. "The power was brand new."

"Yeah, but—"

"Okay, okay." Brandon waved. "Right now, how about we go with 'Calling powers good,' yes?" He looked at Sadie. "I mean, you've been dealing with the invisibility thing for a couple of months now and haven't gone poof, so that's a good sign, isn't it?"

"Yes," Sadie said, nodding.

Brandon turned to Connor. "And you have something to tell us that makes the invisibility thing even better, I bet. Right?"

"I do."

"Great," Brandon said. "Should we sit?" He gestured to the kitchen table. It was covered with a spray of old newspapers, some imprinted with moisture rings from glasses and cups no longer there.

"Uh, yes, let me just . . ." Connor scooped the papers and tossed them in a disorderly pile near the back door. "I'll take those out to the recycling bin later. Have a seat." He scurried over to the sink.

Sadie and Brandon sat. Connor picked up a dishrag, soaked it under the faucet and wiped off the table. Mildew and sour scents from the rag weaseled into Sadie's nose. She forced her expression to stay neutral.

Brandon did not. "Ugh, Connor, you need to wash that thing."

"The dishrag?" He lifted it to his nose then jerked it away. "Oh. Right. That is horrible." He tossed the wet rag on top of the old newspapers. Ink blurred around the edges of the fabric.

Connor brought his laptop to the table and sat between Sadie and Brandon. He unlocked the screen.

"There is some history in our family regarding the power of invisibility, but it hasn't manifested for many generations, so our understanding diluted over the years." He clicked on a file. "But no more. In fact, our little research project has delivered a boon of information."

On the screen in front of them was the image of what seemed to be an ancient document, its script fancy and flourished, the paper caramelized like parchment. The title read: "The Calling Compendium."

A buzz shivered from Sadie's scalp to her toes. "How old is this?"

"We believe it was written about five hundred years ago." Connor scrolled down the screen, zipping past sections of ornate script until he came to the word he was looking for: *Invisibilis*. He pointed to the header. "That little word right there added to the challenge of finding what we needed. We were looking for English. Whoever wrote this used Latin. Tricky bas—, uh, scribes. Tricky scribes."

Sadie smiled.

Brandon leaned forward. "Is all of it written in Latin?" He squinted.

"Only the headers. The rest is English but in fancy writing and fancy words and, well, archaic words, some I even had to look up in the dictionary. And all of which make the document difficult to read." Connor opened a second file. "Thankfully, Alexander transcribed it for us into good ol' Times New Roman." He scooted back while Sadie and Brandon both moved closer to read what was on the screen.

Connor's phone buzzed.

Sadie glanced at the phone's screen and saw "report from HQ" before Connor snatched it up.

"Speak of the devil," Connor said. "I have a text from Alexander. Let me address this."

Sadie returned her gaze to the computer and scanned the page for anything seeming to describe how to start invisibility or stop invisibility or even make it all go away. But she didn't get far, frustrated by the language. "At least *invisibilis* is a word I could guess has to do with invisibility," Sadie said. "But check out the next header." She pointed farther down the screen where it said: "*Periculum ad Candidatum.*"

"Wow," Brandon said. "Sounds like an infection or something."

"I know, right?"

After a quick stint of typing on his phone, Connor returned to the conversation. "All right, how about I spare you more reading and give you the abridged version of our helpful discovery?"

"Please yes," Sadie said. "But first, do you know what '*Periculum ad Candidatum*' means?"

"Ah, well, yes," Connor said, "and it's definitely something you don't want to experience. The header translates to 'risk to the candidate' and goes on to describe how, if the Calling's candidate is in some sort of peril, the powers not yet manifested will be rushed to the candidate in a kind of emergency onslaught. And it's supposed to be quite painful."

"Oh." Sadie stared at the Latin words.

"But that won't happen to Sadie," Brandon stated.

"It will not," Connor said. "Sadie is safe under the cloak while her powers manifest. No peril here." He stood and leaned against the counter. "So, let's focus on the priority at hand—invisibility. Once fully manifested, at a minimum you'll have total control over the ability to become invisible. And once mastered, it's easy to trigger— you still your mind, focus and—what was the word you used? Poof. You just focus and poof."

Sadie suspected it wasn't as simple as that.

"Why am I disappearing parts of my body while I sleep?" Sadie asked. "I'm not focused then."

"I suspect some subconscious part of you is aware of the power coming in, or maybe you read something or watched something that mentioned invisibility," Connor said. "And once the invisibility happened to you that first time, there's no doubt you've had invisibility thoughts on the brain."

"Makes sense," Brandon said.

Connor continued. "And after you wake up and see part of yourself gone, you get pretty focused on not being invisible and everything returns to normal. Yes?"

"Yes." Sadie took a deep breath. "Do we know how long until this power is all in? I don't want to mess up and get stuck in invisible-land by accident." Sadie had learned that Yowie who shapeshift can sometimes get stuck in the form they shifted to and worried the same thing could happen with invisibility.

"It takes a lot of energy to sustain invisibility," Connor said. "Alexander and I don't believe it's possible to keep it going for long, so consequently you couldn't get stuck that way. Your body would run out of invisible-juice and you'd reappear."

"That's a relief." A tightness in Sadie's upper body eased. "For now, let's train so I'm able to restore myself if it

21

happens in public. I can work with the full power after it comes in. Which is hopefully in the spring or summer since there's the whole freezing aspect to consider. Nessa was right about that part."

"Freezing?" Brandon asked.

"A while back, Nessa and I were talking about powers we'd wish for—it was after Derek started calling me a witch."

Brandon nodded.

"Anyway, during that conversation, she said she'd like invisibility except for the fact that you'd always be cold because you couldn't wear clothes since the clothes wouldn't be invisible."

"That may not necessarily be a problem." Connor walked over to the computer and scrolled further down the document. "See this section here?" He tapped the screen. "This states there are varying degrees of invisibility power."

"Meaning . . . I could make both me and my clothes invisible?"

"Potentially, yes," Connor said. "You could make yourself, your clothes, maybe even nearby objects and people invisible. But it's a rare level of skill in those who have this power."

Brandon's hand shot up. "I call dibs. Make me invisible. I volunteer."

Connor chuckled. "She has to master the power over herself first. And there's no information about how long it will take for the power to be fully realized, especially for someone of her age." He flicked a stray piece of lint off his shirt. "In the records we've reviewed, no one as young as Sadie has ever begun manifesting this power."

"Not surprised," Brandon said. "She's an overachiever."

"Agreed." Connor looked at Sadie. "But there's no reason we shouldn't start practice sessions for this and other potential powers. It can't hurt, and the more you know ahead of time, the better."

"I haven't finished reading all the documents you sent me," Sadie said. "Which reminds me, one of the interesting things I read said Garrison Devine is a descendant of one of the most famous criminal families in Australian history."

"What, like, famous assassins or something?" Brandon asked.

"No, but they ran a crime organization like the mob."

"When was this? Are they still around?" Brandon unlocked his phone. "I can look it up."

"Ahem. As fascinating as this is," Connor said, "we should get back to the topic at hand." He looked at Sadie. "You don't have to first finish reading everything I gave you. This isn't a one-two-three type of process. This is more of a let's-get-you-ready-as-fast-as-we-can process."

"But you just said she's protected," Brandon said.

"She is," Connor said. "And I have great confidence she will continue to be protected. But that is no reason to delay training."

"I'm not delaying it," Sadie said. "I'm just being . . . methodical. It's how I learn best. Methodically."

"I appreciate that my dear, I do. But there is no established method for preparing you for what's coming other than practice."

"But I'm learning everything I can about Devine."

"That's not even half the battle, and I think you know that," Connor said. "Consider your Tae Kwon Do training—

did you learn the full history of Tae Kwon Do before practicing your first stance or kick or punch?"

"No . . ."

"And yet you've excelled at Tae Kwon Do. Would you be more accomplished if you'd read documents and history before beginning your training?"

"That's different," Sadie said.

"Is it?" Connor asked.

"I need to know what I'm up against."

"On that point, we agree." Connor sighed. "And we already know what you're up against. There are things hap—" He shut his mouth and paused. "After we lost your grandmother, we all needed time to heal, to grieve, and we took some time to be still with that process. And I know we're all still shaken by her loss, you most of all. But Sadie, you need to focus, to prepare."

"I know," Sadie said. "It's just . . ."

"If you're worried about having enough time for this stuff," Brandon said to Sadie, "and school or whatever, I can help. I'll train with you, and we can study together—I'll do whatever I can."

Sadie didn't want to do more training. She wanted to do less. But at the moment she didn't see a way to make that happen.

"Fine, I'll practice with the powers I already have, but that's it. I'm not messing with any halfway power like invisibility until it's ready. It's too risky."

Connor shook his head. "But it's not—"

"No." Sadie crossed her arms. "Healing power and shifting to Yowie. That's it."

"And memory wipes," Brandon added.

Sadie huffed. "I'm not wiping anyone's memory just for fun. So how will I practice that one?"

"Memory wipes are one skill we may have to work with more in theory than practice," Connor said. "But I'll see what I can come up with."

"Sounds like more reading," Sadie said. "I knew reading was good."

"Regardless, I'm glad you're willing to start some hands-on work. In fact, I also want you to spend more time trying to tune into Yowie energy. I know you're not able to sense it yet but keep practicing. If you don't mind, we'll dive in with a short session on that and the other skills right now." Connor clasped his hands. "Then I better get you home since I presume Lena is expecting you for dinner."

Sadie considered everything coming at her, like an asteroid targeting Salton. She wished with all her might that the asteroid was light-years away.

"Yeah, okay, let's do some training now," she said. "Then dinner. And you're joining us. Lena said so. If you want to."

"Ah, well, I guess I can pull myself away from frozen burritos for one night." Connor shut the laptop. "Let's get practicing so dinnertime comes that much sooner."

✳ ✳ ✳

Sadie lay in bed mulling over the conversation with Connor and the powers she had. She healed easily and was able to heal others, and what had started as an unexpected ability to accidentally make people fall asleep had morphed into the skill of being able to wipe memories. She didn't understand how she would master that one and hoped she'd never have to use it.

She could shift into Yowie form. She'd done that once already even though it was a creature she'd been afraid of becoming. But her parents had been Yowie, and Mamo, and great-uncle Connor, too. She felt connected to them through being Yowie, even if it meant a fight in the future. She shoved aside thoughts of the battle to come with Garrison Devine and those loyal to him.

Sadie hadn't been able to cue any invisibility during her first practice session with Connor. But he was confident the power would become manageable.

She glanced at her computer, wishing she had more time and more interest in coding and hacking like she did before the Calling, before losing Mamo. Sadie touched her fingers to the hawk's eye pendant, a gift from Mamo meant to balance the powers of the Calling as they came to her so she wouldn't be overwhelmed. She wished for the hawk's eye to slow everything down, to help keep the cloak in place, to make sure it protected everyone from her Clan's most powerful Yowie, Devine, who wanted her and her family dead to ensure his place in power.

The words *"Periculum ad Candidatum"* floated through her mind.

She needed the cloak to stay locked in place.

Sadie held up her hand, took a deep breath in through her nose, and out through her mouth. She zeroed in on her pinky finger and closed her eyes. She relaxed, she focused, she asked for her pinky finger to disappear.

Sadie opened her eyes.

Her pinky finger was invisible.

THREE
A New Threat

"Uncle A?" Jason took off his boots and hung his jacket on a coat tree by the door.

"Here," Uncle Alexander said, walking into the living room from the kitchen with Finn.

Jason unclipped Shay's leash and removed her harness. She bolted, chased, and tumbled into Finn, Uncle Alexander's muscled pit bull mix. The dogs wrestled and growled, mouthing each other's limbs, their white bodies blurring into a tangled blob.

"Careful. Watch the—" Uncle Alexander snatched up a glass he'd set on the coffee table seconds before the dogs pitched into it. "Points to me for that save."

"Totally," Jason said. "I'll let them run around in the backyard for a few minutes."

"Good idea."

Jason signaled for the dogs to follow him. He opened the back door, flipped on the floodlights, and the dogs rocketed into the yard.

Not wanting to leave them outside too long with their short coats, Jason watched until panting took precedence over chasing, then asked them to come. Three Skyfish passed overhead without attention from either dog. They shook, trotted inside, and collapsed on beds by the living room fireplace.

Jason sat on the couch across from Uncle Alexander.

"Don't get too comfortable." Uncle Alexander stood. "We're heading down to the gym."

"Can I talk to you for a minute first?"

"Of course." Uncle Alexander sat back down and Jason told him about the encounter on the path. His uncle pinched the bridge of his nose. "You're uncertain what you saw?"

"Yeah," Jason said.

"What does your gut tell you?"

Jason's gut didn't waiver. He knew what he saw. It was the same creature he'd seen from his bedroom window the first night back from London. "I don't want to say. What if I'm wrong? I don't want to cause a big issue if there isn't one."

Uncle Alexander cocked his head. "You believe you saw a cryptid?"

Jason nodded.

"Why is that an issue?"

"Because it was a Bigfoot or a . . . a Yowie," Jason said. "And no one needs any more Yowie around here, especially after everything that happened. And what if it's nothing? What if the creature is just passing through?" Jason suspected otherwise.

"Hold on a minute." Uncle Alexander picked up his cell phone and typed in a message. A *whoosh* sounded as he sent the note. A response arrived quickly. "Connor says there is no new Yowie energy in the area." He looked up from the communication. "Are you aware Yowie can sense how many of their kind are nearby? Have we covered that in your training?"

"Sadie told me."

"Okay," Uncle Alexander said. "So, given that there's no new Yowie here, we can count on things being status quo."

"For sure?" Jason asked.

"Yes. The Yowie you saw, or more likely an indigenous Bigfoot, has always lived around here."

"Oh, but no one's ever seen it except me and Shay." The dog thumped her tail at hearing her name then went back to sleep.

Uncle Alexander set down his phone. "Could be an older member of the species, one who has lived remotely for some time. Perhaps it's now coming in closer to town because its hunting skills have diminished."

"So should we all Bigfoot-proof our garbage cans?" Jason flopped into the back cushion of the couch. "Seems like a stretch."

"Did the creature seem hostile?" Uncle Alexander asked.

"Nah. Just stared at us for a few seconds then took off." Jason considered what he knew about Bigfoot and Yowie. There was no distinct physical difference between Bigfoot of North America and the Yowie of Australia. It was behavior that separated them: Bigfoot preferred isolation, living remotely, and minimizing contact with humans. Yowie were more inclined to live closer to human populations, and they didn't shy from conflict with humans if the situation warranted. But they rarely sought it out.

"That's good news. We probably won't notice it close to town again, at least not anytime soon." Uncle Alexander stood. "Regardless, we will keep our eyes peeled and our ears open for any strange sightings or goings-on."

Jason stood to follow Uncle Alexander down to their training room. "And we don't need to tell anyone else about this, right? Since this Bigfoot is part of the status quo like you said, and it's probably already gone and all that?" Jason didn't want Sadie or anyone else to over-analyze and wonder if a Yowie who wanted her dead might be nearby when there was really nothing to worry about.

"As long as nothing too unusual happens, there's no need to inform anyone yet."

"Which reminds me," Jason said. "I wanted to ask if you know why there are more Skyfish around."

"I've noticed their numbers increasing as well." Uncle Alexander closed his eyes and rubbed his temple.

Jason slouched. "You think it means something's up, right?"

"Between the Skyfish sightings and this Bigfoot sighting, it is possible." Uncle Alexander opened his eyes and zeroed in on Jason. "Let's just say we need to be on alert."

Jason's spirits sank, and an always-there burl of unease twined tighter in his mind.

✳ ✳ ✳

"Stop. Enough." Jason hunched and breathed heavily. "I need a break."

"We've only been practicing for thirty minutes," Uncle Alexander said. "And you had two weeks off for the holidays.

We need to learn how that affected your powers, if at all. And we still haven't discovered your new maximum voltage since infusion with the Lex coin."

"Infusion?" Jason wiped his face on a towel.

"I had to call it something. Until we understand exactly how the coin boosted your Guard powers, I'm calling it 'infusion.' It's easy for me to remember." He moved into a fighting stance. "Let's go again. Activate your powers and fire at me. I'll block you with mine."

Jason straightened and tossed the towel aside. Energy built in his spine and arms and legs. Sparking blue light engulfed his body and circled his head.

Uncle Alexander activated his own Guard powers, blue bolts of electricity zipped from his hands.

Jason raised his arms and fired at Uncle Alexander.

Uncle Alexander deflected Jason's attack. "That's it, Jason," he hollered over the electric din. "Now increase your power if you can."

The bolts from Jason's body thickened and cracked. Uncle Alexander shielded his eyes and leaned into the crash of light building between him and Jason.

Jason surged and purple bolts joined blue. White light blinded. He willed his power higher.

Uncle Alexander took two steps back.

Jason ratcheted up his intensity.

Uncle Alexander skittered backward again.

Jason knew he could do more. Knew he could break through his uncle's defense. Knew he could destroy him.

He had the power to kill.

Jason snuffed his energy and ducked, evading a bolt from Uncle Alexander. He bent and gasped for air.

"What happened?" Uncle Alexander hurried over and knelt next to Jason. "Are you okay? Did I hit you?"

"No, I'm fine." Jason moved to sit, still breathing hard.

Uncle Alexander scanned his face. "Did your powers fail? Are you feeling all right?" He put his hand on Jason's forehead.

"I said I'm fine." He jerked his head away. "I just . . . got tired. It was a lot and I'm tired." He stood and walked to his water bottle. "I told you I needed a break."

Uncle Alexander sat on the floor. "Can you describe to me what you saw or felt before your powers stopped? Were you lightheaded?"

"My powers didn't stop. I stopped my powers." He took a drink of water.

"Mid-session like that? While my powers were still active?"

"Yep." Jason took another drink and looked at anything except Uncle Alexander.

"Why would you do that?" Uncle Alexander stood. "I could have killed you."

And I could have killed you.

"You're sure nothing interrupted your powers?" Uncle Alexander asked. "Think through it. Was there anything different?"

Jason jutted his chin. "You mean other than everything that's different since the coin? This power is huge. It is definitely different since the coin."

"Well yes, but I mean—"

"Uncle A, I don't want to use my powers any more today, and I don't want to talk about it, okay? Can we please do something else?"

Uncle Alexander ran one hand through his hair, pushing away bangs that had fallen into his face. "What's going on, Jason?"

He sighed. "It's just, I have so much power now. It's freaking me out a little."

"Does it feel out of control? Beyond your ability to manage?"

Jason shook his head. "No, it's not like that. It's just a lot to deal with. Isn't there something else we can work on for a while?"

Uncle Alexander paused. "I suppose we could run more lab tests on the coin. Do you have it with you?"

"Always." He removed the coin from his pocket and tossed it to his uncle.

"Let's take it up to the lab and see if we discover anything new." Uncle Alexander eyed the coin a moment and clutched it in his hand. "Will you humor me with one more activation of your powers while we're here?"

Jason blew out a breath.

"You don't have to aim at anything, I won't fight against you," he said. "I just want to see how much power you can generate when you don't have the coin on your person, okay?"

Jason nodded and set down his water.

"When you're ready," Uncle Alexander said.

A few seconds later, Jason summoned his powers, freeing them to escalate unfettered without his uncle as an opponent.

Uncle Alexander's eyes saucered.

Jason turned toward the mirror to discover he had transformed into a fiery figure, blue and purple, electric bolts twisted and wrapped through the surrounding air. In a flash he doused the display.

"Well, that answers that question," Uncle Alexander said. "You most certainly do not need to be holding the Lex coin to activate your upgraded powers."

"I guess not." Jason noticed a buzz of energy still coursing through him.

"In one of our sessions, we'll see if distance from the coin matters," Uncle Alexander said. "We'll leave it here or at your house, and train outside, farther and farther away, and see if your powers decrease. Sound good?"

"Sure." Jason took another drink of water. He'd practice with Uncle Alexander, but Jason's gut told him he could be anywhere, with or without the coin, and he would still be infused with its power.

✳ ✳ ✳

After ninety minutes of training and testing the coin in Uncle Alexander's lab without learning anything new, snow had started to fall. Uncle Alexander offered to drive Jason the few blocks separating their homes.

"We can walk," Jason said. "I have my boots, and Shay doesn't mind the weather."

"Nonsense. What kind of uncle would I be, sending my sweat-drenched nephew out into a dark and icy night?" Uncle Alexander zipped up his parka. His car keys jangled as he removed them from a hook by the door to the garage. "Care to join us for the ride, Finn?"

Finn jumped up and hurried across the floor, her toenails clicking with each step. She leaped into the backseat next to Shay and sat.

Uncle Alexander pulled out of the driveway. Flakes like shredded cotton balls floated onto the windshield and were swiftly swept off the glass by the wipers. He eased onto the street, his knuckles bulging against his grip on the wheel. He kept his speed to a crawl. "Was it supposed to snow tonight?"

"Not that I heard." Jason checked an app on his phone. "Says the snow should be done before midnight. Supposed to be sunny tomorrow."

"I like the sound of that." Uncle Alexander rounded one corner, then another into Jason's neighborhood.

Finn and Shay sprang to alert stances.

"Finn, sit," Uncle Alexander said, checking the dogs in the rearview mirror. "Both of you. You know better than—"

Woof! Finn leaned forward.

"Stop!" Jason flung out his arm to brace the dogs.

Uncle Alexander hit the brakes and slid to a slow stop on a patch of ice. Standing still in the headlights, its eyes glowing, was a cryptid, a Bigfoot, brown and shaggy and frosted with snowflakes. It darted into the dark.

The dogs whined.

Jason's heart pounded.

Uncle Alexander turned toward Jason and the dogs. "Everyone okay?" He stroked Finn's chest.

"I think so." Jason lifted himself up to see over the seat and check on Shay. She licked his face. "We're good." He scratched her behind the ears, then faced his uncle.

Uncle Alexander blew out a breath. "Tell me that's the same one you saw earlier."

"I can't be a hundred percent certain since it was farther away, in the shadows," Jason said, "but my gut tells me it was. And it's the same one I saw the first night we got home from London."

"But you haven't seen it since then, not until today?"

"Right." Jason rubbed Shay's nose, thrust through the gap between the seat and the headrest. "Do you know for sure that was a Bigfoot? Not a Yowie?"

"I suspect you already know the answer to that question."

"Well, it didn't attack us," Jason said.

"Which is Bigfoot behavior." Uncle Alexander shifted under the strap of the seatbelt. "But it shouldn't be here, in town."

"So we have to assume it *is* a Yowie. We need to warn Sadie." Jason took his phone from his pocket.

Uncle Alexander placed his hand on Jason's, stopping him from unlocking his phone. "Something's not right."

"Yeah, I know. Sadie, and her uncle, and everyone could get hurt." Jason tapped his screen.

Uncle Alexander stopped Jason's hand again. "No, that's just it. The cloak from the Calling is powerful and Sadie is protected. She's well-hidden in Salton until all her powers are fully realized, and Connor would have informed us if something had changed in that regard." He ran his hand through his hair. "And, if by some remarkable chance the Calling's protection had failed, given Devine's history and mission, there would be more than one Yowie in the area, and none of them would have revealed themselves to you or me or anyone else while searching for Sadie." He nodded to himself. "The creature we saw must be a Bigfoot. And maybe it's ill, or maybe it's just old, as I hypothesized earlier." He turned to face Jason. "Sadie is not in danger."

"You're sure about that?" Everything Uncle Alexander said made sense but Jason's apprehension didn't ease.

"I'm sure," Uncle Alexander said. "The creature we saw is not a Yowie looking to harm Sadie." He removed his foot from the brake and lightly pressed the gas. The wheels spun then gripped pavement and inched forward. "I'll let Connor know what's going on, just for his awareness, but there's no need for alarm."

Shay whimpered and licked Jason's face.

FOUR

Wiped

The snow didn't stop. By the time Jason climbed out of bed late in the morning, daylight disguised by clouds peeked through his bedroom blinds. He sifted through clothes on his floor, sniffed a T-shirt, and put it on along with a hoodie and jeans. Heading downstairs, Jason ignored a heavy drag of emotion. He passed Kyle's room, his closed door barely muffling the rumble of snores. Della's door was open but her room was empty and Jason remembered she'd stayed at a friend's house last night.

He focused on the scent of bacon wafting from the kitchen.

"Good morning." Dad flipped a pancake, and the griddle steamed. Shay sat on the floor next to him ready to catch any stray bit.

"Good morning." Jason licked his hand and swiped at a patch of his hair he felt sticking straight up. "Smells good."

"Pancakes. Bacon." Dad pointed the spatula at each item. "Of course it smells good." He smiled and loaded up a plate, handing it to Jason.

"Thanks." Jason sat at the kitchen table. "You were out late last night."

"I had dinner with a friend and talked a little business." He tossed a bite of bacon to Shay, served himself, and sat down.

"Did you go to the Salton Spoon?" Jason asked.

"Actually, we tried Chez Martina, the new place Martina Vincent opened in the remodeled Victorian house on the edge of town."

"Did you like it?"

"I was impressed," Dad said. "I expect it will give the Spoon a run for its money. But I heard your evening was more exciting than mine."

"You talked to Uncle A?"

Dad nodded. "He called this morning."

"He doesn't think the Bigfoot is a big deal." Jason poured himself some juice.

"Your uncle is a good judge of these things."

"Yep. Gotta go with him on this one." Jason looked out the window at the piling snow.

"Crazy amount falling," Dad said. "We have close to a foot already with no sign of it letting up. I'm glad we don't have to drive anywhere, though I am heading out a little later to walk Della home from her sleepover."

And hopefully, the Bigfoot is staying in its nest, away from Salton.

"Do you want me to go with you to pick up Della? In case the Bigfoot is out there?"

"Nah. Alexander said it would avoid us, if it's even nearby," Dad said. "You stay home and hang out, maybe get some studying done. Weather like this makes it easier to study."

Jason stopped mid-chew. "Nothing makes it easier to study."

Dad grimaced. "Mouth empty before talking, please." He held up his hand to block the view.

"Sorry." Jason washed down the food with some juice.

Dad continued. "I meant weather like this limits the number of choices you have, so homework is an easier choice."

Jason shook his head. "No. It's Saturday. Homework is never a choice on a Saturday."

"But if—"

"Dad—did you do homework on Saturdays when you were in high school? Ever?"

He pursed his lips. "I can't say that I did."

"See?" Jason stood and served himself more pancakes. "Besides, I didn't get any homework. Guess my teachers are taking it easy on us this first weekend after the break."

"Not even in biology?" Dad asked. "I thought biology was a tough class."

"It was tough to catch up after London, but Sadie and Nessa helped me," Jason said. "I have no doubt Ms. Feinstein will torture us again, but not this weekend."

"Good." Dad sipped his coffee and held the mug in his hands a moment. "But hey, besides homework, I wanted to touch base with you. This is a tough time of year for us. January eighth is only a few days away.

A lump in Jason's belly burned. For three days he'd managed to quash it, to ignore it, to beat it into submission.

He didn't fight it now. "It sucks, Dad."

Dad nodded. "It does."

"Every bad thing that happened to us was because of Mom and the stupid crap she did. Most people get to look at New Year's Eve as a clean slate or whatever, but we're still in our bad year." Jason clenched and unclenched his jaw. "January eighth, the day everyone in town thinks she died—that's our New Year's Eve." He swallowed hard. "But even then it doesn't feel like I'm getting a clean slate. It doesn't feel like I'll ever get a clean slate." Jason bit his lower lip.

Dad put his hand on Jason's forearm and squeezed. "I've struggled with the same feelings. And I agree, there's no clean slate coming our way."

Jason tipped his head back and stared at the ceiling.

Dad squeezed Jason's arm again. "But here's the thing. We don't need anyone to give us a clean slate, and for that matter, I don't think anyone is given a clean slate. Life is messy and hard and full of challenges, and all of those things ding and chip and mess up our slates. There's no getting around that."

Jason looked at his dad. "So, it just always sucks."

"Not necessarily," Dad said. "Because we have a choice. We can let the dings and chips drag us down, or we can learn from how those dings and chips came to be, sweep them into a corner, and move forward with a clean slate we create ourselves."

Jason half-smiled at Dad's woo-woo talk. "What if the old dings and chips unsweep themselves?"

"Then you look at the messy parts, see if you missed a lesson the first time around, or maybe you're just getting a reminder of how far you've come. But take from the dings whatever you can use—lessons you learned, ideas you created, plans you may have considered—and move them out of the way again."

"And do that every year?"

"Do it whenever you damn well need to do it," Dad said. "Keep the good, let go of the bad, move ahead."

Jason paused. "You make it sound easy, but I think it's really hard to do that."

"It is absolutely really hard." Dad put his arm around Jason's shoulders. "But you, and your brother and sister, are really, really strong."

"This week still might suck," Jason said.

"Yep. But hopefully it will suck a little less knowing we're all going to make our own clean slates afterward."

Jason picked up a piece of bacon. "And if we have more bacon. Everything's better with bacon."

Dad jumped up. "And ice cream. Want some?"

"Now? For breakfast?"

"It's almost lunchtime." He opened the freezer. "You in?"

Before Jason could answer, Brandon walked into the room wearing his parka. "Hey, g'morning." He waved at Jason's dad, then addressed Jason. "Sadie wants us to come over. Something's up."

"Everything okay?" Dad asked.

"I think so?" Brandon snagged his own piece of bacon. "She just texted that Jason and I should get over there ASAP."

The Bigfoot flashed in Jason's mind. "I'll grab my coat." He called to Shay and they were out the door.

✳ ✳ ✳

Sadie's garage door was up and she was waiting inside. "Lena figured you could brush off the snow here and leave your wet things in the mudroom."

Jason and Brandon both stomped their boots and shook snow off their hats and coats.

Sadie handed a towel to Jason. "For Shay."

The dog had shaken off most of the snow, but Jason ran the towel down her back and soaked up snowflakes still melting into her fur.

Sadie kneeled and kissed Shay's face. "Nice to see you, sweet girl." Shay wagged her tail.

A couple minutes later, Sadie led them into the living room where a man sat on the couch with Grandma Lena. Jason recognized him as Sadie's neighbor, Mr. Templeman. He delivered the mail for their neighborhood. Mr. Templeman was only in his mid-thirties, but today he seemed older. He was hunched, almost shriveled.

Grandma Lena sat next to him and patted his arm. "It's all right. You sit here as long as you like."

Jason wondered where Colette was, but he also wondered if he should care. He liked her a lot, and she liked him, but she was his first real girlfriend and Jason wasn't always sure what he was supposed to do.

"Mr. Templeman?" Sadie gestured toward Jason and Brandon. "These are two of my friends. I think you know Jason Lex?"

"Of course, of course." His voice was subdued, almost sad. "Your dog is one of my route favorites." Shay softened her ears and walked over to Mr. Templeman for a scratch and a pat. She sat on the floor between him and Grandma Lena.

Mr. Templeman turned to Brandon. "You must be their house guest, last name Shaw, isn't it?"

"Wow, that's impressive." Brandon reached to shake Mr. Templeman's hand. "Brandon Shaw. It's nice to meet you."

"Very nice to meet you, too."

"So, what's up?" Jason asked. "Is your mail truck stuck? We can help push you out."

Mr. Templeman's back stiffened. "I'm not going back out there. Not anytime soon. Not while that thing is out there."

Crap. Jason knew where this was going. But how? The Rampart hides creatures like Bigfoot from being seen by ordinary humans.

Unless the Rampart was damaged.

"Mr. Templeman was finishing his mail delivery on our block when a monster attacked his truck," Sadie said, her eyebrows raised.

"Came out of nowhere." Mr. Templeman trembled. "I'm driving along, nothing but white everywhere I see until suddenly this thing, all brown fur and teeth, jumps in front of Mel—that's what I call my truck—and *wham!* The thing slams its huge furry fist into Mel. Leaves a deep dent. And you know what I did?"

Jason and Brandon shook their heads.

"Nothing. Not a darn thing," Mr. Templeman said. "I didn't know what to do." He picked at a bit of dried skin on his thumb. "I'm still not sure I understand what happened."

"What did the, uh, monster do next?" Jason asked.

"Oh, it took off like it had rocket boosters on its feet." Mr. Templeman stared at an empty spot on the coffee table. "How can something that big move so fast?"

"I heard a noise from my bedroom and got up to look out the window," Sadie said. "I saw Mr. Templeman sitting in his truck and went out to see if he was okay. I told him to come in and take a break. Then he told us what happened."

"*Are* you okay?" Brandon asked. "Did you get hurt?"

"I don't know," Mr. Templeman said, still staring at the coffee table. "I mean, physically, I'm fine, I think. But I must be losing my mind. I can't have seen what I did." He sucked in a breath and gawked at Grandma Lena, his eyes wild. "You can't tell anyone about this!" He bolted to standing, Shay scurrying out of his way. "I made it up. I made it all up." He forced a fake smile on his face. "Ha ha, the joke is on you. I had you all going for a few minutes, didn't I?"

Grandma Lena stood and put her arm around Mr. Templeman. "Jerry, no one here thinks you're losing your mind. We believe you." She eased him back down on the couch.

"You do?" He glanced from Grandma Lena to Sadie and Jason and Brandon, then back to Grandma Lena. "Have you seen that monster too?"

"I don't need to," she said. "You're an upstanding member of our community, and your word is good enough for me."

Mr. Templeman relaxed.

"Can I get you something hot to drink?" she asked. "Your feet must be frozen from trudging through the snow all morning."

"I could use a strong cup of coffee."

"Coming up." Grandma Lena stood. "Kids, there's hot chocolate if you're interested. Come on into the kitchen and help yourselves. And Jerry?"

He glanced up.

"Are you okay visiting with Shay for a few minutes?"

"Of course." Jerry patted his fingertips to call Shay. She shuffled over and snuggled against his legs.

Everyone else followed Grandma Lena out of the living room. She filled the coffee maker with water and turned to Sadie. "Did you call Connor?"

"Yes, and texted him, too. He hasn't responded."

Grandma Lena scooped coffee into a filter. "Then you have to handle this."

Sadie stepped backward. "No way. I'm not ready."

"Handle what?" Brandon asked.

"She needs to wipe Jerry's memory." Grandma Lena pressed the start button and the coffee maker gurgled.

"Cool," Brandon said.

Sadie grimaced.

"Or . . . not cool." Brandon mouthed the word "sorry" to Sadie.

"Cool or not," Grandma Lena said, "it has to be done." She turned back to Sadie. "Has Connor shown you how to do a memory wipe?"

"No. I mean, yes, but we only talked about it, and I've read some things. But I've never done it, not for real." Sadie sank into a chair. "Can't we just tell Mr. Templeman he was in an accident? That he bumped his head and imagined seeing a monster? I mean, maybe that's what happened. I didn't see anything when I looked out the window."

"He didn't imagine it," Jason said. "I saw it yesterday. Uncle A did, too."

Brandon smacked his arm. "Dude, why didn't you tell me?"

"Because I only saw you two minutes before we headed over here and it was too cold to talk while we were walking." Jason put a mug of milk into the microwave. "Plus, Uncle A thought the Bigfoot would be scared enough after seeing us that it would head back to wherever it came from."

"So it's a Bigfoot, for sure?" Sadie asked.

"Yeah," Jason said. "Which is why Connor didn't sense its energy—not a Yowie." Jason hoped that was true.

"That's good," she said. "That's really good. But let's wait for Connor to do the memory wipe. I can't do it. I don't want to do it."

Grandma Lena pulled a chair next to Sadie. "Sweetie, you saw how scared Jerry is. He doesn't know how to cope with what he saw." She tucked a section of Sadie's hair behind her ear. "If he believes what he saw, he'll tell other people about it which will not go well for him since he has no proof. Or, if he doesn't believe what he saw, he'll think he's losing his mind, or worry about his health, or who knows what else." She patted Sadie's knee. "The kindest thing to do is to wipe it from his memory."

"Okay, I get it. But let Connor do it," Sadie pleaded.

"There's no time to wait for Connor," Grandma Lena said. "Jerry won't stay here all day. The storm won't keep him from walking to his house down the block."

Sadie dropped her face in her hands. "I wish I only had the power to make him fall asleep instead."

Brandon chuckled. "Not that long ago, you hated accidentally doing that to people."

"I hate the idea of memory wipes, too. Besides, what if it doesn't work?" Sadie asked. "What if I don't have the full power yet?"

"Worst case scenario," Grandma Lena said, "you're not yet capable of memory wipes and we find out while attempting it on Jerry. But given we know you were making people fall asleep, there's a good chance the power has fully manifested into the ability to wipe memories."

Sadie slowly shook her head.

"Don't worry," Brandon said. "You've got this."

"And you'll be helping Jerry." Grandma Lena stood, removed a mug from the cupboard, and filled it with fresh coffee. She gave the cup of coffee to Sadie. "Hand Jerry the mug. When you're both touching the cup, initiate a connection with him. Have you synced yourself to a passphrase for triggering connections?"

"Not really," Sadie said. "When we were talking about it, I was joking with Connor that I should say something like, 'Did you know that dogs rule and cats drool?' But Connor likes cats. I mean, I like cats, too, but I really, really like dogs. It's just—"

"Sadie." Grandma Lena squeezed Sadie's shoulder.

"Oh, sorry."

"Nothing to be sorry for, but we need to focus. Use that passphrase."

"But I didn't officially choose it."

"It's the best we have."

"Okay, so hand him the mug and use the passphrase," Sadie said. "Got it." She bit her lower lip.

"Actually," Grandma Lena said, "since you're new at this, it would be better if you're able to touch his skin. It will give you a stronger connection."

"Oh my god." Sadie adjusted her hands so one was on the mug's handle, and the other resting underneath it.

"Once you're connected, shift your position so your fingers are at the base of his skull."

"What?" Sadie's eyes darted from Grandma Lena to Brandon and back. "I don't want to put my hands on his head."

"It's key," Grandma Lena said. "Especially while this power is new to you. You're working with the memory center in his brain and the closer you are to the area, the better. You connect, you suggest he's sleepy, and go from there."

"Oh my god." Sadie scrunched her eyes. "Why isn't Connor here?"

"He had something to deal with this morning and must still be busy with that," Grandma Lena said. "But listen."

Sadie opened her eyes and focused on her.

"Don't remove your touch until you're finished or he'll snap out of it and you'll be in for an awkward conversation. Okay?"

Sadie nodded.

"How do you know all of this?" Jason asked Grandma Lena.

She looked at him. "Hmm?"

"I was just wondering how you knew what she's supposed to do."

"Oh, Willene told me about memory wipes," Grandma Lena said. "And I've chatted with Connor a bit."

Jason was once again impressed with how much Grandma Lena knew about things.

She turned back to Sadie. "Ready?"

"No."

Grandma Lena smiled. "Off you go. I'm right beside you."

Jerry had his cell phone out and was typing a message. He glanced up as Sadie approached with the mug. "Let me just finish sending this note to my wife."

"If you don't mind, Jerry," Grandma Lena said, signaling Sadie to hurry forward, "the coffee mug is hot and I don't want Sadie to burn herself."

"Oh, sure thing." Jerry set down his phone and reached for the cup. His pinky finger touched the side of Sadie's hand.

"Uh . . . ," Sadie said, "did you know that dogs rule and cats drool?"

Jerry gave Sadie a perplexed look. "Excuse me?" He pulled the cup toward him.

Sadie moved with the mug. "You're feeling tired after everything you saw today."

"No, I . . . well . . . I do feel a little tired." Jerry's hands dropped away from the mug. One of Sadie's hands fell with his, maintaining physical contact with his skin. He leaned back into the couch, his eyes glazed.

Sadie handed the mug to Grandma Lena, then leaned over Jerry until she could reach the fingers of her free hand behind his neck. She moved around him and propped her hip on the armrest of the couch.

If Jason hadn't known what was going on, he would have thought Sadie was leaning in for a kiss. The image grossed him out.

Sadie spoke to Jerry. "You saw some strange things today, or amazing things . . . uh . . . some scary things."

"I did," Jerry said, his eyes open as if in conversation.

"You should forget all of them," Sadie said.

"Are you sure?" Jerry asked. "I think I want to remember everything."

Sadie's eyes flicked up to Grandma Lena. "Keep going," she mouthed.

"I'm sure you don't want to remember them," Sadie said. "Remembering them makes you tired. You don't like to be tired."

"You're right. I don't like to be tired."

"So, forget the scary and strange and amazing things you saw today, and you won't be tired."

"I will feel better if I'm not tired," Jerry said.

"That's right. And you deserve to feel better."

"What about the dent in his truck?" Brandon whispered.

Grandma Lena vigorously shook her head, but it was too late.

Jerry's eyes cleared. "Oh! That thing! That monster!" He squirmed in his seat. "It punched Mel! It could have come through the windshield!"

Sadie struggled to keep her fingers on the back of his neck. She grabbed onto his shoulder to keep from falling off the armrest.

Jerry suddenly focused on Sadie's face. "What are you doing? This isn't right." He pushed against Sadie's arm. "Get away from me."

"Don't let go, Sadie." Grandma gestured to Jason and Brandon. "Boys, hold onto him."

"What? No!" Jerry started out of his seat but Jason and Brandon pressed him back down. "You can't do this. Get your hands off me."

Sadie shifted positions and added her other hand behind Jerry's neck.

"This is wrong. Get away from me." Jerry continued to thrash.

Sadie, wide-eyed, looked at Grandma Lena. "Now what?"

"Tell him again," she evenly whispered. "And add to the exchange all that just happened. Everyone else listen, no talking."

Brandon squashed his lips into a thin line.

Jason hated holding Jerry against his will.

"Mr. Templeman," Sadie said, her voice jittery, "did you know that dogs rule and cats drool?"

"Get away from me."

"You're feeling very tired."

"I want—" His eyes lost focus. "I want to lie down."

Sadie swallowed. "You feel tired."

"I do feel tired."

"You're tired because of the amazing and scary things you saw today."

Jason and Brandon released their hold and stepped back. Sadie went through the same statements she said before and Jerry agreed it was better to forget so he wouldn't be tired. She included that he should forget everything that happened in her house, except that he'd had a nice visit with Grandma Lena.

"You stopped your truck after it was dented . . . uh . . . by an icicle," Sadie said. "An icicle fell and dented your truck."

"That icicle came out of nowhere and dented Mel," Jerry said.

"Yes, and it surprised you," Sadie said.

"I'm lucky it didn't come through the windshield."

"Yes," Sadie said.

"I'm lucky I didn't get hurt."

"Yes," Sadie said again. "You are very lucky."

"I think I feel better," Jerry said. "But that icicle scared the crap out of me."

"You don't feel scared anymore, and you don't feel tired anymore." Sadie watched Jerry's face while he seemed to process the statements.

After a moment, he spoke. "You're right, I don't feel scared or tired anymore."

"You feel good," she said.

"I feel good." His eyes remained unfocused.

Sadie slid off the armrest, removed her hands, and swiftly stepped to the side.

Jerry's eyes closed for a few seconds, then opened. "Well, Lena, I should get home." He stood. "Okay if I take a rain check on that coffee?"

"Certainly," she said.

He put on his coat. "Thanks for having me over. It was nice to visit with everyone." He bent to pet Shay. "And I'll bring you a dog biscuit on Monday."

Grandma Lena walked him to the foyer and opened the front door.

"Wow! The snow has really been dumping," Jerry said. "I had no idea it was supposed to snow so much today. This is amazing!"

Sadie cringed. "I did too much," she whispered to Jason and Brandon.

"It's just snow," Brandon said. "He's enjoying it. He's happy."

Jerry said one more goodbye as he stepped outside. Grandma Lena closed the door after him and returned to the living room.

"Did I ruin him?" Sadie asked, a hint of panic in her voice. "Have I erased every 'amazing' thing in his life?"

"No, not at all," she said. "Only whatever he considered amazing today. You were specific enough."

"But I could have been better. I need to be better." Sadie covered her mouth with her hands, then dropped them. "We practically kidnapped him. And I had to get so close, and touch him, and hold on to him." She shook her head. "I am never doing a memory wipe again. Never." She wrapped her arms around herself. "Never."

Grandma Lena pulled her close. "You did good, Sadie."

"I could have ruined Mr. Templeman's life. What if I had erased everything?"

"It would take a great deal of power to do that, and if you ever find yourself with that much power in your possession I know you would only use it for good reasons." Grandma Lena squeezed Sadie again. "You should feel good about this. I don't doubt Willene is smiling down, proud of how you helped Jerry."

Sadie leaned into Grandma Lena. "I miss Mamo."

"We all miss her." She kissed Sadie's forehead.

"What do we do now?" Brandon asked. "About this Bigfoot, I mean."

Jason shrugged. "I have no idea. I'll talk to Uncle A. Maybe there's a trap and release program or something."

"Like trap it and zap it." Brandon mimicked Jason's hand gestures when firing his blue bolts.

Jason's jaw tensed. "I'm not going to kill it. I don't just go around killing things."

Brandon stopped and put up his hands. "Whoa, dude. Never said anyone should kill anything. I figured you could set your phasers to stun, or whatever. Make it easier to move it to its new home."

"Oh. I didn't . . . I thought . . ." Jason shook his head. "Sorry."

Brandon swatted Jason on the arm. "No worries. We're good."

They all took seats in the living room and Jason picked up his cup of now-lukewarm chocolate. "Where's Colette?"

"She went out this morning to meet a friend," Grandma Lena said.

"A friend?" Jason looked at Sadie. "Nessa?"

"No idea," she said. "Neither of them mentioned anything to me."

"Huh." Jason hadn't realized Colette had made friends with people outside of their circle.

"I'm sure she's fine," Sadie said.

"Yeah, of course she is. No biggie." Jason took his phone from his pocket. "I'll call Uncle A, let him know what's up. Be right back." He stepped out of the room and texted Colette: "Hi. How are you?"

The message showed delivered. No response came. He typed another note: "Anyway, we're at your place. Talk to you later." He pressed send, then called Uncle Alexander and updated him on everything that happened.

"I haven't sensed any problems, but obviously something is wrong with the Rampart since Jerry was able to see this creature," Uncle Alexander said. "Have you noticed any issues?"

"Nothing other than the extra Skyfish," Jason said.

"I'll do some checking. And we also need to take some action to deal with this rogue Bigfoot." Uncle Alexander discussed a few ideas with Jason. "I'll let you know if I figure out anything about the Rampart."

"Okay," Jason said. "Talk to you later."

Even after chatting with Uncle Alexander for a few minutes, there was still no response from Colette.

Jason went back into the living room where everyone sat quietly like they were worn out. "Uncle A wants us to track the Bigfoot and find its nest, if it has one nearby. He thinks we should try to relocate it since interactions with humans don't seem to be scaring it off."

"That's all well and good," Grandma Lena said. "But there will be no searching for Bigfoot in this weather."

"He said it's important." Jason took a seat.

"My son thinks every cryptid-related activity is important." Grandma Lena waved her hand. "And, yes, this Bigfoot needs to be dealt with. But your safety is important, too, and wandering around in the wilds of Salton during a snowstorm is not smart. Everyone stays home, Alexander included."

Brandon laughed. "Can you even ground him? He's, like, forty-whatever years old."

"From age four to his forties, Alexander has never been keen on listening to the voice of reason," Grandma Lena said. "But there will be no Bigfoot hunting today."

✳ ✳ ✳

A couple hours later, Jason sat at his desk and looked at his computer screen while Shay snoozed on his bed. Sadie had invited Brandon and Jason to spend the afternoon watching movies but Jason declined. It felt weird hanging out with them without Colette there, too.

She still hadn't responded to his texts.

He thought about texting her again but decided he shouldn't.

Or maybe he should—wasn't it good to check on her? Make sure she was okay?

Or would that be annoying?

Was he worried about her? Or just curious about where she was, and who she was with?

Was he . . . jealous?

Jason dismissed the thought. He was being stupid. He and Colette were good.

Brandon's words from earlier replayed in Jason's head: "I just figure when you like a person, you spend time with them. That's all."

Colette knew Jason liked her, didn't she? And she liked him.

Didn't she?

But it was different in Salton than it had been in London. In London, it felt like just the two of them, Colette and Jason. In Salton, there were a lot more people their age.

A lot more guys.

Maybe she liked someone else.

"Aaahhh." Jason tossed his phone in his desk drawer and flopped onto his bed next to Shay. She snuggled in close and lay her head-on his chest, her breath sputtering under her jowls. Jason stroked her back. "At least I know you still like me."

✳ ✳ ✳

Jason woke Sunday morning to a text waiting from Colette: "Hi, sorry, just got your texts. Silenced phone at library yesterday, then watched movies with S and B, didn't check phone until now."

The library?

He was bummed he didn't stay for the movies after all. And he didn't like that Colette said nothing about who she was with. Jason decided not to respond and set his phone on the nightstand.

A few seconds later he changed his mind: "Hi. Thanks for letting me know."

Animation on the screen showed her responding: "And thanks for checking on me. That was sweet."

Tautness in Jason's chest eased a little. "You're welcome," he typed. "Glad you're good. Crazy day yesterday."

She wrote back: "Sadie told me. Wow."

There was a pause before she typed more: "Would be nice to see you, but still snowing so Lena wants us to stay home. See you at school tomorrow."

"Yeah," Jason texted. "See you tomorrow."

Relief washed over him.

Colette still liked him.

FIVE

Gone Rogue

To Jason's disappointment, the snow tapered off early Sunday afternoon giving plows plenty of time to make the roads passable and ensure school was in session Monday morning. But at least there hadn't been any more reported Bigfoot sightings.

"Guys," Dad called up the stairs. "I'm driving Della to school today. If you're ready to go in fifteen minutes, I'll drop you off on the way."

Jason wasn't about to miss a chance to avoid icy sidewalks and slushy paths. "I'll be ready," he hollered.

"Me too," Kyle called from his room.

In the kitchen a few minutes later, Della sat at the table finishing her breakfast and Brandon sat next to her, his laptop open. Shay snoozed at his feet. Jason made a pretend move to muss Della's hair but she blocked him. "Nope. Move along."

Jason laughed.

"You're getting fast, Della," Brandon said.

"He's just getting slow." She smirked.

"Hey, now. Little sisters are supposed to be nice to their big brothers." Jason finished throwing together his lunch, adding an orange at the last minute. He munched on a protein bar.

Kyle walked in. "You know, Dad, I'd like to remind you I get my driver's license next month."

"If you pass the test," Dad said.

"A given," Kyle said. "Anyway, if you get me a car, I can do things like drive us to school, and take Della to her dance lessons and appointments, and you can just chill."

"Somehow the thought of you driving does not give me a feeling of chill." Dad poured creamer in his travel mug of coffee.

"Well it should," Kyle said. "Your life would be better, my life would be better—it's a win-win."

"Hmmm. And what kind of car am I supposed to buy for you?" Dad asked.

"I mean, it has to be practical." Kyle opened the refrigerator and peered inside.

Dad aborted a sip of his coffee. "Did you just say 'practical?'"

"Yeah." Kyle had a jug of milk in his hand. He took off the lid and moved the opening toward his mouth.

"No." Dad pointed at the milk jug.

Kyle stopped, paused as if considering how serious Dad was, and took a glass from the cupboard. "Okay, I figure if I will be driving my dear brother and sister around, not to mention our fine friend Brandon, the car should have four doors."

"I agree," said Dad. "Hypothetically."

"And it should get decent gas mileage so it's affordable."

Dad's expression shifted from amused to perplexed. "Also agree. Again, hypothetically."

"And the car should be reliable. Have a solid history." Kyle downed the glass of milk and wiped his mouth on his sleeve.

"While I'm not impressed with your apparent inability to use a napkin," Dad said, "I am impressed that you've given this car thing some serious thought. And maybe someday, far into the future, we can talk more about it. But right now we have to go." He circled his arm in the air signaling everyone to action. "And dress accordingly, meaning wear your coats. You'll have to walk home this afternoon. I'm taking Della to her appointment."

Jason put on his jacket. "Do you still like Dr. Abernathy, Dell?"

"Yeah," she said. "It's fun talking to her. Especially since she knows about the secret stuff."

Jason flung his backpack over his shoulder. "That's good. Will you keep going twice a week?"

"Yep." Della headed to the garage. "Mondays and Thursdays. I'm glad the League found her for me."

Jason squirmed a little. Her words, "I'm glad the League," reminded him of "I'm thankful for the League," a phrase the League-bots in London repeated over and over until they were free from mind-controlling serum they'd unwittingly consumed, Dad and Della included.

"I'm glad too, Della," Dad said. He winked at Jason.

Jason had worried Della would struggle after everything that happened in London. But with Dr. Abernathy's help, she was her happy self again. As long as they kept the secret about her parents, Jason figured Della would only get better.

* * *

"Later, bro." Kyle left Jason at the front door of the school and was deep in the flow of students before Jason had a chance to respond.

"Yeah, have a great day, you're the best brother ever," Jason said under his breath. Six Skyfish zoomed into the building, then back outside.

"Who are you talking to?" Sadie asked from behind Jason, making him jump.

"Jeez, did you just magic yourself here? Maybe you are a witch."

"You're hilarious."

"And to answer your question, I was just having a one-sided conversation with my self-centered older brother," Jason said. "Where's Colette?"

"She's here somewhere." Sadie headed toward their lockers and Jason fell in step. They turned a corner and found Mr. Whitfield, the head janitor, blocking off a double-doorway with orange cones and yellow caution tape. One door hung askew.

"Good morning, Mr. Whitfield," Sadie said. "Everything okay?"

He looked up from his work, a troubled expression on his face. "Oh, Sadie, good morning. Hello, Jason."

"Hey, Mr. Whitfield."

He shook his head. "No, things are not okay. First, this door drops off its hinge in my hands. Then I find broken pallets, storage blankets shredded, boxes tipped over, and it smells like a kennel full of wet dogs and cats had some sort of shindig I wouldn't care to witness."

Jason peeked inside the area and saw upturned cabinets and files. He scrunched his nose at the stench. Three Skyfish zipped out of the room and over his head.

"Do you want some help cleaning up?" Sadie asked. "Mr. Bond would probably excuse me from history class. I'm ahead on my assignments."

"Thank you for the offer but your classes are important," Mr. Whitfield said. "I can handle this."

"Do you have any idea what happened?" Jason asked.

"A vandal, or vandals," Mr. Whitfield said. "They jimmied the outside door and made themselves quite at home while they wrecked the place. I even found a rotisserie chicken container from the grocery store and some banana peels. I can't say for sure who made this mess, but I have my suspicions."

Derek Goodman had caused problems before so it seemed likely he had caused this one, too.

But Jason wasn't so sure.

"Sorry you have to deal with this," Sadie said. "Let us know if you change your mind about wanting help."

"I'll manage. Don't you worry," Mr. Whitfield said. "You two had better get going or you'll be late for first period."

Jason and Sadie said goodbye to Mr. Whitfield and continued down the hall.

"If we had time, I'd find Derek Goodman right now and tell him what I think of him," Sadie said.

"I don't think it was Derek. I saw something that looked like fur stuck to a piece of pallet. Plus, the hairs on my neck are buzzy which usually means cryptid."

"Huh. So the Bigfoot broke in. But why would it do that?"

"Who knows? Maybe it needed shelter from the weather? Maybe it enjoys breaking and entering?"

They arrived at their lockers. Jason opened his and emptied books from his backpack. "This is just a weird one."

"Weird and getting weirder." Sadie opened her locker. She squealed as a folded piece of paper fell toward her.

"I didn't know Yowie had a fear of paper." Jason removed the books he needed for algebra, his first class of the day.

"Ha ha." She retrieved the note from the floor and unfolded it. Sadie *tsked* and showed the message to Jason.

Scrawled in block letters were the words "I KNOW WHAT YOU DID."

There was no signature.

"Derek?" he asked.

"Who else?" She crumpled the paper and threw it into the bottom of her locker.

"What does he think he knows this time?" Jason shut his locker. "That you made it snow more than expected?"

"I have no idea." She slammed her locker shut. "But one thing I do know—I will never help Derek Goodman with anything ever again."

"And I one hundred percent back you on that plan," Jason said.

They headed down the hall.

"Anyway, where were we?" Sadie asked. "Oh yeah—the actual, real problem of a destructive Bigfoot."

"Yep. And we need to do something about it." Jason glanced toward where Colette had her locker but didn't see her.

"Can we look for it this afternoon?"

They stopped at an intersection where they'd each head a different direction to their respective classes.

"The snow will probably be too deep for another day or so," Jason said, "but I'll get Uncle Alexander to bring Shay and Finn over here after school. They can at least get the scent outside the door where Mr. Whitman said it broke in. Uncle A will want to see it, too."

"Okay, let me know if you need me to do anything." She started down the hallway, her pace brisk. "I'll see you later."

Jason turned and headed to algebra with a step less enthusiastic than Sadie's.

* * *

That afternoon, Jason watched from inside the school, waiting for Uncle Alexander to arrive with Shay and Finn. He pulled up and parked his truck after most of the students were gone. Jason stepped outside and Shay and Finn bounded up to him, their leashes dragging behind.

"Thanks for coming over," Jason said, gathering up the dogs' leashes while greeting them both with pats and scratches.

"Not a problem at all," Uncle Alexander said as he dropped his car keys into the brown leather messenger bag over his shoulder. "This is a fine opportunity to kill two birds with one stone, as they say. Shay can do more real-world training with Finn, and we'll get closer, hopefully, to sorting out the problem with this Bigfoot. As for the Rampart, that's a problem for which I don't have a solution."

"You figured out the problem?"

"Yes," Uncle Alexander said. "It seems your mother damaged the connection to the vortex when she was working to destroy the Rampart, and now we have a rip in the Rampart that leaves most of Salton vulnerable."

"So we fix it, right?"

Uncle Alexander shook his head. "The damage has reconfigured the edges of the Rampart from the sugar mill, where your mother centered her attack, around Salton. Thankfully, it seems Salton and a small portion of the surrounding area is the only location where the Rampart's protections are reduced, but this is something not seen before, and we don't have the resources and skills to repair it ourselves." He bent and scratched Finn's ears. "I've informed the League and they're analyzing the situation. They'll come back to us when they have a solution."

"In the meantime, people in Salton can see the Bigfoot."

"I'm afraid so," Uncle Alexander said.

"Sadie might get more practice with her memory-wiping skills," Jason said. "At least the Skyfish aren't visible, even without the Rampart. Seeing them would really freak people out."

"Indeed it would. We may learn it's the damage to the Rampart that's causing them to be more active," Uncle Alexander said. "I notified the League about the change in their behavior as well. We'll see what they come back with. In the meantime, we should focus on the task at hand."

"Let's head around back. That's where the Bigfoot broke in." Jason led the way behind the building, the dogs both working their noses along the ground as they walked. Melting snow dripped from the eaves like a waning waterfall.

"There won't but much in the way of visible tracks given how fast things are melting," Uncle Alexander said. "But with luck the dogs will find a scent."

Finn's and Shay's ears perked. The dogs increased their speed. Jason and Uncle Alexander shifted into a jog.

They reached the breached door, and both dogs ramped up their scenting. Shay licked at the crack between the door and jamb, sniffed deep, and repeated the action. Finn examined the gap between the bottom of the door and the pavement, then the dogs switched and seemed to check each other's work. Finn pawed at the door and vocalized more than a whine but less than a bark.

"We can't go inside, girl," Uncle Alexander said.

Shay looked from Finn to Uncle Alexander. She barked.

"Same goes for you," Jason said.

Finn sat and Shay followed.

"Your instincts were right. The Bigfoot was here," Uncle Alexander said to Jason. He walked away from the door, eyeing the ground.

"If you find something," Jason said, "promise me you won't lick it."

Uncle Alexander walked toward the trash bin and opened the lid.

Oh no . . .

He waved Jason over and called the dogs.

"Please don't climb in there," Jason said.

"Not me—"

"Nope, not me either," Jason said. "Or Shay. Or Finn. We all have strict 'no dumpster diving' clauses in our contracts."

"I need that bag of garbage, the one on top of the pile. It's likely to have items Mr. Whitfield threw out while cleaning up the storage room today."

"Still not getting in the dumpster," Jason said.

"You don't need to." Uncle Alexander gestured to parts of wooden pallets piled nearby. "Just bring those pieces over to me."

Jason drug over the pieces of wood. Uncle Alexander stacked them and stepped onto his makeshift platform. It wobbled under his weight and Jason jutted his arm to break a near fall.

"I'm fine, I'm fine." Uncle Alexander stepped off and shifted the pieces into a closer-fitting configuration. "This should do it." He climbed back up and the stack teetered again, forcing him sideways off the pile.

"Okay, you win." Jason stepped onto the wood and hoisted himself onto the edge of the dumpster. He leaned over, breathed in the rotten, mildewy, putrefied air, grabbed the bag of trash in question, and hoisted it out onto the ground.

"Thank you," Uncle Alexander said. "You're a good—"

Jason wiped his hands on Uncle Alexander's jeans. "Only fair. We're a team."

Uncle Alexander grinned. "Well played, nephew."

Meanwhile, both dogs were pawing and snorting and sniffing at the trash bag. Uncle Alexander opened the bag and Finn focused on an empty rotisserie chicken container.

"Mr. Whitfield said he'd found one of those in the mess," Jason said.

Finn and Shay both made methodical passes over the plastic, slowly sniffing the dish.

"How do you know they're not just interested because it's still covered in chicken grease?" Jason asked.

"Because they're not trying to eat it."

Duh. Jason chided himself for not noticing the significance of their behavior right away.

A moment later the dogs moved from the trash and traveled their noses along the ground, Shay just behind Finn. They stopped at the edge of the schoolyard and looked at the cottonwood trees in the distance.

"As they say in the movies," Uncle Alexander said, "it went thataway."

Jason shook his head. "You need to see some new movies." He headed toward the trees.

"Hold on."

Jason stopped.

"These January days are short. The sun's going down and we're not properly dressed," Uncle Alexander said. "Nor do we have any gear to restrain or move the Bigfoot if we find it."

"Okay, let's get whatever we need and we'll head out tomorrow morning." Jason shoved his hands in the pockets of his coat.

"You have school tomorrow."

"I can skip school."

"And then your father and grandmother would come after me," Uncle Alexander said.

"But we can't put this off. We need to deal with the Bigfoot before someone else sees it. Or it does more damage."

"I agree." Uncle Alexander pulled a knit cap out of his coat pocket and pulled it onto his head. He tossed the garbage back into the bin. "I'll take the dogs and search for it tomorrow. I'll see if your dad might come along."

"I'm going, too," Jason said.

"You ask your father if he'll excuse you from school to go Bigfoot hunting." Uncle Alexander turned and started back toward the car with Finn trotting at his side. "But I'm betting good money he says no."

Jason and Shay hurried to catch up. "I'll take that bet. This is important enough to skip school. Dad will totally say yes."

✳ ✳ ✳

"Absolutely not." Dad took off his reading glasses. "Your uncle and I can handle it. Plus, I'd never turn down a chance to take a nice long walk with Shay."

Shay rolled onto her back, feet in the air, asking for a belly rub. Dad complied.

Jason put his hands on his hips hoping Dad would understand the seriousness of the situation. "But this is important."

"It's not more important than school." Dad's voice changed from grown-up to coochie-coo. "Is it, Shay. This silly Bigfoot isn't more important than school, right? I know you agree with me. Yes, you do. You're such a good girl."

Shay's tail *thwumped* against the floor.

Jason dropped to a slouch on the couch.

Brandon walked in from his basement room. "What's up?"

"Dad and Uncle Alexander are searching for the rogue Bigfoot tomorrow," Jason mumbled.

"Cool," Brandon said. "Count me in."

"Great," Dad said.

Jason bolted upright. "What?"

"I'm kidding," Dad said. "You're going to your brick and mortar school, Brandon's going to his online school, and I'm adventuring off into the wilds of Salton to find me a Bigfoot." He said the last few words using an old-timey prospector accent.

"You are such a dork, Dad."

"Darn tootin'. Now y'all best be gitten up them stairs and, uh . . ." He changed back to regular Dad voice. "Do whatever they said in the Old West when they meant 'go do your homework.'"

Jason stomped upstairs. Brandon and Shay followed him into his room and Shay sprung onto the bed, curled into a C, and closed her eyes. Jason stared out the window.

"That is not a good idea," Brandon said.

Jason turned. "What's not a good idea?"

"I know you." Brandon straddled Jason's desk chair. "I can hear what you're thinking and I'll tell you right now that going outside in the way-below-freezing-degrees-night is a dumb idea."

"I could find it." Jason pointed from himself to Brandon. "*We* could find it."

Brandon copied the gesture. "*We* aren't stupid. It's pitch black outside."

"Hello. Flashlights."

"Hello." Brandon showed the screen of his phone to Jason. "Twelve degrees."

Jason crumpled to a seat on the floor. "Fine."

"Anyway, I thought you weren't in the mood for Guard stuff right now."

"I'm not," Jason said. "That's why I want to get this taken care of. Chase that thing out of here and go back to everything being calm. Normal."

"Normal." Brandon stood. "From the guy who can turn into a blue fireball."

"Okay, new normal."

Shay's head lifted and she stared at the window. Her hackles spiked.

"Uh-oh." Brandon hurried to the window.

Jason jumped up and joined him.

A low rumble rose from Shay.

In the neighbor's yard across the street, a dark figure slid into shadow.

Woof! Shay was on her feet and down the stairs.

Jason and Brandon scrambled after her.

She fast-scratched at the front door. Jason sped up behind her and reached for the handle.

"Do not let her out," Dad bellowed.

"But the Bigfoot is out there," Jason yelled.

Dad hurried toward them. "All the more reason for everyone to stay in here."

"No—this is what we do." Jason again reached for the doorknob.

"Not—" Dad lurched forward and grabbed Jason's hand, yanking it back. "Not tonight. Not—" He released his grip and held his hands up. "Not like this. And especially not this week."

A twinge winged through Jason's chest at the memory of his mom missing on a snowy night.

Kyle and Della came down the stairs.

"What's going on?" Kyle asked.

Jason rubbed his wrist, more surprised than injured. "Dad, I can handle this."

Shay sat next to Jason while Brandon eased to the side and lowered himself to sitting on one of the bottom steps.

"I know you can handle it, son," Dad said, his voice suddenly seeming tired. "I believe you can handle anything that comes at you. But I don't want you to have to handle everything that comes at you, on your own, without a plan and without . . . without a team." He blew out a breath. "You did that in London, Jason, and you were incredible. But you shouldn't have had to. You should have had me. You should have had your uncle. You should have had Della, all of us, by your side."

Della shrugged one shoulder and nodded.

A knot knitted in Jason's throat. He swallowed it down.

Dad continued. "We didn't know what we were getting into in London. But we know what we're dealing with here. And nothing's going code red at the moment. So please, let's come up with a plan. Let's work this as a team."

"Go team Lex! Woot!" Kyle hollered from the stairs with his fist in the air.

Brandon glanced toward Kyle and shook his head.

Jason noted Shay's body language and realized the threat had passed. "Sure, Dad," he said. "We can work on this one together."

"Thank you." Dad hugged Jason. Shay smushed between their legs. And Jason didn't miss his mom.

SIX
Tests

Jason's anxiousness about the Bigfoot lessened through the week. Dad and Uncle Alexander's trek with the dogs on Monday had revealed few clues. They confirmed the Bigfoot spent a lot of time in the cottonwoods, but between deep snow and numerous scent tracks, they could not find it or its nest.

The rest of the week passed with no new sightings. A pseudo-spring brought fifty-degree temperatures changing the white landscape to a combination of bare trees, dry pavement, and charcoal-colored piles of plowed snow. Even Wednesday, the anniversary of the day Jason's mom "disappeared," came and went without feeling as bad as he'd feared. Maybe he was over it. Maybe everyone in their family was finally over what she had done.

Jason hoped the last few cryptid-free days and better weather meant the Bigfoot had come to its senses and disappeared into the wilderness for good.

Colette waited while Jason and Sadie sorted through their lockers deciding what they needed to bring home for the weekend and what they'd leave at school. Nessa walked up, stopped, and peered down the hallway one direction, then down the other, her muscles twitchy like she was prepared to take flight.

"Are you looking for someone?" Sadie asked, shutting her locker.

"Yes." Nessa rose on her tiptoes and gazed over the heads of passing students. "Kyle."

"Come over to the house," Jason said. "If he's home you can see him all you want."

"No." Her eyes showed shock at the suggestion. "I don't want to see him."

"I'm confused," Colette said. "I thought you liked him."

"I do." Nessa shuffled behind Jason and Sadie so she was close to the lockers and blocked by their bodies. "But I've run into him, like, eighteen million times this week and he will totally think I'm stalking him."

"Are you?" Sadie grinned.

"Shut up, you know I would never," Nessa said. "Not for real, anyway." She executed another tiptoe check. "And this week I have made zero moves to put myself in his path, yet it keeps happening. It's like the fates are taking my embarrassing comment from Monday, about him tutoring me in PE, and torturing me with it every time I turn a corner."

"So, now what? You can't keep hiding here," Jason said. "Because I'm going to bail."

"Me too," Colette said. "I'm with him." She tilted her head toward Jason.

He felt a flush on his face he hoped no one noticed and smiled at Colette.

"And I have to get to Tae Kwon Do," Sadie said. "Do you want to come?" she asked Nessa.

Nessa took a breath, squared her shoulders, and moved out from her tucked-in spot. "No, it's okay. I'm good." She linked arms with Sadie and Colette. "I will walk out with you and not worry about it. And if we run into him, he'll know that I have people, and I'm with my people, and I don't need to be stalking Kyle Lex because I am hanging with my people."

They stepped into the flow of students.

"You still sound like you're worried," Sadie said.

"Nope." Nessa raised her chin. "I'm just me, doing me things, heading home on a Friday afternoon after a normal, Nessa-esque week at school."

"Good," Colette said. "And I think we should do something fun-esque together this weekend, just us girls. What do you think?"

"Love it," Sadie and Nessa said in unison.

They unlinked arms outside the school. "Sleepover tomorrow night?" Nessa asked. "Junk food and bingeing our shows at my house?"

"I'm in." Colette looked to Sadie.

She nodded her head. "It's a date."

"Yay!" Nessa clapped her hands. "Come by around seven. I promise it will be snack heaven." She hugged Sadie and Colette and headed toward home.

"What about me?" Jason asked as Nessa walked away.

"You and Brandon can spend some quality time together," Sadie said.

"Maybe we'll go to a movie or something." Jason adjusted the strap of his backpack.

"As long as it's nothing Colette and I want to see." Sadie checked her phone. "I've got to get going so I'm not late to Tae Kwon Do. Brandon's meeting me there. I'll let him know you'll be asking him on a date." She smirked.

"Hilarious," Jason said. "Though I am pretty fun. He might like hanging out with me more often after we have our own 'fun-esque' evening together."

Sadie laughed and waved goodbye.

Jason laughed too, but he did find it strange that two of his best friends now spent more time with each other than they did with him. He reached for Colette's hand. "Can I walk you home?"

She put her hand in his. "I'd like that."

✳ ✳ ✳

Sadie made her way into downtown Salton for her lesson with Master Kim. In the distance, the sign on the front of the dojo shone in large red letters: Tae Kwon Do. Figures of male and female black belts frozen in side-kicks anchored the sign.

Someone tapped Sadie on her shoulder. She turned.

Derek skittered back a few steps and pointed at her. "I know what you did."

"Go home, Derek." She turned back toward the studio.

He ran around and stood in front of her. "You'd better stop."

"Get out of my way." Sadie tried to walk around him but he blocked her.

"I will tell people." His voice growled.

She crossed her arms. "Tell people what, Derek? That I healed your hand? Is that what you'll say? Because Ms. Feinstein didn't believe you so why should anyone else?"

"So, you admit it." Derek stood taller like he'd just proven a case in court.

"Admit to healing your hand with some magic spell?" Sadie glared at him. "We're not friends, Derek, and you're not nice to anybody. So even if I could heal your hand, why would I?" She stepped forward and this time Derek let her pass. She'd walked a few stern steps when Derek yelled again.

"You've done things to other people, too. I know it."

Sadie ignored him.

"Yeah, you better keep going," Derek called after her.

She fought down the urge to try going full Yowie and scare the crap out of him. But that would only bring more trouble. She quickened her pace to the dojo.

✳ ✳ ✳

After her encounter with Derek, Sadie leaned over the sink in the women's locker room and breathed deep. Her heart pounded in her ears, in her neck, in her chest. She closed her eyes and focused on calming her system.

Derek Goodman isn't worth the energy.

She changed into her white dobok and tied the blue belt around her waist. Sadie paused a moment, then repeated to herself the tenets of Tae Kwon Do: courtesy, integrity, perseverance, self-control, indomitable spirit.

She hadn't been courteous to Derek. *How can you be courteous to someone like him?* She'd have to work on that.

Sadie took another deep breath and splashed water on her throat.

Her heart rate slowed.

She stored her stuff and exited the locker room.

Brandon was in the hall, already dressed in his dobok with a white belt. He waved at Sadie. She sat down next to him and told him about the incident with Derek.

"Jeez," Brandon said. "I know you don't need me to do it, but I kind of want to kick his ass right now."

"I considered doing the same thing," she said. "But whatever Derek's deal is, it's his issue, not mine."

Brandon gave Sadie a sideways glance. "That's very chill of you."

"Ha. I wasn't chill at all about twenty minutes ago," she said. "But I'm better now. And class will help me blow off more steam."

"I wish I was chill, but I'm kind of freaking out." Brandon leaned in and lowered his voice. "Master Kim encouraged me to test for my yellow belt tonight."

"That's great," Sadie said.

"Except I'm not ready."

"Yes, you are. You've been practicing."

"But I'm not ready *today*," he said. "I'm not in the right mindset. I didn't expect to be testing."

"There is no ready today or ready tomorrow," she said. "You're ready every day."

Brandon gave her a look like he didn't know if he wanted to agree or disagree. Then he released tendons holding his posture taut. "You're right. I'm ready. And crazy nervous." He rubbed his hands together. "But ready."

After class, Sadie watched Brandon test with the other students, moving through their forms and demonstrating their skills. Brandon's performance was clean, precise, and he was awarded his yellow belt.

Sadie congratulated him with a hug.

"I still have a long way to go before I catch up with you," Brandon said as they put on their coats.

"*If* you catch up with me."

He stopped in place and squared his shoulders. "Challenge accepted."

Sadie laughed.

They walked outside where Lena was waiting in the parking lot. As they climbed into her car, Sadie heard Lena finishing a phone call.

"Not what any of us want to hear," Lena said, "and I'm picking them up now so I'll talk to you later."

"Everything okay?" Sadie asked.

"Nothing for you to worry about right now," Lena said.

The comment caught Sadie's attention. *Did that mean she was talking about something to worry about later?*

"How was class tonight?" Lena asked.

Sadie told her of Brandon's achievement.

"My goodness." Lena pulled into traffic. "Congratulations. Impressive work in such a short time."

"Thanks," he said. "I'm going to send a note to my parents and tell them the news."

While Brandon typed, Sadie noticed an orange glow out in the distance. "What is that?"

"Looks like a fire." Lena stopped on the side of the road. "We'd better report it."

Sadie dialed 9-1-1 on her phone and put it on speaker. She told the dispatcher what they saw.

"Fire crews are on scene," the dispatcher said. "It's a small brush fire, already contained. We'll send out an emergency alert message should anything change but for now there's nothing to worry about."

"Okay, thanks," Sadie said.

"Thank you for calling in the report." The dispatcher disconnected.

"Strange time of the year to have a fire, especially considering how much snow we just had." Lena stared out at the flickering light.

"Maybe someone was camping," Brandon said, looking up from his phone.

"Also an odd time to be camping, but not unheard of." Lena put the car in gear and eased back onto the road. "I'm glad to know it didn't get out of hand."

✳ ✳ ✳

Sadie woke the next morning and willed the invisible right side of her body, from her cheeks to her toes, to reappear. She was pleased it only took a few seconds. She still couldn't manage more than small transitions from visible to invisible, but she practiced in her room every evening, keeping her progress, or lack thereof, to herself. Sadie wanted to take it slow.

She wanted the Calling to take it slow.

Sadie headed downstairs to the kitchen and heard Lena talking on the phone.

"What is the total number now?" Lena asked the person on the other end of the line, her voice tense.

Sadie stayed outside the room and listened.

Lena took a deep breath. "One is already too many, but nineteen?"

Nineteen . . . nineteen what?

"You and I both know their return is unlikely, not given the history of past disappearances."

Sadie's stomach dropped. Was Lena talking about Yowie in Sadie's Clan disappearing? Connor had told her Garrison Devine had eliminated others who didn't agree with his leadership.

Another pause.

"We may be getting close to having to do that," Lena said into her phone. "It's not my first choice—"

Sadie decided she didn't want to hear anymore and stepped into the kitchen.

"I'll call you back." Lena disconnected her call. "Good morning," she said to Sadie.

"G'morning." Sadie removed a mug from the cupboard. "Who were you talking to?"

"Connor," Lena said.

Sadie's angst increased. "Is he okay?" She poured hot water from the tea kettle.

"He's fine. But he'd like to see more training from you."

"I'm doing as much as I can right now," Sadie said, her eyes fixed on her mug. "And I had a crash course on memory wipes. That should count for something." She dunked an orange-ginger tea bag in the steaming cup.

"I know you," Lena said, "and you always want to do your best."

I want to do my best to stay cloaked, to protect everyone . . .

"Don't you?" Lena asked.

Sadie stopped dunking and looked at Lena. "Yeah, I do."

"That's all I wanted to hear." Lena stood. "That's all Willene would want as well." She squeezed Sadie's shoulder and exited the kitchen.

Sadie pushed the thought that Devine was hurting people out of her mind. She told herself Lena was probably talking about something else. Sadie had jumped to a wrong conclusion. She'd misunderstood. Everything was fine as long as the cloak was in place.

She carried her tea upstairs, took a shower, and found her phone buzzing when she shut off the water. There was a message from Jason to her and Colette: "Break-in last night at the new place, Chez Martina. Meeting Uncle A there in twenty minutes to see what's up. Come if you want."

"Count me in," Sadie typed.

"Me too," was Colette's message.

A little jolt of eagerness zinged through Sadie. It would be good to do something besides think about training for the Calling.

SEVEN

An Enemy Returns

Jason, Brandon, and Shay found Uncle Alexander and Finn standing with Sadie and Colette on the front porch of Chez Martina, the old Victorian-style house remade into a new restaurant on the outskirts of town. Uncle Alexander had his brown leather messenger bag slung over his shoulder as usual. A sheriff's car was parked on the road but Jason didn't see anyone in uniform.

"No other Lexes joining us today?" Uncle Alexander asked. "Your dad was quite enthusiastic during our search earlier this week. I expected he would want to tag along today, too."

"Dad was already gone when I got up," Jason said. "He was taking Della to dance class, then he had some other thing afterward. I don't remember what. And Kyle—"

"Still asleep," Brandon said.

Jason brushed away hair that had blown into his eyes. "Yeah, it is before noon."

"Right," Uncle Alexander said. "He's far from being a morning person."

"So, what's the situation here?" Sadie asked. Finn's leg kicked when Sadie found an appealing spot to scratch.

"Let's go around back and take a look." Uncle Alexander led them through the sunny but dormant gardens and down a narrow path along the side of the house. Rounding the corner, they came to an expansive backyard with a covered patio attached to the house. An assortment of tables dotted the flagstone surface, all the tables seeming old, and none of them matching. A mishmash of chairs continued the mismatched theme. Strings of lights waved beneath the canvas patio cover, and a double screen door led into the house. Strategically placed portable heaters stood watch.

"Did somebody steal their good tables?" Jason asked.

Sadie *tsked*. "Rude."

"What?"

"Not being all matchy-matchy is totally in," Sadie said. "And I think it's adorable."

"And you need to cut back on watching the remodeling shows on television," Jason said.

"I dunno," Brandon said. "It does look pretty cool."

Jason stared at Sadie and Brandon. "What is happening?"

"Yes, what is happening is the question of the morning," Uncle Alexander said. "But whether the tables match is not the problem. In fact, nothing here," he gestured at the patio area, "is of issue. Our situation lies in the carriage house where Martina stores food and supplies for the restaurant."

Farther back on the lot, nestled near the edge of the cottonwoods, was a second house almost as large as the first. It had expansive, heavy barn doors. One door dangled on a single hinge.

That looks familiar.

Uncle Alexander poked his head in the opening. "Sheriff Gunderson?"

"You can come in, Alexander," the sheriff said. "All clear."

They traipsed inside and Jason's eyes took a moment to adjust from the bright light outdoors to the muted light of the carriage house.

A look of surprise crossed Sheriff Gunderson's face. "Brought the whole crew with you, huh?"

"Yes, well I'm, uh . . . I'm on uncle duty today, so here we are."

Uncle duty? Jason resisted making a face so he didn't call attention to the oddball comment.

But Sheriff Gunderson was well-versed in Uncle Alexander's quirky history with cryptozoology. The sheriff then looked at Jason. "You kids can't be trusted to stay home by yourselves? Still need a babysitter?" He used his authoritative voice, a voice of which Jason had been on the receiving end more than once since moving to Salton.

"Uh . . ." Jason's mind raced to find a response that didn't make everyone seem brainless.

The sheriff smiled. "I'm kidding. You're all welcome to look around but there's not much to see. I walked through this place with Martina and she said everything seemed in order. Maybe she'll later find a few food items missing, after she has time to do an inventory. But for now, she says everything looks good. Broken door out front is the only clear damage."

"Thank you, sheriff." Uncle Alexander ran his finger along the top of a cardboard box labeled "dinner plates."

"No problem." The sheriff tucked a notepad into his breast pocket. "And I realize Martina said it was all right for you to take a look around, but can I ask why it is you're interested?"

Uncle Alexander stopped and stared at the sheriff for a moment. "Ah, well, I'm quite fond of this old place and its architecture."

"Are you?" Sheriff Gunderson wiped his brow with a handkerchief. "I understand you enjoy researching the weird monster-things some people say they've seen—"

"Cryptids," Uncle Alexander said.

"That's right—cryptids," the sheriff said. "But I didn't know you were also interested in architecture."

Jason recognized an undercurrent of judgment in Sheriff Gunderson's tone and wondered if he sounded like that more often than not, even when he was talking to his kids or his neighbors, whether or not he was investigating a crime.

Uncle Alexander's brows raised. "It's not so much the architecture itself, sheriff, but what has lived in these walls for over one hundred years since the house was built."

Now a look of surprise crossed Sadie's, Brandon's, and Colette's faces.

Uncle Alexander continued. "Historical documents I've researched contain solid evidence that this structure has been, and may continue to be, infested with Mongolian Death Worms." He shook his head hard. "And those, dear sheriff, are not creatures we want escaping from the walls and into Salton. The destruction they could cause with their acidic systems would be catastrophic. When I found out the building had been damaged, I needed to get over here as soon as I could to inspect it." He put his hand on Sheriff Gunderson's shoulder. "For the safety of all of Salton."

"Right," the sheriff said. "But you mean, if they're real."

Uncle Alexander dropped his hand by his side. "Oh, they're real, sheriff. The Mongolian Death Worm is absolutely real and you do not want to tangle with one." He put his arm around Jason's shoulder. "Just ask Jason."

"Uh, yep." Jason glanced at his uncle who still had his gaze fixed on the sheriff. "They spit acid. Really . . . burny acid."

"Well . . ." The sheriff put on his hat. "Thank you for, uh, keeping Salton safe." He shook Uncle Alexander's hand. "It's good knowing we have you on our team. Now you all have a good day." He gave both dogs friendly pats on their heads and left the carriage house.

"Should we get out of here, too?" Colette asked. "I do not want to see a Mongolian Death Worm."

"No worries," Jason said. "He made up the whole story. Right, Uncle A?"

"I confess I did," he said. "The sheriff already believes I'm off my rocker, and when I heard that note in his voice, I decided to have a little fun." He turned to Jason. "Thank you for playing along."

"No problem, though now he thinks I'm off my rocker, too."

"Not at all. He'll just assume you're a good nephew humoring your half-baked uncle." He walked deeper into the carriage house. "Now let's inspect things and see if we notice anything Martina and the sheriff might have missed."

It didn't take long before Jason noticed bits of brown fur settled on stacked boxes of replacement dinnerware, and Uncle Alexander found a void in the freezer where packages of frozen meat had been. Gallons of ice cream appeared to have been rearranged to disguise the empty spot.

"So, we still have a Bigfoot problem," Sadie said.

"Yes, we do." Uncle Alexander pinched the bridge of his nose. "Though an odd one. There's no mess."

"Mess?" Brandon asked.

"Yes." Uncle Alexander turned to Jason and Sadie. "Correct me if I'm wrong, but the storage area at school was damaged, items were broken, things were out of sorts after the visit from the Bigfoot, correct?

"Yeah," Jason said. "And it stunk. It doesn't stink in here."

"But that *was* Bigfoot fur Jason found, wasn't it?" Sadie scanned the room.

"I believe so." Uncle Alexander opened the freezer and examined the contents again. "I suppose it's possible the ice cream wasn't so much rearranged as it was pawed, pushing it unintentionally into that spot . . ." He shut the door. "The creature must have been here for only a minute or two before it was somehow startled and took off. It wasn't here long enough to do any damage beyond the door."

Brandon looked around at the ceiling. "Are there any cameras?"

"Martina didn't see a need for them when she remodeled the property," Uncle Alexander said. "Salton isn't exactly a hotbed of crime."

"Just a home for a rogue cryptid," Jason said. "We need to find this thing."

✳ ✳ ✳

Uncle Alexander retrieved a rope and two tranquilizer dart guns from his car. If they found the Bigfoot, the plan was to tranq it and restrain it somewhere out of sight. They'd drive back at night, hopefully be able to park close to wherever they'd bound the Bigfoot, and load it into a cage in an enclosed truck bed. Uncle Alexander would later, with Dad's and Connor's assistance, drive the Bigfoot deep into wilderness away from Salton and release it unharmed.

Within seconds of Jason offering the dogs the cryptid fur he'd found in the carriage house, they scented a trail and led everyone into the woods. The dogs were excited and focused and kept a quick pace hiking farther and farther through clutches of cottonwoods and wide-open space. Thirty minutes passed with no Bigfoot sighting.

"How long do we follow the dogs?" Brandon puffed through the words.

"I'm asking myself the same question," Uncle Alexander said. "I'm surprised we're already this far out and still going. I expected to discover a nest before now, and closer to town."

"Should we split up?" Sadie asked. "Cover more territory?"

"Perhaps," Uncle Alexander said. "We have two tranq guns, and Jason knows how to shoot. Though I'm not sure we should split up the dogs since they're both zeroed in on the same direction, and Shay is still in training."

Just then, both dogs froze and looked to the right.

Everyone halted behind them and peered in the same direction.

"I don't see anything," Brandon whispered to Sadie. "Do you?"

"No, but why are we whispering?"

"In case the dogs are listening for something," he said.

Uncle Alexander gave them a thumbs up.

Jason watched as both dogs sniffed the air, paused another moment, then started again on a trail only they could sense.

"I guess it was nothing," Jason said to Uncle Alexander.

"Nothing worth—"

The dogs froze again and looked to the right. Shay cocked her head.

Jason scanned the area but nothing caught his attention. After a few more seconds he expected the dogs to resume their search, but they still didn't move.

"I think I heard something," Colette said, inching closer to Jason. "It sounded like a howl."

The dogs held their gaze.

More seconds passed.

Then Jason heard it.

A howl, or whine, emanated from something in the distance, but how far away was too hard to tell. He tapped Uncle Alexander.

"I hear it." Uncle Alexander removed binoculars from his messenger bag. He swept the landscape and then lowered the glasses. "I'm not seeing anything."

The sound rose again, but closer. The dogs kept their gazes locked.

Colette stepped behind Jason and grabbed onto his arm.

"You've seen plenty of Bigfoot at League headquarters," Jason said, keeping his voice low. "What's so scary about this one?"

"The ones I've seen are healthy and friendly," she said. "Not wild and destructive. So I'll just stick close to you, if you don't mind."

Jason didn't mind, not even a little.

A second later the sound wailed again, closer, and Colette jumped. Jason ignited fire in his fists.

"Wait," Sadie said. "That sounds like a kid."

Twigs crunched as something approached. Finn sat but Shay remained standing and half-growled, half-whined.

From behind a copse of trees came a boy, dressed in jeans and T-shirt but no jacket. He was crying.

"Hello, there," Uncle Alexander said.

The boy jumped, not realizing anyone was around. He stared for a moment then ran over and latched onto Uncle Alexander's waist, his tears flowing harder.

Uncle Alexander patted the boy's back. "It's all right, you're all right. Are you cold?" He signaled Jason to give the boy his jacket.

Jason hurried out of his coat and hung it around the boy's shoulders.

"Are you out here by yourself?" Uncle Alexander asked as he helped the boy maneuver his arms into the sleeves.

"Yeah," he said. "I was with my brother but he ditched me."

"That's terrible," Sadie said. "How long have you been out here?"

The boy shrugged. "I dunno. I was trying to find Derek but I couldn't find him. And then I couldn't find home either."

Derek? "Your brother isn't Derek Goodman, is he?" Jason asked.

The boy nodded. "Do you know him?"

"Yeah," Jason said. "We go to school with him." He glanced at Sadie and saw the disgust on her face.

The boy stiffened. "Are you friends with him?"

"Not even a little," Jason said. "Hope that's okay with you."

He smiled a bit. "Yeah, that's okay with me. I don't like him very much."

Totally understandable.

Colette bent down to his eye level. "What's your name?"

"Ash."

"Ash Goodman," she said. "That's a nice name."

"Dunaby," he said. "I'm Ash Dunaby. We have different parents."

Jason was taken aback. *Different parents? He must mean different dads.*

Shay stepped closer to the boy, her nose twitching as she worked scents around him.

Ash jumped. "I don't like dogs."

"She won't hurt you," Jason said. "She's just curious."

He scrambled behind Uncle Alexander. "No, no, no. Bad dog."

"No, really." Jason stroked Shay's head and asked her to sit. "She's a good dog. See?"

"Just keep her away from me." Ash had an edge to his voice.

Finn stood and Ash backed up farther. "I don't like dogs."

"Okay, okay." Jason took Finn's leash from Uncle Alexander and walked both dogs a few more feet away.

Uncle Alexander stepped up to Ash and put his arm around him. "Why don't we get you home. We were just about to head home ourselves. We can give you a lift."

Ash kept his eyes on the dogs. "Okay."

They headed toward Chez Martina, and Ash, who shared he'd recently turned ten years old and seemed proud of every one of his years, told Uncle Alexander his address.

"He doesn't live too far," Uncle Alexander said after they got back to the restaurant. "Would you all mind waiting here with Finn? I'll drop Ash off, then come back and give everyone a ride home. All right?" He loaded the rope and tranquilizer guns into his trunk.

"Sure thing, Uncle A," Jason said.

Ash returned Jason's coat and waved from the passenger seat of Uncle Alexander's car, his eyes fixed on the dogs as they drove off.

Jason suggested waiting on the patio and they headed that way.

"Poor kid," Brandon said. "I can't believe Derek ditched him out there. What if something had happened to him?"

"Derek is a horrible human being," Sadie said. "If he even is human."

"It *was* mean of him to do that," Colette said. "I don't suppose there could be a good reason for it?"

"To ditch a kid in the wilderness? In the winter? Without a coat?" Jason put one of his hands in his pocket.

"I can't think of any good reason to do something like that."

They gathered around one of the larger tables on the patio and sat. Jason looped each dog's leash on a chair leg near the edge of the patio enabling them to move from shade to sunshine. The dogs plopped down on a sunny patch of winter-brown grass.

"What's next?" Brandon asked. "More of the same out here tomorrow?"

Jason shifted his chair so his legs were in the sun. Heat soaked into his jeans. "Probably. If the weather's good."

Sadie checked her phone. "No snow or anything in the forecast. It will be warm all week."

"Then Uncle A and I will be out here. Or he may even want to come back this afternoon." Jason placed his hands on his thighs to warm his fingers. "But you guys don't have to come. It could be a whole lot of nothing. Feel free to—"

Hairs zinged on the back of his neck.

Both dogs sprang to standing and froze facing the cottonwoods behind the carriage house. Shay's hackles crept up her spine, shifting her coat from smooth to spiked.

Finn's front paw hovered midair. Her tail straightened like a metal rod.

Neither dog twitched.

Jason watched the trees but saw nothing. He moved toward the leashes.

A bass-drum growl rumbled in Finn's chest. She placed her paw forward on the ground. The legs of the chair semi-anchoring her scraped across the stone.

Shay's growl joined Finn's.

Jason unclipped their leashes. With his hand behind his back, he signaled the others to stay put, to not move, to avoid making a sound. He remained as transfixed on the trees as Finn and Shay.

Seconds later came a crash of branches and the dogs bolted.

Jason gave chase.

A Bigfoot fled through the brush up ahead and dodged behind thick stands of trees, Finn and Shay not far behind.

Jason was no match for the speed of the dogs but he willed himself faster, scraping through bramble and whacking with his arms to smash branches away.

He had to catch up. He had to get to the dogs, afraid Shay could get hurt still early in her training.

The dogs barked.

A lion-like roar followed.

Fear flooded Jason and he activated his power.

His arms fired blue and purple.

He veered around a corner and skidded to a halt, his breath coming hard.

On a boulder about forty feet away was the Bigfoot, its eyes wild and terrified. Splotches of its fur seemed singed.

Finn and Shay guarded the base of the stone, fixed on the Bigfoot, ready to block its escape.

The Bigfoot roared again but the dogs didn't budge.

Jason's mind raced. What was he going to do? He didn't have a tranquilizer gun. He didn't have ropes.

Sadie, Brandon, and Colette hurried to a stop behind him.

Sadie gasped. "What?" She gulped air. "It can't be. It can't." She sucked in a breath. "She's supposed to be dead."

Sadie rushed to Jason's side. "Kill her! You have to kill her!"

"What are you talking about?" Jason asked, not taking his eyes off the Bigfoot.

"That's Merinda." Sadie shoved Jason forward. "She killed Mamo!"

The Bigfoot crouched and snarled.

The dogs maintained focus.

The Bigfoot dragged a clawed hand across the rock.

The dogs didn't flinch.

"Do it, Jason," Sadie yelled.

"How are you sure it's her?"

"I saw her in Yowie form." Sadie sucked in more air. "That is Merinda."

Confusion and conflict collided in Jason's brain. The Bigfoot—Yowie—deserved to die. Didn't she?

Yes. Because she's Merinda. The traitor. The bounty hunter that tried to take Sadie.

The woman who killed Mamo.

But Jason had to be sure.

So many innocent people had died in London. Too many.

"Are you hearing me?" Sadie asked. "Kill her."

The creature remained crouched. It peeled back its lips and growled out a long, slow *raareee* sound, then silenced.

Shay sat. Finn moved closer to her, standing between Shay and the creature.

Good girl, Finn. Jason appreciated Finn was prepared to keep Shay safe, her training clearly lacking. She should not be relaxed, she should not be sitting. Jason kept his powers engaged and ready.

"What are you waiting for?" Sadie flung her arms, sunlight glinting off her bracelet.

The creature raised up.

Jason increased his power. "Stop, Sadie. You're antagonizing it."

"I'm antagonizing it?" She moved into Jason's peripheral line of sight. She pointed at the Yowie. "She. Killed. Mamo. Do you get what I am saying? How am I antagonizing Mamo's murderer? How is that even possible?"

He saw rage in Sadie's eyes. He knew that feeling. He knew the inclination to want someone dead. To make them pay.

To kill.

But he couldn't do it. He shouldn't do it.

Jason scrunched his eyes a second. He tried to think.

What made sense?

What should he do?

Uncle Alexander's words about problem-solving came to mind: *"What do we know about the situation?"*

Jason knew he had to stop this creature before something else happened.

Before someone else got hurt.

"Get back." Jason stepped forward. He reduced the intensity of his powers and aimed at the creature.

It leaped from the rock and over the dogs.

Jason fired, hitting the creature's leg.

It landed, tumbled and recovered, and limped fast toward deeper wilderness.

"Get her," Sadie yelled.

Jason aimed, ready to fire again, but the creature disappeared into the shadows. The dogs did not give chase.

Sadie crumpled to the ground. Tears flowed. Brandon hurried over and sat next to her.

"We'll get it . . . eh, her, next time," Jason said. "Uncle A and I will come back with the ropes and everything, and the dogs have a solid scent on her now so it shouldn't be too hard to find her."

Sadie threw a handful of mushy dead leaves at Jason shoes. "Get away from me."

"I said we'll get her. It's fine."

She stood and squared off with Jason. "It's not fine. You let Merinda get away like she's just some sweet little confused animal that lives in the woods. I told you who she was and you know what she did."

"I have to be sure," Jason said. "I'm not going to kill every cryptid we meet."

Sadie's eyes flashed. "So you don't trust I know what I'm talking about? You didn't believe I knew who she was? That I'd seen her before?" She backhanded the air. "Who would you believe, huh? And what are you going to do now? Catch her and make her take a DNA test?" She crossed her arms. "Will that be good enough for you?"

"I don't know."

"You're right, Jason, you don't know," Sadie said. "You have no idea what we went through while you were in London."

Jason felt anger rising at Sadie's unfairness. "I know it was bad."

More tears welled in her eyes. "'Bad' is a half-assed way to describe it. We went through hell. I went through hell. And you just let the woman who put us all through that hell run off to live happily ever after in the woods."

"I will get her." Jason's voice rose.

"And find her a nice new place to live." Sadie turned her back to Jason.

"That's not what I said."

Sadie spun to face him. "You should have killed her."

"Oh, yeah?" He took a step forward and raised his hands palms up. "Why didn't you kill her? Why didn't you shift into Yowie and beat the crap out of her? Rip her arms off or whatever it is you Yowie do to destroy your enemies?"

"Shut up, Jason," Sadie said. Brandon tried to put his arm around her but she shrugged it off. "You don't know anything about what I'm going through."

"I know you're not ready," he said. "I know you've been hiding from your powers. Is that why you didn't shift? Is that why you didn't kill her yourself? And now you're pissed because I wouldn't do your dirty work for you."

Sadie clenched her jaw and stepped up to Jason, stopping only a foot away. "I'm pissed because that woman, that Yowie," she pointed in the direction the Yowie had run, "destroyed my life. And you chose her over me." She stormed off.

Brandon shook his head at Jason and hurried after her.

Colette came closer with the dogs, both now on their leashes.

Shay leaned into Jason's leg.

"You okay?" Colette asked.

Jason stared after Sadie. "Nope," he said. "Definitely not okay."

EIGHT

Powerless

Sadie jiggled the knob of Connor's locked front door. She pounded her fist on the wood. "Connor, let me in." She poked the doorbell.

Ding-dong-ding-dong-ding-dong.

"Connor." She yelled this time.

"Maybe he isn't home," Brandon said.

Sadie took out her phone and punched Connor's name. The call connected and started to ring just as he opened the door.

"What is it?" His eyes flicked with worry between Sadie's and Brandon's faces.

Sadie pushed past him and Brandon followed.

"Has something happened? Is everyone okay?" Connor closed the door and joined Sadie and Brandon in the living room.

Sadie paced. "Merinda is alive."

"What?" Connor glanced from Sadie to Brandon and back. "That's not possible."

"It is possible," she said. "We just saw her. And Jason let her get away." She crossed the room to the spot where Mamo had fought with Merinda, where Merinda had stabbed her, where Mamo had died. The room had been remodeled and reconfigured since then, walls opened to flow to the kitchen, but Sadie knew where she was standing. She returned to Brandon and Connor.

"You saw her, too?" Connor asked Brandon.

"I saw a Yowie," he said, "and if Sadie says it was Merinda, then it was Merinda."

Connor sat on the couch. "But . . . after Merinda was killed, I no longer sensed her. And the level of Yowie energy hasn't since changed."

Sadie crossed her arms. "You said yourself your skills were rusty because you hadn't used them in a while. You missed her."

"Or could it be because she was hurt really bad?" Brandon asked. "It just seemed like she was gone?"

"I suppose it's possible." Connor's face contorted in confusion. "But how would I not have known about her as she healed? Unless . . ." He stood and headed into the kitchen and returned with his laptop. He scrolled through something on the screen, then stopped. "Yes, here it is. After a traumatic injury that results in brain damage, a Yowie's energy will be unlikely to carry a personal signature as they may, one, not know who they are because of amnesia or similar, or two, be in such a state that they must relearn any number of things, from speech to basic functions like dressing, feeding themselves, and so forth."

He shut the computer. "So, in simplest terms, if she isn't the person, the Yowie, that she was before what we perceived as her death, no Yowie would sense her energy as Merinda."

Connor stood and looked out the front window. "She shifted to starling, and Shay snatched her out of the air and shook her until we thought her neck was broken. There's no doubt in my mind that the shaking by Shay would have caused brain damage." He rubbed a spot on the side of his head. "It is also likely that Merinda has been in bird form for the entirety of her recovery thus far, only recently having healed enough to have the energy to shift to Yowie." He was talking more to himself than anyone else. He sighed and turned toward Sadie. "I'm so sorry, my dear. This is not good news for any of us."

Sadie's lip quivered. "We have to get her."

"And we will." Connor returned to the couch and signaled for Sadie to sit. He took out his phone. "I'll call Alexander and we'll discuss next steps. We must trap her somehow, which shouldn't be too hard with her reduced faculties."

Sadie ground her teeth. "No."

Connor stopped.

"Let's go now." She wagged her finger between herself and Brandon. "We saw the direction she went. The three of us can go after her right now."

Connor set down his phone. "I don't think that's a good idea. We don't have a plan or any weapons at hand."

"We have you," she said. "You're a Yowie."

"I'm in no shape to take on Merinda."

"Sure you are. Jason wounded her today." Acid bit into Sadie's throat as she recalled Jason's betrayal. "She'll be easier to get now."

Connor looked at the carpet. "I think we're taking things a bit too quickly."

"Fine." She snipped the word at Connor. "Brandon and I will do it."

Brandon closed his mouth tight before speaking. "Don't get me wrong. I'm one hundred percent on board for getting Merinda. But how are you and I going to take on a Yowie, even a wounded one? I don't have any super-skills, and you . . ."

She crossed her arms again.

"Well, have you shifted to Yowie again since that night?" Brandon asked.

Sadie had shifted to Yowie that night without even realizing she'd done it, and she'd battled Merinda who was also in Yowie form. With Shay's help, Sadie had defeated her.

Or so she thought.

Sadie hadn't shifted to Yowie again. She didn't need to. She didn't want to.

And now she didn't know if she could.

"No, I haven't." Sadie dropped onto the couch.

Connor had encouraged her to try, to practice at home. First, she made excuses about being busy and not finding time to practice. Then she'd told him she'd tried but was unable to shift.

But she'd never tried.

As long as the Calling couldn't see Sadie as ready, couldn't count on her having the ability to fight Garrison Devine, couldn't expect her to save everyone, she'd have more time under the cloak.

Hidden.

Safe.

Everyone in Salton was safe under the Calling's cloak.

But now there was Merinda. In Salton. Under the same cloak.

"What if she has a way to contact Devine and his people?" Sadie asked, her voice now small and tired.

Connor leaned forward and patted her knee. "I doubt she knows her name much less anything about you or Garrison." He leaned back and had a twinkle in his eye. "And besides, Yowie aren't great communicators."

"That's for sure," Brandon said. "She was just all *grrrs* and *arghs* and *roars*." He bared his teeth.

Air puffed with a hint of a laugh from Sadie's lungs. "I guess that's true."

She knew going after Merinda tonight wasn't a smart idea. She let the idea go for the moment.

But Sadie knew one more thing.

She had to stop Merinda before Merinda hurt, or killed, someone else Sadie loved.

NINE

Too Easy

Uncle Alexander returned to Chez Martina after dropping Ash home, and Jason relayed everything that happened with Merinda.

And with Sadie.

Uncle Alexander hurried toward the cottonwoods. "Show me where this took place."

Jason and Colette led Uncle Alexander to where they'd encountered the Yowie. The dogs scampered in and out of the brush sniffing and snorting on grasses and branches but didn't indicate a path to follow.

Uncle Alexander hunched. "Ah." He scraped dirt into one of the bags he carried to clean up after Finn during walks. "Blood sample. Though not much to work with, I'm afraid. Your blast may have cauterized the wound." He stood. "We need to refine our training with the new variable strength of your powers." He scanned more of the area.

"I lowered my intensity before I fired," Jason said. "I guess that was stupid. Not enough blood for you, and not enough killing for Sadie."

Uncle Alexander came over and put his arm around Jason's shoulders. "She'll be okay. She needs to process things."

"She doesn't need to process how much she hates me," he said. "She made that clear." He smacked a dry leaf dangling on the tip of a nearby branch.

"She might surprise you," Uncle Alexander said. "She's angry and upset, and I can't blame her. Merinda caused a great deal of damage to her and her family, and subsequently to all of us. But with a little time, I trust she'll come to realize her anger is misdirected at you."

"Maybe I'll call her later," Jason said.

"Ah, well, it would be best to give her some time . . . for now." He squeezed Jason's shoulder.

"Should I tell Lena what happened?" Colette asked.

"Definitely," Uncle Alexander said. "I'll talk to her as well."

Colette nodded. "I just hope it's not weird staying with them now."

"I'm certain it will be fine," Uncle Alexander said. "If I know my mother, she'll help Sadie through this in no time, and she won't let anyone living under the same roof be uncomfortable for long. But if need be, you're welcome to stay with me for a few days. The guest room is always available."

"Thanks," Colette said.

Uncle Alexander exhaled. "Between Bigfoot hunting, finding lost boys, and learning our Bigfoot was a thought-to-be-dead Yowie, it's been a long day." He headed out of the cottonwoods. "And it's still early in the afternoon."

"The rest of the day has to be easier." Jason and Shay trudged along the trail with Colette, following Uncle Alexander and Finn. "How was Ash when you dropped him off?" Jason asked.

"He was fine," Uncle Alexander said. "No worse for the experience. He seemed rather indifferent to it all once he was settled in the car. He pointed out where to turn, which driveway was his, and dashed off as soon as we stopped."

"Was Derek there?" Jason asked.

"I didn't see any other kids, but I met Mr. and Mrs. Dunaby. Interesting couple."

"How so?" Colette asked.

"Well, they came outside when I pulled up. I got out of the car and said hello, but neither of them responded. If I hadn't walked over and introduced myself, I'm not sure they would have spoken two words to me." He cocked his head to the side. "As it is, I still only heard three words from them. Mr. Dunaby said, 'hey' when I introduced myself, and 'well, thanks,' when I left. She never spoke."

"They didn't ask questions?" Jason unclipped Shay's leash, and she leaped into the backseat with Finn. "Like about why you had their kid in your car?"

"No," Uncle Alexander said. "I told them we'd been hiking and met Ash on the trail and offered him a ride home. I didn't mention Derek had abandoned Ash—I figured that information should come from him. Perhaps after he shares the story with them, they'll have a more emotional reaction." He slid into the driver's seat. "But as it was, they acted as if there was nothing unusual about the situation."

"Weird." Jason fastened his seatbelt.

"It takes all kinds of people to make the world go 'round, I suppose." Uncle Alexander started the car.

"That's something we all know for sure," Colette said.

✳ ✳ ✳

Uncle Alexander pulled up in front of Sadie's house, put the car in park and set the brake. "I'll walk in with you, Colette. We can bring my mom up to speed together, if she hasn't already heard from Sadie." He opened the car door.

"That would be lovely." Colette unlatched her seatbelt. "I'd much rather you tell Lena what's going on. I'm not sure what to say." She turned toward Jason. "I'll talk to you later."

"Yeah, later." Jason scratched the chests of both dogs as he watched Colette and Uncle Alexander enter the house. His uncle came out about ten minutes later.

Jason moved from the back seat to the front. "How'd it go with Grandma Lena?"

"As well as to be expected." Uncle Alexander turned the key in the ignition. "She's upset to learn Merinda is still alive. But you know how strong your grandmother is. She'll hardly let this put a dent in her day. She was already on me to find a solution to this problem."

"Yep, that sounds like Grandma Lena," Jason said. "How was Sadie?"

"Not home. She and Brandon are at Connor's place."

"Did you tell Grandma Lena about me and Sadie?"

"I did. She'll talk to her." He pulled away from the curb.

"Good." Jason leaned into the seatback. "She'll tell Sadie she shouldn't be so mad at me."

"But why shouldn't she be?" Uncle Alexander asked.

Jason jerked his head to look at his uncle. "What do you mean? She's totally wrong. I didn't do anything."

"That's just it."

"That's just what?" Jason's voice pitched higher. "A little while ago you said you thought Sadie's anger at me was . . . was . . . misdirected. You said it was misdirected, but now you think she *should* be mad at me?"

"I'm saying I understand why she is mad at you," Uncle Alexander said.

Jason crossed his arms. "Then you're the only one who does. Because no way she should be mad at me."

Uncle Alexander pulled off to the side of the road and turned to Jason. "Why didn't you do as Sadie asked?"

"I attacked the Yowie-what's-her-name, Merinda." Jason's words came fast. "I used my powers, I fired at her, I burned her leg and knocked her to the freaking ground."

"But Sadie told you the Yowie murdered Mamo. Didn't she?"

"Yeah, but—"

"Did you believe her?"

"Well, yeah, but—"

"But you lowered the magnitude of your power."

"Yeah—"

"You chose to disregard what Sadie had told you. You didn't trust her."

"I did, I do, but—"

"But what, Jason?" Uncle Alexander's tone was urgent. "What were you thinking?"

"I was thinking I didn't want to kill someone again!" The words blurted out. An inhale of air caught in his throat and he swallowed.

Uncle Alexander said nothing.

Jason took another breath. "So many people and cryptids died at the League, and they didn't deserve it. Because of the serum, because of the mind-control, they didn't know what they were doing. They didn't mean to be bad. And they died." He took another breath. "And I killed them. Me. I killed them like it was nothing."

Uncle Alexander squeezed Jason's knee. "It wasn't nothing."

"I know," he said. "But it was so easy. We were fighting, and I amped my powers, and I used them against everyone. I didn't even think about it."

"You were fighting for your life, for the lives of your family, for your friends," Uncle Alexander said. "For Colette."

He shook his head. "I thought Colette and Della were dead. And I wanted Rick dead because he killed them. And hurt you. And hurt Dad. And everyone."

"That's understandable."

"But Uncle A, you don't get it." Jason closed his eyes a moment, picturing the final battle at the League. "It was so easy. Too easy."

"What do you mean?"

"I mean . . . I think I mean . . ." Jason scrunched his fists into his forehead. "What if I'm like Mom? Mom killed Grandpa Tate like it was nothing. Rick wanted him dead, so she killed him. Her own dad. Your dad. Like it was easy."

Uncle Alexander's hand gripped harder on the steering wheel. "You're not like your mother."

"And I don't want to be like her," Jason said. "But what if I am? What if I inherited some bad juju gene from her that gets worse as I get older? You said she was great until high school, and then she started to change. *I'm* in high school."

Uncle Alexander paused a moment, then a slight smile crossed his face.

"What's funny?" Jason's shoulders slumped. "I knew I shouldn't have said anything."

"I'm proud of you," Uncle Alexander said.

He looked at his uncle. "Huh?"

Uncle Alexander put his hand on Jason's forearm. "I'm proud of you."

"For what?" Confusion whirled, slippery in Jason's mind. Hadn't Uncle Alexander heard him? Wasn't he listening?

"You did the right thing today, with Merinda." He nodded. "Even though your best friend asked you to do something different, you followed your own moral compass and made a sound decision. A good decision." He shrugged. "That's a far cry from what your mother would have done."

A knot in Jason's chest untangled a tiny bit. "But in London . . ."

"You were fighting for your life and, frankly, for the lives of hundreds of people you didn't know," Uncle Alexander said. "The situation called for you to defend not only yourself but also those people and cryptids who couldn't defend themselves. You weren't fighting for your own gain like your mother or Rick would have done. You were fighting for the good of others."

The knot wriggled looser. "It doesn't feel good."

Uncle Alexander sighed. "You've been dealt a tough hand, Jason. You and Sadie both. No one should have to go through what you've been through, and especially at your age. What you've had to deal with isn't right, it isn't fair, it isn't even a little bit okay." He shifted in his seat to more fully face Jason. "But you've handled it incredibly well. And no, innocents should not have died. But that is not on you. The death and destruction at the League—that's on Rick. All of it. Whether by his own hand, or his control and manipulation of others, it's all Rick."

"And Mom."

A sadness shaded Uncle Alexander's face. "And your mom. But not you. And it never will be you." He gripped Jason's shoulder. "You'll never be like your mother."

"Promise?"

Uncle Alexander faced forward in his seat. "I don't have to promise. You don't have it in you to choose the dark side."

The knot floated apart but a few small strands stuck, knitted in the center of Jason's chest.

"One thing I did promise to your grandmother is that we'd quickly come up with a plan to deal with Merinda." He signaled and checked for traffic. "If you're up for it, let's work with your powers this afternoon. I'd also like to talk to Connor and get his input."

Jason shied away from the cold of Shay's nose in his ear. "I'm up for it. The sooner we deal with Merinda, the sooner Sadie can stop hating me."

✳ ✳ ✳

Two hours later, Jason lay on the floor of the gym in Uncle Alexander's basement. Sweat streamed down his temples, into his hair, and dripped on the mat. Shay lay at his side. She licked off a trickle of moisture.

"Ugh, that is gross," Jason said, secretly relieved that the tickle of water was gone. She moved in for another taste but he scooted a few inches sideways. "No baths, thanks. I'll take a shower." Her tail thumped the floor.

"Good work today," Uncle Alexander said. "You're getting quite a good sense for the different levels of intensity at your disposal. Have you been practicing outside of training?"

Jason raised onto his elbows. "Some, over break. But I didn't want to overdo it like before. I swear every time I get a little tired or something, I hear your voice in my head lecturing me about overtraining."

Uncle Alexander chuckled. "Good. And I was right about the overtraining."

"As you continue to remind me." Jason reached for a towel and wiped off his face and neck.

"It is a pleasure to do so." Uncle Alexander waved Jason over to the monitor at the end of the room. "Look at this."

On the screen was a still image of Jason engulfed in a fiery ball of blue that reached about three feet beyond his outstretched arms and above his head. Uncle Alexander pushed play and the outer edges of the energy pulsated, almost vibrated, like water in a bowl that's been bumped.

"What are you feeling here?" Uncle Alexander asked.

"Hot."

"Too hot? Painfully so?"

"No," Jason said. "Just like sauna-hot."

"Good. What else?"

"I don't know. Maybe kind of rattly? Like I have pebbles pinging inside me."

Uncle Alexander bobbed his head up and down. "Tell me more about that sensation."

Jason pushed the towel over his head, absorbing sweat from his hair. "I don't get what it is, I mean, I don't know what I'm supposed to do with it. After a few seconds, I drop the power down a couple notches because it feels weird and I want to stop feeling weird."

"I have a theory," Uncle Alexander said. "Are you up for one to two more exercises?"

Jason slumped. "What about overtraining? I'm wiped, and I'm hungry."

"Okay, one attempt. For your dear uncle." He switched off the monitor. "And if you overdo it and collapse into a heap, I'll take full responsibility, and you can mock me endlessly for years to come."

Jason huffed. "Fine."

"Excellent." Uncle Alexander slid a table away from the wall and closer to the center of the room. "Besides your ability to use heat and electricity at varying degrees, firing bolts, and blasts, I believe you have some control over sound waves." He rubbed his hands together with anticipation, placed a medicine ball on the table, and grinned. "And if that's the case, you should be able to direct sound waves and move the medicine ball off the table." He directed Jason onto the mat. "Generate the level of power that feels like pebbles vibrating inside of you and concentrate on moving the medicine ball."

Jason readied his hands.

"No," Uncle Alexander said. "You should attempt it without using your hands."

Jason arched one brow. "So, I'll mind-move the ball off the table?"

"Perhaps. Or perhaps not. That's what we're hoping to learn."

"Okay, then. Here goes I-don't-know-what." Jason's hands, still down by his sides, turned blue as he initialized his Guard power.

"Hold on, hold on," Uncle Alexander yelled.

Jason extinguished the energy.

Uncle Alexander called to the dogs and hurried behind a blast wall installed at the far end of the room.

"Seriously? For a medicine ball?"

"This is new territory," Uncle Alexander said through the Plexiglass window. "Safety first."

Jason rolled his eyes and ignited his powers. He leveled them up, increased them again, then maxed into the blue orb.

Energy waves rippled.

The sensation of tiny stones rattled under his skin.

He focused on the medicine ball. It vibrated. It jiggled. It quaked in its spot.

Wham!

Both table and ball crashed into the far wall.

Jason pitched onto the floor and immediately cut his powers.

Uncle Alexander touchdowned his arms from behind the safety barrier.

"Not sure why you're celebrating." Jason pushed himself to standing.

"Because that was fantastic." Uncle Alexander stepped out and walked over with Jason's water bottle. "My hypothesis is sound."

"Was your hypothesis that I'd kick my own butt?" He drank from the bottle.

"Of course not. We have some work to do." Uncle Alexander inspected the damage where the table had chunked off crumbles of drywall. "But once mastered," he turned toward Jason, "you could apprehend our targets without burning them, without injury."

"Unless I knock them into a wall. Or something harder."

"As I said, we have some work to do. But we'll get there, and quickly. The Lex coin seems determined to have you master your new skills sooner rather than later."

Jason pulled the coin out of the pocket of his sweat pants. "No new images or anything. Still the coat of arms on one side and the Lex name on the other."

"Doesn't surprise me. There's no need for the coin to send us any signals if we're on the right track. Which I'm certain we are."

"I still wish we could ask it things." Jason rubbed a spot of tarnish with his towel. "Like what are we supposed to do with Merinda?"

"I have an idea about that." Uncle Alexander headed toward the stairs. Jason and the dogs followed him up to the main floor. "I talked to Connor earlier. He believes Merinda is suffering from brain damage and doesn't realize who she is, which is why he didn't sense her. And he's on the same page as us—he is not inclined to, well, terminate Merinda when we find her, regardless of the horrible things she's done. Connor would like to see her brought to justice."

They went into the kitchen. "So, we catch her and turn her over to someone? Like who?"

"Connor doesn't trust anyone within the Clan. He has no way of knowing who is loyal to Garrison Devine and who isn't." Uncle Alexander handed an apple to Jason and removed some string cheese from the refrigerator. "I suggested to him we simply send her to the League of Governors."

Jason shuddered at the memory of rigged trials and extreme punishment he'd seen at the League while it was being run by Rick, before Jason had helped set things right again. "Now that they aren't all whacked there, yeah, that's a good idea," Jason said. "Maybe we'd even get to see Barty and Elizabeth. But let's make them come and get Merinda. I'm not up for another trip to London yet."

"You and me both." Uncle Alexander bit into an unwrapped string cheese.

Jason unwrapped two for himself. He peeled off strings for Shay and Finn, then bit into both of the remaining tube-shaped cheeses at the same time. "Sadie won't like it."

"Sending Merinda to the League?"

"Sending Merinda anywhere," Jason said. "She wants her dead."

Uncle Alexander thought for a moment. "She's upset now, but she has a good head on her shoulders. She'll want to do the right thing."

"Not the Sadie I saw today."

"No, but she'll calm down," Uncle Alexander said. "And she'll support the plan."

Jason hoped as hard as he could that Uncle Alexander was right.

TEN

Attack

Sadie said goodbye to Brandon and Connor and headed home.

"Hello," she called as she entered her front door.

Lena hurried from the kitchen and swept Sadie into a long hug. "Are you okay?"

Sadie held tight. "Better than I was." She released Lena's embrace. "It really sucks though."

"Yes, it does," Lena said. "No doubt about it. I've tasked Alexander with finding a solution for us as fast as he can. He and Jason both."

Sadie's muscles tensed. She stepped around Lena and came face to face with Colette.

Colette gave a small wave. "Hi."

"Hi." Sadie averted her eyes and moved past Colette, into the kitchen. Footsteps followed. Sadie opened the pantry door and peered inside, bracing herself for a conversation she didn't want to have.

"I understand you're upset with Jason," Lena said.

Sadie moved to the refrigerator and grabbed a yogurt. She peeled back the foil lid and snatched a spoon from the drawer.

"And I understand why you're upset with him," Lena continued, "but with time, the two of you will come to an understanding."

Sadie shrugged and spooned yogurt into her mouth.

"Obviously such a thing won't happen today, nor do I expect that it would. But what should happen today is that you and Colette talk." Lena picked up her handbag and looked from Sadie to Colette. "Yes, Colette is seeing Jason, but she isn't Jason, and it's unfair to allow any frustration you have with him impact the relationship you have with her." Lena put her hand on the door to the garage. "I'm going to the post office and grocery shopping. I'll be back in about an hour. Are you still going to Nessa's tonight?"

"I doubt it," Sadie said, taking another bite of yogurt.

"Well, that would be a shame," Lena said. "If ever there was a day in need of a little fun, it's this one. You two should discuss it." She opened the door. "I'll be back soon."

Colette took a half step forward. "Do you want to talk?"

Sadie stared at the ceiling. "I don't know what I want right now."

"How about biscuits?" Colette walked to the pantry, pulled out a bag of mini chocolate chip cookies and held them up using her formerly-sling-bound arm. "Biscuits, or I mean, cookies seem to be good for any situation."

Lena was right, wasn't she? It wasn't fair to be mad at Colette.

Sadie signaled for Colette to bring the cookies to the table. "Cookies are a fine dessert to follow yogurt." She sat.

Colette sat next to her. "Are they? Is that an American thing?"

"It's a universal thing," Sadie said. "Cookies go with everything." She took a handful from the bag and popped one into her mouth.

Colette smiled and grabbed her own handful. "I'm sorry you're upset with Jason. I don't know what to say."

"You don't have to say anything. It's not you. But I can't be around him for a while."

"I understand. But I hope you two can work things out soon. He feels terrible about what happened."

"I don't want to talk about him," Sadie said.

"I get it. I just wish I could make you feel better, outside of a cookie bender," Colette said. "One thing I can say is I know how you feel. If I'd had the opportunity to kill the Governess the moment she ordered the execution of my father, I might have—" A choke cut off Colette's words. She shook her head slightly. "Of course, we found out later she was being controlled by Rick Shannon."

"What about now?" Sadie asked.

"Now?"

"Yeah. What if Rick Shannon, who we all believe is dead, showed up in Salton, with amnesia? Would you want to kill him?"

Colette leaned back in her chair. "Maybe?"

"You don't know for sure?"

"It's such an improbable situation," Colette said. "And so much has happened since then, and there were so many things going on I didn't know. And killing someone . . ."

"You couldn't do it." Sadie ate another cookie and surmised weakness in Colette.

"It's more that I don't want to do it. I don't want to kill anyone." Colette tucked her dark hair behind her ears. "Even if I were fighting for my life, I hope I'd never have to kill someone. I'm not sure I could deal with that."

"Merinda didn't—doesn't—have a problem with killing." Sadie crushed crumbs of cookie between her fingers.

"No, it seems not. And she's done a lot of damage, caused a lot of pain."

"And she should pay."

"Absolutely," Colette said.

Sadie would make Merinda pay. For herself and for Mamo. And Mamo would agree with what Sadie was considering, if she were here. Mamo was herself trying to kill Merinda when Merinda got the upper hand.

Wasn't she?

"Sadie?" Colette touched Sadie's arm.

She snapped her attention back to the room. "Huh?"

"I asked you if you still wanted to go to Nessa's," Colette said. "Could be good for us to have some fun, get our minds off things for a while."

"Oh, right." Sadie couldn't do anything about Merinda tonight. Not by herself. Not without a reliable ability to shift into Yowie. "That's a good idea. We should go to Nessa's."

"Brilliant. And hopefully she'll have more biscuits." Colette bit into the last chocolate chip cookie. The gnarl of badly healed bones in her forearm was obvious as she raised her hand to her mouth.

"How's your arm?" Sadie asked.

Colette pushed her arm to straighten it until it stopped short, a bend locked in her elbow, and the bump jutting out. "Still good."

"I wish I could have done more to fix the damage," Sadie said.

"You've already done so much." Colette moved her arm left and right. "Compared to life in a sling, I can't complain."

"Maybe my healing power will improve with the Calling." *Someday. Not now. Not soon.* "We can try again then if you want to."

"I don't want to be a bother."

"Don't be silly," Sadie said. "I'd love to repair all of the injury if I can."

Colette's eyes shimmered and she covered her mouth.

"What's wrong?" Sadie placed her hand on Colette's knee. "I didn't mean to upset you."

"You didn't." Colette sniffed. "I just feel so lucky to have you, and everyone here, in my life."

"Aww." Sadie leaned over and hugged her. "We're family."

"That's exactly how it feels to me," Colette said. "Thank you."

Both Sadie's and Colette's phones buzzed at the same time with a text message from Nessa: "Come over earlier! I want my girls here! Friends don't let friends do junk food alone!"

"What do you reckon?" Colette asked Sadie.

"Well, I wanted to spend more time practicing, trying to shift to Yowie before going to Nessa's," Sadie said. "But that would probably be a waste of time anyway."

"Why do you say that?"

"I worked on it with Connor today but couldn't generate even a hint of Yowie. He said I was too tired, too worked up from everything that happened. Told me to take a break for a while."

"You should listen to your wise great-uncle," Colette said. "Plus, junk food and girl talk and bingeing all of our favorite shows sooner rather than later."

"How can I resist all of that?" Sadie picked up her phone. "When should I tell her we'll be there?"

"How soon can you get your things together?" Colette asked. "I can be ready in twenty minutes."

Sadie texted Nessa: "See you as soon as we can get there."

A second later came a return message from Nessa with a heart-shape-eyed emoji.

*** ✳ ✳ ✳ ***

Sadie and Colette walked up the path to Nessa's house in the waning light of day. The front door opened and Nessa dashed outside. She wore green pajamas decorated with images of cakes and pastries and pies.

"Besties!" She hugged Sadie and Colette. She pranced her bare feet on the cold sidewalk. "Hurry hurry hurry. Inside now. Too cold on toes." She scurried into the house with Sadie and Colette close behind.

"First, PJs." Nessa pointed toward the guest bathroom. "We are all loungey all the time."

"No argument from me," Colette said.

"Me either." Sadie headed into the bathroom where she and Colette changed. Afterward, they helped Nessa carry from the kitchen to the family room a bowl of peanut M&Ms, a tin divided with three flavors of popcorn, a package of red licorice, a container of donut holes dipped in powdered sugar, and another bowl with chocolate-covered raisins which Nessa said were healthy, "Because fruit."

Just as they started to dig in, the doorbell rang. Nessa jumped up. "That must be the pizza."

"You ordered a pizza, too?" Sadie asked.

"Because we need veggies," Nessa said. "And all the better if veggies come with cheese and bread and tomato sauce. And tomato sauce counts as more veggie. Or fruit."

Colette turned to Sadie as Nessa exited the room. "She is the queen of the sleepover. We need to up our game."

"No doubt," Sadie said.

"And there are ice cream bars in the freezer," Nessa yelled from the other room. "The kind with caramel in the center."

"Can she be knighted for these skills?" Sadie asked.

"I'll send a note to the monarchy first thing tomorrow." Colette snapped off a bite of licorice.

A few minutes later, Nessa returned with paper plates, napkins, and a steamy hot, veggie-loaded pepperoni pizza. She plopped down on the couch. "Let the yum begin." She served herself a slice and sighed.

"We were talking about you while you were gone," Sadie said.

Nessa stopped mid-bite, appearing distressed.

"Yes," Colette said. "We were saying how amazing you are, and this will be the best sleepover of our lives to date."

Nessa squealed and resumed biting into her slice. She chewed and smiled and swallowed. "I live to serve."

"Is your mom out of town?" Sadie asked.

"Yeah, still on the road," Nessa said. "Always on the road. And my dad and brother are off to a car show, then they're going to a midnight premiere of a horror movie which I have zero desire to see. So, we basically have the house to ourselves all night."

"Nice." Sadie high-fived Nessa.

"Right?" Nessa ate another bite of pizza. "And next on our agenda is girl talk, starting with you, Sadie. Let's talk Brandon."

"Let's not."

"C'mon," Nessa said. "You're not weaseling out of that hot topic."

"Well," Colette said, "I propose we start with a different topic. I want Nessa to tell us what was going on with the whole act of evading Kyle this week."

"Good idea," Sadie said. "What was up with that?"

"I told you already," she said. "I kept running into him and I didn't want him to get the wrong idea."

"And you really weren't trying to run into him," Sadie said.

Nessa placed her hand on her heart. "I swear."

Something in Nessa's demeanor seemed off. "What aren't you telling us?" Sadie asked.

"Nothing. That's the whole story." Nessa took another bite of pizza.

"Ah." Sadie pointed at Nessa. "You're blushing."

Nessa covered her face with a napkin. "I'm not."

"You definitely are," Colette said.

"Spill." Sadie twirled her finger in the air. "Give us the real scoop.

Nessa glanced from Colette to Sadie. She set her plate on the coffee table and placed her hands in her lap. "On Monday evening, Kyle called and asked if I wanted to hang out with him." Her face was unemotional.

"What?" Sadie clasped her hands together. "That's great."

Nessa's expression remained neutral.

"It's not great?" Colette asked.

"I don't think so." Nessa shook her head.

"Why not?" Sadie asked. "You've been crushing on him forever. This is like the dream-come-true phone call."

"No, it isn't. And I'm so embarrassed."

"And I'm so confused," Sadie said. "Why are you embarrassed?"

"Because he only called me after I made that dumb comment at lunch that day, saying he could tutor me in PE. Which I totally didn't mean to say." She held her fisted hands up by her face. "He must think I meant, well, you know, like I meant something else."

"Like what?" Colette asked.

"He knows you didn't mean that," Sadie said.

"Mean what?" Colette asked again.

"She's afraid he thinks she meant something that has to do with taking their clothes off."

"Oh!" Colette looked at Nessa. "Did you mean that?"

"No!" Nessa flung a few M&Ms in her mouth. "But why else would he suddenly call me, the same day I said that to him?"

"Because he likes you," Sadie said.

"Because he thinks I'll take my clothes off." She filled her mouth with more M&Ms.

Sadie chuckled. "He does not think that. One, he knows you. He's known you for years. He knows you're not that kind of person."

Nessa chewed on her mouthful of candy.

Sadie continued. "And he's been around us more the last couple of months. He's gotten to know you better, and I think he likes you." She picked an olive off a slice of pizza and ate it.

"But he called me *that day*," Nessa said.

"So?" Sadie asked. "I think it was because of you he came and sat with us at lunch."

"Right," Colette said. "That makes sense. It was odd for him to say he wanted to spend more time with Jason." She turned back to Nessa. "Kyle definitely likes you."

Nessa swallowed. "Really?"

"Totally," Sadie said. "So, what did you tell him when he asked you out?"

"Nothing. I . . . I pretended the call dropped."

Sadie smacked Nessa's knee. "You hung up on him?"

"This is exactly why I didn't tell you."

"Because you were a dork, and I'd tell you so?" Sadie asked.

Nessa shrugged. "Yes."

"Did he call you back?" Colette asked.

"A couple of times." Nessa stood. "I'll get us more drinks."

"Sit." Sadie pointed to the couch.

Nessa dropped back into her spot.

Sadie crossed her arms. "I'm guessing you didn't answer his calls, and you haven't called him back."

"Your guess is correct." She picked up a piece of licorice.

"And you were dodging him at school because you didn't want to talk to him," Colette added.

"You are both so smart," Nessa said. "I'm so lucky to have you."

"Yes, you are. And we want the best for you." Sadie picked up Nessa's phone. "Which is why we will hold your hand while you call Kyle. Unlock your phone."

"Now?" Nessa waved both hands in the air. "No way. There's no way I can call him now after a whole week has gone by."

"Then I'll call him." Sadie picked up her own phone, punched Kyle's number, and put it on speaker.

"No—" Nessa covered her mouth with her hands when she heard Kyle's voice.

"Hello?"

"Hey, Kyle. It's Sadie."

"Hey, what's up?"

"I'm here with Nessa. She mentioned you tried to reach her this week."

Nessa buried her face in a couch cushion.

"Yeah, we got cut off."

"She has been embarrassed to call you back—"

Nessa bolted upright, her eyes wild, her face beet red.

"—because so many days went by without calling you. But her phone wasn't working, so I told her I'd call you and explain, and that you'd see it was no big deal."

Nessa fell face down, smothering herself again in a cushion.

"Oh, yeah, that's totally no big deal," Kyle said. "Can I talk to her?"

Nessa yanked the cushion off her face. "No, no, no, no, no." She mouthed the words.

"Sure," Sadie said. "Let me get her for you." She held her phone out to Nessa.

Nessa breathed out a silent breath and fanned her face with both hands. She took the phone. "Hey, Kyle. Sorry about not calling you back." She steadied her voice and took the call off speaker.

Sadie and Colette left the room, giving Nessa a sense of privacy, but listening from the kitchen. Sadie heard Nessa agree to something, say a couple of "uh-huhs," and a little while later Nessa squealed. Sadie and Colette headed back into the family room.

Nessa barreled into them with a bouncing hug. "I'm going on a date with Kyle Lex next Friday. You are the best besties ever. Dream come true. Dream come true. Yay me."

※ ※ ※

Hours passed with more pizza, more candy, and five straight episodes of their favorite show about demons and angels fighting to take over the world for good, for evil, or for their own self-interests.

"One more episode?" Nessa asked. "I have to find out if they stop the meat-suit guy."

Sadie yawned and checked the time on her phone. It was almost one a.m. "I can't stay awake long enough to watch another episode."

"Neither can I." Colette scrunched into a pillow.

"Now you're making me sleepy," Nessa said, "with your yawning and your pillow hugging."

"Maybe we can watch the next episode in the morning," Sadie said. "I want to find out what happens, too. But now, sleep."

Nessa left and came back with a trash bag. "My dad hates it when we leave food containers and stuff in the inside garbage. I'll take it out."

They helped her fill the bag with the pizza box, plates, and napkins. Nessa carried the bag outside while Sadie and

Colette put the containers of snacks on the counter in the kitchen.

A moment later, Nessa came in along with a bitter blast of air. "Oh, my gosh, it's cold outside." She rubbed her arms. "Start spring now, please."

"If only it was that easy." Sadie helped herself to a glass of water and they all headed up to Nessa's room.

Nessa flopped onto the larger, lower bed of her bunk beds and Sadie climbed up top. Colette crashed on an air mattress on the floor.

"Goodnight, besties," Nessa said.

"Goodnight," Sadie and Colette each said in return.

Soon Sadie heard soft sleep breath coming from both Nessa and Colette. Sadie replayed the evening, thinking about how much fun she'd had, how good it was to hang out with Nessa and Colette . . . her thoughts smeared and blended and faded . . .

Clang!

Sadie bolted upright.

"What was that?" Colette asked in a whisper.

"Probably a raccoon." Nessa got out of bed and went to her window. "They sometimes get in our garbage."

"See anything?" Sadie asked.

"No, it's too—"

Crash!

Nessa jumped.

Sadie climbed down and joined her at the window. "Did it tip over the garbage?"

"I think so." Nessa craned her neck to peer down the side of the house. "But I can't see—" She gasped and skittered backward. "Someone's out there."

"What?" Sadie scanned outside, her pulse quickening. Colette hurried to join her.

"Do you see anyone?" Nessa asked.

Sadie watched for a long moment, then stepped away from the window. "No. You probably just saw the raccoon's shadow or something.

"Okay, good." Nessa crawled back into bed. "I shouldn't eat so much sugar. My mom says it makes me jittery."

As Sadie started her climb to the upper bunk, Colette noiselessly grabbed her arm and pulled her toward the window.

Staring up at them, breath steaming from its mouth and its nose, was the Yowie.

Merinda.

She bared her teeth then darted toward the back of the house.

Sadie's adrenaline spiked. "Did we remember to lock the doors?"

"They're locked," Nessa said. "I always lock them when my dad's not here."

"I'll just double-check," Sadie said. "And I'll, uh, fix the garbage can so there's no mess when your dad gets home." She hurried out of the room with zero intention of going outside but determined to scope out what Merinda was doing.

Bam bam bam.

Sadie stopped at the top of the stairs. The noise had come from the sliding glass door to the backyard.

"What was that?" Nessa yelled.

"Uh, not sure," Sadie said.

A few seconds later, Nessa stood by Sadie's side, tucked close.

Colette joined them. "What do we do now?"

Sadie turned to Nessa. "Do you have any baseball bats or anything like that?"

The pounding noise came again. Louder. Harder.

"Oh my god, oh my god, oh my god." Nessa's eyes widened. "We need to call the police."

"I already called for help," Colette said.

Sadie shot her a look and Colette gave a nod. Sadie turned back to Nessa. "We should try to scare them away."

"Them? How many people are out there?" Nessa hunched down.

Sadie hunched next to her. "I mean 'them' in a generic way. But we need to be ready to defend ourselves before the police get here, just in case. Any bats? Or anything?"

"Mudroom," Nessa said. "My brother's baseball stuff is in the mudroom."

"I'm going down there." Sadie looked at Colette.

"Me too," she said.

Sadie turned back to Nessa. "You can wait here."

Nessa stood. "No way. I've seen enough scary movies to know that staying by yourself is a bad idea."

Bam bam bam.

Nessa muffled a scream. Her eyes teared. "Why are they doing that?"

Sadie put her arm around Nessa. "C'mon. We'll be okay."

They started down the stairs and moved toward the back of the house. Sadie peered around a corner first, checking the glass patio door. No one was there. *Hopefully, she's gone.* She waved Nessa forward.

Boom!

Nessa screamed.

Merinda was pressed into the glass, her hands above her head, her mouth steaming the window, her body lit by floodlights.

Boom boom boom! She pounded her fists on the window.

Nessa stifled another scream and ducked behind the counter with Sadie and Colette. "Oh my god! What is that thing?"

Neither Sadie nor Colette answered.

"Where are the sirens? Why don't we hear sirens?" Nessa's hands were shaking.

A scraping sounded, scratching and clawing. Sadie peeked out and saw Merinda using her feet, left foot then right, gouging her claws into the lower third of the glass. She growled.

Sadie pulled herself back behind the counter.

Nessa held her hands over her ears and scrunched her eyes.

Colette pulled Nessa close, eyed Sadie and mouthed, "What now?"

Sadie scooted farther away. She shut her eyes. She focused on Yowie. She needed to shift into Yowie. *C'mon, c'mon, c'mon.*

Boom boom boom!

Come on! Sadie steeled her fists and her jaws and gut. She demanded her Yowie come out, transform her, make her ready to fight.

She opened her eyes. Still Sadie. "Damn it."

"What's it doing?" Nessa asked.

Boom boom boom!

"Oh my god," Nessa said. "It wants to get us. It wants to get in."

Sadie stood and stepped out from behind the counter.

"No, don't go over there." Nessa grabbed for the leg of Sadie's pajamas. The fabric slipped through her grasp.

"Sadie," Colette said. "You can't."

Sadie ignored them, strode to the glass and faced Merinda with her arms raised in the air. "Get out of here!"

Boom boom—

Merinda stopped and stared at Sadie. She bared her teeth.

Sadie marched up and smacked her hand onto the glass in front of Merinda's face, the charms of her bracelet clanking against the surface.

Merinda's head snapped back.

"Get away from us!" Sadie whacked the window again.

Merinda lurched forward, unafraid. She compressed her forehead onto the window and glared down at Sadie like she dared her to strike again.

Sadie punched the spot.

Merinda roared and pounded both of her fists into the window. *Boom boom boom boom boom boom boom.*

"Look what you did," Nessa yelled. She was standing now, gawking at the scene. "Make it stop! It's going to break in!" She scrambled for a knife, pulling one from a butcher block on the counter. Colette followed suit.

Boom boom boom.

Sadie rushed to the mudroom and came back with a bat. She held it like she was ready for a pitch. She would clobber Merinda as hard as she could, to stop her from getting to Nessa and Colette, to stop her from hurting anyone else.

Crack.

A line formed at the bottom of the glass, laced into the etches made by Merinda, and traveled about a foot before stopping.

"Oh my god, oh my god, oh my god." Nessa pointed the knife at the door, holding it with two quaking hands.

Colette shook her head at Sadie, a knife in one hand and a cutting board with a handle in the other.

Boom boom boom.

The crack widened and traveled higher.

Tears streamed down Nessa's cheeks.

Sadie's heart banged in her ribs and her head.

Boom boom—

Blue light smothered the white of the floodlights.

Merinda spun and ran.

Bolts of blue chased her, hit her. Smoke or steam, Sadie didn't know which, wafted from Merinda's back but she didn't stop. She cleared the fence and vanished from sight.

Relief mixed with anger washed through Sadie. *Jason let her get away.*

Brandon appeared at the patio door, his face anxious. Jason stepped up next to him, his arms still glowing.

Sadie unlocked the door and Brandon slid it open, rushed inside, and wrapped Sadie in his arms. Jason doused his power and hurried to Colette.

"Are you okay," Brandon asked Sadie. "Are you hurt?"

"I'm fine. I'm so glad you're here." She pulled away from him and went to Nessa.

She was shaking all over. Nessa's mouth hung open, tears spilled from her eyes, but she made no noise. She just stared.

Sadie took the knife out of her hands and led her to a chair. "Nessa? Are you okay?"

Nessa shook harder.

Brandon removed his coat and hung it around her shoulders.

Sadie rubbed Nessa's jiggling hands. "Ness? Can you hear me?"

Nessa looked at Sadie but didn't seem to see her.

"Ness? Are you with me?"

A moment later Nessa's eyes focused. She wrapped her arms around herself. "Sadie, what was that thing? What happened?" Her teeth chattered. She reeled toward Jason. "And what . . . how . . . what did you do?"

Sadie pulled a chair closer to Nessa and sat. "We need to talk."

Nessa refocused on Sadie but didn't speak.

"We need to talk about everything, okay?"

Nessa nodded and hiccuped air. She had almost stopped shaking.

Sadie hated seeing Nessa so upset. Before tonight, it had seemed safer for Nessa not to learn about cryptids. But now things were different. Sadie would explain to Nessa what she had seen, and finally, Sadie wouldn't have to keep secrets from her.

Colette pulled another chair close, and Brandon and Jason hopped up to sit on the kitchen counter.

Sadie held one of Nessa's hands in hers. "So, the creature that came here tonight, that's a Yowie."

"A what?" Nessa asked.

"A Yowie," Sadie said. "Yowie are like Bigfoot."

"Bigfoot," Nessa said.

"Yes," Sadie answered.

137

Nessa scanned everyone's faces. "Are you guys messing with me?"

Colette patted Nessa's knee. "We wouldn't do that to you."

"So you're telling me that Bigfoot are real and these . . . these . . ."

"Yowie," Sadie said.

"Yeah, these Yowie are real."

"Yes," Sadie said.

"But no one knows about them," Nessa said. "Even though they attack people's houses in the middle of the night and scare the crap out of them."

Sadie rubbed Nessa's arm. "They don't attack like that very often. Tonight was kind of a problem."

"Ya' think?" Nessa didn't wait for an answer. "But wait—if they're real, how does no one know about them?"

"A lot of people know about them," Jason said. "All over the world."

Nessa's brows drew together. "All over the world?"

Sadie sent Jason a look to stay quiet. "That's a bigger picture story, and we'll get to that," she said to Nessa. "But I want to explain what happened tonight so you realize everything is okay."

"Oh sure, go ahead." Nessa wiped remains of tears from her cheeks with the backs of her hands.

"Well, the Yowie you saw is named Merinda, and it's my fault she came here tonight. I think she was looking for me."

"So, this Yowie has a name? Merinda?"

"Yes," Sadie said.

"Do they all have names?"

"I guess so." Sadie hadn't ever considered it, but she didn't see why a Yowie wouldn't have a name.

"And why is this Merinda looking for you?"

"Well, she's been looking for me for a long time," Sadie said. "To turn me over to some bad Yowie."

"Are you serious?" Nessa's breathing shallowed.

"Yes."

"Why do they want you?" Nessa swallowed hard.

"I, well, I'm part of a family that the leader of the Yowie want dead," Sadie said. "It's a long story."

"I bet. But keep going. Why do they want you and your family dead?"

Sadie noticed shortness in Nessa's tone. "Because I'm supposed to take over and lead, and the Yowie who's in charge now doesn't want that to happen." *Wow, that sounds so dumb saying it out loud to her.*

"Oh, so these Yowie choose teenage girls from small towns to lead their faction or whatever?" Nessa's lips flattened to a thin line.

"It's a Clan," Sadie said. "And I get it, it's so weird—"

Nessa jumped up and turned toward Jason. "And what are you? A wizard? Shouldn't you be at some magical academy?"

"I'm not a wizard," Jason said. "I'm a—"

"Just stop." Nessa flung off Brandon's coat onto the kitchen table. "You all suck. I thought you were my friends." Her eyes welled with tears again.

Sadie stood. "We are your friends. Of course, we're your friends. We're best friends."

"Best friends don't do things like this to each other."

"I'm sorry I've been keeping secrets from you," Sadie said. "I didn't want to."

"Just stop with the whole game, Sadie." Nessa crossed her arms. "And get out. You can all take your huge prank and get out. And tell Kyle to stay away from me, too. I assume that's who was in the big gorilla suit." She stormed into the family room.

Sadie hurried after her. "No, Nessa. I'm telling you the truth." Nessa plopped onto the couch and Sadie sat next to her. "Please, I promise you everything I've talked about is real."

A giant gulp of air whisked into Nessa's lungs and she wailed it out. "Get out of my house."

"No. Ness." Sadie tried to hug her but Nessa shoved her away. "Get out."

Sadie watched Nessa for a moment. "Please, Nessa, please listen."

Nessa stood and ran up the stairs. Her bedroom door slammed.

Brandon, Colette, and Jason stepped into the family room. Brandon sat next to Sadie. "Now what?"

"I have no idea." Sadie leaned her head-on Brandon's shoulder and fought back tears of her own. "Why doesn't she believe me?"

"She can't deal," Brandon said. "That was a lot to come at her in one night."

Sadie sat up. "But she has to know we would never play that kind of joke on her. We just wouldn't."

"From her perspective, maybe a prank is a more logical conclusion," Colette said. "Think about it—she saw a monster trying to break into her house and hurt her, and Jason's arms were weapons against the monster, and she learns all of this is real, and there are more monsters where that monster came from. Or, your mind offers the idea that your friends played a cruel prank on you." She shrugged. "What would be easier to believe?"

Sadie covered her face with her hands. "I've got to get her to listen to me."

"I'm not sure that will happen anytime soon," Colette said.

"I know you don't want to hear from me," Jason said. "But I have an idea."

She looked up. "You're right. I don't want to hear from you."

"Well, I'm sharing my idea anyway." Jason folded his arms across his chest. "You can wipe Nessa's memory."

"No," Sadie said. "No way."

"She's freaking out," Jason said. "And she hates you, hates all of us. You can't leave her like this."

"I wouldn't have to leave her like this if you had just stopped Merinda when I told you to."

Jason threw his hands up in the air. "Okay, fine, this whole situation is my fault. Blame me and hate me forever. But right now, Nessa cannot deal and you can help her."

Sadie stood. "I said no. I will not mess with Nessa's head."

"Whatever. I'm out of here." He headed toward the back door. "See you back at the house, Brandon." The sliding glass door opened and clunked closed.

"God, he is so annoying." Sadie pushed her hands through her hair.

Colette sat in an armchair across from the couch. "Sadie, Nessa is so upset."

Sadie *tsked*. "Not you, too."

"Make it three," Brandon said.

She sucked in a breath. "I can't." Sadie paced across the room. "I can't do that to her."

"You'd be doing her a favor," Colette said. "And saving your friendship, our friendship. There's no talking our way out of this with her." She shrugged. "I'd never forgive friends who I believed did something like this to me."

"Wiping Nessa's memory is better than losing her," Brandon said. "Isn't it? And you can't leave her feeling so upset."

Sadie's posture sagged. "Okay, you're right. You're both right." She headed upstairs, determined.

"You're going to do it? Just like that?" Colette asked.

"We don't have a lot of time," Sadie said. "Her dad and brother will be home soon."

"I'll come with you." Colette dashed up the stairs after her.

Sadie knocked on Nessa's door. "Ness?"

"I told you to go."

"We, uh, we have to get our stuff." Sadie turned the knob and opened the door. "Okay?"

"Fine. Get it and get out." Nessa pulled her covers over her head.

Sadie entered and sat on the edge of Nessa's bed. "Can we please talk? Please give me a chance to explain?"

Nessa swept the covers off her face and glared. "There's nothing you can say to make this better. You—" She pointed to Colette. "Both of you are the suckiest friends ever." Her voice broke. "Please just leave." She flipped on her side so her back was to Sadie and Nessa.

Sadie glanced at Colette and took a deep breath. "Nessa." She placed her hand on Nessa's exposed hand.

"Get off me." Nessa yanked her hand.

Sadie increased her hold. "Did you know dogs rule and cats drool?"

"Let—" Nessa's hand went slack. "I just want to go to sleep."

"You're very tired." Sadie scooted onto the bed, closer to Nessa, maintaining her touch while she ran her hand up Nessa's arm and stopped with her fingers at the base of Nessa's skull.

"I am really tired."

"You saw some scary things tonight, and they made you tired."

"They were so scary."

Sadie's eyes watered. "Forget every scary thing you saw and heard. Then you won't be tired."

"I shouldn't forget," Nessa said. "It seems important to remember."

"It's not important to remember," Sadie said. "Forget everything that upset you, like it never happened. And you'll feel good and happy and rested. You'll sleep in tomorrow and have no memory of anything that happened tonight. Okay?"

"Okay," Nessa said. "Can I sleep now?"

"Yes. Go to sleep." Sadie removed her hand.

Nessa's breath moved softly in and out.

Sadie eased herself off the bed, smoothed the covers, and started gathering her things.

"Shouldn't we stay?" Colette asked. "Finish the sleepover?"

"I can't. I just want to go home." Sadie stuffed her hairbrush in an outside pocket of her bag. "She'll sleep late. We'll text her in the morning and tell her we woke up early and headed home to help Lena with something. She'll be fine with that."

"Okay."

They grabbed the rest of their things and made their beds, tiptoed out of the room, and headed downstairs.

"How'd it go?" Brandon asked.

Sadie shrugged. "Fine, I guess. Let's get out of here."

✳ ✳ ✳

Sadie slept fitfully. She couldn't stop thinking about everything that had happened.

Finally falling asleep around six a.m., Sadie woke a few hours later when the vibration of her phone rattled against the top of her desk. It was a text message from Nessa to her and Colette: "I can't believe you both bailed on me last night. AND without even calling. Last time I plan anything fun for us."

What? A whoosh swept through Sadie pulling heat and air from her face and chest. *No, no, no.*

She typed: "What do you mean?" Then she backspaced and deleted the message. Sadie knew what Nessa meant. To her, Sadie and Colette had never arrived at Nessa's house last night. They'd never eaten pizza. They'd never watched their show.

They'd never had fun.

You'll sleep in tomorrow and have no memory of anything that happened tonight.

Sadie had erased too much of Nessa's memory.

She had to fix this. How could she fix this? Her mind raced.

There was a knock at her door. "Are you awake?" Colette asked.

"Come in, come in," Sadie said. "What do we do now?"

Colette, her phone in her hand, sat on Sadie's bed. "Can you give them back to her? Her memories? The good ones?"

"How would I even try? Where do memories go? Are they still in her head somewhere?" Sadie didn't try to answer the question. "I broke her. I messed with her head, and I broke her."

"You didn't break her. She's just mad at us."

"Oh my gosh." Sadie snatched up her phone and typed: "Nessa, I am so, so, so, so sorry. Please don't hate us."

Nessa responded. "Where were you? Did you do something fun without me? Maybe you and Colette don't really need me as a friend since you have each other now."

"Oh, dear," Colette said to Sadie, distress engulfing Colette's face. She typed a message: "No, we love you! But we were stupid last night." She hit send.

"What do we say happened?" Sadie asked Colette. "I don't know what to tell her."

Colette started typing again: "And so sorry. Something went wrong with my injured arm last night. Lots of pain. Sadie had to take care of me and we forgot our plans. So, so sorry." She hit send and shrugged.

Sadie stared at her screen. Nessa wasn't responding. "She hates us," Sadie said. "I'd hate us."

"She can't hate us. Can she?"

"Maybe I left some of those hate feelings in her head last night when she thought we were playing a trick on her." Sadie slapped the bed and fell back on her pillow. "Figures I'd wipe away too much, but leave some of the crappy stuff just to make things worse."

"I don't think that's possible. You didn't tell her to forget everything but remember some bad stuff."

"But she hates us, doesn't she?"

Colette opened her mouth to answer but then shut it and shook her head.

Sadie tossed her phone aside. "Everything is so screwed up right now. Why is this happening?"

Both of their phones vibrated. Sadie sat up, snatched her phone and checked the screen.

"Is your arm okay?" Nessa asked in her text.

"It's much better, thank you," Colette responded. "But we're still stupid. Will you forgive us?"

A long moment passed with no message from Nessa. Finally, a note: "Please don't do this to me again, okay?"

"Never!" Sadie typed and followed it with a long string of Xs and Os.

"Same from me!" Colette sent her message following Sadie's.

Sadie fell back onto her bed again, relieved but anxious about her friendship with Nessa going forward. How could she keep this up? How could they all keep lying to Nessa when she was such a big part of their lives?

Sadie couldn't handle losing Nessa.

ELEVEN
Secrets Exposed

The morning after everything that happened at Nessa's house, Jason shuffled into the kitchen, groggy from too little sleep. He hated fighting with Sadie. He hated being mad. He hated how unfair she was being. And he hated that it all had kept him awake.

Brandon and Della sat at the kitchen table eating oatmeal. Shay left her spot watching for bits of anything edible, trotted to Jason for a pat, then returned to her falling-food post.

Della laughed and pointed at Jason. "Your hair is sticking straight out of the side of your head."

Jason shrugged. "Whatever." He took a bowl from the cupboard and dished oatmeal from the pot on the stove. "Where's Dad?"

"He just left," Brandon said. "He was meeting a friend for coffee."

"Huh." Jason grunted, sprinkled brown sugar on his oatmeal and added milk.

Della got up and put her bowl in the dishwasher. She headed out of the kitchen.

"Where are you going?" Jason asked, his tone stern.

Della kept walking. "To watch TV."

"Better not watch that stupid cartoon I hate."

"I can watch whatever I want," Della yelled from the living room. Audio blared as she clicked on the television.

Jason *thunked* his bowl onto the table and sat.

"Dude," Brandon said, "what's your problem?"

"My problem?" Jason dropped his spoon and it clanked against the rim of his bowl. "Oh, I don't know. Maybe it's the killer Yowie that's wandering around. Or that Sadie used to be one of my best friends but now she hates me." He shoved back from the table and stood. Shay skittered sideways. "And maybe you're another best friend that hates me."

Brandon shook his head and looked at his oatmeal.

"Well?" Jason asked, fired up for a fight.

"Well, what?"

"You hate me, too."

Brandon stared. "I don't hate you."

"But you're on Sadie's side."

"This isn't about sides." Brandon sprang from his seat and picked up his bowl. "I get why you didn't kill Merinda the first time we saw her. She didn't seem like a threat in that moment. Totally on board with you there." He rinsed his bowl. "But last night she was attacking, trying to break into Nessa's house and hurt them, maybe kill them. And all you did was scare her away."

"That's not—"

"I was there, Jason. I know what happened."

"We don't know for sure what Merinda was doing."

Brandon's chin jutted. "She was banging on a glass door she had already cracked. What do you think she was doing?"

"I don't know."

"I do," Brandon said. "She was attacking."

"And I stopped her."

"But what about tonight? And tomorrow night? And the next night? Or morning? Or afternoon?"

Jason's body slumped and he stared up at the ceiling.

"Not to mention the fact that she's part of the whole Garrison Devine crew," Brandon said.

"Connor said she doesn't know who she is."

"So, she's just chasing Sadie down for some random reason?"

Jason sat on a stool and slumped onto the kitchen island. "I get it. It doesn't make sense."

"And Nessa—"

"I know, I know." Jason lowered his face onto his crossed arms. "That was horrible." His voice was smothered between his arms and the countertop.

Brandon paused a moment. "Why didn't you take Merinda out?"

Jason raised his head and propped his chin on his hand. "I just couldn't."

"Are you afraid?"

Was that the problem? Was he willing to let his friends get hurt, or even killed because he was afraid of killing anyone else himself?

No. He would never knowingly let someone get hurt.

Would he?

"No, I'm not afraid."

Brandon crossed his arms. "Well, last night was bad, Jason, really bad. I'm trying not to be mad at you, but you didn't do enough."

I didn't do enough. Jason rubbed his hands down his face. "How was Nessa after I took off?"

"Sadie wiped her memory after all. She was asleep when we left," Brandon said. "I walked Sadie and Colette home then headed back here."

"Does my dad know we were gone?"

"I don't think so."

"That's good." Jason bent and scratched Shay behind the ears. "I worried Shay would wake him up since she couldn't come with us. But I couldn't risk her not being prepared for another encounter. Not without Finn to help."

Brandon nodded. "Good call."

"At least you approve of one of my decisions."

"Hey, bottom line for me," Brandon said, "is I don't want anyone to get hurt."

"Neither do I," Jason said.

"Then you better figure stuff out and fast. This Merinda thing is far from over."

✳ ✳ ✳

Jason called Uncle Alexander and told him what had happened.

"Bring Shay and let's head out," Uncle Alexander said. "We need to find Merinda."

"Okay, I'll be there in a few." Jason clicked off the call and texted Colette, asking her if she wanted to come with him and Uncle Alexander.

"I don't think I'm up for it," she typed. "Not after everything."

Jason replied: "I get it. I'll talk to you later, hopefully with good news."

"Okay," she wrote back. "Good luck."

Jason headed downstairs and told Brandon where he was going. "Wanna come?"

"Nah," he said. "I'm going to stay close to Sadie today."

"And she definitely doesn't want to come with me," Jason said.

"Pretty much."

Anger fought with sadness in Jason's head. He forced the feelings aside, slipped Shay's harness over her body, and clipped it in place. He put on his coat. "Be sure Kyle's here with Dell if you need to leave before my dad gets home." He attached Shay's leash with a *click*.

"No prob," Brandon said.

"And Uncle A's calling my dad and Connor to get their help today."

"So, your dad *will* know we snuck out."

Jason cringed. "Oh, yeah."

"This is when I'm extra glad my parentals are not around," Brandon said. "The wrath when rules are broken is not fun."

"That's for sure." Jason dreaded the conversation to come. He headed toward the door. "See you later."

"Yeah." Brandon waved. "Good luck."

Jason followed Shay out and closed the door behind him. Brandon's was the second wish of good luck Jason had received today. He figured he needed all the luck he could get.

✳ ✳ ✳

Jason and Shay arrived at Uncle Alexander's house to find
Connor scurrying from his car carrying a box.

"Hey, Connor."

He stopped and seemed surprised to find Jason standing
there. "Oh, hello, Jason. You got here fast."

Jason raised his brows. "Not that far of a walk."

"Of course not." He pointed to the open hatch of his
SUV. "Would you mind grabbing that box and bringing it
inside?"

"No problem." Jason pushed the looped handle of
Shay's leash onto his wrist and loaded his arms with a flat
but heavy cardboard box.

Connor clicked a button on his key fob and the hatch
eased to a close. They all headed inside the house.

"I have the rest of the boxes, Alexander," Connor
called. "I was lucky to enlist Jason's assistance."

"I'll be right there," Uncle Alexander said from the
kitchen.

Connor set his load on the floor in the living room, and
Jason followed his lead, Shay by his side. He unclipped her
leash and she dashed into the kitchen to find Finn. Jason
heard the back door open and a scramble of paws
pounding outside.

Uncle Alexander walked into the room. He opened one
of the flat boxes. "All the parts are here?"

"Yes," Connor said. "With this box and the other one."
He pointed to the second box Jason had carried in.

"Parts for what?" Jason asked.

"To confine and secure Merinda in the back of my
truck after we've tranquilized her," Uncle Alexander said.
"We'll bring her back here and keep her in a holding pen
downstairs until the League of Governors can take her into

custody. Your father will help us search and, assuming we're successful, he can help load her into the truck. I just need to text him a meeting place when the time comes." He looked up from the box of parts. "He's not too happy with you, by the way."

"Yeah, I figured." Jason stuffed his hands in the pockets of his hoodie. "Why doesn't he meet us here?"

"He's busy with something else at the moment."

Dad had been busy a lot lately, which usually meant a new project at work. "And our plan is still to catch Merinda and turn her over to the League?"

"Why wouldn't it be?" Metal clanged as Uncle Alexander dug through the box.

"I just thought, since she hunted Sadie down last night, maybe you'd want to do something . . . bigger."

"We can't be certain she was hunting Sadie," Connor said. "Could have been a coincidence Merinda was there last night."

Jason jutted his chin. "That would be a big coincidence."

"I agree with Jason," Uncle Alexander said. "Merinda was likely there for a reason and since Colette is new in town, she wasn't the attraction. That leaves Nessa and Sadie and, well, odds are on the idea that she was after Sadie."

Connor sighed. "I suppose you're right."

"Whether she's aware of who she is or not, it's clear now there is something inside Merinda driving her to go after Sadie," Uncle Alexander said. "We need to trap her as soon as we can."

"How are we even going to find her?" Jason asked. "She's never where we think she'll be."

"We'll take the dogs down Nessa's street first and around the outskirts of her yard," Uncle Alexander said. "They should get a solid scent, especially if you wounded her."

"I'm not sure what I did. I didn't notice any blood, just smoke, or steam, so I might not have hit her at all."

"Even so, we should get a good trail to follow from there." Uncle Alexander unpacked more metal parts and grids from the boxes.

Jason turned to Connor. "You're coming with us?"

"No, I'm afraid you're on your own for the search," Connor said. "I've pressed upon Sadie that we need to get her ability to shift into Yowie back on track and she agreed to come over later to train." He looked at his watch. "In a little over an hour."

"Good," Jason said. "She needs to help."

"No one wants to stop Merinda more than Sadie." Connor glanced at Uncle Alexander. "But she did carry quite a load while you were in London. I feel bad this has yet to be resolved for her, and for all of us."

A twinge of guilt snaked into Jason's head. Sadie had unwillingly received a crash course in everything Yowie and Calling and Clan, turning her life upside down while Jason was gone. It was easy to forget what she'd been through since he hadn't been here to help.

But he was here now. He could help her now, even if she did hate him. He just hoped his help would be good enough for her.

"If you have everything you need from me," Connor said, "I'll be on my way."

Uncle Alexander looked up from a metal bracket he was tinkering with. "Yes, I think we're all set. Thanks for bringing this over." He waved his arm over the pieces and parts.

"No problem," he said. "And it's easy enough to put together. Match the letters, tighten the latches, and you'll be good to go. Call me later with an update, would you?"

"Of course," Uncle Alexander said.

Connor headed to the door. "Good luck."

Good luck. Jason hadn't ever hoped as hard as he did now that those words imparted extra advantage.

Uncle Alexander checked his phone. "I'm glad our good weather is holding." He signaled Jason. "Let the dogs in, would you? We'll put this cage together in the truck, then get going ourselves."

"Sure." Jason walked through the kitchen and opened the back door where he found the dogs baking in sunshine on the deck. They jumped up and came inside. Jason hunched and pet both dogs who smelled like warm fur and winter air.

After Jason and Uncle Alexander set up everything in the truck, Jason called the dogs, Uncle Alexander flung his messenger bag onto the floor of the back seat, and the four of them headed to Nessa's.

※ ※ ※

As Uncle Alexander predicted, after they arrived on Nessa's street the dogs quickly honed in on Merinda's scent and pulled Jason and Uncle Alexander to follow the trail. Since they needed to continue on foot, Uncle Alexander tucked his keys under the floor mat and left the truck at Nessa's. He asked Jason's dad to pick up the truck and meet them at the park, its edges skirting the open space on the edge of town.

A little later, Dad got out of the truck and zeroed in on Jason. "You and I are going to have a long talk."

"Yeah, sorry." Jason scuffed his foot on the asphalt.

"Sorry doesn't cut it," Dad said with the voice you didn't question. "You gave me your word that we would tackle this as a team."

"I know, but it was an emergency—"

"All the more reason to wake me," Dad gestured to Uncle Alexander, "wake your uncle. Hell, wake the whole town if you have to. Rally the troops."

"I know, I get it."

"Do you?" Dad's eyebrows raised. "Do you get it?"

"I do, Dad. I just . . . I just have to remember that I have troops." He kept his head down and looked up at Dad's face.

Dad's expression softened. "We're a heck of a good team when needed."

"I remember." Jason glanced from Dad to Uncle Alexander. "And with the dogs, we're that much better."

"That we are," Uncle Alexander said.

As if on cue, the dogs whined and pulled against their harnesses, urging them all to move.

Dad locked the truck and they headed into the cottonwoods.

The dogs' noses moved from ground to air to passing bushes, and they pressed onward, their tails wagging, their ears perked.

The energy of the dogs seemed boundless.

With each passing moment, Jason felt certain the next minute would reveal Merinda. He was anxious. Ready. He kept a low, blue glow dancing across his palms.

He wouldn't let her escape this time.

He couldn't.

He might not get another chance before Merinda hurt someone, before she killed someone.

Finn and Shay turned to the right and led them deep into a thicket of brush, forcing them into single file. Finn pulled on Uncle Alexander, Shay walked in front of Jason, and Dad brought up the rear.

Branches scraped through Jason's hair and scratched against his coat. He shielded his eyes from sudden *thwaps* of twigs and wondered how they'd fare against Merinda in such a snug space. He was comforted by the fact they'd at least hear her coming. There was no stealthy moving inside the tangle of tree limbs.

"Whoa." Uncle Alexander ducked.

Five Skyfish flew into Jason's chest and presumably out his back. "Ugh."

"What?" Dad asked.

"Skyfish," Jason said. "Probably just flew through you, too."

"I felt nothing," he said.

Uncle Alexander craned his neck. "You wouldn't. No one does."

"Weird," Dad said. "Even though you've told me that before, I thought I'd have to feel something if it ever happened to me."

"It's probably happened to you many times before today, Zachary," Uncle Alexander said. "Skyfish are abundant. Though they don't often move in groups like that."

The dogs continued moving forward but slowed their pace. A moment later they paused, examined a group of branches, turned further to the right and continued their quest. After a couple of minutes, they stopped again to smell the ground.

They now stood in a widened section where Jason, his dad, and Uncle Alexander could easily stand side by side. It reminded Jason of the cove near home where he'd first met Sadie, only this space was bigger, and he could stand upright. Branches of bushes canopied over their heads, and sunshine filtered in between wood and the dried leaves determined to hang on through winter.

Across from them was another cove in the branches, wide, but tight and low where Jason imagined he could lie down. Shay moved gingerly toward the space, her nose twitching at an accelerated tempo. She leaned into the gap and breathed deep, wagged her tail, and sat. Jason bent and looked inside but saw nothing.

"Shay seems pleased with herself," Dad said.

Finn copied Shay's actions and sat next to her.

"With good reason. But hold on," Uncle Alexander removed his binoculars from his bag and looked through the trees. "As I suspected." He handed the binoculars to Jason who lifted them to his eyes.

"Is that black from the fire a few days ago?" Jason asked, handing the glasses to his dad.

"Yes," Uncle Alexander said. "It's a much smaller area than I expected, given how much of a glow I saw."

Dad gave the binoculars back to Uncle Alexander. "Looks like about four hundred feet from here."

"Give or take." Uncle Alexander returned the binoculars to his bag. "And we need to get over there."

"But the dogs led us here, and Shay acts like she found something," Jason said. "Shouldn't we look around here, first?"

"We've seen all there is to see," Uncle Alexander said. "This is Merinda's nest."

Jason stiffened and scanned the surrounding area.

"But this is only a briefly-used nest." Uncle Alexander pointed to the burn. "I suspect that is where she lived before."

"And she accidentally started a fire?" Jason asked.

"Perhaps. Let's go discover what there is to learn." Uncle Alexander called Finn and she fell into step at his side.

Jason called Shay. She took another look inside the part of the nest she'd investigated, gave a slight wag of her tail, then joined Jason as they pushed their way out of the cove and onto a more open path.

A short time later, they might have found themselves shoving through another dense copse had it not been for firefighters who had chainsawed a route. Shreds of branches and leaves littered the ground. Char scented the air.

Jason noticed a slight filmy residue on some trunks and branches. "Did they use fire extinguishers?"

Uncle Alexander nodded. "They wouldn't have been able to get a firetruck close enough to use the hoses."

"Good thing it was wet out here to begin with," Dad said.

Jason glanced down at the mushy muddle of organic debris, most of it unmarked by fire. "But how did it even start?"

Uncle Alexander hunched and reached into a low-topped cove similar to the one Shay had examined during their last stop. He pulled out a handful of burnt debris and sniffed it. "Odd." Finn and Shay were also smelling what he held in his hand, and alternately driving their heads deep into the space from where he'd taken it, and sniffing more. "There's an odor of something, like lighter fluid."

"Did she try to build a fire?" Dad asked. "Is she capable of building a fire?"

"It's not out of the realm of possibility," Uncle Alexander said. "But given her injury, and the likely brain damage, it seems unlikely she'd have the mental capacity to do so."

"But what else could it be?" Jason asked.

"I'm not sure, but something seems off." Uncle Alexander flicked the debris onto the ground and wiped his hand on his pants. "She would have slept in this more enclosed, drier area, and would build a fire out here." He waved his hand around where they stood. "If she built one at all. Having a fire isn't a priority for Yowie. They are well insulated against the cold. And a fire's more likely to reveal them."

"I noticed what looked like burn marks in her fur yesterday," Jason said.

"Interesting," Uncle Alexander said. "An accidental consequence I suppose. It seems she herself is lucky there's more wet matter out here than dry or she may well have been severely injured. I'm still baffled, though, why she would attempt a fire where she slept."

"Because everything else was too wet?" Dad suggested.

"Perhaps," Uncle Alexander said. "Maybe with her compromised faculties, she simply didn't realize what she was doing."

Finn, deep in the low clearing where Merinda had slept, shuffled out rear first, her mouth full of newspaper and hay which she spit onto the ground. Uncle Alexander examined the newspaper, its edges burned. "This is dated the day of the fire."

"Meaning she'd just built her nest that day?" Dad asked. "Or refreshed it with new material? I'm guessing the hay is nesting material, right?"

"Hay, yes," Uncle Alexander said. "It's easy to come by on the farms and ranches around here. But newspaper, no. It's not generally a nesting material of choice. And newspapers aren't easy to come by, at least not in any quantity. This is odd."

"Well, we know she's messed up," Jason said. "She must be using whatever she can find. Maybe someone left their newspaper in the park or something."

"Possibly. But—"

Finn and Shay growled.

Sticks crunched.

Jason spun and ignited his powers, his arms glowing purple and blue.

Uncle Alexander swung the tranquilizer gun off his shoulder and aimed.

Dad sprang to a fighting stance.

A figure in shadow, about sixty feet away, ran from them, crashing through trees, away from the nest.

Jason moved to give chase but Uncle Alexander grabbed his arm and nodded toward the dogs who watched but didn't react. "Human," he said.

"Who is it?" Jason extinguished his powers.

Dad snatched the binoculars out of Uncle Alexander's bag and adjusted the view. "Can't tell. I only see them from behind and they're moving too much to get a clear view. But I can see they're wearing a navy-blue parka. It might be a kid."

Jason looked but was unable to find the person in the binoculars. They were too far away or moving too fast, or both. "Do you think they heard us?" He replaced the lens caps and put the binoculars away. "Or saw any sparkly blue light?" He wriggled his now-normal fingers in the air.

Uncle Alexander sighed. "Since we're in a sunny spot your powers would not have been obvious. And I think that person was too far away to have heard anything of interest."

"I hope you're right."

"If it becomes an issue," Dad said, "we'll deal with it." He checked the time on his phone. "In the meantime, we're about done. We don't have a lot of daylight left."

"Good point," Uncle Alexander said. "I'd like to spend a few more minutes examining the area, perhaps take a few pictures, and we'll go. I'll drive you back to your car, Zachary."

"Or how about this idea," Dad said. "After we're finished here, why don't we order pizzas and you and Finn join us for dinner? We can strategize our plan for tomorrow, and pick up my car later."

"I like your thinking," Uncle Alexander said.

"But what about Merinda?" Jason asked. "We can't wait for tomorrow. What if she goes after Sadie again? Tonight?"

"I'll update Connor and your grandmother," Uncle Alexander said. "They can keep a watch on things tonight, and your dad and I will get back out here tomorrow."

"You're sure Sadie, and Colette, and Grandma Lena will be okay?" Anxiousness inched up Jason's spine.

Dad chuckled. "Have you forgotten who showed up to help save the day in London?"

"Right." Jason had never been as happy to see Grandma Lena as he had been that day. "She and Connor can handle it." He put his hands in his coat pockets. "And I realize tomorrow is a school day, but please let me come with you guys to find Merinda."

Dad put his hand on Jason's shoulder. "Let's see how things go tonight. If she attacks again, we'll all go after her tomorrow."

His edginess still firing, Jason helped Uncle Alexander take all the photos he wanted.

***

The sun sat low in the sky as they hiked out of the towering trees, the light changing from bright on blue to dull on dusky gray.

Dad tapped a contact on his phone and put the call on speaker.

A woman with an Italian accent answered. "*Ciao*, Za Zena's, may I help you?"

"Hi, Zena," Dad said. "It's Zachary Lex."

"Oh, Mr. Zachary! So good to hear from you. Are you placing your usual order? One pepperoni, size extra-large, and one veggie, size extra-large?"

"Yes, please. And Alexander, my brother-in-law, is eating with us, too." Dad looked at Uncle Alexander, ready to add to the order but Zena didn't hesitate.

"Oh, Mr. Alexander, he likes the Canadian bacon and tomato," she said. "I'll add one extra-large, you'll have plenty of leftovers. Makes nutritious and delicious breakfast, *si*?"

Uncle Alexander nodded.

"*Si*," Dad said.

"*Grazie, grazie,*" Zena said. "Your order will be ready in twenty minutes, *si*?"

"Perfect. Thank you, Zena."

"It is my pleasure. We'll see you soon."

Dad disconnected the call.

"I'd say that's a lot of food, but Kyle is like a food vacuum," Jason said.

"You don't exactly eat like a bird," Dad said. "Neither does Brandon."

"Fair point." Jason's stomach growled. "And now I'm starving."

A few minutes later they arrived at Uncle Alexander's truck and piled in. They drove into town, parked in front of Za Zena's, and Dad gave Jason his credit card. "Don't drop the pizzas on the way out."

"I'll guard them with my life." Jason opened the door and went inside the shop.

"Mr. Jason," Zena said from behind the counter. "I need seven more minutes for your pizzas to be perfect. They must be perfect." She handed him a paper cup and a lid. "You help yourself to soda while you wait, *si*? My treat."

"Thanks." Jason took the cup and filled it with ice and cola. He showed off his prize, grinning through the store window at Dad and Uncle Alexander. Dad shook his head but smiled back at Jason.

Someone walking along the sidewalk across the street caught Jason's eye. It was Colette. Jason started toward the door.

"Hey, Zena, I'll be right ba—"

Jason froze.

A second person walked up to Colette and gave her a hug.

It was Derek Goodman.

Colette had hugged Derek Goodman.

Colette was hanging out with Derek Goodman.

He watched them walk into the Salton Spoon.

Colette . . . with Derek Goodman.

And Derek was wearing a navy-blue parka.

TWELVE

Busted

Jason said nothing to Dad and Uncle Alexander about seeing Colette with Derek. He kept quiet, scratched Shay's back, and considered the situation.

Was there a logical explanation for her to be with Derek? Maybe they had a class together, and she was helping him with his homework. He was certain Derek wasn't helping Colette.

Colette was smart.

Derek wasn't.

Jason flexed his fingers.

They must be studying.

But Colette didn't have her backpack with her.

And she'd *hugged* him. She'd hugged Derek Goodman.

"Jason?" Dad's voice snapped him out of his funk.

"Huh?"

They were parked in the garage at home. "The pizzas. Can you manage them?"

Jason unlatched his seatbelt. "Yeah, I've got them."

Uncle Alexander removed the dogs' harnesses and followed them into the house. "I'll feed Finn and Shay."

A couple of minutes later, Jason was in the kitchen with everyone including Kyle, Della, and Brandon. Jason reached for a plate.

"Hands," Dad said. "Wash. All of you."

A line formed at the kitchen sink as everyone, even Uncle Alexander, took turns soaping, washing, and drying. Jason then loaded a plate with three slices—two pepperoni and one veggie. He sat at the table next to Brandon.

"Are you on a diet?" Brandon smirked.

Jason faked a laugh. "This is my appetizer."

"I heard your uncle and dad talking. Merinda-hunt was a bust?" Brandon bit into a slice of pepperoni.

"No sightings," Jason said. "At least not of Merinda. But someone was watching us. Might have been Derek."

Brandon's brows furrowed. "Goodman? What was he doing out there? Ditching his little brother again?"

"No idea. We're not even sure it was him. We didn't see his face, just his coat."

"And you know what coat Derek wears?" Brandon asked.

"No, it's just . . . something else happened."

Uncle Alexander, standing next to Dad at the end of the kitchen, started talking about next steps to capture Merinda.

Jason leaned into Brandon and lowered his voice. "I'll tell you later."

"We found two of Merinda's nests," Uncle Alexander said. "Which is good. Unfortunately, she'll sense that we found the newer one, so it's likely she'll relocate. And she won't return to the burned nest."

"Burned?" Kyle asked.

Uncle Alexander explained what they'd seen. "Even if she somehow started the fire, it scorched her bedding and she won't accept that nest as a safe space anymore. So, we have to figure out where she'll go next."

"Like to Sadie's house," Brandon said.

"I wish I could say for certain that will not happen," Uncle Alexander said. "But Merinda's behavior isn't tracking with what's normal for a Yowie. I already spoke to Connor, and he'll spend the night at Sadie's home. He'll be able to shift to Yowie form if needed."

Colette is probably not even at home right now. She's probably still with Derek. Jason tensed his fist.

Uncle Alexander continued. "Sadie is still having trouble activating her power to shift."

"Connor says she's too stressed, that she's trying too hard," Brandon added.

Jason dismissed a dart of guilt about Sadie being upset.

"But I'm heading over there tonight, too," Brandon said. "Connor and I are staying in the living room, like a first line of defense. I'll do the online school thing after I get home in the morning. Uh, if you're cool with that, Mr. Lex."

Dad turned his back to everyone, murmured to Uncle Alexander, and Uncle Alexander nodded.

Dad faced the room. "That's fine, Brandon. Just be careful."

"And you'll call us at once if you see or hear anything that could be Merinda." Uncle Alexander said it as an order rather than a question.

"Yep." Brandon waggled his phone. "I've got you on speed dial."

"Good." Uncle Alexander pulled cheese off a slice and popped it in his mouth. "Zachary and I will resume the search with the dogs in the morning."

Kyle raised his hand. "I'm in."

"Unless we have an urgent situation, you will go to school," Dad said.

"But—"

"No buts. School unless it's otherwise discussed in the morning."

Kyle slumped in his chair and stuffed half of a slice into his mouth.

✻ ✻ ✻

Jason cleared the table. Brandon dumped pizza crusts in the garbage and put the plates in the dishwasher. Dad wrapped leftovers, some going in the refrigerator, and some going home with Uncle Alexander.

Dad checked his phone. "I need to send a quick email, then we can get my car, and I'll drop off Brandon. I'll be back in a bit."

"No rush." Uncle Alexander dried his hands on a towel.

Brandon pulled Jason aside. "What were you going to tell me?"

"Upstairs," Jason said. He and Brandon headed up to Jason's room and closed the door. He told Brandon about seeing Colette with Derek, and Derek's navy-blue parka.

Brandon dropped onto Jason's bed. "Hold on. You saw Colette, our Colette, hugging Derek? Are you sure?"

"One hundred percent."

"Dude, that sucks."

"I know."

"She hasn't told you she's tutoring him or something?"

"No," Jason said. "Besides, do you hug tutors?"

"Nope, I don't think hugging your tutor is a thing."

Jason sank to a seat on the floor. "I have no idea what to do. One part of me wants to yell at her, ask her what she was doing with him. But another part of me doesn't want to talk to her at all. Ever. Never again."

"So, both sides of you are mad."

"All sides of me are mad." He picked at a loose thread in the carpet. "How can I not be mad? I've tried to come up with a regular reason she'd even know him that well, much less hug him, and I can't think of anything. Can you?"

"Not really."

"I mean, even when we've talked about Derek, she hasn't mentioned how well she knows him." Jason spat the words. "So she's . . . she must be . . ."

"You think she's cheating on you."

"Yeah." Jason fell back and stared at the ceiling. "With Derek Goodman of all people. *And* he's the person who was spying on us out there today."

"You don't know that for sure," Brandon said. "And I'm not sure about any of this. Colette's cool. I don't think she'd cheat on you."

"Except that she is."

"It looks like it, but talk to her. Give her a chance to explain."

Dad called from the bottom of the stairs. "Brandon, let's go."

"On my way," Brandon yelled back. "Gotta go," he said to Jason. "I'll text you if she's home."

"I don't care if she's home," Jason said.

Brandon stood. "Yeah, you do. I'll text you."

※ ※ ※

Jason stayed glued to his phone. After forty minutes, a text from Brandon arrived: "She's here. Just her. No new friends."

"Very funny," Jason replied. "Thanks for telling me."

"She seems totally normal. You should talk to her."

Jason considered it for a moment and his temper rose again. "Can't deal."

"Do deal. You've gotta be wrong," Brandon wrote.

Jason replayed the sight of Colette hugging Derek.

He wasn't wrong.

He typed a message to Brandon. "Hope no Merinda tonight. Call if needed."

The phone showed Brandon was typing a reply. "Okay. And Colette says hi."

Jason didn't respond. He clicked off his phone.

THIRTEEN
Leveling Up

Sadie sat on the couch close to Brandon. Colette stretched out on the floor near the fire, and Lena and Connor sat on a second couch opposite the first. A sleeping bag and two pillows were piled in the corner, along with a set of sheets and a blanket. It was close to ten p.m.

"All right, everybody." Lena stood and picked up spent mugs of cocoa. "As nice as it is to have some quiet time together, this is still a school night and not a slumber party."

"I am super-tired." Sadie stretched.

Brandon stood and took her hand, pulling her up to standing next to him. "I'll see you in the morning." He gave her a hug.

"Unless Merinda crashes the party," Sadie said.

"Positive thoughts," Lena said. "We all need a good night's sleep. Merinda can keep herself outside and far away from us unless she comes by to turn herself in so the League of Governors can bring her to justice."

Sadie kept her mouth closed. But how would any sentence given by the League be enough justice after all Merinda had done?

Lena turned to Brandon. "You have your sleeping bag and pillow. Do you need anything else?"

"Nope, I'm all set."

"And Connor?" Lena asked. "Anything more I can get for you besides the bed linens and pillow?"

"Not at all. You're an excellent hostess."

"If that were true, you'd be in a bedroom instead of on the couch," Lena said. "Thank you for staying over tonight."

"Not a problem. This is what family does for each other."

More hugs were shared, everyone said goodnight, and Sadie went up to her room. She changed into her pajamas, glad to have time alone.

Sadie plopped into bed but left her lamp on. She rolled onto her side.

What kind of friend was she? She kept secrets, and she'd put Nessa's life in danger. Merinda could have hurt Nessa, if not worse. And Sadie was incapable of stopping her.

Sadie couldn't shift.

She couldn't turn invisible.

She wasn't even sure her Tae Kwon Do skills would have made a difference if she'd had to use them on Merinda before Jason and Brandon showed up.

Jason.

This was all his fault. If he'd done as Sadie had asked, if he'd stopped Merinda when he had the chance, none of this would have happened. Nessa and Sadie would still be Nessa and Sadie.

She tamped down tears. She would not cry because of Jason Lex.

She would figure this out on her own and deal with Merinda.

Sadie moved from her side to her back and closed her eyes. She breathed deep. She needed to relax. Connor told her she was too stressed, too anxious, and he was right.

She took more deep breaths, stilled her thoughts, and slowed her heart rate.

Mamo's voice played in her head, telling Sadie she was strong, stronger than Mamo had realized.

Sadie touched the tips of her fingers to the hawk's eye pendant. She took another deep breath, held it a moment, then breathed out. She repeated the action again, and again, calming her mind.

When she was ready, she concentrated on her right hand. She imagined it fading, her skin color clearing, any outline of knuckles or fingers or bones erasing.

Her right hand tingled.

She carried the concept up her arm, to her shoulder, across her chest and over her face and scalp. She watched in her mind's eye as she erased her left arm, her torso, her hips, and both legs, her feet.

The tingling intensified.

Sadie lay there a moment, experiencing the buzz of energy while solidifying invisibleness in her mind.

A moment later, she opened her eyes, pulled her right arm from under the covers and held it in front of her face.

And saw nothing.

She whipped the covers off and jumped out of bed.

And saw nothing.

No toes, no feet, no legs, no hips.

No pajamas.

She hurried to a mirror and checked her reflection. She found nothing but the dim glow of her bedside lamp revealing the edge of her headboard against the wall behind her, and the shapes of pictures hanging above.

Sadie rushed to flip on her overhead light.

She flung her hands in front of her face. Nothing.

She looked down. Nothing.

Sadie was invisible, pajamas and all.

"Oh my gosh, oh my gosh, oh my gosh." She kept her voice to a whisper.

She sat on the edge of her bed and eyed where her pointer finger should be. Sadie took a deep breath and set her will to return her finger to normal, to make it visible.

The tingling in her finger seemed to fade, but the invisibility remained, and seconds later the potency of the tingling returned. She took another breath, concentrated, focused, and willed her finger to appear.

The tingling faded.

An outline formed.

Color filled in.

Her finger floated in the air in front of her.

Oh my gosh.

Sadie swallowed hard, picked up a hand mirror with her left hand, giving it, too, the illusion of levitation, and focused her attention on the rest of her body. She followed the same path as she had in her mind before, traveling up her right arm.

Her arm reappeared.

She directed her focus across her chest, face, and scalp.

All reappeared.

She watched as she willed visibility to her torso, legs, and feet.

The tingling stopped and Sadie was whole.

❋ ❋ ❋

After Sadie was showered and ready for school, she walked into the kitchen and found Lena and Colette sitting at the table eating breakfast.

"Brandon and Connor are already gone?" Sadie asked.

"Yes," Lena said. "They left a little over an hour ago."

"Too bad for them because watch this." Sadie picked up Lena's coffee cup, held it high, and made her arm disappear leaving the cup seemingly floating in midair.

Lena and Colette gasped.

Sadie returned the cup to its place on the table and reappeared her arm. "Ta-da."

"That's wonderful, Sadie," Lena said.

Colette clapped her fingertips together. "Brilliant."

"I worked on it last night." Sadie took a glass out of the cupboard and filled it with almond milk. "Once I got going, and maintained focus, the rest came easy. Now I can turn it on and off like a switch."

"You even made your clothes disappear," Colette said. "You've already leveled up."

"That is impressive," Lena said. "Connor doesn't know yet?"

"Nope. You two are the first to hear," Sadie said. "Or see. Or not see."

Lena took a sip of her coffee. "He'll be thrilled. I'm guessing this achievement also opens the door for the next phase of powers from the Calling, whatever they may be. And you'll regain your power to shift to Yowie soon, if you haven't already."

"Maybe." Sadie turned her back on Lena and opened the pantry door.

"Can I help you find something in particular?" Lena asked.

"No," Sadie said, "I'm just looking for something breakfasty."

"We have eggs." Lena gestured to the refrigerator. "You have time to make some before you have to leave for school."

"I'm good." Sadie held up a protein bar. "This is all I need." She turned to Colette. "Ready to go?"

"Give me two shakes. I need to grab some stuff in my room." Colette dashed out of the kitchen.

Lena patted a chair next to her. "Come sit with me."

Sadie carried over her almond milk and protein bar, and sat.

"What's going on with you?" Lena brushed hair off of Sadie's face and tucked it behind her ears.

"Nothing. It's just crazy around here." She peeled open the wrapper.

"I mean in the last few minutes," Lena said. "You were pleased with your new power, as you should be. But things changed when I mentioned the Calling."

Sadie's mouth dropped open. "Are you psychic or something? Or am I that obvious?"

"It's the latter. You would not be a good poker player." Lena smiled. "So, what's up?"

"It's just . . ." Sadie sighed. "What if the Calling made a mistake? It should have picked Mamo, or Connor, or someone else who can handle it."

"The Calling wouldn't have selected you if you're unable to handle it."

"It must have misread the signs or something," Sadie said, "because there's no way it should be me. I couldn't help when Nessa was so scared. Look how messed up that whole situation is now."

Lena nodded. "I understand." She took another sip of coffee.

Sadie sat back and frowned. "Wait—aren't you supposed to say something like, 'don't worry, these things take time, it's all going to work out, just hang in there, Sadie?'"

"Do you need me to say that?"

"I don't know. Maybe?"

"Hmm. Well," Lena said, "I don't believe I will. You already know that speech."

"Okay, then I guess I'll just think whatever and go with the flow." Sadie bit off a hunk of the bar.

"You need to do more than that." Lena stood and refilled her coffee. Steam wisped above the cup. "Things are changing whether you want them to or not. Merinda is a threat right now. Garrison Devine is a threat in your future. But—" She shut her mouth.

"But what?" Sadie asked slowly, afraid of the next words she'd here.

Lena sighed. "He's a threat right now, outside of the cloak. Members of your Clan—"

"I know." Sadie didn't want to hear more of what Lena was about to say. "But I can't help anyone if I'm not fully prepared."

Lena zeroed in on Sadie's face. "The Calling is your opportunity to be prepared, to deal with these threats."

"But . . ." Sadie's breaths shortened.

Lena sat and put her hand on Sadie's knee. "I understand you're scared, I do, more than you know. But more challenges are coming. You can ready yourself, or you can keep trying to hide. And you don't strike me as the hiding type. Preparing yourself gives you, gives all of us, a fighting chance. The other option, slowing things down and hoping for the best, well, it lowers our odds."

"But that's just it," Sadie said. "If I only had to worry about me, that would be okay. But I have to worry about you and Colette and Brandon and Connor, my whole Clan—everybody. I have to protect everybody."

Lena squeezed Sadie's hand. "Ah, but you're thinking about it the wrong way. All of those people you mentioned, and more—even those in your Clan who you've never met— we're all on your team. You don't have to fight to protect us. We'll all be fighting *with* you, to stop Merinda, to stop Garrison Devine, to stop whatever or whoever else needs to be stopped. Together."

Sadie stared into Lena's eyes. Her mind bounded through thoughts of fear and fighting.

"Whether you're ready, or can handle the Calling— that's up to you." Lena pulled her into a side-hug. "But you are not alone."

Sadie sat back. "But everyone here is safe with the cloak in place."

"The cloak is temporary."

"But at least it's here."

"To give you time to prepare. Use it."

A swirl started inside Sadie. It was like the anxiety she had before a test when she didn't feel like she'd studied enough. "What if it's too late?"

"What if it's not?" Lena kissed Sadie's forehead.

Colette bounced into the room. "I'm ready."

Sadie jumped.

"Oh, sorry," Colette said. "I interrupted something. Should I leave for a few more minutes?"

"No, no." Lena waved her forward. "You're fine. We were just having a little chat."

"And we should get going." Sadie stood, finished the almond milk and protein bar, and put the wrapper in the garbage.

"I'll drive you," Lena said. "No reason to let you walk alone while Merinda is out there."

"Can't agree with you more," Colette said.

The comments hit home. If Sadie was prepared, if she had focused on training, if she had been more open to the Calling, she could manage a walk to school with Colette.

She could manage Merinda.

Maybe, with help, she could even manage Garrison Devine.

✳ ✳ ✳

While Lena drove them to school, Sadie texted Connor and told him about her invisibility.

He wrote back: "Fantastic news, my dear! Amazing!"

Sadie couldn't help but smile. She sent another message: "Can I come over right after school? I want to show you and also work on shifting again."

"Of course," Connor wrote. "I'll pick you up."

He'd pick her up because it was too dangerous for her to walk to Connor's on her own. Untrained. Unprepared.

"Thanks." Sadie did not like needing to be protected.

She sent another text, this time to Brandon, updating him and inviting him to join her at Connor's after school.

"Invisibility is cool—you rock," he replied. "I'll be there."

The car slowed to a stop in front of Salton High. Sadie told Lena about going to Connor's.

"And I'll walk home with Jason," Colette said.

"All right," Lena said. "Have a good day."

Sadie and Colette headed into the school.

"Eat together at lunch?" Colette asked as she turned toward her locker.

"Uh, I'll be in the library studying."

"Right," Colette said. "You don't want to be around Jason."

Sadie shrugged. "Nope."

"Got it." Sadness soaked through Colette's voice. "I'll see you in history class."

"Yeah. Bye." Sadie walked down the hall and peeked around the next corner where she had a view of her locker next to Jason's. He was standing there, locker door open, looking at his phone. An expression of surprise washed over his face.

Sadie guessed Brandon had texted him about her invisibility.

Jason typed something back, grabbed what he needed for class, and shut the door. But instead of heading his usual direction, away from where Sadie stood, he walked toward her.

Crap. I don't want to talk to him.

Sadie ducked into a doorway, dark because the classroom was unused. She activated her invisibility. The tingling sensation coursed through her.

Jason walked by without a glance, as did every other student in the hall. Sadie smiled to herself. *Yep, invisibility is cool.*

Seconds later, the door of the assumed-to-be-unused classroom punched into her when a teacher walked out, momentarily pinning Sadie onto the wall. She suppressed a cry and seized a spot on her arm where she expected a bruise would come until her healing power intercepted it.

Sadie then received a stub into her foot, not realizing her foot stuck out in the hall. She watched a girl stumble, save herself from falling, but lose her grip on her phone. It crashed on the floor and other students pointed and laughed. The girl's face flooded red as she grabbed her phone and hurried away.

Sadie winced. *Okay, invisibility is not entirely cool.*

Students continued to pass by and Sadie hesitated about reappearing. What if she caught someone's eye? How would she explain it? She waited for the crowd to thin but worried she'd be late to class.

Then the tingles started to weaken.

An outline of her hand appeared.

Crap.

She willed the tingles to increase, to maintain her cover.

They powered lower.

There was nothing she could do.

Sadie tucked herself as deep into the doorway as she could, closed her eyes, tried to concentrate and hold on until there were fewer students, fewer chances of being discovered, and hoped no one would notice her reentry if she failed.

"What the what?"

Sadie looked toward where the voice had come.

Kyle gawked at her, his eyes shocked open. "What did you just do?"

She checked her hands, her torso, her legs, her feet. All there. "You can see me?"

"Yeah, I can see you," Kyle said. "You scared the bejeezus out of me."

"Can you see all of me?" She pointed at her face. "Even my head?"

Confusion crawled over every feature on Kyle's face. "Would I be talking to you if I couldn't see your head?"

Sadie stepped forward and glanced down the hall. "Okay, good. Bye."

"Wait—what just happened?"

"New, ya' know, thing," Sadie said as she hurried away from him. "I'll tell you later. Gotta run." She left Kyle looking dumbfounded. She grabbed her stuff from her locker, rushed to her first class, and skittered into her seat as the late bell sounded.

✻ ✻ ✻

At Connor's that afternoon, Brandon laughed after Sadie told the story about dodging Jason and scaring Kyle.

"It's not that funny," she said.

"No, it really is." Brandon grinned. "Especially the part about Kyle. I wish I could have seen his face."

"But I tripped that girl." Sadie grimaced.

"And you should feel bad about that," Brandon said. "That was mean."

Sadie *tsked.* "I didn't do it on purpose."

"I know, I'm just giving you a hard time." He bumped his shoulder into hers. "She'll be fine. After a few sessions of therapy."

"Thanks a lot."

"I'm kidding! She'll deal. It's all good."

"I hope so," she said. "And needless to say, I kept the invisibility switch in the off position the rest of the day."

"Did you see Nessa?"

"Yeah, she's okay. Big hugs all around so we're good, at least for now." *Until she catches me in another lie or I do some other stupid thing to her.*

"That's good," he said. "How was Jason?"

"Never saw him."

"How did you manage not seeing him the entire day?" Brandon asked.

"I took everything out of my locker this morning and carried it all day so I wouldn't have to go back," she said. "Plus, I know his schedule. And I may have skipped a couple of classes."

"You can't do that every day."

"Sure I can," Sadie said. "At least until I transfer into different classes."

Connor walked into the room with a tray of lemonade. "Here we go, a bit of after school refreshment." He set down the tray. "And whenever you're ready, Sadie, do feel free to show off your new skill."

Connor and Brandon sat on the couch, looking at Sadie as if she were on stage. She raised her hands palms up, concentrated, the tingles intensified, and she disappeared like a burning match snuffed out in water.

"My word," Connor exclaimed. "That is extraordinary. Outerwear and everything. And I can see right through you."

"Wow," Sadie said. "I hadn't even thought about that part of things."

"It's truly as if you aren't even here," Connor said.

"Unless you touch me." Sadie turned to Brandon. "Hold out your hand."

Both Brandon and Connor thrust their hands forward.

Right, they can't tell where I was looking. She put one of her hands in each of theirs and squeezed. "See? Or I mean, no see? I'm still bumpable, which I learned the hard way today."

She reappeared and brought Connor up to speed about what had happened at school.

"We'll take that into consideration as we train with this skill," he said. "And I'll enlist Alexander's help for more research. Since you can transform clothing, and we know there have been cases of including other people and items in invisibility, perhaps there's another level where your mass is also not noticeable to others."

"Which reminds me." Brandon held his hand out again. "Try to make me invisible."

Sadie took his hand, concentrated, flipped the switch and disappeared. "Hold on." She focused on Brandon's hand. The tingles amped but Brandon's hand remained unchanged. She tried again but to no avail. She reappeared. "Sorry."

Brandon released her hand. "No worries. But I'm always up to play guinea pig whenever you want to try again."

"Thanks." She leaned in and kissed Brandon on the cheek.

"Oh, well, now, uh . . ." Connor drank a mouthful of lemonade and set down the glass. "We should get to the rest of our training and see if we can find your inner Yowie. Shouldn't we?" He gulped two more swallows of lemonade. "I think we should. Let's get to it." He stood. "Come along, you two." He waved for them to follow.

They went downstairs to a room similar to the training room at Uncle Alexander's house. There was a partition at the far end, but it wasn't a safety wall. It was a privacy wall.

"All right, Sadie." Connor gestured to the end of the room. "Off you go."

She crossed the room and stepped behind the partition. Anxiety surged. Sadie had tried to shift a few times before, standing right here behind this wall, and she always failed. She took a deep breath, slipped out of her regular clothes and put on a pair of baggy sweats and a sweatshirt that read "Salton High School" across the front. She also removed her necklace and charm bracelet, not wanting to break them again like she had when she shifted to Yowie the first time.

"Whenever you're ready, my dear," Connor said. "Deep breath and see yourself as Yowie. Powerful, majestic."

"Majestic?" Sadie asked. "Are you serious?"

"Yes. We Yowie are magnificent creatures," Connor said. "Strong. Practically invincible."

Practically invincible, but not wholly invincible.

"Focus."

"Okay, okay," Sadie said. "Give me a minute." She'd felt confident before coming in to practice. She'd figured out the invisibility thing, so why not shifting to Yowie? She'd done it before. She knew it was in her somewhere.

Wasn't it?

Sadie closed her eyes and focused.

She pictured Yowie.

She pictured strength.

She pictured fur and claws and height.

Her body tingled.

"No." She scrubbed the effort, opened her eyes and examined her hands.

"What is it?" Connor asked.

"I was tingling, like when I turn invisible," Sadie said. "But I'm not trying to turn invisible."

"Ah, that's Yowie energy," Connor said. "It isn't specific to any one power—it's part of every power."

Sadie stepped from behind the wall. "But I didn't notice it when I wiped Jerry's or Nessa's memories." A pain pinged her heart, thinking about Nessa.

"Memory wipes channel calming energy, but shifting and activating invisibility—those take extraordinary energy, energy you will feel, energy you can gauge as it's working."

A thought dawned on Sadie. "Oh, so that's why I felt the tingling decrease even though I wanted to keep my invisibility active, right? I was losing Yowie energy."

"Exactly. But don't be hard on yourself for running out of steam. You'll build up your resources as your skills increase, with practice, and with the will of the Calling. And what you can already do with invisibility . . ." Connor starbursted his fists over his head. "It's mind-blowing."

Goosebumps traveled along Sadie's back. "Thanks, Connor."

"Don't thank me," Connor said. "You're the one doing the dazzling. Do you want to try again?"

"Yeah. For sure." She stepped back behind the wall which she didn't need since she'd already changed clothes, but not being watched helped her concentrate. "Thinking Yowie."

"You've got this," Brandon cheered.

Sadie closed her eyes and focused, but nothing changed.

She stopped, took three deep breaths and tried again. She closed her eyes. She concentrated. She scrunched her brows.

Nothing came. Not even a tingle.

"Aaahh," She dropped to her haunches. "I can't do it."

"Try again, Sadie," Connor said. "Think about Willy."

Yeah. Mamo. I can do this for Mamo.

Sadie stood and exhaled a breath. She closed her eyes. She focused.

Tingling started in the tips of her fingers. It traveled through her arms. It zipped through her shoulders.

Then it stopped. Extinguished. Gone.

"Dang it, dang it, dang it." Sadie smacked her hand against the wall.

"I have an idea." Brandon ran over and poked his head behind the partition. "Think about Merinda, but think about her the day you stopped her, the day she and those two dudes had us tied up. We were in trouble, but you shifted and saved us. Okay?"

Sadie opened her mouth to reply but Brandon had already hurried away, returning to his spot next to Connor at the far end of the room.

Sadie considered what he'd said.

The day she had stopped Merinda.

The day she, Yowie-she, had saved them.

Saved them so she wouldn't lose them.

A fire fueled Sadie's focus. She closed her eyes.

Concentrated.

Tingles coursed through her.

They ramped in intensity.

Heat flooded her, and a moment later, the sweatshirt and sweatpants lay in tatters at Sadie's feet.

She was Yowie.

FOURTEEN

Confrontation

Jason *clunked* his locker closed at the end of the school day and startled to find Colette standing next to him.

"I missed you at lunch today," she said.

He avoided eye contact and lurched past her. "I had stuff to do."

She fell into step next to him. "Like what?" Her voice carried gaiety.

"Just stuff." Jason increased his pace.

Colette hurried to keep up. "You didn't miss much. Sadie spent lunch in the library, so it was me and Nessa eating with some other people."

Other people, like Derek Goodman.

Jason walked faster.

"Are you late for something?" Colette asked as she dodged students in the hall.

"I've gotta go." He banged through the front doors of the school, Colette right behind him.

"Why are you in such a hurry?"

"I said, I've got to go."

"Jason." She grabbed his arm and pulled him to a stop. "What is up with you?"

He tugged his arm away. "I don't want to talk about it."

"Well, okay. But will you at least walk me home?"

"I can't." He started down the sidewalk toward home.

"Hold on." Colette double-stepped and stopped him again. "I get that something's bugging you, but I don't get why you would let me walk home alone."

His anger flared. "I'm sure someone else can walk you home."

"Uh . . ." Confusion crossed Colette's face. "Sadie has already left, and Nessa is staying after to meet with a school committee she's part of. But I guess I could try to find Kyle . . ."

"Or Derek," Jason said. "You can go find Derek and he can walk you home."

Colette's mouth dropped open.

"And he can give you a nice big hug."

"Oh . . ."

Jason crossed his arms. "Yeah, I know about you and Derek. So don't bother lying about it."

She shook her head. "It's not what you think."

"I think you met him at the Salton Spoon, and he hugged you. Did that happen?"

"Yeah, but—"

"Then it's totally what I think."

"But that's not the whole story."

"Are you tutoring him or something?"

"No, but—"

"So what else is it besides you like him and he likes you?" The lining of Jason's lungs contracted. "Guess you don't have to keep the big secret anymore. You can sit with him at lunch every day from now on."

Colette yanked on Jason's sleeve and pulled him to a quieter spot in front of the school. "I'm not seeing Derek. We were paired up for a class assignment and I got to know him a little. He needed someone to talk to."

"And you didn't bother to tell me you were working on a class assignment with him."

"No," she said, "because you hate him."

"With good reason." Jason's chin jutted. "He's a jerk."

Colette huffed. "I get that he's been a jerk to you, but he's always been nice to me."

"Great." Jason sneered. "Go be his best buddy." He stormed away from her.

"Do not do this," Colette called after him. "Not after everything. Not after London." Her voice caught in her throat.

Jason stopped but kept his back to her.

"Listen," she said. "Walk me home, and listen."

He wanted to ignore her.

But he also wanted to understand, to hear what she had to say, to learn he was wrong, and Colette was still his girlfriend.

He nodded.

Colette walked up to him and they started down the sidewalk to her place.

She took a deep breath. "Derek has a horrible home life."

Jason's voice amped. "Have you been to his house?"

"No, I haven't been to his house," she said, her tone calm. "Please, just listen."

He steadied himself. "Go ahead."

"Derek's parents are dead," she said.

"Not true. Uncle A met them."

"He met the Dunabys—Derek's step-mom and her new husband. She remarried after Derek's dad died. Derek's mom died when he was even younger."

For a moment, Jason felt sorry for Derek. "That's a huge bummer, but hello, we've had sucky stuff happen with our parents, and we aren't jerks to everyone."

"You're right," she said. "But we've at least had people to talk to." A slight downturn moved over her lips. "He's had no one."

"He has his step-mom."

"She doesn't pay much attention to him."

"He has other friends," Jason said. "Why not talk to them?"

She shrugged. "I guess he has to be the tough guy with them."

"But not with you."

She shrugged again. "I was the new girl and knew nothing about him, so I wasn't afraid of him or anything. I just talked to him."

"And you liked him." Given everything else he knew about Derek, Jason didn't understand how anyone could like him.

"He was nice. And at the beginning, he didn't know I was with you."

A flutter loosened tightness anchored in Jason. *Colette was with him.*

"Why didn't you tell me about being friends with him earlier?" he asked.

"I've brought him up a few times but you and Sadie both dislike him so much," she said. "And he obviously doesn't like either of you. It was a weird position to be in. But I only saw him in class, so I didn't think it was a big deal."

"But you've seen him outside of class."

"Yes. But only two times, and only because he was upset."

Jason stopped walking. "Wait—two times?"

She gestured for him to keep walking with her. "Last night was the second time. The first was the day of the big snow when Sadie had to wipe Mr. Templeman's memory."

The day Jason had wondered where she was.

"Derek texted me that morning saying he was worried about a friend in trouble, that things at his house were messed up, and everyone was yelling at him. He asked if I'd meet him so he could get out of there."

"Sounds like a jerkwad way to ask you out on a date."

"It wasn't like that," she said. "I met him at the Salton Spoon and he was really stressed. The way he was talking about his friend made it sound like they were in serious trouble, like they might hurt themselves."

"Who was he talking about?"

"He didn't say, but I figured it must be one of the guys he hangs out with."

Jason definitely didn't know any other friends of Derek Goodman.

"Anyway, after a few minutes, he got agitated and said he had to go. He practically ran out of the Spoon," Colette said. "I finished my hot chocolate and decided to head to the library."

"And last night?"

"Last night was weird, too," she said. "He called me, very upset, so much so I could barely understand what he was saying. I agreed to meet him, and when I walked up to him on the street, he was crying. That's why I hugged him."

Another pang of sympathy wiggled into Jason. He forced it out.

"And that's the only time I've ever hugged him," Colette said. "He seemed so lost."

"And then what happened?" Jason asked.

"We sat at a table and he stared at his glass of water, not saying a word. I asked him a few questions, and he'd look up at me, it would seem like he was about to answer, and then he'd say nothing and go back to staring at his glass. After about twenty minutes I excused myself and called Lena for a ride home."

"That's it?" Jason stopped in front of Colette's.

"That's it," she said. "I'm sorry I didn't tell you about Derek sooner. It's only a casual friendship, and I never expected to see him anywhere but in class. But I did feel uncomfortable after I met with him the first time, and I should have said something to you."

Jason considered everything he'd been thinking, every wrong thing he'd believed about Colette. "I'm sorry, too." He reached for her hand. "I should have asked you about him instead of being so mad."

"It's okay." She moved in closer. "At least you care enough to get mad. We'll just do better, both of us, from now on, okay?"

"Okay."

"Do you want to come in for a while?"

"Nah," Jason said. "I don't want to risk being here when Sadie gets home."

Disappointment etched her face. "I'll talk to you later." She turned and walked toward the front door.

"Colette?" Jason called, and she turned. "I care a lot. About you. I care a lot about you."

She smiled. "I care a lot about you, too." She continued into the house.

FIFTEEN

Swarmed

The week passed with no sign of Merinda. Connor spent nights at Sadie's, and each day Dad and Uncle Alexander, along with Connor and the dogs, had searched without success. There had been no new attacks or sightings.

By Friday afternoon, Jason had only seen Sadie a handful of times. He always said hello, but she never responded.

"Can I share your locker for a while?" Jason asked Colette as he was gathering what he needed to take home for the weekend. "Just until things get worked out between me and Sadie?"

"I guess so," she said. "But I don't like being in the middle of this. I hate seeing you fighting with each other."

"There's no fighting. She won't even speak to me."

"I wish I could tell you that would change soon," Colette said, "but she won't talk to me about you, and I've tried. We can talk about anything else but you."

"It sucks." He closed his locker. "How is her Yowie and invisibility stuff going?"

"Still training though she hardly needs to. She barely has to think about it to make the shifting and invisibility work now."

Jason flung his backpack on one shoulder and weaved his arm under the second strap. "That's awesome. Wish I could see it."

"Aw, I'm sorry." She put her hand in Jason's. "I hope things get better soon for all of us."

"Me too," he said. "Let's go. I'll walk you home before I head to Uncle A's."

✹ ✹ ✹

Sweaty from Tae Kwon Do, Sadie showered in the locker room and changed her clothes while other students buzzed around her, changing and chatting and showering. She checked her phone and found two text messages from Nessa addressed to her and Colette. The first message read: "OK, my crush on Kyle Lex is officially

O
V
E
R

He just showed up at my door and said he was here to take me out on a date. I mean, hello, call me first. Make a plan. Don't just show up."

The realization of what had happened gouged Sadie in the gut. *Oh no, oh no, oh no.* Nessa hadn't remembered her date with Kyle because Sadie had wiped it.

She tapped on the second message from Nessa: "And he had the nerve to get mad and say I should have called him and told him I didn't want to go out with him. Excuse me? Something is off with that guy. Can't believe I ever liked him."

Sadie plopped onto a bench and reread the messages again and again. How had she forgotten this big of a deal? How could she fix this?

She covered her face with her hands.

Sadie couldn't fix it. She couldn't convince Nessa she had plans with Kyle, not without messing her up more.

Sadie had ruined it.

She'd ruined Nessa's longtime crush on Kyle and stolen the joy Nessa had when he'd asked her out.

Sadie pressed the heels of her palms into her eyes. Her phone slid off her lap and dropped to the floor. Merinda, Jason, the Calling—she hated everything right now.

"Excuse me."

Sadie looked up at a red-headed woman standing over her, her long curls twisted into a messy bun on top of her head. She held out Sadie's phone. "You dropped this."

"Thanks." She tossed her phone into her bag.

"Are you okay?" The woman sat on the bench opposite Sadie. "Can I get you water or anything?"

"Any chance you have a time machine so I can go back and fix a problem I caused?"

A soft smile turned up the corners of the woman's mouth. "I wish I did. There are a few problems in my past that I wouldn't mind changing." She stood. "But if it's any consolation, I've learned that most of the problems in our past aren't as bad as we think they are. Everything will likely work out."

Sadie disagreed but didn't want to argue the point. "I hope you're right."

"Since I'm fresh out of time machines, is there anything else I can do?" she asked.

"No, I'm fine," Sadie said. "Thanks for offering."

"You take care," the woman said and exited the locker room.

✳ ✳ ✳

Jason rose early Saturday morning and headed downstairs. Brandon was cooking eggs, supervised by Shay, and Dad was about to go out the door with Della.

"Shay still needs her breakfast," Dad said. "I'm dropping Della at dance class, then we can head to Alexander's. I just hope we find Merinda today and wrap this up."

"Me too," Jason said. The sooner Merinda was dealt with, the sooner he could repair things with Sadie. At least he hoped he could. He picked up Shay's bowl.

"Is Kyle ready to go?" Dad asked.

"If you consider walrus-snoring ready to go, then yeah." Jason filled Shay's bowl with kibble. She twirled three times as he walked the bowl to her spot and dug into her meal the second he placed it on the floor.

"Fine," Dad said. "But he'd better not complain about us going without him today. I'll be back soon."

"Okay." Jason waved at his sister. "Have fun, Dell."

"Thanks. You, too," she said as she sauntered out the door. "See ya', Brandon."

"See ya'." Brandon dropped two slices of bread in the toaster and turned to Jason. "So, what are our odds today?"

"Of finding Merinda? Not great," Jason said. "Uncle A's wondering if she took off."

"Sadie would not like that."

"I'm guessing she's not coming with us today?"

"No way," Brandon said. "If you're in, she's out."

Disappointment matted in Jason's mind.

"Besides, she's stressing over Nessa. Nessa was supposed to go on a date with Kyle last night but Sadie wiped it from her memory." Brandon buttered toast now sitting on a plate next to his scrambled eggs. "I guess Kyle showed up at her house, ready to take her out, and she had no clue."

"No way." Jason winced at the discomfort both of them must have felt.

"Yeah, not good for anyone," Brandon said. "Sadie was upset after Tae Kwon Do last night. And she hasn't replied to a text I sent this morning."

"That sucks," Jason said. "I get why she'd be upset. And Nessa and Kyle, too." He wondered if that was why Kyle hadn't bothered to get up on time. Maybe he was embarrassed. Or pissed. Or both.

Brandon carried his plate to the table. Shay came over and sat next to him, watching the floor for falling crumbs. "I just want things to settle down around here. Sadie's mad at you, you're mad at Colette—it's too much."

"I'm not mad at Colette," Jason said. "I was wrong about her and Derek." He explained what he'd learned.

"Today is looking up," Brandon said. "Here's hoping Merinda is next on our list of things to make better."

"Yes, please." Jason started cooking his own meal of eggs and toast.

✳ ✳ ✳

Less than an hour later, Jason, Brandon, Shay, and Dad stood in Uncle Alexander's driveway with him and Finn. The sun shone in a cloudless sky.

Connor pulled up in his SUV. "Good morning, fellow hunters. Good day for a search, isn't it?"

"Hopefully better than every other day this week," Dad said.

"Do we have any new ideas about where Merinda might be?" Jason asked.

Uncle Alexander sighed. "Unfortunately, no. The fact that she switched from highly active to zero signs of activity makes me question if she's still in the area. But I think we should revisit the newer of the two nests and see if anything has changed."

Shay looked up in the sky and whimpered. A bright glob that wasn't the sun glowed in the distance overhead. Jason squinted. Hairs on his neck prickled.

Uncle Alexander continued. "I thought we also might sprinkle corn starch around the nest area, making it easier to see tracks or other marks made if she visits the nest."

"Uncle A?" Jason held his hand to shield his eyes.

"Of course, whatever we do needs to be nontoxic and in no way harmful to the environment."

Finn barked.

"Uncle A—look." Jason pointed to the glow coming closer.

Uncle Alexander and everyone else turned and gazed up.

"That isn't . . . is it?" Uncle Alexander asked.

"I'm pretty sure it is," Jason said.

"Pretty sure it's what?" Brandon asked. "It's moving fast."

"You can see it?" Jason asked.

"Yeah."

"It's a swarm. Everybody in the vehicles." Uncle Alexander started his truck while Jason and Brandon piled in with the dogs. Dad jumped into Connor's SUV.

A few seconds later, dozens of Skyfish flocked the cars then shot away, shimmering iridescent colors, flashing silver and gold. Uncle Alexander yanked his transmission into gear and followed their glow, once again high in the sky.

"Please tell me those are Skyfish," Brandon said, gripping the dashboard and grinning up through the windshield.

"Those are Skyfish," Jason said. "But I have no idea what they're doing. It's not usually a good thing when they swarm."

"Why I can see them?" Brandon asked.

"Because of the swarm." Uncle Alexander accelerated as the Skyfish moved faster. "Now let's see where they lead us."

"What about Merinda?" Jason grabbed onto an armrest.

"One challenge at a time," Uncle Alexander said. "Swarming Skyfish seems to be the most pressing issue at the moment."

Away from downtown Salton, the Skyfish changed direction. Uncle Alexander wrenched the wheel and turned onto a dirt road that split corn fields hosting yellowed and spent stalks. Connor missed the corner but Jason soon saw them following again.

Ruts tossed them inside the cab. Jason braced himself against the door. Another sudden turn sent Brandon sliding into him then bouncing him back when Uncle Alexander corrected.

"Sorry," Uncle Alexander said. "Tricky here on these farm roads."

After two more turns and two more stretches of bumpy ride, the Skyfish dove into a gray-weathered barn with planks of wood missing and holes in its roof. It had no door and looked like it hadn't been used in decades.

Uncle Alexander stopped the car about seventy feet away and put it in park. "This is unusual." He killed the engine but left the keys in the ignition.

"What were you expecting?" Brandon asked.

"That's a good point," Uncle Alexander said. "I guess I wasn't expecting anything since we're in new territory here." He got out of the car. Jason and Brandon followed, the dogs bounding out after them.

Connor pulled up with Dad and they both exited their vehicle.

"What's happening?" Dad asked.

"Not sure," Uncle Alexander said. "Jason and I will investigate with Finn and Shay, and Connor, too, if you're feeling up for it?"

"Absolutely," he said. "Lead the way."

"What do you want us to do?" Dad gestured between himself and Brandon.

"Stay here for now," Uncle Alexander said. "Without powers, I prefer you remain out of harm's way. I'll signal you when and if we know it's safe."

Dad nodded.

Jason, Uncle Alexander, and Connor traipsed toward the barn with the dogs, weaving through overgrown weeds and dried grasses.

Before they reached the structure, indistinct yells came from inside the building followed by a Yowie-roar.

Merinda.

The dogs bolted.

Jason sprinted after them with Uncle Alexander and Connor close behind. He skittered to a stop inside the door. Cool air smelled like musty hay and old wood. The dogs both stood still, alert, and watching the scene. Seconds later, the swarm of Skyfish zipped through the roof, away from the site.

Merinda, cornered, rose to full height and swiped at Derek and Ash who were now yelling and screaming over Merinda's growls. Derek pulled at Ash. Ash flailed and fell to the ground. Derek grabbed a cattle prod with one hand and tugged on Ash's hair with the other.

Jason moved to ignite his powers but Uncle Alexander stopped him. "Not with the boys here. Keep her cornered. Connor will back you up."

Connor nodded.

"I'll get the boys out of here and then we'll deal with Merinda," Uncle Alexander said.

Jason signaled the dogs forward. "Hey," he yelled at Merinda as he approached. She jerked her head toward the sound. "Back off."

She hunched and bared her teeth.

"And you two," Uncle Alexander said to Derek and Ash. "Let's get you out of here."

"That thing hurt me," Ash yelled, scurrying away from Merinda. "And he made it hurt me." He pointed at Derek.

"Shut up, Ash-hole." Derek shoved Ash. Ash recovered his balance and drove his head into Derek's torso knocking them both to the ground. The cattle prod flew from Derek's hand.

Merinda roared.

The dogs watched, waiting for instruction.

Jason internally amped his powers, readying them for launch. "Stop," he yelled at Merinda and Derek and Ash.

No one listened.

"You wanted that thing to kill me." Ash had scrambled onto Derek's chest and was pummeling his face, in part blocked by Derek's arms. "Just like when you left me out there by myself."

Uncle Alexander grabbed Ash by the scruff of his coat and hauled him off, but before Derek could stand Ash escaped Uncle Alexander and was on Derek again. "You tried to make it kill me."

"Get off me." Derek rolled his weight and pinned Ash. "You didn't even get half of what you deserve."

Ash hocked a loogie onto Derek's forehead. "That's what you deserve."

Merinda growled and rose partway to standing.

Jason scanned the space, from Merinda to Derek and Ash, ready to react.

Derek scowled and shook his head. Ash writhed, but the loogie dropped off Derek's face and onto Ash's neck.

"Enough." Uncle Alexander pulled the boys apart.

Ash weaseled away from Uncle Alexander and picked up the cattle prod. "I'll show you, Derek." He switched on the prod and marched toward Merinda, fury on his face.

Finn stepped in front of him and he stopped. He turned to Jason. "Get your dog, or I'll zap it."

Heat fired into Jason's skin. "Not if you know what's good for you." He twitched his head, and Shay moved to stand next to Finn.

Ash pointed the prod. "I'll do it."

Shay's hackles rose, and she took a half-step toward Ash.

"Get out of here, Ash," Jason said. "Or I'll help Derek feed you to the monster."

"You said you didn't like Derek." Ash spit the words.

"You threatened my dogs," Jason said. "Now, I don't like you either."

"Asshole." Ash stomped off with the cattle prod.

Jason couldn't believe this was the same kid they'd met in the cottonwoods. He suspected that day was all an act.

Jason focused his attention on Merinda who seemed calmer but was still on edge, still cornered. Patches of her fur were soaked with blood trickling from open wounds on her legs and torso. She teetered like she was off-balance, but didn't fall.

Uncle Alexander and Connor were challenged with escorting the boys out of the barn, keeping them apart and leading one away from the other. Jason heard Uncle Alexander suggest the boys wait separately, in the two cars, until he and Connor could drive them home. Jason knew Uncle A really meant memory erased first, then a ride home.

"Hey," Uncle Alexander said, his voice tense.

Derek and Ash were fighting again, bodies hitting hard on the ground, calling each other names and landing punches. For a split second, Jason thought about leaving the barn to help but no way would he leave Merinda unattended.

More minutes passed, and after yet another round of scrapping, it sounded like Uncle Alexander, Connor, and Dad had the boys pulled apart for a third time.

"Ash, you sit in my truck, and Derek, in Connor's car," Uncle Alexander said. "We'll drive you home."

"You're not the boss of me," Ash said. "Get a life, freak-man."

"You need to show more respect—wait. Hold on," Uncle Alexander yelled.

Jason heard footsteps racing away, first one set, then another. *Guess it's no memory wipe and no ride home.*

A moment later, Connor reentered the barn.

"Derek and Ash took off?" Jason asked.

"Yes, they did," Connor said. "A couple of little scoundrels." He changed his tone from serious to sing-songy. "Merinda," he said as he approached.

Panting, she stood and cocked her head.

"Do you know me?" Connor asked as he moved closer.

"What are you doing?" Jason asked. He signaled the dogs to his side.

"Having a little chat while your uncle gets what we need out of the car." He plastered a fake smile on his mouth and kept his voice pleasant, sweet.

"Right." Jason remembered they needed a tranquilizer gun. "Good. Nice chat."

Merinda stared at Connor.

"Do you think she recognizes you?" He checked the dogs' body language. Both were relaxed, not alerting on any potential danger. "It kind of seems like she might."

"It's possible, I suppose." Connor practically sang the words. "I sense familiarity in her. She could be coming back into herself as she heals."

"I don't get why she isn't trying to run, to get past us."

"Maybe she's tired, or maybe she enjoys visiting with us," Connor soothed. "She's safe. Nothing to worry about."

Uncle Alexander stepped into the barn. He held the tranquilizer gun low, pointed at the ground, mostly out of view. "Everything okay in here?"

"Almost too okay," Jason said. "The dogs are chill, and she hasn't tried anything since Derek and Ash left."

"That may change in an instant," he said. "Be prepared to keep her contained in here."

"Okay." Jason checked his powers.

Both dogs' ears perked and they looked toward the doorway.

Sadie entered the barn, breathing hard, a scowl coating her face like a mask.

Dad and Brandon hurried in after her.

"I tried to keep her outside," Dad said.

"It's okay, Zachary," Uncle Alexander said. He turned to Sadie who was glaring at Merinda. "We have everything under control in here, Sadie. But I'd appreciate it if you'd keep watch outside, make sure Derek and Ash aren't hanging around."

"I'm staying in here." Her fists clenched.

"It would be better—"

She flicked her gaze to Uncle Alexander. "I said, I'm staying." She returned her regard to Merinda. "I want to make sure she doesn't get away. Again."

Jason blew out a breath, feeling the zing in Sadie's words.

"All right. But Brandon and Zachary, it would be better if you put some distance between us."

They both left the barn.

Uncle Alexander nodded to Jason and Connor. "Ready?"

Jason and Connor nodded.

Uncle Alexander raised the tranquilizer gun and pulled the trigger.

Merinda rose and roared and leaped into the air, clearing the path of the dart.

As she landed, a second Yowie plowed into her and drilled Merinda into the ground. Air gushed from her lungs. She scrambled to stand.

Jason's arms engulfed.

Connor and Alexander hollered.

Sadie was Yowie and battling Merinda.

The enemies roared and clawed and cried.

Jason reoriented, looked for an opportunity to strike, to help Sadie. But he couldn't fire without chancing injury to her. He couldn't risk it.

He wouldn't risk it.

The two Yowie tumbled and growled.

Blood spurted.

Sadie kicked Merinda.

Merinda *thudded* onto the dirt floor near Connor. Then she jumped up and rushed toward Sadie.

"Oh my god. Oh, no! Sadie!" Connor's clothing ripped and he transformed to Yowie. He flung himself into the fray, pulling at Sadie, pinning her arms, roaring in her ear. Merinda, bleeding, scrambled away.

What is Connor doing? Jason checked Uncle Alexander who looked as dumbfounded as Jason felt.

Sadie backhanded Connor, hurling him off her and onto the ground. She chased after Merinda.

Connor returned to the fight and countered Sadie again.

"What do we do?" Jason yelled to Uncle Alexander.

He repeatedly adjusted the aim of the gun. "Just be ready."

The dogs were both fixed on the fight.

Connor swiped one of Sadie's legs. She dropped to one knee then leaped up and pivoted, shoving him back. He buckled and fell, restored to human form but naked and gasping for air.

Jason rushed over and pulled him away.

Connor reached his hand toward Sadie and Merinda. "Stop, stop." The words whispered from his throat as he worked to catch his breath.

Sadie pinned Merinda in a corner, the fur of her powerful arm mixing with Merinda's coat.

She leaned in and compressed Merinda's throat.

Merinda's eyes bulged.

Uncle Alexander fired a dart into Merinda's thigh.

Connor found his voice. "Stop, Sadie! She's not Merinda! She's your mother! SHE'S YOUR MOTHER."

Sadie sprang back, releasing her hold.

The Yowie they thought was Merinda slumped to the floor.

And Sadie slumped next to her.

SIXTEEN
A Return

The Yowie who wasn't Merinda lay unconscious on the floor of the barn. Sadie, still in Yowie form, breathed hard and stared at the inert Yowie's face, its lips swollen, its nose bleeding.

"Sadie." Connor, one eye puffy and discolored and closing in on itself, pulled shredded remains of his clothes over his body. "She's Elly. She's your mother." He puffed through the words. "I'm certain it's her."

Sadie's Yowie eyes glanced at Connor, then she scrambled to her feet and ran out of the barn.

"Sadie," Connor called after her but she didn't stop.

Dad and Brandon hurried in.

"What happened?" Brandon asked. "Is Merinda dead?"

"She's not Merinda." Jason filled them in with a condensed version of what had happened.

"Whoa." Brandon ran a hand through his hair.

"If you would be so kind, Zachary," Connor said, "there's a bag in my trunk with a change of clothes. I planned for such a development."

Dad dashed out of the barn and returned with the bag and a blanket. He held the blanket to give Connor some privacy.

"I sensed familiarity with her, Elly, from the start." Connor rose slowly to his feet with an assist from Uncle Alexander. "It wasn't until I was close to her, when she fell near me, that the familiarity became knowing."

"It's a good thing you identified her when you did," Uncle Alexander said. "And now let's get medical treatment for both of you." He checked Elly's pulse. Finn and Shay joined him at Elly's side, sniffing and wagging. "Zachary, please bring my truck down, as close to the doors as possible."

"You got it." Dad wrapped the blanket around Connor's upper body and rushed out again.

"Brandon, call the paramedics for Connor."

"Nonsense," Connor said. "I'm fine. No need to summon the cavalry. All I need is rest."

"What about Sadie?" Brandon asked. "You know, her healing power."

"Right," Uncle Alexander said. "I'm still getting used to her having powers. Though after the last few minutes, I'm certain I won't forget about her being a Yowie."

"I'd much rather spend time with my great-niece than some random doctor," Connor said.

"We'll start with Sadie, and see how that goes, okay?" Uncle Alexander gestured to Brandon. "Would you help Connor to his car? He'll be warmer there. His coat is in tatters."

"You bet." Brandon pulled Connor's arm over his shoulder, and they slow-stepped toward the door.

"And if you can contact Sadie," Uncle Alexander said, "please ask her to return."

"Got it," Brandon said.

"What can I do?" Jason asked.

Uncle Alexander scanned the area, then pointed. "Grab that section of wood that's fallen from the wall and bring it over here. We can use it to slide Elly closer to the truck."

While Jason collected the wood, Uncle Alexander activated his Guard power and cauterized Elly's visible wounds.

"Can Sadie fix Merin . . . uh . . . Elly, too?" Jason set the boards next to Elly's body.

"Obvious wounds, yes," Uncle Alexander said. "But we can't perceive what's going on internally. And I also don't understand the extent of Sadie's healing power so we'll need additional expertise."

"Hold on." Jason grimaced and waved his hand in front of his nose. "What is that stench?"

"That would be Eau de Unwashed Yowie."

"Did she roll in cow manure or something?" Jason asked.

"No," Uncle Alexander said. "But living for years in the wilderness rarely leaves one smelling fresh. Not to mention the added odor of burnt fur."

The rumble of an engine approached, filled the space, then silenced. Dad reentered the barn. "The truck's right outside the door."

"Good," Uncle Alexander said. "Now, can the two of you maneuver Elly onto her side? I'll stop any bleeding from wounds she may have on her back."

THE FORGE OF BONDS

Jason and Dad heaved her mass and Uncle Alexander scanned for injuries. "Ah, no open wounds, though she has a few that seem recent, but not so recent as tonight."

Jason and Dad returned Elly to her previous position.

"Probably from me," Jason said.

"Two were from you, but there were several smaller ones," Uncle Alexander said. "Not sure where she would have received those kinds of injuries."

Dad lowered his head near her face and listened to her breathing. "I'm no Yowie expert, but her breathing seems fine. Steady."

"Good." Uncle Alexander examined the boards next to Elly's body. "Now we just need to get her off the floor and onto the planks."

"Do you believe this Yowie is Sadie's mom?" Jason asked.

"It makes as much sense as her being Merinda, a Yowie they were certain they'd defeated a few months ago." Uncle Alexander checked Elly's pulse again. "And I have no reason not to trust Connor's senses in this situation."

"Yeah, true." Jason hoped Connor was right and Sadie had her mom again.

A moment later, Finn and Shay perked their ears.

Derek stood inside the door, rocking from one foot to the other. "Is it dead?"

Jason rose and blocked his view. "Get out of here, Derek."

"I just want to know if you killed it." He wrung his hands. "Did you kill it?"

Behind him, Jason heard Dad and Uncle Alexander wrestling Elly onto the wood slide. "No, we didn't kill it."

Derek bowed his head. "Good, that's really good."

Huh?

"I gotta go." Derek raced out.

Jason paused a moment, then hunched to help Dad and Uncle Alexander. "I don't understand what just happened."

"Derek has a heart after all," Dad said.

Jason rolled his eyes. "Doubtful."

With a final shove, all of Elly's upper body lay on the boards. They grabbed her feet, dragged her across the dirt floor, and considered how to lift her into the cage inside the enclosed truck bed.

"We can help," Sadie said, walking up with Brandon. She had hints of nearly healed bruises on her chin and her forehead, and her eyes were rimmed red. She wore a baggy gray sweatshirt and a pair of sweatpants.

"Connor needs you first," Uncle Alexander said.

"Already done," she said. "But I still think he should see a doctor. I'm not sure if I fixed everything that I . . . he . . ."

"We'll get him checked out," Uncle Alexander said. "And as for lifting Elly, with the five of us together, we just might get this done."

Sadie and Uncle Alexander stood on one side, Jason and Dad on the other, and Brandon at Elly's feet.

"On three," Uncle Alexander said. "One, two, three."

They lifted together but Uncle Alexander's and Sadie's side thrust faster, unbalancing the boards and nearly dumping Elly onto Jason and his dad.

"Ease up, Uncle A," Jason said, repositioning the makeshift stretcher. "You don't realize your own strength."

"But I do realize my own strength." Uncle Alexander side-eyed Sadie. "That wasn't me."

They slid Elly into the truck.

"It was Sadie?" Jason asked.

Brandon grinned. "My girl. She's got skills."

"New skills, I guess," she said, examining her arms as if they might look different.

Uncle Alexander signaled the dogs to join Elly in the truck bed. "Yowie strength without being in Yowie form— it's noted in The Calling Compendium. An excellent ability to add to your repertoire."

"Yeah," Sadie said, her tone void of enthusiasm. "I guess so."

"All right, next steps," Uncle Alexander said. "Zachary, please drive Connor to the hospital. We all want to be certain his injuries aren't severe."

Sadie covered her face with her hands.

"He'll be okay," Brandon whispered to her.

Uncle Alexander continued giving direction. "Jason, please ride with Elly and the dogs, in case the tranquilizer wears off. It shouldn't, but better safe than sorry."

Jason hopped into the truck bed.

"And we're taking Elly to my house for treatment since we obviously can't take her to a public hospital," Uncle Alexander said. "I've already notified the League. They're sending a team to assist."

"What about me?" Sadie asked.

"You're welcome to come with us, or go with Connor if you prefer."

Her mouth opened and closed as her gaze flicked from Connor's car to Elly. "I should make sure Connor's okay. Can I come to your house later?" she asked Uncle Alexander.

"Of course, Sadie. You're always welcome."

Her lips quivered. "Thanks."

"Keep us posted about Connor, okay?" Uncle Alexander closed the shell of the truck.

Sadie nodded and then walked to Connor's car.

※ ※ ※

Sadie sat in the waiting room with Brandon. It was empty except for the two of them and the receptionist behind the desk at the far end of the room. A television in the corner blared an infomercial about spray-on makeup.

Jason's dad came out of the examination area. "The doctor is with Connor now. He told the doc he fell down the stairs."

"He must hate me," Sadie said.

"Not at all," Jason's dad said. "In fact, he's asking for you. Both of you." He stood. "I have to go pick up Della, but I'll come back and give you all a ride home."

"That's okay," Sadie said. "Lena is on her way."

"Then just call if you need me." He turned to Brandon. "I'll see you at home later. Keep me posted."

"Will do, Mr. Lex." Brandon stood and spoke to Sadie. "Let's get in there."

Sadie didn't budge. "I think I should stay here."

"But he wants—"

"I hurt him. He wouldn't even be seeing the doctor if it wasn't for me."

Brandon returned to his seat. "You didn't do it on purpose."

"All I could think about was making Merinda pay for—" A sob lodged in her vocal cords. She blew out a breath. "I was so angry at him for trying to stop me."

"So . . . uh . . . so you *tried* to hurt him?"

"No, I just wanted him to let go of me." She shifted her gaze to her lap. "I wanted him out of the way."

"You didn't realize he'd get hurt."

"But I should have known, shouldn't I?" She swallowed hard and looked Brandon in the face. "I wanted to stop her. I was determined she wouldn't get away again. What if I'd . . ."

Brandon was silent for a moment. "But you didn't. You didn't kill her."

A tear slid down Sadie's cheek. "I could have killed my own mother. My mom." Another tear fell. "What if I had killed my mom?"

He pulled her into a hug. "But you didn't. You didn't mean to hurt Connor, and you didn't kill your mom. It's okay."

"I'm not sure it is," Sadie said, her voice muted by Brandon's shirt. "So many things are not okay right now."

A hand pressed into her shoulder. "Sadie?"

Lena stood over her.

Sadie jumped up and hugged her hard. Her tears flowed with sniffs morphing to hiccuping gasps.

"There, there, it's all right." Lena stroked her hair. "Everything will be fine."

"You don't know," Sadie hiccuped, "what I did."

"Alexander brought me up to speed." She pulled out of the hug and looked Sadie in the eye. "And you have something to celebrate with the return of your mom."

"Nothing feels worth celebrating right now." Sadie sniffed.

Lena led her to a seat on a waiting room bench and signaled Brandon to pull a chair close. She held Sadie's hand. "Now listen up. We're taking things one at a time, starting with Connor. How is he?"

"Jason's dad said he's okay," Sadie said. "But we haven't talked to the doctor."

"Then we start there, though I expect the doctor will have nothing of urgency to report," Lena said. "And as for your mother, Alexander said her situation is unchanged. She's unconscious but stable, and the League medical team will arrive within the hour."

"All the way from London?" Brandon asked. "That's super-fast."

"They're sending one of the US-based teams," Lena said. "And leveraging a few cryptid powers in the process to speed up travel."

"Cool." Brandon smiled and nodded.

"What else has you upset?" Lena asked Sadie.

She swallowed and lowered her eyes. "Jason. I need to talk to him."

"So, you'll talk to him and he'll listen," Lena said. "And if I know my grandson, and I know him very well, he'll do whatever it takes to work things out between the two of you." She patted Sadie's hand. "What else?"

"Me." Sadie searched for words. "Something's wrong with me."

"What do you mean?"

"I almost did a horrible thing."

Lena paused a moment. "Yes, you *almost* did. Almost being the key word here because you didn't do it, and I don't believe you would have even if Connor hadn't stopped you."

Sadie's chest ached. "But I thought about it. I'm a terrible person." Tears tumbled down her cheeks.

"Now on that point, I disagree," Lena said. "I've known you for a long time and never have I even remotely considered the idea that you are a terrible person." She angled her head. "But in light of recent events, I do have one question for you."

"Okay." Sadie choked out the word.

"If I could push a reset button and you had today to do again, would you make the same choices?"

Sadie stiffened. "No." She shook her head resolutely. "I'd do everything differently. Everything." *Even before today, I'd do things differently* . . .

Lena smiled and patted Sadie's knee. "Of course you would. Because you are a good person who learns from her mistakes." She stood. "Now let's go check on Connor."

Sadie took a deep breath and followed Lena to Connor's room.

✳ ✳ ✳

The conversation with Connor's doctor was brief. She prescribed pain medication, instructed them to keep a precautionary watch on his "could be much worse" bruises to be certain they healed as opposed to declined, and suggested he use bags of frozen peas to ice the slight swelling around his eye. Before long they were in Lena's car and heading home.

"Lena, this isn't necessary," Connor said as they pulled into the garage. "I'll be just fine at my place. Please drive me there."

"I'll do no such thing." Lena pushed a button and the garage door started to open. "We want you here with us. And it gives me an opportunity to be a better hostess and provide you with a comfortable bed as opposed to the couch."

"But Lena—"

"Not another word." She opened her car door. "Inside with you."

Connor got out of the car. "I see why you and my sister got along so well."

Lena smirked. "She taught me everything I know about commanding people to do my bidding."

"Clearly." Connor chuckled. "And I admit, I'm grateful for your hospitality." He moved gingerly toward the steps into the house.

Sadie hurried to his side. "Do you need some help?"

"Oh, no, I'm okay. Just a bit of stiffness settling in. I think I used a few new muscles today. Or rather some old ones that had been in retirement for a while."

"All right." Sadie dropped back to stand next to Brandon and wait for Connor to pass.

"On second thought," Connor said, "since you're the reason I rediscovered these muscles, maybe I should make you pay me back with a little assistance."

She returned to his side and steadied his arm. "Whatever you need. I'm so, so sorry about everything."

"You were on fire today." He held onto the handrail with his right hand and Sadie's arm on his left. "There was a moment I wasn't sure what would happen. Your power was tremendous."

"I shouldn't have . . . I didn't mean . . ."

He stopped inside the door and faced her. "Perhaps you could clean my house every week for the next eighteen months to make up for everything you put me through today."

Sadie cringed at cleaning up after Connor's slovenliness but she didn't hesitate to respond. "You've got it. What else can I do?"

"Make me dinner five days a week."

"Done. What else?"

"Do my laundry."

"Okay. What else?"

Connor laughed and started to make his way to the kitchen. Sadie and Brandon followed. "Did you hear, Lena? I have an indentured servant."

"I heard," Lena said. "How long are you going to torture her?"

"Only for a month or two." He laughed again.

"Ah, I get it," Brandon said.

"I don't," Sadie said. "What are you laughing about?"

"My darling great-niece," Connor said, taking Sadie's hand in his. "All is forgiven and you owe me nothing."

"But . . . no," Sadie said. "What happened today—"

"What happened today was difficult, but also wonderful." Connor released her hand and eased into a chair at the kitchen island.

"Because we found my mom." Sadie said the words but didn't feel excitement about the Yowie that was supposedly her mother.

"Yes, because we found your mom," Connor said. "But you've also given me great hope."

Sadie shook her head. "Hope? In what?"

"In you. In the Calling. In defeating Garrison Devine." His eyes lit. "You demonstrated power well beyond your years. By no means should you, a young and inexperienced Yowie, have been able to counter my attack with such ease." He *tsked*. "If I'd known what I was getting into, I simply would have asked Alexander to dart you rather than try to stop you myself."

"Oh." Sadie's mind whirled.

"So, you see my dear, you didn't realize your power, so you can't be blamed for how you used it against me," Connor said. "And now that I have a painfully clear understanding of your abilities," he pointed to his now-barely-black eye, "we'll train together even harder so you can harness and develop that power. Deal?" He held out his hand.

Sadie took his hand and shook. "Deal. But I am super-sorry I hurt you."

"So am I. And I will be for a few days." He smiled.

Colette rushed into the kitchen. "I was hoping you were in here. Jason just called me." She hugged Sadie. "Why didn't you tell me you were going to the barn?"

"I didn't plan it," Sadie said. "Brandon texted me they'd found her, and I couldn't think about anything else but getting there and . . ." She swallowed. "And making sure Merinda didn't get away again."

"And I apologize for not asking you if you wanted to come to the hospital with me," Lena said. "I just rushed out the moment I heard they were there. I figured we'd have plenty of time to catch you up when we got back."

"I'm mostly caught up after talking to Jason." Colette turned to Connor. "But are you okay? What did the doctor say?"

"Sadie took care of the hard work." He pointed to his eye. "And I'm just fine. I'll be sore for a day or two, that's all."

Lena's phone rang. "It's Alexander." She answered and set the phone on the counter. "Alexander, you're on speaker with all of us."

"I'm glad you're all listening," Alexander said. "Nothing to worry about, but we have a slight issue here I thought you should be aware of."

"What's that?" Lena asked.

"Well, the medical team arrived, and I led them down to the lab where Jason and I were able to move Elly. She is safely and comfortably strapped down, just in case she wakes and is disoriented. We don't want her to hurt herself or someone else. Which I mention again to emphasize the fact that there's nothing to worry about."

"All right, Alexander," Lena said. "What happened?"

"Well, when I led the team into the lab, it seemed that Elly had disappeared."

"What?" Connor's eyes widened.

Uncle Alexander continued. "But in reality, Elly is right where we left her. She is merely invisible."

SEVENTEEN

Crash

"Sadie, Brandon, and Colette are on their way over," Uncle Alexander said to Jason. "Your grandmother will stay with Connor."

"I thought he was okay," Jason said.

"She's just being cautious, and there's nothing either of them can do here." Uncle Alexander peered into the windows next to the open door of the lab where three people wearing medical scrubs, masks, and safety glasses worked on the invisible Yowie. An IV dripped into space. A pulse registered on a monitor connected to a finger that didn't seem to exist.

"How do they even know what they're doing?" Jason asked.

Uncle Alexander gestured to the glasses the medical team wore. "Those do more than protect their eyes."

A member of the medical team gripped air where Elly's arm should be, tapped two fingers on an invisible spot, and inserted a syringe with an attached needle. Blood flowed and filled the tube.

"This is like watching a magic show," Jason said.

Uncle Alexander's phone buzzed. He tapped an icon and unlocked the front door. "Do you think Sadie remembers how to activate the elevator?"

"For sure," Jason said.

A moment later, the elevator, otherwise disguised as a walk-in closet, opened and deposited Sadie, Brandon, and Colette along with Finn and Shay.

"Hey," Sadie said to Jason.

"Hey," he answered, glad Sadie was speaking to him, even if it was only one word. Colette walked over and stood next to him.

Sadie and Brandon looked into the lab.

"I guess we have no idea if she's still in her Yowie form or not, huh?" Sadie asked.

"The medical team does, but we don't know much yet," Uncle Alexander said. "Other than she's stable, and she'll likely wake up soon unless the team has decided to keep her sedated." He turned to Sadie. "You're welcome to go in if you'd like."

Sadie shrugged, almost in slow motion. "I don't know what I'd do in there. I can't see her. And I don't even know her. I'd be in the way."

"Just say the word if you change your mind," Uncle Alexander said.

Sadie nodded and stared into the room.

Uncle Alexander paused. "I do have a question for you, Sadie."

"Sure," she said. "What is it?"

"What made you so certain this Yowie was Merinda?"

"I ran into her a few times when I was out walking with Shay when all the earlier stuff with Merinda was happening," Sadie said. "I knew neither Mamo or Connor had shifted, so I assumed I'd seen Merinda."

"But wasn't Merinda in Yowie form when you fought with her?" Uncle Alexander asked.

"Yeah, she was." Sadie smoothed a section of her hair. "But it was so crazy then, everything was happening fast. She was up close during the fight, and I'd only seen her from a distance before then. And both Merinda's and . . . Elly's fur is pretty much the same color." Her cheeks reddened. "I really screwed up. I screwed up a lot of things."

"Hmm, well . . ." Uncle Alexander said. "I understand how it could be easy to mistake the two of them."

Sadie tucked her hair behind her ears. "Uh, Jason?" She gave a light tug on his sleeve. "Can I talk to you for a minute? In private?"

His stomach flip-flopped. "Yeah. Sure."

"You can use my office." Uncle Alexander pointed down the hall.

Jason led the way to Uncle Alexander's office and Sadie closed the door behind them. Sadie sat in a chair. Jason hopped onto the front edge of the desk and worked to still twitchiness in his legs.

"I will try really hard not to cry," Sadie said.

Oh god, please don't cry, please don't cry. "I can get Brandon." Jason pointed at the door.

"No, that's okay. I want to talk to you," she said. "Because, wow, I owe you a huge apology. I'm sorry about everything."

"It's okay."

"But it's not. I said some horrible things." She paused. "I tried to get you to do a horrible thing." Sadie swallowed hard. "I didn't really want you to kill her, even if she had been Merinda. I was freaking out, totally overreacting, and you were right to say no. I'm so glad you said no."

"I'm not sure what to say now . . ."

"You don't have to say anything," Sadie said. "But, well, do you forgive me for everything I said? And for being so mad at you?"

"Totally," Jason said. "One hundred percent. It's not like I haven't been a dumbass before. And you've forgiven me."

"So, I'm a dumbass?" Sadie half-smiled.

Jason canted his head from side to side. "I gotta say, you were kind of a dumbass."

"And I one hundred percent agree with you." Sadie sucked in a quick breath. "Thanks for not killing my mom." Her voice cracked.

Don't cry. Please don't cry.

"Not a problem," Jason said quickly. "I promise never to kill your mom."

"Friends again?" Sadie asked.

"Friends always." He jumped off the desk and hugged Sadie, then stepped back. "So, I've been dying to see you show off your new skill."

"The invisibility?"

"Yeah. I mean, the whole Yowie thing would be cool too, but now is probably not a good time," he said.

"Definitely not. But I can do invisibility." As if she were flipping a switch, Sadie disappeared and reappeared.

Jason's jaw dropped. "That. Is. Awesome."

"I have to admit, I'm kind of a fan of it myself—"

A high-pitched beeping noise sounded from down the hall. The office door opened just as Jason reached for the handle.

Uncle Alexander stood in the doorway. "Come now." He rushed away. Jason and Sadie followed.

"Elly's crashing," Uncle Alexander said as they stood outside the room where Elly, no longer invisible but still in Yowie form, lay on the bed.

"What happened?" Sadie asked.

"It's unclear," Uncle Alexander said.

The medical team scurried around her, calling out stats and meds and orders.

Seconds ticked away.

Alarms screeched.

"Oh my god," Sadie said. "She can't die. Not now. Not after everything."

Brandon took her hand in his.

A new alarm pierced the air.

The medical team raced to hang bags and open syringes.

"Sadie," Uncle Alexander said. "You can go in there."

She blinked rapidly. "I have no idea what's wrong with her. I have no idea what to do."

"Just activate your healing power and talk to her," Uncle Alexander said. "You can't hurt her."

"I . . . okay." Sadie hurried into the room and sat on a stool near Elly's fur-covered face.

One of the medical team looked at Sadie, then at Uncle Alexander. He nodded, and the medical personnel continued their work.

Sadie placed one hand on Elly's forehead, and the other on her chest. She closed her eyes, then leaned close to Elly's ear. Jason saw Sadie's lips move but he couldn't tell what she said, until the last three words: "Please don't go."

She kept her hands in place and bent over to lay her cheek on Elly's shoulder. Alarms and frantic shouts continued to rend the air.

Colette moved closer to Jason and leaned into him.

Shay put her front feet up on the windowsill, whined, then retreated to a corner of the outer room with Finn.

Another moment passed then all the alarms silenced.

The team stepped back and checked the monitors.

A flat green line traveled across a dark screen.

"Oh, no . . ." Colette whispered.

Sadie, keeping her face on Elly's fur and her eyes closed, encircled her arm around Elly's head. Sadie linked her fingers with her other hand on Elly's chest.

Beep.

One bump in the green line.

The medical team moved in but Sadie, eyes still closed, shook her head. They stopped.

Beep.

No one moved.

"C'mon green line, more beeps. Give us more beeps." Jason gripped Colette's hand.

Beep.

Pause.

Beep.

Pause.

Beep.

Beep.

Beep.

The bumps in the green line increased in speed.

"Yes," Brandon said. "Keep going."

Beep. Beep. Beep.

The medical team exchanged looks of surprise and reengaged with activities around their patient.

Sadie stood. She took one of Elly's hands into hers. "Please, wake up."

The beeps settled into a steady rhythm.

A faint shimmer flickered through Elly's fur. Sadie released her hand and stepped back.

The glow amplified. The medical team paused while one of them covered Elly with a sheet.

A moment later, the shimmer faded, Elly's fur slicked to skin, and the patient was in human form.

Long hair, dark mixed with auburn like Sadie's, lay tangled and knotted around Elly's face. Her skin was pallid behind smattered blood, her mouth pale except for a cut crusted brown, and her eyes were still closed. One of the medical team declared Elly's vitals stable.

"Remarkable," said another member of the team.

Sadie ducked out of the room and stood next to Brandon.

"Nice work, Dr. Callahan," he said.

"Thanks."

"Though you might need a shower now," Brandon said.

Sadie sniffed her fingers. "Right? All I can smell is Yowie."

"Yeah," Jason said, smiling. "You are ripe."

One of the medical team left Elly's side and stepped outside the lab. She pulled down her mask.

"How is she?" Uncle Alexander asked the doctor.

"Stable," the doctor said. "Amazingly so. We're continuing to pump her full of fluids, and we have her on a course of antibiotics. She has quite a few wounds at various stages of healing, and some show signs of infection."

"Can you tell what happened?" Jason asked. "How she got hurt?"

"They look like burns, but I can assure you they aren't from Guard bolts," the doctor said. "These are different, smaller. But numerous. And some are deep. I can't explain it. But she's safe now. And since she's shifted into her human form it will be that much easier to treat the wounds."

"Why is she still unconscious?" Sadie asked.

"Her injuries combined with the sedative, not to mention the fact that she's somewhat malnourished, well . . ." the doctor shrugged. "I'm not surprised she's still asleep. But it's nothing to worry about now. We're also getting her some nutrition and expect she'll wake soon."

Sadie cast her gaze to the floor.

"Is something wrong?" Brandon asked Sadie.

"It's just . . . my healing . . . my healing wasn't enough." She wrapped her arms around herself. "Just like with Mamo."

"Well," the doctor said to Sadie, "I can't speak about what happened with this Mamo person, but I can tell you the only reason our patient here is stable, and alive for that matter, is because of you. You saved her life. You have an extraordinary gift."

"Thanks," Sadie said softly.

Brandon nudged his shoulder into Sadie's and a slight smile crossed her face.

"I'm heading back in there." The doctor replaced her mask. "I'll call you if anything changes, but for now everyone can relax, get some rest."

"Thank you, doctor." Uncle Alexander shook her hand.

❋ ❋ ❋

Sadie woke the next morning when the horizon only hinted at daylight. A cluster of nerves clamped in her belly.

I wonder if Mom . . . Elly . . . is awake yet?

I wonder if she'll recognize me?

What if she's not really my mom?

Before coming home the night before, Uncle Alexander asked the medical team to take a sample of Sadie's blood for comparison to the Yowie.

"Just to be certain," Uncle Alexander had said.

Sadie had acted like it was no big deal, but the blood draw had planted a seed of doubt, and the seed had germinated and sprouted overnight.

"It doesn't matter," she said to herself. "If she's not my mom, she's not my mom." Sadie got out of bed, scanned her body to make sure each part was visible, and headed into the bathroom wondering if she'd inherited her invisibility from the Yowie who might be her mother.

When she walked back into her room, she found a message on her phone: "Elly is awake. Come by whenever you like."

Sadie dressed, pulled her hair into a ponytail and hurried downstairs. She found Lena in the kitchen with her usual cup of coffee.

"You're up early," Lena said. "Did you get Alexander's message?"

"Yeah." Sadie grabbed an apple. "Is it okay if I go over there right now?"

"Of course. Colette and I will join you a little later, after she's up."

"Sounds good." Sadie's heart thumped like she'd just finished a session at the dojo. "I'll see you then."

✳ ✳ ✳

Sadie rang Uncle Alexander's doorbell. A starburst of rising sun peeked through the tips of tall nearby trees, splattering light across his porch. The door opened.

"Good morning," Uncle Alexander said.

"Hi. Thanks for texting me."

"Of course." He waved her forward. "Come in, come in."

Sadie stepped inside. Finn trotted over, her mouth open, her tail wagging. Sadie bent to Finn's level. "Good morning, sweet girl." She scratched Finn behind the ears and kissed her forehead. Finn licked Sadie's cheek.

"Thank you," Sadie said. "A kiss from you or Shay is the best way to start the day."

"I have some news that may add to the good start of your day," Uncle Alexander said.

Sadie bit the inside of her cheek and followed him to the elevator, but he didn't go inside.

"The DNA results came back. The woman downstairs is Elly Callahan," he said. "She's your mom."

Sadie's thoughts twirled through her mind. Even though Connor had told her the Yowie was her mom, even though she had believed him, she now had data. The niggling idea that Connor might be wrong was snuffed out.

Her mom was alive. And awake. And Sadie was about to see her, to talk to her.

"One more thing I want to mention before we go to the lab," Uncle Alexander said. "She hasn't used human speech for a very long time, so don't be alarmed if she seems a bit off. Her brain has a lot of catching up to do. It basically has to access archived information which can take some time." He opened the door to the closet elevator.

"So, she can't talk?" Sadie asked.

He stepped into the elevator and Sadie followed. "She can speak," Uncle Alexander said. "But she might struggle to find a word, or use an incorrect word when she's trying to convey something. The doctors believe this is temporary but there's no saying how long it will take before her verbal capacities are restored."

The elevator doors opened and they stepped out.

Elly reclined on the bed inside the lab, propped up on pillows and still covered with a sheet and blanket. But now she wore a white V-neck T-shirt, her face and arms were clean of blood and dirt, and her hair was pulled into a scrunchy, though Sadie could see it was still tangled. Elly's eyes were closed.

"Oh, she's asleep again," Sadie whispered to Uncle Alexander. "I'll go back upstairs and wait."

Elly's eyes opened. "Someone there?"

Uncle Alexander nodded at Sadie. "I'll wait out here."

She stepped into the room and stopped at the foot of the bed. "Hi. I'm Sadie." Her insides felt jiggly and taut at the same time.

Elly brows furrowed and she scratched a spot on her back.

"I'm . . ." Sadie stopped. It felt weird to say, "I'm your daughter," to a woman she didn't know. "I'm Sadie Callahan."

"Calla-han?" Elly asked, breaking the name into two parts.

"Yeah," Sadie said. "Like you."

Elly tilted her head. "Same name."

"Same last name, yeah."

"Closer, come sit."

Sadie sat in the same spot as the night before. Elly's skin smelled medicinal, like rubbing alcohol and soap, but the wild fur fragrance still wafted from her hair.

Elly stared at Sadie's face. "I saw you. I know."

"Uh . . . you mean you saw me out in the cottonwoods?" Sadie asked. "With Shay? The white dog?"

"Shay bark." Elly nodded.

"Yes, she barked. We saw you a couple of times, and she always barked."

Elly nodded. "I know. I get you. I watch to get you."

Sadie racked her brain trying to decipher what Elly meant. "You mean you watched for me and Shay?"

"You. Watched you."

Goosebumps tingled across Sadie's arms. "I don't understand."

Elly's eyes scrunched shut. "You. I m-m-must." Her eyes sprang wide open. "I must get you. I watch to get you."

"Oh, uh . . ." Hairs rose on the back of Sadie's neck. "Last weekend at the house—"

"Yes yes." Elly pushed herself toward Sadie. "I get you at the house." She breathed hard.

Sadie's heart pounded. She inched the stool back but Elly snatched Sadie's wrist in her hand.

"I get you. I get you."

"No, let go." Sadie twisted her wrist in Elly's grip.

Uncle Alexander rushed in. "Elly. Stop." He grabbed onto the hand that held Sadie and pulled her free. She jumped up and skittered backward, rubbing her wrist where her bracelet had dug in.

"I must get you." Elly pointed at Sadie's wrist. "I know."

Uncle Alexander looked at Sadie's wrist. "You wanted to get Sadie?" he asked.

Elly shook her head. "No." Tears welled in her eyes. "I know."

A thought clicked in Sadie's mind. "Wait, you know the bracelet?"

"Yes." Elly's voice pleaded. "I know."

"You were staring at my bracelet that day, with me and Shay."

"Yes."

"And you knew it was yours," Sadie said, recalling the look on the Yowie's face. She'd thought it was Merinda wanting to take the bracelet that had belonged to Sadie's mother. "You remembered."

Elly relaxed back into her pillows. "Remembered, yes. I knew. I had to get."

"Oh." Sadie moved to unlatch the bracelet. "You want it back."

"No, no." Elly waved her hands.

Sadie stopped. "I don't understand."

Uncle Alexander stepped close and put his hand on Elly's forearm. "Take a few deep breaths and think, take your time. You have the words for what you want to say. It's all in there."

Elly closed her eyes and breathed deep. "Bracelet, I knew."

"Yes, you recognized the bracelet," Uncle Alexander said.

She nodded and took another breath in, then out. "Then . . ." She breathed deeply again. "Started . . . remember."

"You started remembering . . . who you were?" Uncle Alexander asked.

"Small," Elly said.

Beats whooshed blood through Sadie's head.

"Only bits and pieces," Uncle Alexander said. "You didn't remember everything right away."

"Yes," she said. "But . . . one . . . thing knew." She opened her eyes and pointed at Sadie. "Get you."

Sadie's hope crumbled. This woman, this Yowie, her own mother had gone after Sadie, had tried to get her that night at Nessa's.

"Get her," Uncle Alexander said. "You wanted to hurt Sadie?"

Elly's eyes widened and she frantically shook her head. "No. Get her . . . sss . . . sss . . . you . . ." She took another breath and blew it out. She locked eyes with Sadie. "Ssssafe. Get you safe."

Tears flooded Sadie's eyes. She stared at her mom trying to process what she'd said.

"Ah, your instincts told you to protect Sadie," Uncle Alexander said.

Elly's entire body relaxed. "Yes. Protect Sadie."

A titter mixed with a cry crawled from Sadie's throat. "You scared the crap out of me."

"Sorry." Elly reached for Sadie.

Sadie hurried over and hugged her. "I'm glad you're here."

"Me . . . too." Elly stroked Sadie's hair. "Me too."

EIGHTEEN
King

Sadie spent a few more minutes with her mom, but she soon showed signs of fatigue.

"We should let Elly rest," Uncle Alexander said. "Her body and mind are working overtime as she heals."

Sadie nodded and stood. "I'll be back a little later, okay?"

"Okay." Mom squeezed Sadie's hand. "Soon."

"Soon," Sadie said, then followed Uncle Alexander out of the room. One of the medical team stepped in to check vital signs.

Sadie and Uncle Alexander headed upstairs. The front door opened and Connor peeked his head inside.

"Knock knock," he said. "I heard the bolt unlock."

"Yes, I saw you on the camera," Uncle Alexander said. "Come on in."

Connor entered the house. "How is our patient this morning?"

"She's good, resting." Uncle Alexander brought him up to speed about the DNA test results and the conversation Sadie had with her mom.

"Ah." Connor looked at Sadie. "She was hunting you down, but not in the way we presumed. It was maternal instinct enhanced by her Yowie connection to you, her child, that drove her."

"Her Yowie connection?" Sadie rubbed her temple where a light headache was forming.

"Yes," Connor said. "Our ability to sense Yowie energy is stronger with our close family members, especially parent and child. Elly must have that connection to you."

"I guess so," Sadie said. "But how is she even alive? Didn't they find her body after the car accident?"

"I've been pondering that," Connor said.

Uncle Alexander invited everyone to sit in the living room.

"And to answer your question," Connor continued, "no, we never found her body. But being a Yowie, knowing she had the ability to shift to things other than human, and given the severity of the fire that engulfed the car, we assumed she'd shifted into something else, something small, and was caught in the flames."

"Why would she do that?" Sadie asked.

"Perhaps to better enable an escape? Squeeze out of a space too small for a human?" Connor shrugged. "It was all speculation. I searched for Elly in the surrounding area for quite some time, but there was no sign of her Yowie energy. I accepted the presumption that she'd died in the fire."

"And I didn't die in the fire," Sadie said.

"Someone got you out." A slight smile flit across Connor's face. "You were sitting a few yards away, in your car seat, playing with a plastic set of keys, happy as a clam." He sighed. "Considering the facts we now have, I suspect your mom is the one who rescued you, probably in Yowie form so she'd have the additional strength at her disposal. Then perhaps she went back for your father. Whatever happened after that, well, it wasn't good. Your father lost his life, and the accident injured your mother such that she lost knowing who she was and became stuck, if you will, as a Yowie. She wandered off before help arrived, and we never realized she was still alive."

Sadie erased an image of her dad in the fiery car and focused on her mom. "How is she here now, in Salton, when the accident happened back east?"

"Score another one for instinct," Uncle Alexander said. "Her innate connection to you likely brought her here. I'm curious about how long she's been in the area. It may be she's been here for years but wasn't revealed until the rip in the Rampart. If that's the case, at least one good thing came from that bad situation." He took a deep breath and stood. "Would anyone like something to drink? Coffee or water?"

"Coffee sounds like an elixir to me right about now," Connor said.

"Water would be great." Sadie stood. "Can I help?"

"No, no. Stay here and relax," Uncle Alexander said. "I'll be right back."

She returned to her seat on the couch next to Connor. She stared at her hands.

"Are you okay?" he asked.

Sadie looked up. "Yeah. I mean, there are just so many 'what ifs.' Like what if I'd never run into her in the cottonwoods? What if I hadn't been wearing her bracelet? What if we'd never figured out she wasn't Merinda? And what if I'd . . ."

Connor patted her knee. "None of those 'what ifs' happened, nor can they happen now. Elly is back, Elly is getting better, and you have your mom again."

"Yeah." Sadie blew out a breath. "But wow, so much has happened to me in the last few months. I'm not sure how to deal."

"That is not an uncommon feeling," Connor said. "In my experience, the best path forward is to take things one at a time. One moment, one project, one problem, one challenge. Whatever it is, tackle one thing, then move on to the next."

"And today's problem is my mom."

"Not a problem, if you ask me." He smiled.

She considered the situation for a moment. "Right. I mean, it's uncomfortable because I don't know her, even though she's my mom, which is weird. But that's not really a problem."

"You'll get acquainted with each other soon enough."

Uncle Alexander walked in with two cups of coffee and a glass of water. "Here we go." He distributed the drinks and sat. "I heard you talking about what constitutes a problem, and we do have one problem we need to consider: Derek and Ash."

Connor's brows furrowed. "Those scoundrels. We need to wipe their memories."

"Yes," Uncle Alexander said. "Though how we'll do that, I'm not sure. I'm also curious how they ended up in the barn with Elly in the first place."

"Did they follow you there?" Sadie asked.

Uncle Alexander sipped his coffee. "They were there when we arrived. And if it weren't for the Skyfish leading us, we wouldn't have ended up at the barn."

"You believe the Skyfish meant for us to follow them?" Connor asked.

"I do," Uncle Alexander said. "And as I reflect on it, I suspect they've been showing us that something was out of sorts for some time. And once they swarmed the way they did, well, it's clear something disturbed the Skyfish."

"Something about my mom," Sadie said.

"It's possible." Uncle Alexander pinched the bridge of his nose for a moment. "Or it could be the combination of the rip in the Rampart and Elly's being seen by so many people throwing off the balance. I can't be certain. I'll give it more study, and observe how the Skyfish behave going forward. In the meantime, we should figure out how to manage a memory wipe for Derek and Ash."

"Colette might be able to help." Sadie relayed the story Colette had shared about her friendship with Derek. "He might meet her somewhere, and we could wipe his memory then. And it's a stretch, but maybe she can get him to bring Ash with him."

"An ambush," Connor said. "Not my favorite *modus operandi*, but it may be our only option."

"It's a good idea," Uncle Alexander said. "And we can focus on Derek and Ash while we give Elly more time to recover. The doctor said she's more likely to be asleep than awake over the next few days."

"Should I spend more time with her?" Sadie asked. "Use more of my healing power?"

"I'm sure every minute you spend with her is beneficial, regardless of your healing power." He breathed in curls of steam from his coffee. "But rest is key for Elly now. How did the doctor put it?" Uncle Alexander reflected for a moment. "Oh, yes." He looked at Sadie. "You pulled Elly back from the brink, changed her trajectory, pointed her body in the right direction, and gave her the strength to move toward the finish line. All Elly has to do is rest and let it happen."

"Sounds like a pretty good deal to me," Connor said.

The memory of Mamo telling Sadie her healing power would be a treasure ran through Sadie's mind. Mamo was right, and this wasn't the first time Sadie had been thankful for her ability to heal. She only wished Mamo was here to see what Sadie had done, to see Elly again.

To be a family.

But Sadie had her great-uncle Connor now. And Colette. And Lena. Even Uncle Alexander seemed as much Sadie's uncle as he did Jason's.

And Jason. It felt good to be friends with him again.

And she had Brandon.

And now she had her mom back in her life.

Sadie had a family. A wonderful family.

And she would protect them all.

✳ ✳ ✳

Early afternoon, Jason, Shay, and Colette arrived at Uncle Alexander's, along with Brandon who gave Sadie a hug. Finn, snoozing on one of the beds near the fireplace, raised her head, yawned hello, and fell back to sleep. Shay cozied up on a bed next to her.

Uncle Alexander started a discussion about the Derek and Ash situation.

"I can probably get Derek to meet me," Colette said. "But I'm not sure about Ash. I didn't even know Derek had a brother, or sort of brother, until we met Ash out in the cottonwoods."

"And they weren't exactly chummy at the barn," Brandon said.

"An understatement." Uncle Alexander ran one hand through his hair. "But let's hear what he says. At the very least, maybe Derek will come and we'll be able to wipe his memory."

"How about this?" Colette read aloud the message she'd typed, ready to text to Derek: "Heard what happened last night. Are you and your brother okay?"

"That works," Sadie said. She sat close to Colette and watched her screen. It seemed like Derek wouldn't respond, but then an animation indicated he was typing. His response came: "I'm fine."

Colette read the note to everyone. "He doesn't seem too keen on talking. And no mention of Ash."

"No surprise there," Sadie said. "Write back and offer to meet him. Find out if he's up for that."

"And if he wants to meet, I'm going with you." Jason crossed his arms.

"Several of us will go with Colette to meet Derek," Uncle Alexander said. "And those who go will be in hiding, including you."

"But he needs to know—"

Uncle Alexander held up one finger. "Not open for debate."

Jason pressed hard to keep his mouth closed.

Colette typed another message: "Want to talk? I can meet you." A response arrived. "He says he can't because he has homework," she said.

"Like he does his homework." Jason threw his hands in the air. "That's a huge load of bull—"

"Jason." Uncle Alexander gave Jason a look like he was about to send him to his room without supper.

"Sorry."

"So, I guess that's it, then." Colette set her phone down on the coffee table. "Is there a plan B?"

"Do we have any insight about where he likes to spend his time?" Connor asked. "Perhaps we can intercept him somewhere?"

"He likes to hang out at the Salton Spoon with Colette," Jason said with a twang of annoyance in his tone.

"Oh my gosh, will you stop," Colette said.

"Okay, sorry, sorry," Jason said. "Derek just bugs the crap out of me."

"Clearly. But this here," she waved her hands over the phone, "is us working together to solve a problem. This is not about me being friends with Derek."

"You're right." Jason sat on the end of the couch. "I'm being stupid. I'll stop. All good."

"Thank you." Colette's phone buzzed and she looked at the screen. "It's him. He says he wants to talk, and do I want to meet at the barn where everything happened."

"Is it just me?" Sadie asked. "Or is that a little creepy?"

"It's not," Colette said. "Derek's not like that. And it's the middle of the afternoon."

"If you're comfortable meeting him there," Uncle Alexander said, "it would be a good place for Connor or Sadie—"

"I vote Connor," Sadie said.

Connor nodded. "That's fine with me."

"For Connor," Uncle Alexander continued, "to do the memory wipe. We can get there before him and conceal ourselves."

"There were bales of hay stacked in the corner," Connor said. "Alexander and I could hide there."

Jason raised his hand. "And me. Not letting Colette meet Derek without me."

Uncle Alexander looked at him askance. "Can you control yourself? Follow our instructions? Not act unless we ask you to take action?"

"Totally." Jason stood. "I'm going."

"I'll stay here with my mom unless you need me," Sadie said.

"Me too," Brandon added.

"Not a problem, you two stay here." Uncle Alexander turned to Colette. "Tell Derek you'll meet him there. Let's go."

✻✻✻

Thirty minutes later, Jason crouched behind a wall of hay stacked four bales high. He shifted his position to avoid dried stalks trying to poke through his pants.

Connor and Uncle Alexander sat on a bale next to him. Colette stood in the doorway opposite their spot, waiting for Derek.

"Remember, stay calm and quiet," Uncle Alexander whispered to Jason.

"I've got it," Jason whispered back, irritated that Uncle Alexander had reminded him for something like the thirteenth time.

A few minutes later, bicycle wheels crunching on gravel approached the barn. Jason peered through a tiny gap between bales. Derek rode up on his bike, dismounted, and leaned the bike against the barn just outside the door. One side of his face seemed puffy.

"Hi," Derek said. He walked up to Colette and opened his arms for a hug.

"Oh, hi." She lightly embraced Derek and stepped back.

Jason forced himself to relax, to let it go.

"Thanks for meeting me here," Derek said.

"No problem." Colette pointed. "Your eye looks bad. Are you okay?"

"I'm fine." He pressed the tips of his fingers onto his cheek. "Stupid Ash."

"Yeah." She waved her arm around the large space. "What happened?"

Derek walked past her, deeper into the barn and farther away from Jason, Connor, and Uncle Alexander. The plan had been for Connor to get behind Derek when his back was turned, but Derek wasn't making that easy.

"Didn't all your friends tell you?" Derek climbed onto fencing around an old stall. He had a direct view of the hay bales.

Colette stood near him. "I, uh, haven't talked to anyone much today. I read a text that said you and Ash were fighting."

"That's it?" Derek's brows scrunched. "No one told you about King?"

"King?" Colette asked.

"The big monster. I think it's a Sasquatch."

"Uh . . . a Sasquatch?" Colette shifted her weight from one leg to the other.

A puzzled expression settled on Derek's face. "You for real don't know about the Sasquatch?"

"I don't know about any Sasquatch," Colette said. Jason sensed relief in her voice that she was technically telling the truth.

"Well, I'm not making it up. You can ask them—Jason, Sadie, that homeschool dude Sadie hangs out with—they all know about it."

"Is that what you wanted to talk about? The Sasquatch?" Colette scanned the area like she was looking for a place to sit.

"I guess." Derek jumped off the fence and sat on the floor. Colette sat near him. "And I guess you don't know if it's still alive."

"Why wouldn't it be?" she asked.

"Because I wouldn't be surprised if they killed it. King—that's the name I gave it. I mean, King was alive when I asked Jason, at least he told me King was alive," Derek said. "But his uncle is some science guy, and guys like that always want to kill things and dissect them." He cleared his throat. "Doesn't matter. It was just a dumb monster."

Colette paused. "How long did you know about the . . . Sasquatch?"

"I found it a couple of months ago when I was hanging out in the cottonwoods, just trying to get away from everyone."

"Everyone at home?"

He shrugged. "Just everyone." He flicked a dead bug laying on the floor. "King scared the crap out of me the first time. I'd been asleep in this kind of secret spot where I thought no one could find me. And I wake up to the smell of something like fish-butt, then I open my eyes and all I see is fur and teeth."

"That would scare anybody."

"Yeah, I hauled ass out of there, and got all scraped up on the branches," he said. "I was sure the thing was going to grab me, but when I turned around it was gone."

Jason wondered if Elly had hidden or used her invisibility.

"I headed out the next day with a cattle prod."

Colette gasped.

"No way I'd let some monster get me." Derek scrunched his brow. "I'm not stupid."

"Was it there? Did you hurt it?" Colette's voice wound tight with anxiety.

"I went back to the same area but didn't find King anywhere," he said. "But I had one trick up my sleeve. I brought one of those roasted chickens with me."

Jason flashed on the roasted chicken container they'd found at Salton High.

"I set that chicken on the ground in the same area where I'd seen the Sasquatch before, and I waited. Sure enough, here came King."

Colette covered her mouth with her hands. "And you used the cattle prod."

Derek's eyes widened. "No way. That was only for protection, just in case I needed it. But King was cool. He just watched me while I watched him eat that whole chicken. Nothing left, not even bones."

"And that's it?" Colette's shoulders relaxed. "You didn't hurt her . . . er, King?"

"I didn't, but a lot of bad things happened to King after that, and those were my fault." He brushed dust off his shoes.

"What do you mean?"

"I kept bringing food for King, but everyone at home thought I was eating more than my fair share. I got yelled at a lot. My step-mom said I was lucky to have a place to live since I didn't have parents anymore and said she'd kick me out if I didn't stop hogging the food."

"Oh, I'm sorry . . ."

"That's nothing," Derek said. "The bad part is Ash started following me, and he found out about King. And he started messing with King just to mess with me. He realized King was nice, so Ash did whatever he wanted to King, knowing King wouldn't hurt him. He threw smoke bombs in King's house, or lair, or whatever. And firecrackers. And then he started using the cattle prod."

"Oh my god."

"King would bat at the cattle prod as it zapped him, but Ash got meaner and meaner and he'd hold it on King until King ran or I could tackle Ash. But sometimes I wasn't there."

Colette grimaced. "That's horrible."

"Ash sucks," Derek said. "And King started acting moody, getting angrier and more nervous. I tried to hide him somewhere else, away from Ash. I even put King in the school one weekend but he wouldn't settle down. Not that he could have stayed there anyway. It was just until I could find somewhere else for him to go. But he headed back to his lair." He stared at the ground and shook his head. "That's when Ash tried to burn King alive. Doused him and newspapers with lighter fluid and tossed a lit match."

Colette sucked in a breath. "That was the fire."

"I ran as hard as I could when I saw the flames," Derek said. The firefighters had it out by the time I got there. And I didn't notice Ash or King anywhere."

"And the day of the snowstorm, when you said a friend was in trouble?"

"It was King," Derek said. "He was scared and acting crazy. I saw him in run through town from the window of the Salton Spoon."

"*That's* why you left so fast."

Derek nodded. "I chased after him, and I watched him slam his fist into Mr. Templeman's mail truck."

As if a lightbulb lit above Jason's head, he put two and two together. Derek saw Mr. Templeman's encounter with Elly, so he had to have seen Sadie invite Mr. Templeman inside. And if Derek talked to Mr. Templeman after that, and realized he no longer remembered seeing Elly, it was no wonder Derek thought Sadie was a witch.

"I had no idea what to do," Derek said.

Jason leaned close to Uncle Alexander. "Speaking of which, what are we doing?"

Derek jumped up. "Did you hear something?"

Uncle Alexander glared and held his hand signaling Jason to hush.

Jason shut his mouth.

Colette stayed seated. "I didn't hear anything."

"You sure?"

"Yeah, but maybe there was a mouse or something," she said. "This old barn is probably full of them. So, what happened last night?"

Jason barely breathed while Derek stayed silent for another moment.

Finally, he spoke. "Yeah, okay. Last night."

Jason dared a peek. Derek had returned to sitting on the floor.

"I went to visit King at the beginning of the week, but I couldn't find him," Derek said. "And later when I saw Ash, he had this smart-ass look on his face and made this asshat comment that any friends I had were idiots. He also showed me a key he was wearing around his neck and said he had hidden treasure that I'd never find. But he's always a jerkwad, so I blew it off."

Derek scuffed his shoe across the dirt floor. "A couple more days passed, I still hadn't seen King, and then Ash told me one of my idiot friends was going to be a dead idiot friend. I knew Ash had done something to King. I had to find out what it was, and Ash figured I'd try to follow him, so he got me in trouble. He made it look like I'd stolen money from my step-mom and she locked me in a dog kennel in my room."

"What?" Colette's tone screamed outrage.

"It's no big deal," Derek said. "I've had worse. And I've learned lots of ways to get out."

Sympathy weaseled into Jason.

"Last night, after she let me out to eat dinner, my step-mom was too drunk to realize I'd taped the lock. I snuck out and followed Ash here, to the barn." He gestured at the stall. "He had King chained in there."

Jason looked through the slats and saw links of chain lying on the floor. He shuddered thinking about Sadie's mom in that situation.

"Oh my god . . ." Colette covered her mouth with her hands.

"Ash was burning King with the cattle prod and King was howling," Derek said. "I broke into a full run, slammed Ash to the floor, and ripped that key off his neck. Then I flew into the stall and unlocked the padlock that held the chain around King's waist. Ash zapped me good, too." Derek pulled his jacket and shirt off one shoulder.

Jason could see the angry red welt from across the room.

"But it didn't matter," Derek said. "I got King free."

"That was really good of you," Colette said.

He shrugged. "What Ash was doing to King, it wasn't right. It's one thing for him to be a jerkwad to me, but King didn't deserve that."

"Neither do you," Colette said.

Derek shrugged again. "Things went crazy from there. King jumped out of the pen and Ash chased him with the cattle prod. I tackled Ash. We were fighting and rolling around and got close to King and King swatted Ash across the room. It was the first time I'd seen King fight back, if that's even what he was doing. Ash pitched a fit, said I was trying to get him killed. That's not what I did, but I don't think I've ever been so pissed off. I wanted to beat the crap out of that little maggot. But then everyone else showed up and pulled me and Ash apart."

"Wow, Derek," Colette said, "I'm so sorry you had to go through all of that."

He stared into the empty paddock. "I just wish I knew King was okay."

"And the name? King?"

"Like King Kong," Derek said. "Seemed like a good name for him."

"It's a great name." She paused a moment. "If you want, I can ask about King, see if anyone knows what happened."

Derek's eyes widened. "I don't want Jason or any of them to know about it, to know I asked again."

"I won't say anything. I won't even tell them we talked."

Jason detested the notion that Colette seemed to be sharing a secret with Derek, at least from Derek's point of view.

"Promise?" Derek asked.

Colette stood and brushed off her pants. "I promise. And unfortunately, I need to get going. I'll text you if I learn anything, okay?"

"Yeah, okay." Derek stood. "Do you want to head back to town together?"

"Uh, sure," Colette said. "I have a bike outside." She walked toward the door and Derek followed.

"Oh, I didn't see a bike when I came in."

Just before Derek exited the barn, Connor hurried up behind him and sent Derek into what Jason thought was a memory-erasing trance. Derek crumpled, and Uncle Alexander caught him under his arms and eased him to the floor.

"I wasn't sure what else to do," Colette said. "I just hoped you could get to him before he saw I didn't have a bicycle."

"You did the right thing," Connor said.

"Shouldn't you be telling him to forget stuff?" Jason asked. "And think happy thoughts or whatever?"

"Actually, no," Connor said. "We have a bit of a problem, and we need to talk about it before I erase anything. I put our friend Derek here into a deep sleep state until we figure things out."

"What's the issue?" Uncle Alexander asked.

"His history," Connor said. "Everything he knows. This isn't a matter of someone seeing a cryptid one time while out having a picnic. Yesterday evening wasn't the one and only time Derek encountered Elly. He has months of history with her, regardless of what name he calls her. Not to mention the fact that his step-brother, Ash, shares the history. Derek's memories of Elly are woven throughout his life."

"I see what you mean." Uncle Alexander pinched the bridge of his nose.

"What if you asked him to forget everything he associates with King?" Colette asked.

"If Ash was not in the picture, your suggestion would be good," Connor said. "Though there'd be a chance Derek would need the occasional tune-up, if you will, since such a large cache of memory could leak into the conscious brain." He sighed. "But without wiping Ash's memory at the same time as Derek's, and knowing Ash's inclination to pester Derek with what he knows—"

"'Pester' is putting it nicely," Colette said.

"Yes, it is," Connor said. "Regardless, it won't take more than one or two taunts from Ash to crumble a wall around Derek's memories that I otherwise seemingly erased."

"So, the memories you or Sadie wipe aren't deleted," Jason said.

Connor shook his head. "No. More like archived behind a password-protected firewall. And in Derek's case, Ash has the password."

"Then you stay here with Derek," Jason said to Connor, "and we'll go find Ash and bring him back here so you can wipe them both at the same time."

"I'm not sure how we could get Ash to come with us," Uncle Alexander said. "If we could even find him."

"He does seem to be the slippery sort," Connor said.

Jason held up his hands. "Then what do we do?" He looked at Uncle Alexander.

Uncle Alexander looked at Connor. "You're the expert."

"I think the best tactic, for now, is to implant the suggestion, as strongly as I can, that Derek tell no one what he knows about King—using his term for Elly—outside of the people he saw at the barn." Connor rubbed his hands down his face. "Even then, we must hope for a good outcome. While it is similar, implanting a suggestion differs from blocking off a memory or memories, so I can't say for sure how well it will work."

"Seems to be our only option at the moment," Uncle Alexander said. "Let's do it."

"Wait—can you also make him forget talking to Colette?" Jason asked.

She lightly swatted his arm. "Stop worrying about him."

"I'm not talking about that," Jason said. "He thinks she has a bike and they're riding home together. I mean, I definitely don't want Derek off riding bikes with my girlfriend." He felt heat flush his face. "But I'm talking about how we fix it so he doesn't walk out of here and wonder why Colette doesn't have a bike."

"Good catch, Jason," Uncle Alexander said. He turned to Connor. "Can you erase that bit of their conversation?"

"I can," Connor said.

"Good." Uncle Alexander looked at Colette. "Tell him you've texted Lena for a ride, and she wrote back and said I'll pick you up on her behalf, just in case Derek says he'll wait with you."

"Okay," Colette said. "But I doubt he'd wait since he didn't want me to tell anyone we talked."

"True, but it covers our bases just in case." Uncle Alexander blew out a breath. "Ready?"

Connor nodded and set to work on Derek. Everything seemed to go according to plan, Derek rode away on his bike, and a few minutes later Jason, Colette, Connor, and Uncle Alexander were in the truck heading home.

Sitting next to Colette in the back seat, Jason's mind spun as they bounced over ruts and bumps in the road. He leaned forward. "What if Derek knows about me? He followed Elly a lot. He saw what happened to Mr. Templeman's truck. What if he saw what happened at Nessa's?"

Connor looked at Uncle Alexander. "I didn't implant any suggestion about not talking about Jason."

"Or Sadie," Jason said. "I think he knows more about Sadie, too."

Uncle Alexander took a deep breath. "I'm not sure what we can do other than hope Derek chooses to keep anything he might know to himself. I can't imagine how he'd gain from telling anyone our secrets. And given his experience with Ash, perhaps Derek realizes it's best not to reveal such information."

Jason leaned back in his seat. "I hope so."

"I want to know what we can do to help Derek," Colette said.

"Help him with what?" Jason asked.

"With his home life," she said. "That woman, his step-mother, sounds horrible. Derek shouldn't be treated that way."

"I'll call Sheriff Gunderson," Uncle Alexander said.

Colette sat up. "Oh, no, we can't do that. Derek will think I called the sheriff. I promised him I wouldn't tell anyone we talked."

Connor angled to face her. "We can't get help for Derek without calling the authorities."

"And I never would have thought I'd be talking about getting help for Derek," Jason said.

Colette looked at Jason with astonishment.

"I'm totally on board with helping him," Jason said. "He's in a sucky situation. I just mean I never thought I'd ever want to help Derek Goodman with anything since he's been nothing but a jerk since the first day I met him."

Colette's expression softened. "Well, we can't call the authorities yet. Let me talk to him about it first. And can I text Derek and tell him King is okay?"

Jason crossed his arms. "I don't think we should say anything else to Derek about any of this stuff. The more we tell him, the harder it will be to eventually erase, right Connor?"

Connor canted his head from side to side. "It's already such a complex web, I doubt it would make much of a difference, especially since we're talking about a short note regarding Elly's, or in this case King's, condition."

"Makes sense," Uncle Alexander said. "I don't think it would hurt anything, and it secures Derek's trust in Colette. That may be helpful in the future." He paused. "Our bigger concern is Ash. He has zero trust in any of us after last night, and we can't exactly kidnap him to wipe his memory. Plus, he seems far less likely to keep his knowledge of Elly a secret."

"Not that anyone would believe an obnoxious little kid," Jason said.

260

"True," Connor said. "And at least Elly is out of his clutches. But I admit, I wouldn't mind getting my hands on that slimy little bas—uh, rascal, and give him the what for. That kid needs some serious discipline in his life."

"Sadly, it may take more than being grounded and losing privileges to turn that boy around," Uncle Alexander said. "He held Elly captive and tortured her. He's committing serious criminal acts."

"We should report Ash to the League," Colette said. "He's a threat to the treaty between humans and cryptids."

"I was thinking the same thing," Uncle Alexander said. "The League of Governors can legally take action against Ash and wipe his memory, and once that's done, we can handle the situation with Derek."

"I hope the League can fix more than Ash's memory," Jason said. "That kid is messed up."

"Indeed, he is," Uncle Alexander said. "Indeed, he is."

NINETEEN
A Home

A few days later, Sadie stopped by Uncle Alexander's house on her way home from school, like she had every day since they'd found her mom. Conversations with her mom had been limited by Elly's ability to speak until the last two days when Elly's speech improved exponentially. Even so, Sadie hesitated to push too much while her mom was still recovering. She punched in the code Uncle Alexander had given her to unlock the front door. "Hello?"

"In here, Sadie," he called. "I was just heading down to check on your mom."

Sadie hurried to join him. They stepped off the elevator into the room outside the lab. One of the League doctors treating Elly came out to greet them.

"Good news," she said. "Our patient is well enough to be released from our care."

"That *is* good news," Uncle Alexander said.

"She simply needs to continue a regimen of rest and good nutrition while she returns to full strength."

"How long will that be?" Uncle Alexander asked.

"At the rate she's been healing, especially given her condition when she came in, I estimate she'll be close to one hundred percent within a few weeks." The doctor gestured into the room where Elly sat in the bed wearing hospital scrubs. "And she can go home now. I'm sure she'll be happy to be out of the lab. We're packing up our gear and League transport will be here for us soon."

Home? Sadie clasped her hands. *Where was home for Elly?*

Uncle Alexander thanked the doctor and asked Sadie to follow him down the hall to his office. He closed the door and leaned against the front edge of his desk. "Lena, Connor and I talked about where Elly could live."

Sadie thought through options but couldn't land on any of them.

Uncle Alexander continued. "Elly is more than welcome to stay in my guest room, and I'll make sure she has everything she needs. Or she could stay with Connor if she prefers."

"Okay . . ." Sadie felt uncertain, almost confused.

"Lena is also willing to help Elly heal if you'd like your mom to move in with you. And perhaps Elly has other ideas. We can discuss those with her of course, though given her history, I suspect she does not." He paused a moment. "Regardless, she will not be left destitute, and it's your choice whether you invite her into your home."

The options for Elly flip-flopped in Sadie's mind. One second she wanted her mom with her and Lena and Colette, and the next she wanted Elly to stay somewhere else.

Elly was her mom. She should move in with Sadie.

But Sadie barely knew her.

But she's Mom. My mom. And she loves me. Doesn't she?

And I should take care of her, shouldn't I?

"I can't decide," Sadie said. "I . . . I have no idea."

"Then let's do this," Uncle Alexander said with a soothing tone in his voice. "I will invite Elly to stay with me. Assuming she accepts my offer, you can come and go as you like, spend whatever time with her you like, take all the time you need with her. As far as I'm concerned, Elly can stay here for a few days, a few months, or a few years. Okay?"

"Okay . . . but I don't want to hurt her feelings." Sadie swallowed. "She'll feel bad if she expected to come home with me, but now she's not."

"She'll understand. She's probably as anxious about getting to know you as you are about her. This is the best choice for both of you."

"If you think so."

"I do," Uncle Alexander said. "And I'll share my opinion with Elly as well."

Sadie felt a surge of relief.

"Let's go tell her the good news." He opened the office door and they headed to the lab.

"There you are," Elly said as Sadie entered.

Elly opened her arms and Sadie hugged her, though it was still more like hugging an acquaintance than a mom.

"I so enjoy your visits," Elly said to Sadie.

"You'll enjoy the visits even more in a less-lab-oriented space," Uncle Alexander said. "The medical team has released you, and I have a guest room ready and waiting for you upstairs, if you'd like."

"Oh." Elly looked from Uncle Alexander to Sadie, then back to Uncle Alexander. "That's very gracious of you. But I don't want to be a bother."

"No bother at all," he said. "It will be nice to have the company. And it will be nice to see more of Sadie, too, since I'm sure she'll spend plenty of time here."

"Totally," Sadie said. "I'll come by and hang out every day."

"I'd like that," Elly said. She reached over her shoulder and scratched a spot on her back. "And I hope sometimes you'll bring the dogs."

"Finn lives here," Sadie said. "And Shay is Jason's dog, but he brings her over whenever he's training with Uncle Alexander."

Elly turned to Uncle Alexander. "You're a dog trainer?"

"Well, in a way, yes, since Finn and Shay are an important part of our work," he said, chuckling. "But that's only a small element. Jason and I are Rampart Guards."

Elly's eyes lit up. "I didn't realize I was in the company of elite Rampart Guards. That's wonderful. I'm delighted Sadie has you both as friends. And it's no wonder the dogs didn't give me away."

"What do you mean?" Sadie asked.

"Some of you were in my nest one day, including a man I don't know."

"That man would be Zachary Lex, Jason's dad," Uncle Alexander said. "You were nearby?"

"Nearer than you think," she said. "I was asleep in my nest, tucked under the bramble when a cold snout pressed onto my nose."

"Ah . . . Shay acted like she'd found something," Uncle Alexander said. "But you were invisible."

Elly smiled. "Exactly."

"And neither Shay nor Finn sensed you as a threat. They alerted just as they should have." Uncle Alexander ran one hand through his hair. "Fascinating."

"They did the same thing the first time I came face to face with them, the day Jason wounded me with what I now realize were Guard bolts."

Sadie cringed inside at the memory.

"Both dogs sat rather than attack," Elly said. "I was relieved."

"And we thought Shay's inexperience was the issue," Uncle Alexander said, seeming to think aloud.

"Her training is right on point, if you ask me," Elly said. "Both her's and Finn's. You have two talented dogs on your team."

"Indeed, we do. Why don't we continue the conversation upstairs in the living room where you can visit with Finn, too?" Uncle Alexander asked. "And when you need to rest, just say the word."

"I admit, I would like to get out of this lab," Elly said.

"I'll get a wheelchair." Uncle Alexander started out of the room.

"No need," she said. "I'd like to walk."

Sadie and Uncle Alexander helped Elly out of the bed. "You can lean on me," Sadie said.

"Thank you, sweetheart," Elly said as she put one arm around Sadie's shoulders.

Mamo sometimes called me sweetheart.

They rode the elevator upstairs and settled Elly onto one of the two couches. Uncle Alexander laid a blanket over her lap, and Finn jumped up and snuggled next to her.

Elly stroked the top of Finn's head. "A cuddly dog, a cozy blanket, a new friend, and my dear daughter." The last syllable stuck. She cleared her throat. "This is a wonderful day."

Sadie sat across from her, and Uncle Alexander excused himself after a ping on his phone.

"I'm glad you're getting better," Sadie said.

"Even more than getting better, I feel more normal than I have in a long time." She scratched Finn's ear. "But how are you?"

"I'm fine," Sadie said. "Healthy."

"I mean about all of this." Elly waved her arm. "Me. Back in your life."

Sadie shrugged slowly. "It doesn't seem like that to me, like you're back in my life . . . because . . . I don't remember you being in my life in the first place."

Elly's expression dimmed. "Right. This must be hard for you."

"It's not hard, and it's not easy," Sadie said. "I'm not sure what it is. But Connor says just tackle things one at a time so that's what I'm trying to do."

"Huh. I remember him telling me that when I was a kid," she said. "It's good advice."

Uncle Alexander returned. "Apologies. Your doctor had some final care items to review before leaving."

"Nothing too complicated, I hope," Elly said.

"Just the usual—eat well, stay hydrated, get plenty of rest. I believe we can manage it." He tipped his head to include Sadie.

Elly shifted herself on the couch. "I'm sure I'm in good hands."

A gap grew in the conversation until Sadie blurted a question at Elly. "Can I ask you something?"

"Of course."

"What do you remember?"

"I remember that nasty little kid tormenting me," Elly said. "And I remember not wanting to hurt him even though he may have deserved it. What's his name?"

"Ash," Uncle Alexander said. "The League is on point to deal with him now, though they seem to be having some difficulty locating him. He's out of town with his father."

"But he has school," Sadie said. "Doesn't he?"

Uncle Alexander raised his brows. "Apparently not."

"I hope the League finds him soon," Elly said. "And how he and Derek are in the same family I don't understand. Derek was always very nice to me. He seems a bit lonely, though."

Sadie huffed. "Derek's always been a jerk to me. Jason, too. I mean, I get that his home life is awful, but I *don't* get why that's an excuse to be rude to people."

"These things are usually complicated," Uncle Alexander said.

"Whatever it is, I still think being nice to people and making friends must be easier than being a jerk. But I don't want to talk about Derek." Sadie looked at Elly. "I was wondering if you remember stuff from way back when the car accident happened."

"Oh, Sadie," Uncle Alexander said, "that may be too much—"

"No, it's okay." Elly pulled the blanket over her bare feet. "To be honest, I don't remember much." She stared into space like she was watching a movie play on the air. "It was dark, your father was driving . . . and he was going too fast." She squinted. "You were in the back, in your car seat, and I remember checking on you. Your dad, he wouldn't slow down. Or . . . he couldn't slow down. Why couldn't he slow down? I remember telling him . . ." Her head jerked and a look of surprise crossed her face. "I told him to drive faster. Why faster? The road was narrow, and he was skidding around corners . . . why go faster?"

Elly's eyes widened and she zeroed on Sadie. "Oh my god, it was Devine. His people. They were chasing us, trying to run us off the road."

"You saw them?" Sadie asked.

"They were right behind us. I saw them coming up fast when I turned to check on you. Bright headlights. High speed. We were on our way out of town, trying to hide but they found us."

Sadie covered her mouth. "They caused the accident."

Elly nodded. "We crashed. I shifted to Yowie and pulled you out, then went back for your dad. He was unconscious and pinned in the car." She shook her head like she was trying to loosen something stuck in her brain. "I heard yelling, then there was an explosion . . . and I realized your dad was gone . . . dead." Her eyes glistened. She took a deep breath. "That's the last thing I remember," she said softly.

A pain pinched Sadie's heart at the loss of a father she never knew. "You don't know where you went after that?"

Elly thought for a moment. "I don't have any other memories, not until I saw you and Shay that first time in the cottonwoods. You seemed familiar to me but I wasn't sure why. I just wanted to be close to you."

Goosebumps skittered across Sadie's skin.

"Your memory loss is from brain trauma," Uncle Alexander added. "Which would have otherwise gone unhealed if Sadie hadn't helped you."

"Your father had that ability as well." Elly bolted upright. "Oh my god, the Calling. That's why we were running—because of the Calling picking your father. What happened with the Calling?" Her eyes were wild and worried.

Sadie inched up her hand.

"No," Elly said. "No, no, no, it's not you."

"It is," Sadie said. "Mamo tried to stop it, but she couldn't."

"She needs to try harder. Devine's people killed her son because of the Calling—how can she let them go after Sadie now? What kind of grandmother is she?" Elly tried to push herself to standing. Finn jumped off the couch. "She needs to find a way to take the Calling herself or give it to someone else."

Sadie's eyes watered. She blinked the tears dry.

Uncle Alexander hurried to sit next to Elly and eased her back to her seat. "Elly, she died a few months ago, protecting Sadie."

"Oh." Elly's voice was small, and she sank into the couch.

"The cloak?" Elly asked.

"In place." Uncle Alexander readjusted the blanket on Elly's lap.

"I'm sorry," Elly said to Sadie. "There's a lot I don't know."

"It's okay," Sadie said.

But it wasn't okay. Sadie gritted her teeth.

Elly paused. "I think I'd better go lie down for a while."

Uncle Alexander escorted her upstairs.

Sadie rushed out and headed for home.

* * *

Sadie stormed into her house.

"You're home early," Colette said from the living room. "No training session today?"

"I canceled." Sadie headed for the stairs.

"Oh. Should we write up a shopping list for the store then?"

Sadie stopped. "The store?"

"Yeah," Colette said. "To get stuff for Nessa's birthday."

Sadie tried to think, but her mom and the Calling monopolized most of her mind. "Nessa's birthday isn't until Saturday."

"But we were going to decorate her locker before school tomorrow since we won't be at school on Saturday."

"Right." Sadie walked over and flopped onto the couch next to Colette. "I forgot."

"Are you okay?" Colette asked. "Did something happen?"

Sadie told her the car accident story and how her mom freaked out about the Calling coming to Sadie.

"Wow." Colette shifted to face Sadie. "I mean, I get that she's your mum, and she's concerned, but she also hasn't been around."

"Right? I did not like it when she acted all mad at Mamo," Sadie said. "She has no clue about anything, and here she is saying Mamo is wrong or bad or whatever."

"I get it," Colette said.

"She can't drop into my life and act like she's in charge."

"I agree."

"And I almost invited her to come live with us," Sadie said.

Colette's eyebrows arched. "You did?"

"Well, not really," Sadie said. "I talked about it with Jason's uncle, and he offered to let her stay with him. That seemed like a better idea."

"For sure," Colette said. "At least until you get to know her. We have no idea what she's like."

"I'm not sure *she* even knows what she's like." Sadie sighed. "I need a distraction from all things Elly. Let's think about fun stuff and decorations for Nessa."

Colette stood and Sadie followed. "Have you told Nessa about your mum yet?"

Sadie fell back onto the couch. "No. What do I even say? Oh, guess what, Nessa, my mom's been living in the woods for fourteen years because she had amnesia but now she's back?"

"Those kinds of stories work on soap operas."

"Do they, though?"

"Sort of?" Colette held out her arm and pulled Sadie off the couch again.

"I don't think so," Sadie said. "I have to tell Nessa something. Sometime. Eventually. But at the moment, I can't even decide if I should call Elly 'mom' or 'Elly.' Both seem weird to me. Maybe after I figure that out, I can figure out what to tell Nessa."

"I wish we could tell Nessa everything," Colette said.

"Me too." Sadie linked arms with Colette and they headed into the kitchen.

Lena stirred a pot on the stove.

"Smells yum," Sadie said, inhaling the aroma of garlic, tomatoes, and shrimp. She left Colette's side and peered into the pan.

"Paella," Lena said. "New recipe."

"If it tastes as good as it smells, it's a keeper." Colette washed her hands and took plates out of the cupboard.

"Let's hope." Lena stirred the pot again and set the spoon aside. "I heard you talking about Nessa's birthday."

"Yeah, would you mind driving us to the store after dinner?" Sadie plopped down at the table. Lena pointed at the drawer and Sadie stood to get silverware.

"I need to pick up a few things myself," Lena said. "Do you have plans with Nessa for her big day on Saturday?"

"No," Sadie said. "She's doing family stuff, and that evening she's going out on a date with Kyle." She sang Kyle's name and smiled.

A grin sprang onto Lena's face. "This is new news. When did this happen? For that matter, how did this happen?"

Sadie shook her head. "It wasn't easy. First, I had to explain to Kyle how I'd accidentally erased the conversation they had when he asked her out."

"Actually, that was the easy part," Colette said.

"True," Sadie said. "Because then, Colette and I had to convince him to apologize to Nessa and tell her he'd misunderstood things she'd said."

"He wanted nothing to do with something that made him look like he was in the wrong," Colette said.

"No, I can't imagine Kyle would be fine with such a thing," Lena said. "But you convinced him to go along with your plan?"

"Yes," Sadie said, "because he likes Nessa way more than I realized."

"He wanted another chance to go out with her," Colette added.

"Then we had to talk to Nessa, tell her Kyle felt bad because he'd made a mistake with her, and convince her to give him another chance." Sadie sighed. "It took a little pushing, but she agreed."

"It didn't take *that* much pushing," Colette said. "She still has years of her Kyle-crush-feelings floating inside her."

"Totally," Sadie said.

Colette filled three glasses with water. "After all of that, Kyle called Nessa, Nessa said yes to a date, and all is right with the world."

"And knock on wood," Sadie rapped her knuckles on the kitchen table, "they both have fun tomorrow night."

"I'll think nothing but positive thoughts for a happy outcome." Lena dished paella onto their plates.

✳ ✳ ✳

An hour later, Sadie, Colette and Lena drove into a strip mall parking lot anchored by the largest grocery store in town. Colette pointed out of the car window as they passed a storefront. "Ooh, popcorn."

Sadie glanced over and saw an Opening Soon banner pasted across a plate glass window. In large letters, the lighted sign above the door read: "Poppy's Corn." Below the name, a smaller tagline read: "Poppin' Good and Freakin' Delicious."

"That's it? All they sell is popcorn?" Sadie asked.

"It must be great popcorn," Colette said. "Wait, isn't Poppy's the name of the popcorn Nessa had at her house?"

A tiny twinge of sadness nipped Sadie with the memory of the sleepover, but she comforted herself with the thought of Kyle's and Nessa's upcoming date. "The name sounds familiar. And that was great popcorn. She must have ordered it online."

"I hope they do well," Lena said. "I always like to see a new small business succeed in Salton." She turned down a row of spaces. "Did the sign say when they're opening?"

"Not that I saw," Sadie said.

Lena parked the car and they walked into the grocery store.

Colette squealed and startled Sadie.

"They're here, they're here, they're here." Colette bounced on her toes then dashed toward a table draped in a cloth that said, "Poppy's Corn - Free Samples."

Sadie and Lena followed her over.

"Hello," said the red-headed woman behind the table. "Care to sample a few of our many flavors of popcorn? We're opening our store soon, just down the sidewalk."

"Yes, please," Colette said.

"Me too." Sadie stepped up to the table, as did Lena.

The woman set cups of glazed bronze popcorn in front of each of them. "This is caramel corn, the house specialty and secret recipe." She added cups of pink popcorn flaked with red bits. "This is our cherry cotton candy popcorn."

"Ooh, cherry cotton candy." Colette put a piece in her mouth. "Yum."

The woman set a third cup on the table for each of them. "And here is our quad-cheese popcorn."

Sadie ate a piece. "Oh my gosh, so much cheesy goodness."

The woman looked at Sadie. "You seem familiar to me."

"I do?" Sadie's voice mumbled through another bite of popcorn.

"Do you study Tae Kwon Do with Master Kim?" the woman asked.

Sadie swallowed. "Oh, right." She nodded. "You picked up my phone when I dropped it the other day."

"I did," she said. "I hope everything thing worked out, and you didn't need that time machine after all."

"It did work out, at least that particular thing worked out." Sadie held up her cup of caramel corn. "And free popcorn, so things are definitely better."

"I'm glad to hear it," the woman said.

"When does your shop open?" Lena asked.

"In a couple of weeks. I hope you'll all come to the grand opening weekend. The chamber of commerce is kicking off a revitalization project of the shopping center at the same time, so it will be quite the party. And of course, we'll be giving away more free popcorn." The woman smiled.

"We're in," Colette said. "And we'll bring friends."

Lena scanned one of the flyers stacked on the table. "It sounds fun. And how nice of the grocery store to let you give away your samples here."

"I thought it would be a great way to introduce the business, and the product, in advance of the opening." She leaned across the table. "And truth be told, the owner—who happens to be me—moved here because I'm tired of the big city rat race. I decided I wanted to live in a smaller, quieter place where I might actually get to meet my neighbors." She stepped back. "What better way to meet people than at the grocery store?"

"How did you decide on Salton?" Lena asked.

"My mom lived in Salton until she was fifteen, and always talked about how much she loved it, so when I was looking for a more mellow place to live, Salton was a nostalgic choice."

"What was your mother's maiden name? Perhaps I know the family."

"Johnson, same as me," the woman said.

Lena gave her a perplexed look.

"A bit complicated," the woman said, "but the short story is my mom never married. As for Salton, according to my mom, we don't have any relatives left in town."

"And I'm unaware of any Johnsons here," Lena said, "But how nice that you have the opportunity to return to your roots."

"Yes, and so far, so good," she said. "I'm discovering new places and meeting new people every day."

"That's very nice," Lena said. "Is the store you're opening your first venture into the popcorn business?"

"This is the fifteenth," the woman said. "The flagship store is in New York City but they don't need me on site all the time, and technology makes it easy to connect with them as needed." She shrugged. "So, here I am, giving Salton a go."

"That's quite a change, going from New York City to here," Lena said.

"Yes, but I think it will be a good one." The woman ate a piece of caramel corn from a cup she had near her. "I'm already sleeping better without hearing horns honking and trucks rumbling by at all hours."

"And they say sleep is an important key to success," Lena said.

Sadie wondered if she heard an odd tone in Lena's voice.

"True. But I hope I'll be successful making new friends, too." The woman held out her hand. "To which I should add, I'm Poppy. Poppy Johnson."

"Seriously?" Colette asked. "Your real name is Poppy?"

"What can I say—"

"Your mom loves popcorn?" Sadie asked.

"Actually, she loves the flower." Poppy smiled. "I love popcorn."

"Well, regardless," Lena said, "It's nice to meet you, Poppy. And best of luck with the new store."

Poppy thanked her and waved as Sadie, Colette, and Lena continued into the store. "And I'll see you at the dojo," she called after Sadie

"For sure," Sadie said. "See you there."

✳ ✳ ✳

The next morning, Jason closed his locker and waited for Sadie.

"Friends!" Nessa bopped Jason on the head with a glossy red helium balloon. "Today is a wonderful day."

Static crackled as Jason smoothed his hair. "Why do you have a balloon?"

"It's Nessa's birthday tomorrow," Sadie said.

"And my dearests, Sadie and Colette, surprised me with a decorated locker this morning." Nessa released her hold on the balloon's ribbon. It bounced as it extended above its tie to her backpack.

"So, shouldn't the balloon be with its friends in your locker?" Jason smirked.

"But it's so pretty," Nessa said. "I want to adore it all day."

"And she enjoys attention." Sadie shut her locker.

"Birthday attention is special." Nessa boinged the balloon with a small yank on the ribbon. "Plus, fun." She followed Jason and Sadie into the student traffic.

"Have you decided what you're wearing on your date with Kyle tomorrow?" Sadie asked Nessa.

"No idea," Nessa said. "Can you come over and help me choose something?"

"I can stop by after Tae Kwon Do tonight," Sadie said.

"Oh gosh," Jason said, "as much as I'd love to talk clothes with you, here's my corner. I'll see you at lunch."

Sadie and Nessa said goodbye and Jason continued down the hall. He approached Colette's locker and saw Derek standing next to her. Derek glanced up, spotted Jason, and hurried away in the opposite direction.

Jason walked up to Colette. "What did he want?"

"Nothing. He was just saying hi."

"He says hi to you a lot." Ever since Colette's conversation with Derek at the barn, followed by her text to him about "King" being okay, Jason saw Derek near Colette more than he liked.

"It's not a big deal," she said. "He's just being nice."

"And you're being nice back."

"Jason—"

"I know," he said. "No reason not to be nice, and it's good he trusts you and whatever. Have you talked to him about calling the sheriff on his step-mom?"

"Yeah, he didn't like the idea." She shut her locker. "In fact, he hated it. He said he didn't want to end up in foster care, and at least where he is now he knows how to deal."

Jason and Colette started toward their first classes of the day. "But does he?" Jason asked.

"Does he what?"

"Know how to deal. I don't see how anyone knows how to deal with being locked up by their parents. Or being yelled at for eating too much."

"He was stealing food for Elly," Colette said.

"Yeah, but they didn't know that. It sounds pretty sucky."

"Do I sense some sympathy from you for Derek?" Colette asked.

Jason *tsked*. "No way. I'm just saying he's in a bad situation. Doesn't mean I don't still think he's totally annoying. Because he is."

They stopped outside of Colette's classroom. She smiled at Jason.

"What?" he asked.

"Nothing." Colette kissed Jason's cheek. "I'll see you later."

Moths and grasshoppers and butterflies flicked through Jason's stomach as he watched Colette walk away.

✳ ✳ ✳

Saturday slogged along with no crisis to chase. Jason worked on his mind-move power as he had each day since things had calmed down. Sadie visited her mom in the morning, trained with Connor mid-day, and since Uncle Alexander and Connor spent time with Elly in the late afternoon, Jason, Colette, Sadie, and Brandon were free to play video games and watch movies.

Jason slept through most of Sunday morning since he had no good reason to get out of bed.

When he finally wandered down to the kitchen, he was surprised to find Kyle making pancakes. Brandon sat at the table with a plate of pancakes stacked three-high, soaking in butter and swirled with maple syrup.

Jason's mouth watered.

"Good morning, dear brother." Kyle smacked Jason on his back as he passed. "Long time no see. How're things?"

"Uh, fine." Jason shuffled to the refrigerator and opened the door. "How are you?"

"Good, really good," Kyle said, "Want pancakes?"

"Sure." Jason poured himself some orange juice.

"Sit." Kyle waved a spatula. "I'll bring them to you. How many do you want?"

"Two's good."

"Three's better," Kyle said. "I have three just about ready to go."

Jason slid into his chair and set down his juice. He leaned close to Brandon and lowered his voice. "What is happening?"

"Nessa is happening," Brandon whispered.

Jason sat back and grinned. He directed his attention to Kyle. "So, how was your date?"

Kyle looked up for a moment, then shrugged. "It was fine. Nessa's cool, I guess."

Bewildered, Jason glanced at Brandon.

While chewing a bite of pancake, Brandon slid his phone over so Jason could read the screen. On it was a forwarded message Nessa had sent to Sadie and Colette earlier that day: "OMG Kyle is the dreamiest. SUCH a good time. SO MUCH fun. DID NOT want it to end. And he already asked me out again! THANK YOU for talking me into giving him another chance. You're the BEST of best friends!"

Brandon inverted his phone to hide the screen as Kyle put a plate of pancakes in front of Jason.

Jason reached for the butter. "Are you going to ask her out again?"

"Uh, maybe." Kyle poured batter onto the hot griddle. "She's cool."

"So you said." Jason smeared the melting pats of butter. "But you haven't asked her out again yet?"

"Nah," Kyle said. "Gotta play it cool."

"Sure," Jason said. "Play it cool." For a moment Jason focused on eating until Brandon elbowed him in the ribs.

Jason returned his attention to Kyle. "Since you're so skilled at the whole dating thing, how long do you play it cool before you do ask her out again?"

Kyle flipped a pancake. "At least a few days." He flipped another pancake. "I won't even text Nessa until, like, Thursday to see if she wants to go out Friday or Saturday." Another pancake steamed as the raw side hit the surface.

"For real?" Brandon asked. "You wait that long before you ask a girl out on another date?"

"Yeah," Kyle said. "You don't want to seem too eager." He set down the spatula while he waited for the pancakes to cook. "It's better if girls don't think you're interested."

Jason shook his head. "How is that better?"

"I don't know, it just is," Kyle said.

"Did you read this in some article?" Brandon asked.

Kyle picked up the spatula. "Yeah." He removed the pancakes from the griddle and put them on a plate. "It was a solid article about how to keep girls interested."

"If it was such a solid article, why didn't you follow it?" Jason asked.

Kyle sat at the table. "Huh?"

Brandon tapped his phone. "We know you already asked Nessa out again. She told Sadie."

Kyle's face fell. "Man, I should have known that would happen."

"Yep, you're busted." Jason laughed. "But it doesn't matter. We're glad you both had fun. Nessa's great, and it's better if you ask her out before someone else does."

Kyle halted a big bite of pancake about to enter his mouth. "Other guys want to ask Nessa out? Who?" He dropped the fork. "Who else wants to ask her out?"

"No one I know in particular," Jason said. "I just mean—"

"Maybe I should ask her out now for every weekend for, like, the next three months." Kyle's gaze flicked from Jason to Brandon. "Do you guys think I should do that?"

Jason didn't speak. Brandon kicked him under the table.

"Uh, you could," Jason said. "But you're probably fine just asking one week at a time . . . I mean . . . right, Brandon?"

"Yep," Brandon said. "One week at a time. Or more if you want to because Nessa is super-cool."

Jason kicked Brandon under the table.

Brandon stifled a smile but Jason still saw the corners of his mouth curl upward.

"You're right." Kyle picked up his plate. "I'm going to go text her right now. I'll talk to you guys later."

Jason fake-punched Brandon in the arm.

"What was that for?" Brandon asked, laughing.

"What if he scares Nessa off?"

"Because he wants her to go out with him a million times?" Brandon swept a bite of pancake through a pooling blend of syrup and butter. "That won't scare Nessa. She looooovvvvveeeesss him." He popped the bite in his mouth.

"Yeah, you're right." Jason dug into more of his breakfast.

"Speaking of dates, Sadie and I are going to the movies this afternoon," Brandon said. "You and Colette should come."

"Sounds good." Jason stabbed a whole pancake onto his fork and stuffed it all in his mouth.

Brandon shook his head. "It's no wonder Colette finds you so attractive."

"Shut up," Jason said, his voice stifled by food.

TWENTY
Bright Red

The next Friday, Jason found Sadie and Colette in the hall just before heading into the lunchroom. He slouched in front of them. "Please don't make me sit with Kyle and Nessa again."

"Don't you mean Kessa?" Sadie asked.

"I thought she was going with Nyle as their couple name," Colette said.

"Wouldn't surprise me since she keeps changing her mind." Sadie adjusted the strap of her backpack.

"Whatever or whoever they are, can we please eat lunch somewhere else?" Jason asked. "All Kyle does is make googly eyes at Nessa, and it's kind of disturbing. After four straight days of Kessa or Nyle, I need a break."

"It is weird to see Kyle all mushy," Sadie said. "And honestly, Nessa would be fine with having him all to herself."

"If she even noticed we weren't there." Colette glanced out a window. "It looks nice outside. We could eat in the courtyard."

"Yes. Lunch in the courtyard," Jason said. "Excellent idea."

They situated themselves in the sun on tiers of concrete designed like bleachers. Jason unpacked his lunch.

"How are things with your mom?" Jason asked. "She's always in her room when I've been there to train with Uncle A. Do you think we'll get to meet her soon?"

"Ugh." Sadie shook her head.

"That doesn't sound good," Jason said.

"After that first freak out when Mom ... eh ... Elly found out about the Calling, well, she mellowed out and it was nice talking to her," Sadie said. "She told me stories about her and my dad, and asked all the basic questions like what subjects I like in school, what are my hobbies—you know the stuff grown-ups ask when they're trying to make conversation."

"Totally," Jason said.

"But then she started asking more questions about me and Mamo."

"What kinds of questions?" Colette asked.

"Like why Mamo chose Salton, as if I'd had a deep conversation about it with her at some point." Sadie's lips pursed. "Oh, and Elly asked if I had liked being homeschooled by Mamo. When I said I did like it, and I liked hanging out with Mamo, Elly got this judgy tone and said I probably only liked it because I didn't know any better."

"What's there to know? You go to public school or you don't go to public school." Jason drank from his water bottle.

"Right?" Sadie rolled her eyes. "Elly's also asked about eight million questions about the Calling and what Connor's doing to help me and what training I'm doing and blah, blah, blah. A couple of days ago I told her she should just talk to Connor about it."

Colette brushed a strand of hair out of her eyes. "What did she say?"

"She seemed annoyed." Sadie crumpled a napkin. "I know this sounds terrible, but I've seen Elly every day for almost two weeks and think I need a break." She faked a laugh. "Elly's way worse than Kessa right now."

"Sorry," Jason said. "That sucks."

"Things *could* be better after a break," Colette said.

"I hope so," Sadie said. "And I guess I'll find out because I just decided I'm not going over there after Tae Kwon Do tonight."

"And training with Connor is still good?" Jason asked.

"Yeah," Sadie said. "I do wish I'd been more focused earlier, though."

Jason opened his mouth.

Sadie whipped her index finger up in front of his face. "Don't say it. I know. You were right."

Instead of speaking, Jason smiled and bit into his sandwich.

✳ ✳ ✳

After school, Jason picked up Shay and headed to Uncle Alexander's for training. He punched in the code and walked in the front door. He heard Uncle Alexander's voice coming from the kitchen. An uneasy tone weaved through his speech.

"Shay, sit," Jason whispered. She obeyed and wagged her tail. Jason stayed in the foyer but leaned one ear toward the kitchen.

"Elly, I don't think that's the right thing to do," Uncle Alexander said. "Not at this time."

"She's my daughter," she said. "I should have a say in this."

"I understand why you feel that way." Uncle Alexander sighed. "And technically, Sadie isn't my relative."

"No, she isn't," Elly said.

Another moment passed.

Shay licked the tips of Jason's fingers and he scratched her behind the ears but stayed hidden.

"As I was saying," Uncle Alexander continued with a flintier tone, "Sadie may not be genetically related to me, but she is absolutely part of my family. As such, her best interest is also my best interest. And what you're asking right now is not in her best interest."

There was a pause in the conversation and Jason worried Elly had left the kitchen and might be heading toward him. He prepared to move, to make an excuse about why he was eavesdropping.

He relaxed when she spoke. "I am her mother." Elly said each word as if they granted her access into a secret club.

"Biologically, you are her mother," Uncle Alexander said. "But you haven't earned that emotional place in Sadie's life yet. And if you push her, you may lengthen the time and attention it takes before you truly become part of Sadie's family."

"I've already missed too much," she said. "She has to understand that. She *will* understand."

"Please, just give it a little more time," Uncle Alexander said. "Time is important in this situation."

"Which is all the more reason for me to act now," she said.

Jason decided not to risk hiding his presence any longer. "Hello," he called as if he'd just walked in the door. He unclipped Shay's leash, and she ran to find Finn. Jason took off his coat and hung it on the rack near the door.

Uncle Alexander came out of the kitchen with Elly just behind him. "Oh good, you're here. Let me introduce you to Sadie's mother." He gestured to Elly. "Elly, this is my nephew, Jason Lex."

She held out her hand. "It's very nice to meet you." Her voice had shifted from demanding to warm and welcoming.

"You, too, Mrs. Callahan."

"Please, call me Elly," she said. "After living in the wild for as long as I did, Mrs. Callahan seems way too formal."

"Sure. Okay."

"I've heard you're quite the talented Rampart Guard."

"Oh, uh, I guess," Jason said. "Thanks to Uncle A. He's taught me everything I know."

"I wouldn't go quite that far," Uncle Alexander said. "Jason is talented in his own right. But we make a good team."

"Yeah, we do. For sure." Jason beamed at the mention of team and pointed to the stairs. "Ready to do some training?"

"I am." Uncle Alexander turned to Elly. "If you'll excuse us?"

"Of course," she said.

Uncle Alexander called the dogs and headed downstairs with Jason.

Jason changed into his workout clothes. "Elly seems . . . nice."

"She is," he said. "Though I doubt you came to that conclusion based on the conversation you heard."

"Oh . . . I . . ."

Uncle Alexander waggled his phone. "Camera notified me of your arrival."

"Right." Jason made a mental note to always remember there was no sneaking around Uncle A's house since he'd installed the security system. "Sorry."

"That's all right," Uncle Alexander said. "I mean, no it isn't all right. You shouldn't eavesdrop."

"Yeah. Still sorry."

"It doesn't matter. I have no secrets from you." Uncle Alexander blew out a breath.

"What's her deal?" Jason asked. "What were you talking about?"

"She wants to play a bigger role in Sadie's life, which is understandable since she's Sadie's mother," Uncle Alexander said. "But I'm not sure Sadie's ready for that. She's had and still has many ongoing challenges, and rushing her into another one won't help anything." He rubbed his temple. "Sadie should decide the pace at which she gets to know her mother."

"Even though her mom is the grown-up?" he asked.

Uncle Alexander gave a sarcastic chuckle. "Because adults should always be trusted to make the best decisions for everyone concerned."

Memories flicked through Jason's mind like a flip-book. He thought of his mom, Rick, Merinda, and other adults who'd messed things up. "Nope. Definitely not." He rubbed the Lex coin in his pocket. "Why is Elly in such a hurry?"

"Because of the Calling," Uncle Alexander said. "She seems to think she's the only one who understands the situation."

"Which is not true."

"No."

"So now what?" Jason asked.

"Now we let go of that which we cannot change and do some training."

"Cool," Jason said. "Because I have a surprise for you." He placed the medicine ball on the table in the middle of the room. Before Uncle Alexander could get himself and the dogs behind the blast wall, Jason focused on the ball, then *wham!* He'd lifted the ball and flung it into the far wall. It rolled back toward him.

"Luck or mastery?" Uncle Alexander asked.

"If by 'mastery' you mean I've been practicing until I have this whole mind-moving thing down, then mastery."

"Do it again," Uncle Alexander ordered.

"I can do better than that." Jason waved his arm. "You and the dogs get back a little."

Uncle Alexander called to the dogs. Jason concentrated and lifted the table, flipped it in the air and slammed it onto the floor, top down.

"Remarkable." Uncle Alexander hurried forward and examined the table. "Was it your intention to land it upside down?"

"Yep."

"Can you set it upright again?" Uncle Alexander said. "Do you have that level of control?" He put space between himself and the target.

Jason raised it up, floated it over and set it on its legs.

"Well done, Jason," Uncle Alexander said.

"Thanks. Since things calmed down, I had time to work on this."

"Have you discovered any limitations?" Uncle Alexander asked. "Size or weight of item?"

"Not yet, but I haven't tried it on huge things." Jason pushed his hair out of his eyes. "I thought about testing it with Dad's car but my gut said that might be a bad idea."

"Good for your gut. Neither of us needs to be buying your father a new car."

"Can I try it with your truck?" Jason asked.

"I don't need to be buying myself a new vehicle either," Uncle Alexander said. "Let's focus on other heavy items first. Have you tried this new skill on living organisms?"

"Potted plants."

"But not Shay. Or your siblings."

"No way," Jason said. "Didn't want to chance it."

"Smart." Uncle Alexander pinched the bridge of his nose. "And I can't imagine it should make a difference whether you're moving a living organism versus an inanimate object. But regardless, let's put you through your paces and train with inanimate objects. Once you've proven consistency moving heavier items, you can test your skills on me."

"But if I drop you—"

"You won't," Uncle Alexander said. "You must put your skills to the test. Push the envelope. I have every confidence in you."

An hour passed, and Jason had successfully moved everything available, from heavy free weights to the entire rack loaded with every weight it could hold. He'd lifted Uncle Alexander's desk and set it down. He'd lifted the bed where Elly had been treated and set it down. He lifted a pile of bricks in the furnace room, leftover from when Uncle Alexander's house had been built, then he set them down in the same configuration as before Jason disturbed their dusty pile.

Uncle Alexander coughed. "I didn't think that one through." He waved the air to flick dust away from his face and exited the furnace room. "Let's have you lift me now."

Jason rubbed the back of his neck. "Are you sure?" He followed Uncle Alexander down the hall.

"You haven't missed a beat on any of the items you've attempted today," he said. "You won't hurt me."

"Can you at least lie on the bed, just in case? At least you'd have a softer landing."

"Unless you throw me onto the floor." Uncle Alexander climbed onto the bed.

"I won't throw you onto the floor."

"Just like you won't drop me." Uncle Alexander grinned and lay flat. "Go ahead."

"You better hope you're right." Jason took a deep breath and focused on his uncle.

Uncle Alexander rose into the air, made a slow circle above and away from the bed, then suddenly flipped over, dropped about six inches and stopped, his face now aimed at the floor.

"Jason . . ."

A moment later Uncle Alexander floated higher, rolled languidly until he was face up again, and drifted to settle on the bed now beneath him. He breathed fast.

"You're right," Jason said. "I can move animate objects as easily as inanimate."

Uncle Alexander sat up. "You did that on purpose?"

Jason smiled. "You said to test my skills, push the envelope."

"I do love it when you use my words against me." Uncle Alexander climbed off the bed. "But even so, a good session. This is an excellent new ability to have."

"Now I can catch bad cryptids and turn them into my personal, custom-made helium balloons, but without the helium."

Uncle Alexander gave him an incredulous look. "I hope you're kidding."

"Of course I'm kidding," Jason said. "The bad ones are angry when we catch them and wouldn't be very cute as balloons."

"Regardless," Uncle Alexander said while shaking his head, "keep practicing. But not on the dogs, and not on your siblings."

"How about—"

"Not Brandon. Or Sadie or Colette. No humans without their consent. And no animals."

Jason opened his mouth to speak but Uncle Alexanders spoke first.

"And not on the cars."

"Then what?" Jason whined.

"Go outside this weekend and find some big rocks to play with. You could also test how many you can lift at once," Uncle Alexander said. "The weather is still supposed to be nice, strangely enough. We're having quite a warm winter since that big snow."

"Fine," Jason said. "I guess that's better than searching for a rogue Yowie. At least that project is finished."

"Yes, it's nice to have things settled again. Even the Skyfish seem to have returned to more normal behavior patterns."

"What about dear old Mom's rip in the Rampart?" Jason asked.

"I wanted to talk to you about that," Uncle Alexander said. "I mentioned regular Guard powers can't repair it—this tear is unprecedented and beyond the scope of normal Guard skills. The League is still working on a solution, but I thought we might head to the sugar mill where she created the rift and see if leveraging your new, amped powers might make a difference. Not this new ability but the supercharged Guard bolts."

"I'm game."

"Tomorrow, then?" Uncle Alexander asked. "I'll even let you sleep in."

"Deal," Jason said. "I'll text you when I get up in the morning."

"Good." Uncle Alexander headed upstairs with the dogs and Jason followed.

Elly sat on the couch reading a book. "Finished training so soon?"

"I don't like to overwork him," Uncle Alexander said.

"Yeah, I learned that the hard way." Jason called to Shay and waved at Elly. "It was nice to meet you."

"You too, Jason," she said. "See you again I'm sure."

Jason walked into the foyer, put on his coat, and clipped Shay's leash to her harness. He opened the front door and Shay zipped out, nearly plowing them both into Mr. Templeman.

"Oh, my goodness." Mr. Templeman put a hand up and leaned on the house. "You about gave me a heart attack, uh . . . uh . . ."

"Jason."

Mr. Templeman straightened and snapped his fingers. "Right. Sorry about that, Jason. My mind hasn't been too sharp the last couple of weeks."

"No problem. I hope everything's okay." Jason counted back to when Sadie wiped Mr. Templeman's memory. It was a little over two weeks ago.

"I'm just fine. Working too hard is all, and need a little vacation."

Shay sniffed Mr. Templeman's pant leg as if cataloging everywhere he'd been on his route. "Looks like she smells other dogs I visit with," Mr. Templeman said. "I always wonder how much information dogs pick up with their noses."

"A lot more than we do," Jason said.

"Ha. No doubt about that." He read the label on a package he was holding. "Meanwhile, I have a package for Alexander."

"I'll take it." Jason set the package on a table inside the door.

"Good man." Mr. Templeman scratched Shay under her chin, then turned and headed toward his mail truck. "You have a good rest of your day now, Jason." He waved.

"You, too." Jason yelled to Uncle Alexander about the package waiting in the foyer and wondered if he should tell Sadie about Mr. Templeman being forgetful.

Nah. He said he's working too hard, and she has enough to deal with already.

Jason stepped out into the crisp air with Shay and walked home.

✳ ✳ ✳

Sadie glanced around the Tae Kwon Do studio before and after class, looking for Poppy Johnson, but didn't see her.

"She's not here?" Brandon asked.

"Doesn't look like it." She headed toward the exit with Brandon.

"Are you going to see your mom now?" He held the door, and they both stepped outside to wait for Lena.

"No, I'm taking a break."

"That was fast," Brandon said, his words puffing in the cold air. "More proof she's your mom."

"What do you mean?"

"Sometimes we all need a break from our parents. It's totally normal." He blew on his hands and rubbed them together. "You know I can only spend a few days with mine before I need a time out."

"I never felt that way with Mamo," Sadie said.

"Grandparents are different," Brandon said. "Maybe because they've been around longer, and maybe they relax and remember what it's like to be a kid. But whatever it is, they don't seem to be as uptight as parents."

"Elly is definitely uptight. Being around her has been so hard lately. Plus, with all of the extra training I'm doing with Connor now, I'm really tired at the end of the day." A chill crept inside the collar of Sadie's coat. "Let's wait inside."

Brandon held the door for her and they both watched for Lena from inside the glass.

"So, why is Elly bugging you?" Brandon asked.

Sadie sighed and shared with Brandon what she'd told Jason and Colette.

"Wow," Brandon said. "That's bold."

"Yeah." Sadie shoved her hands into the pockets of her coat. "One part of me thinks, okay, she's my mom, and she has a right to say things about my life. But another side of me is thinking, hold on, you weren't here. You were off hiding in the woods while Mamo dealt with everything, good and bad."

"Totally."

"And—" A breath caught in Sadie's throat. "And if she's questioning all this stuff Mamo did, how Mamo raised me, it makes me wonder if Elly doesn't like the way I turned out."

"No way," Brandon said. "One hundred percent not possible. You're awesome. She has to see that."

Sadie *tsked*. "You sort of have to say that."

"No, I don't. I don't have to say it just like I don't have to hang out with you. But I want to hang out with you because you are awesome."

A small smile crept onto Sadie's face. "You're kind of awesome, too."

Brandon arched one brow. "Just kind of?"

"Okay . . ." Sadie glanced up as if she was calculating a formula. "Kind of times a million."

"I'll take it."

Lena pulled up, and they left the dojo.

✷ ✷ ✷

Shay rushed into the kitchen after returning home from training and slurped water from her bowl.

"I do not get why you don't drink at Uncle A's if you're so thirsty," Jason said as he walked in after her.

Shay flopped onto one of her many beds located around the house. Her tongue lolled and dripped water.

"Do you want your dinner?"

Shay sprung up and hurried to where her food bowl sat. Jason filled it with kibble and she dove into the bits, crunching and swallowing as fast as she could.

"I promise, you are not starving," Jason said.

Shay didn't look up.

The door to the garage opened and Dad walked in. "Did I hear something about starving?" He held a paper bag in front of him.

Della dashed under his arm and into the house. "Dad bought Chinese food."

"Nice." Jason's own hunger switched from silent to insistent.

"I'm going to change my clothes because this sweater is itchy." She ran upstairs. "Don't start without me."

"I'm eating an egg roll right now," Jason called after her.

"Dad, don't let him," she yelled, her voice fading as she moved farther away.

Jason turned to his dad. "Did she have a dance class or something?"

He shook his head. "No, her appointment with Dr. Abernathy was rescheduled for this afternoon. And after I picked her up, I didn't feel like cooking."

"I'm good with that."

Dad unpacked white paper containers. "Set the table, please. And wash your hands first."

Jason washed and took plates out of the cupboard, then grabbed napkins and utensils and set five places at the table. "Brandon isn't home yet, but he should be here soon. What about Kyle?"

"He'll be home in a bit," Dad said.

Della scurried into the room and slid onto her chair. "Okay, I'm back."

"Thank you for letting us know." Jason sat next to her.

Dad put serving spoons into each of the containers and handed one to Jason. "How was your training session?"

Jason scooped noodles onto his plate. "It was great. I have this new—" He abruptly set down the white box and grimaced as he reached into his pocket. "Something is burning." He removed the Lex coin and dropped it on the table.

It glowed bright red.

Someone in Jason's circle was in trouble.

Or trouble was coming.

Or trouble was already here.

TWENTY-ONE
Into the Core

"It's Elly," Jason said to Uncle Alexander as they drove down the road to the sugar mill. "She's why the coin turned red."

"But you didn't discover it until you were home, with your Dad." Uncle Alexander paused. "And Della."

"It's not Della. Not this time."

"The coin has called her out before."

"Yeah," Jason said. "But that was when she was at the League and all dosed up on serum. She's better now."

"Jason . . ."

"She is." Uncle Alexander's truck hit a rut and bounced Jason in his seat. "Besides, she saw the coin glowing, too."

"Did you ask her specifically what she saw?"

Jason slumped. "No. She saw the glow and freaked out about it burning down the house. I didn't ask what the coin looked like to her while she was screaming and searching for the fire extinguisher."

"But the coin wasn't hot."

"Not after I took it out of my pocket." Jason twisted to face his uncle. "But that's another thing. I think it signaled hot to get my attention. It was probably glowing red when I talked to Elly, both when I got there and when I left, and I didn't notice since the coin was in my pocket. It burned me so I'd take it out."

"I suppose that's possible," Uncle Alexander said. "Though improbable. Think about it—neither of the dogs identify Elly as a threat."

Shay nudged Jason from the back seat.

"And the coin didn't signal you with heat while you were in the room with her," Uncle Alexander added. "Plus, we can't ignore Della's history."

"It can't be Della," Jason said. "Not again."

Uncle Alexander sighed. "You said she'd just seen Dr. Abernathy, right?"

"Yeah."

"Perhaps something came up in her conversation with Della that triggered some of Della's old issues or feelings."

Jason stared at his hands.

"Or perhaps there's something going on with Dr. Abernathy," Uncle Alexander said. "We did a thorough background check before bringing her here, but something could have changed."

Jason shrugged. "I'll go with Dad the next time he drops Della off at Dr. Abernathy's office to see what happens." He paused a moment. "But you better watch your back with Elly because I'm pretty sure she's the problem."

The abandoned sugar mill loomed before them and Uncle Alexander put the truck into park. "Please don't jump to conclusions," he said.

"I'm not," Jason said. "The coin sent me a signal." He emphasized the last four words.

"And you may be misinterpreting that signal." Uncle Alexander pointed out the front windshield. "Consider where we are right now. This place brings up bad memories of your mom for both of us."

"Yep. Sucks."

"It's possible you're transferring some of those bad feelings onto Sadie's mom," Uncle Alexander said.

Jason looked at his uncle. "I don't know Sadie's mom well enough to transfer anything. I'm trusting the coin."

"You have a few reasons to wonder about Elly. The conversation you overheard between me and Elly, for one." Uncle Alexander stared at the crumbling building. "And I'm guessing Sadie has shared her feelings of frustration."

"A little," Jason said. "But none of that stuff is enough to make me think Sadie's mom is like my mom."

"No, but emotions can mess with us sometimes when we don't even realize it."

"That's not what this is." He pulled the no-longer-glowing Lex coin from his pocket. "The coin sent a message and I'm paying attention. That's it."

Uncle Alexander turned to Jason. "We don't yet know exactly what that message is, but we'll both be cautious, okay? As for now, are you sure you want to go into the sugar mill?"

"Totally." Jason opened the door and stepped out of the car while returning the coin to his pocket. "Let's do this." He let Shay and Finn out of the back seat.

"All right." Uncle Alexander got out and locked the truck. "Do this we shall."

The dogs ran ahead and sniffed the ground, their ears active, their tails wagging. Jason walked toward the same door he'd snuck in months ago. "How do we get inside?"

"While the building is now owned by the League, there's not enough of it left to warrant security," Uncle Alexander said. "I'm guessing nothing is locked. And once inside, pay attention to where the dogs step. They'll pick the safest path."

They rounded the building, and Jason eyed the camera above the familiar door. The camera hung lifeless, its lens grungy and strung with cobwebs. He pushed down the lever on the door and pulled. It held fast in its frame, but with a tougher tug, the barrier scraped free.

Cool air billowed out mixed with mold and oil and decomposing death. Jason grimaced. "Don't tell me all the dead cryptids are still in here?"

"The League cleaned up as much as they could, but given what happened and the quantity of fallen debris . . . well, it seems likely they missed some body parts."

"But not Mom's body." Jason had watched her fall into the shaft a moment before the core flared.

"No, nothing remains of your mother."

Jason picked tentative steps over rubble and piles of rocks where there used to be passages and hallways. "To the center? Where she tapped into the core?"

"Yes," Uncle Alexander said. "That seems like the most logical place to start."

Finn and Shay led the way over boulders of crumbled concrete. They sniffed and checked and leaped from one rocky pile to the next, careful to avoid snags of rebar and bits of broken glass. They climbed downward, over to the right, then toward the center. Jason and Uncle Alexander followed the dogs' path. The stench of rot grew dense.

"Ugh, that is foul," Jason said, his voice nasal as he tried to breathe only through his mouth.

"I imagine it will be much worse this summer." Uncle Alexander swallowed hard. "At least we have the benefit of winter temperatures keeping the fetor somewhat at bay."

"Let's for sure not come back when it's warmer." Jason pinched his nose and stuck out his tongue. "It's like I can taste everything I'm smelling."

"Try not to think about it. Focus on finding the entrance she made to the core."

The dogs stopped up ahead. Jason and Uncle Alexander stopped next to them. A few feet away was the edge of a crater filled with rock and debris.

"I think we found it." Jason released the pinch on his nose but tried not to inhale more than was necessary. He stared at the pit that was his mom's final resting place.

The mom who was never what a mom should be.

Uncle Alexander moved forward, stepping closer to the edge.

"I don't think you should do that," Jason said. "The dogs stopped for a reason."

A chunk of rubble slipped under Uncle Alexander's right foot and toppled him sideways. He barely regained his balance. "I need to find a gap, a place where the core is leaking." He took a few more steps around the edge of the pit.

Jason's heart raced. "But you can't. It's not safe. And if you fall—"

"I won't fall."

"You *can't* fall," Jason said. "I can't save you." The image of his mother slipping out of his grasp and into the shaft replayed in Jason's mind. He scrambled to the right, away from the edge where Uncle Alexander walked. "Please stop. Let the League figure this out."

"We have to try," Uncle Alexander said. "The League is struggling to find a solution."

"But they'll find one." Jason took a few more steps to keep close to Uncle Alexander. "You need to come back toward me, where it's—"

Uncle Alexander took another step and the ground eroded.

Finn whined and barked.

"Uncle A," Jason yelled.

Uncle Alexander grabbed onto a jutting piece of rebar and held fast, one leg sunk deep into the detritus. "I'm okay."

Jason and the dogs scrambled as close as they could.

"I can't pull myself up," Uncle Alexander said as gravel slid beneath the foot Jason could see.

"Hold on." Jason scanned the area for something that could help, then chided himself as he remembered his new ability. He faced Uncle Alexander and focused. "I've got this."

"Please no tricks this time."

"No way," Jason said. "Here we go." He concentrated on Uncle Alexander, on lifting him, on freeing him.

Bits of rubble rolled around his uncle. Uncle Alexander raised a few inches then sank back.

"Dammit," Jason said.

"It's okay." Uncle Alexander took a deep breath. "Try again."

Jason attempted it another time but the same thing happened. "I can do this."

"No, it's no good," Uncle Alexander said. "The gravitational pull is strong here. It's too much."

Jason remembered the strength of the core's force when his mom had fallen.

"We have to try something else," Uncle Alexander said. "Any ideas?"

Jason frantically looked around. He spotted a long piece of metal that had been part of a bracket mounting a monitor to the ceiling before everything had been destroyed. He grabbed the metal bar, laid on his belly over sharp edges of rock, and hooked his foot on a heavy chunk of concrete. He held the bar as close to Uncle Alexander as he could. "Can you reach this?"

Uncle Alexander stretched one arm forward. "I think so." He grunted as he compelled his arm to reach farther.

Jason stretched.

His anchored toes slipped, then held.

Uncle Alexander's fingertips grazed the bar, and he almost had it but more of the crater's edge crumbled. It pulled him farther into the pit.

Adrenaline shot through Jason.

Finn and Shay squealed and yelped and paced across the rocks.

Both of Uncle Alexander's legs were below the surface. His knuckles practically punched through his skin, tight against his grip. "I seem to be in a pickle."

"You are so not funny right now." Jason pushed himself up and threw the metal bar that was now too short to help. He searched for something, anything he could use to save Uncle Alexander. He scrabbled over concrete and picked up lengths of steel, of wood, of shredded fabric. He touched dried slime and scum and breathed in muck but none of it mattered. Jason had to save Uncle Alexander.

Finn growled. She and Shay had their teeth on something black, something stuck under debris. They both tugged and yanked and Jason hurried over.

More of the crater crumbled and Uncle Alexander sank deeper. "I can't hold on much longer."

"Yes, you can," Jason yelled. "Do not let go. The dogs have something."

Jason lifted off rock and recognized what the dogs had found. "Yes. Good girls." He tossed off more heavy bits, and the dogs pulled harder. Seconds later they'd freed their find from its tomb. It was the tattered wing of an Ahool, about eight feet long and now more bone and fiber than fully formed. Jason rushed back to his uncle. "Grab this."

He floated the end of the bat-like wing to Uncle Alexander who grabbed with one hand, then let go of the rebar and grabbed on the wing with his other hand. "I'm not sure you can pull me up by yourself. My weight, plus the angle—"

"No math," Jason said. "Besides, I'm not by myself."

Both dogs bit onto the wing and yanked. Jason activated his power to move Uncle Alexander with his powers while heaving with his muscles.

Uncle Alexander inched upward.

Jason and the dogs moved back and reset their feet.

They pulled again.

Uncle Alexander came farther out of the pit.

They all tugged a third time until Uncle Alexander reached a solid perch and pulled himself the rest of the way to safety. Finn rushed to his side and licked his face.

Jason hunched and panted next to Shay. He leaned into her scruff. "You two are the best dogs." Shay squealed and wagged and licked Jason's nose. He turned to Uncle Alexander. "Are you okay?"

"Yes, thanks to all of you."

"So, can we bail now?"

"Not yet." He gestured to where he'd almost been sucked into the crater. "We have a little work to do."

Jason came over to see where he pointed. A silvery light glowed at the bottom of a deep hole. "You found the problem with the Rampart."

"I believe so," Uncle Alexander said while he scratched Finn's chest. "A leak in the core that powers the Rampart, resulting in a rip. It's small, which is why only Salton is unprotected by the Rampart right now." He tottered himself to standing on the uneven surface. "But it will likely get bigger if left unattended."

"I don't get what we can do about this on our own," Jason said. "That's the core we're talking about, not the Rampart. The last time someone added energy to the core . . ." He held his hands wide like he was presenting on stage. "This whole mess happened."

"Right," Uncle Alexander said. "And I'm not suggesting we touch the core. In fact, it's vital that we do not touch the core for the reason you just gave."

Jason shook his head. "Then what do we do?"

"We need to seal the leak." Uncle Alexander pointed to all the parts of broken metal and crumbled concrete with metal embedded. "We melt metal near the leak, as much as we can. As it cools, a barrier will form. Then we use your ability to move items, more debris and rubble, into the pit to compact and fill it."

"And just hope we don't mess up and explode everything again."

"You won't. I have every confidence in you."

"Me?"

"This is the perfect assignment for your amped powers," Uncle Alexander said. "My regular level of Guard energy won't be of much use to melt the amount of metal needed, at least not with any efficiency. And I can't move rubble with my powers."

Jason sighed. "Shouldn't I practice more before I start messing around with the core?"

"Just the leak, not the core."

"Yeah, I get it," Jason said. "But still."

Uncle Alexander gripped Jason's shoulder. "We both know you can do this."

Jason blew out a breath. "Okay, but if I screw this up, it's your fault."

"If you screw it up, we all probably die," Uncle Alexander said.

Jason looked at the dogs who were both happily panting and wagging their tails. "I won't screw this up."

✳ ✳ ✳

A couple of hours later, Jason and Uncle Alexander used their Guard powers to analyze the Rampart around Salton.

"One hundred percent functional," Uncle Alexander said. "There won't be any new cryptid sightings in Salton anytime soon. Nice work."

"Thanks." Jason climbed into the truck. "You're buying me lunch."

"Now? It's only a few hours until dinner. Besides, we both stink." Uncle Alexander got behind the wheel. "All I'm inhaling is my body odor, your body odor, and rotting cryptid."

"Thanks for reminding me." Jason leaned into the seat and closed his eyes. "Hopefully your truck won't smell like this forever. And now that I've been reminded of the stench I'm breathing, I've lost my appetite."

"I'll drop you home and owe you lunch." Uncle Alexander started the engine. "Okay?"

"Okay," Jason said. "If you promise me you won't turn your back on Elly."

"I don't think—"

Jason opened his eyes and sat up. "Just promise me."

Uncle Alexander paused a moment then nodded. "Okay. I promise."

✳ ✳ ✳

Sadie invited Brandon to go see her mom Saturday afternoon. Brandon swung by Sadie's to pick her up and they both walked to Uncle Alexander's house.

"I'm a little nervous," Brandon said.

"Why?" Sadie asked.

"Well, because I'm meeting your mom." He squeezed Sadie's hand. "It kind of feels like a big deal. What if she doesn't like me?"

"It doesn't matter if she doesn't like you," Sadie said. "Now, if Mamo hadn't liked you, that would have been a big deal. But she loved you."

"Mrs. C was cool. And she obviously had good taste."

Sadie grinned. "Yes, she did."

"Still, I do want your mom to like me," Brandon said.

"I want her to like me, too." Sadie punched in the code on Uncle Alexander's front door. "So, we're basically in the same boat." She opened the door and walked in with Brandon. "Elly?" Sadie called.

"In the living room."

Sadie stepped into the room with Brandon. Elly lay on the couch with a book and a blanket.

"Hi." Sadie gestured to Brandon. "This is Brandon."

He waved. "Hi, uh . . ."

"Elly." She invited Brandon to shake her hand. "Call me Elly."

"It's great to meet you." Brandon shook her hand then returned to Sadie's side. They both sat on the couch across from Elly.

"How are you feeling?" Sadie asked.

"I'm fine," Elly said, sitting up. "I missed seeing you yesterday."

"Oh, I had Tae Kwon Do after school, and some other stuff to do."

Elly glanced at Brandon then back to Sadie. "I wish you had let me know you weren't coming over." She placed a bookmark and closed her book. "I was expecting you."

Sadie shrugged. "Sorry. I won't always be able to come here every day."

"I understand. But you could let me know so I don't wait on you." Elly set her book on the coffee table. "If you text Jason's uncle, I'm sure he'd be happy to pass on the message until I'm able to get my own phone."

A flint of frustration sparked inside Sadie. She forced herself to ignore it and searched for another topic of conversation. "Have you been outside? The weather is great today. Nice for the bees, and me since I don't worry about the hives being too cold."

"You're keeping bees?" Elly asked.

"Yeah. Mamo and I started beekeeping when I was little."

"I guess that's nice, but I don't want you getting stung," Elly said.

"It's not a big deal," Sadie said. "Besides, you have to upset the bees to get stung, and that doesn't happen often."

"Hmm." Elly dismissed the topic of beekeeping. "Tell me more about Tae Kwon Do." She turned to Brandon. "Is this something you got her involved in?"

Brandon seemed surprised by the question. "No, it's actually the other way around. I started going because Sadie likes it and I thought it sounded cool." He tipped his head toward Sadie. "She's been doing Tae Kwon Do for a while and she's way ahead of me, way more skilled."

"I see." Elly redirected her gaze to Sadie. "And did you and Brandon go do something fun after Tae Kwon Do?"

While the question seemed normal, Elly's tone hinted at annoyed.

"I had something else to do after Tae Kwon Do." Sadie crossed her hands on her lap.

"I see," Elly said in the same tone.

"Is there a problem?" Sadie worked to keep her tone neutral.

Elly shook her head. "No problem. I've just been eager to discuss something with you and was disappointed we didn't get to do that last night." She looked at Brandon. "And today you arrive with unexpected guests, so I feel like I have to postpone the conversation again."

Tendons tightened in Sadie's neck. "You can talk to me about anything in front of Brandon."

Elly huffed. "I'm sure that's not true."

"Anything." Sadie laced her fingers together and stared at her mom. Brandon shifted in his seat next to her.

"Oh," Elly said. "Is he a cryptid?"

"He's sitting right here," Sadie said. "You can ask him."

"Uh, no," Brandon said, "I'm not a cryptid. But I'm up to speed on everything. So, uh, no worries about spilling any secrets because they've already been spilled. Or I've been fully briefed. Or whatever you want to call it." He swallowed. "But yeah, I know what's up with Sadie."

"Then you understand why it's important for her to spend less time with you and more time with me and her great-uncle," Elly said.

"What?" Sadie glared at Elly.

"You know what's coming," Elly said. "We need to prepare you and I want to take an active role in your training."

Sadie stood. "I don't need you to take an active role in my training. I'm good with how things are going right now."

"You're only fourteen years old—"

"Almost fifteen." Sadie crossed her arms.

"Fine," Elly said. "You're almost fifteen years old, but you don't have the age and experience to know what's good for you."

"And you do?"

"I am your mother."

"Not to me," Sadie said. "To me you're some woman who lived in the woods for years. You're just lucky we found you, and lucky I could heal you and your brain injury or you'd still be out there getting chased by a little sociopath with a cattle prod."

Elly held up her hand. "Sadie—"

"No." Sadie shook her head vigorously. "You've been here, as your human self, for barely two weeks. And I don't know you, and right now I'm not sure I even want to know you." She raised her chin. "But what I do know is I am surrounded by great people, and great friends, and great family. We're all working together so I can use the Calling to defend my Clan—our Clan. And maybe in the future you can work with us, too. But right now, you're definitely not needed." She turned to Brandon. "Let's get out of here."

Brandon sprang to his feet.

"Please don't go," Elly pleaded. "I just want to talk."

"So you can tell me more about how you'd do things better than everyone else in my life?" Sadie headed to the front door. "No, thank you." She stalked out of the house with Brandon by her side and slammed the door behind her.

After hurrying for a few blocks, Sadie dropped onto an empty bus bench. Tears filled her eyes.

"These are angry tears, not sad tears," Sadie proclaimed. "I hate that I sometimes cry when I'm furious."

"I get it." Brandon sat next to her. "I mean, I don't get it because that doesn't happen to me, and it would be annoying if it did. But feel free to angry cry in front of me with no judgment."

Sadie wiped her eyes with her sleeve. "It's so not fair."

"That I don't angry cry? One hundred percent agree."

A light laugh snuck out of Sadie. "No, I mean Elly."

Brandon sighed. "Yeah, she's embracing the whole controlling parent thing. I wonder if this is how she always would've been as a mom or if she's just freaking out."

"What do you mean?" Sadie asked.

"Well, it could be this is who she is. Maybe her parents were super-controlling so now she's super-controlling." Brandon shrugged. "Or, she's freaking out because you have this huge Calling thing to deal with. My mom loses it sometimes, and then tells me it's because she cares about me, which seems totally whack. But Elly's deal could be something like that."

"But she doesn't care about me." Sadie sniffed.

"Why do you say that?"

"Because she never came back," Sadie said. "She's been alive all this time, she somehow figured out how to follow me and Mamo to Salton, and then decided to keep living in the woods."

Brandon smiled slightly but said nothing.

"Okay," Sadie said. "Brain injury, not her choice to stay wild."

"Yeah."

Sadie held up one finger. "But now, choosing to be annoying and controlling is all on her."

"True."

"And I don't have to be around her if I don't want to be around her."

"Also true," Brandon said.

Sadie's shoulders sagged. "So, now what do I do?"

Brandon stood and held out his hand. "Now you come with me, we go get hot chocolate, and we talk about how dumb parents can be."

Sadie took his hand. "Best plan ever."

TWENTY-TWO

Betrayed

On Monday afternoon, Jason opened his front door then jumped back. Uncle Alexander stood on Jason's porch poised to ring the bell, Finn at his side. A black sedan waited in the driveway.

"Good, I got here before you left for my place." Uncle Alexander entered the house and removed Finn's leash. "Connor and I have been called out of town for a few days. Do you mind watching Finn?"

Jason shut the front door and unhooked Shay's lead. She raced off with Finn. "Of course not. Where are you going?"

"Some friends of mine—ours—are working on a . . . project and they asked for my . . . eh . . . our expertise."

"What kind of project?" Jason asked, trying to decipher Uncle Alexander's unusual tone.

"Nothing you'd find interesting." He flicked his wrist. "And the friends are no one you've met."

"Okay." Jason knew very few of Uncle Alexander's friends outside of Salton so it was odd for him to clarify the point. "What about training?"

"Continue practicing on your own," Uncle Alexander said. "But don't overdo it. But definitely keep practicing. Everything. Hone your skills." He paced over to the front window and peered out, then returned to the foyer. "Connor is asking the same of Sadie."

"Sure. And since I doubt Sadie will want to do it, should I check on Elly for you?" Jason removed the Lex coin from his pocket. "That would give me a chance to see if the coin reacts. I was going to do that tonight but—"

"No." Uncle Alexander shook his head. "No need to check on Elly. I've arranged for a nurse to be on call should Elly need aid. Plus, she's unsettled about her last conversation with Sadie and prefers to be left alone."

"Yeah, Sadie told me what happened."

"How is she?" Uncle Alexander asked. "Does she want to try again with her mother?"

Jason returned the coin to his pocket. "Nah, she's pretty upset."

"It's just as well she not attempt to mend things while I'm gone." He walked over and glanced out the window again. "I'd like to be present when they talk again."

"Are you looking for someone?" Jason asked.

"Hmm?" Uncle Alexander tilted his head. "Oh, the window. No, I, uh, just wanted to make sure my ride was still here."

"The ride you're paying to take you to the airport? Why would they leave without you?"

Uncle Alexander faked a laugh. "Ha, right. They wouldn't leave without me. I had too much caffeine today.

Not processing well." He moved toward the front door. "I'd better get going. Call or text if you need me."

"Uncle A," Jason said.

His uncle stopped in the doorway.

"We don't have secrets." Jason fingered the Lex coin in his pocket. "You'd tell me if something was up, right?"

Uncle Alexander's body relaxed, and he fixed his eyes on Jason's. "When I have anything definitive, I promise to share. Deal?"

"Deal." Unease flowed through Jason as he watched Uncle Alexander get into the car and drive away.

✳ ✳ ✳

Two days passed with only brief texts from Uncle Alexander to Jason, and Connor to Sadie. Jason trained on his own, but by Wednesday he suggested to Sadie they combine forces and train together.

That afternoon, Jason and Sadie met at Connor's house to use his training room. They were joined by Colette, Brandon, and the dogs.

"I can't believe we didn't do this earlier," Sadie said.

"Right?" Jason gave each of the dogs a chew stick to keep them happy while he trained with Sadie.

"You and Sadie should pool your resources," Brandon said. He and Colette sat on a bench off to the side, near the dogs.

"What do you mean?" Sadie asked.

"Like Sadie, you throw huge rocks in the air," Colette mimicked the move, "and Jason can blast them out of the sky. Like skeet shooting."

"Skeet shooting." Jason glanced at Sadie. "Do Yowie do a lot of skeet shooting?"

She laughed. "Not that I'm aware of."

"Okay," Brandon said, "she throws the rocks up, or something—it doesn't have to be rocks—and you can vibrate the stuff out of the way." He waved his hand in the air. "Whatever that new thing is you do."

"I've been calling it mind-move," Jason said.

Brandon frowned. "Mind-move? That's lame."

"Then you come up with something better." Jason sat on the floor.

"You're using sound waves, right?" Brandon asked.

Jason nodded.

"How about Sound Dog."

Colette laughed. "He doesn't need a superhero name."

"And if I did, it would not be Sound Dog," Jason said. "Just name the sound wave thing I do with my mind. I've got the bolts, I've got the orb—"

"I still think that one should be nuclear-orb." Brandon tossed a piece of lint in Jason's direction.

"Except I'm not nuclear," Jason said with a tone of "duh" in his voice.

"Reverb," Sadie said.

Brandon's brows raised. "I like. Bolts, orb, and reverb."

"I second it," Colette said.

"I like it, too." Jason high-fived Sadie. "Nice."

"Thanks," she said. "But now, Sound Dog, we need to practice."

Jason stood. "Brandon, you will pay for coming up with that name."

"Pay nothing," Brandon said. "You use sound waves, you like dogs—the name works for you."

"Someday, when the time comes, you will pay." Jason grinned.

✳ ✳ ✳

Jason and Sadie tested each other's skills. Sadie, in Yowie form, dodged Jason's bolts, and Jason evaded Yowie maneuvers. Jason rapidly reverbed mats and cushions at Sadie's head and Sadie batted them from the air. Heat built in the room and Brandon and Colette escaped with the dogs.

After the session, Sadie dressed, and she and Jason lay on the floor working to catch their breath.

"You're great at this," Jason said.

"Thanks."

"The invisibility thing, well, I'm totally jealous." Jason sat up and took a swig from his water bottle. "Do you think you inherited that from Elly?"

"Could be. But she can't make clothes disappear."

For a moment, Jason thought about telling Sadie about the coin glowing red, but decided against it. He wasn't certain of anything.

"Have you talked to her again?" he asked.

Sadie sighed and sat up. "No. And I don't even feel bad. Isn't that terrible?"

"I don't think so," Jason said.

"I can't deal with how she wants to take over my life." Sadie wiped her face with a towel. "Like I need anything else trying to take over my life."

"Yeah, that sucks."

"I feel so weird about it. I mean, here she is, the woman who is my actual mom, who I used to wish was still in my life, and I don't know if I even like her."

"I understand the weirdness of not liking your mom." Jason took another drink from his water bottle.

"Oh, sorry," Sadie said. "I didn't mean—"

Jason shook his head. "It's okay. My mom was . . . the person she was. And that person was not a good mom."

"Understatement." Sadie tucked a sweaty piece of loose hair behind her ear. "Still, I'm sorry if I made you feel bad with all my talk about my mom. But I appreciate you listening. I just need to figure out what I want before I talk to her again."

"I agree." Jason stood. "And stay away from her until you know you can trust her."

"You don't think I can trust her?"

Crap. He walked away from Sadie to refill his bottle. "Uh . . . I just meant until Connor and Uncle Alexander get back." Jason scrambled for the right words. "No one knows Elly well enough to be around her without them nearby. And she still needs to rest anyway, right? It's only been, like, not that long since we found her. She can't be better yet. Or maybe she is because you helped her? I mean, it just seems like—"

"Stop." Sadie stood and moved closer to Jason. "What aren't you telling me?"

"Nothing." He kept his back to her but felt her eyes on him.

"I can tell when you're hiding something. Spill."

Jason tipped his head and stared at the ceiling. "The coin was red."

"What?" She hurried to stand in front of him. "The Lex coin?"

"Yes, but I don't know for sure it was because of Elly."

"What did your uncle say?"

"That it might be Della." Jason explained what he'd seen and when he'd seen it. "I've checked the coin about a million times since then when Della's around, and nothing has happened. But I haven't been to Dr. Abernathy's office yet."

"And you haven't seen Elly again."

"Nope," Jason said. "But something's up. The coin, and then this sudden trip to who-knows-where by Connor and Uncle A? Something is definitely up."

Sadie leaned against the wall. "Yeah, it is."

"We all need to just be ready."

"Yeah, we do." Sadie breathed deep.

Jason paused. "And maybe stay away from Elly, at least until they get back from their trip, okay?"

Sadie swallowed hard. "Okay."

※ ※ ※

Jason and Sadie trained together again the next day. Afterward, everyone from the Lex household went to Sadie's house for dinner. Grandma Lena made lasagna, one of Jason's favorites. The pan steamed, fresh from the oven.

"This is very nice of you, Lena," Dad said. He glanced at the pile of pots and pans soaking in the sink. "Maybe too nice. It's a big job to make dinner for this many people."

"Nonsense," she said. "I love to cook. But I hate to clean up. Truth is I'm being selfish by cooking for all of you since I know I won't have to lift a finger after the part I enjoy is complete."

Dad chuckled. "And if it's all right with you, I'll be playing the grown-up card and passing my share of those duties to the kids."

"You should," Lena said. "I'd be disappointed if you didn't."

"Sadie and I have been working out hard," Jason said, "so I don't think we should have to clean up either."

"Nice try, but you're not getting out of it," Dad said. "And the more you all pitch in, the faster it will go."

"Worry about that later," Grandma Lena said. "It's time to eat. Everyone grab a plate and serve yourselves."

"Dibs on head of the table." Kyle, with an already full plate, bumped Jason aside and slid into a seat.

"It's a round table." Jason sat next to Colette.

"But this seat looks out at everyone," Kyle said. "And my back isn't exposed."

Jason long-blinked at Kyle. "I don't even know what to say to that."

Kyle nodded once and ate a huge bite of lasagna.

"Any news from Alexander or Connor?" Dad asked.

"Not really," Sadie said. "All I've heard from Connor are notes that say he'll be gone another day or two. That's it."

"Same with Uncle A." Jason sipped his water.

"What about Ash?" Dad asked. "Any news from the League about him?"

"I was wondering that myself and reached out to Elizabeth at League headquarters just this morning," Grandma Lena said. "She told me they haven't found him, and they're baffled by the whole thing. It's as if Ash disappeared into thin air."

"I don't think the League has ever failed to locate someone." Colette wiped her mouth on a napkin.

"Elizabeth said the same thing." Grandma Lena sprinkled parmesan cheese on her salad. "Highly unusual."

Jason wondered if Ash had done something stupid. "I know Ash is . . ." Jason searched for the right word. "Horrible. But I hope he's okay."

"Me too," Grandma Lena said.

"On another note," Dad said, "Saturday is the grand opening of Poppy's Corn and the Chamber's kick-off celebration of the revitalization project, and I have VIP tickets if you'd all like to come."

"Tickets?" Sadie asked. "I thought it was free."

"This is for early access to the festivities." Dad sat back in his chair. "Poppy's Corn is one of my firm's accounts—we do the architectural design for their stores. I'm not on the account myself, but since I'm on site in Salton I've been helping out with the details for this new location. And for the grand opening, that means VIP treatment which includes early access, and a goody bag with things like a T-shirt, and a gift card to use in the store."

"Sounds fun," Jason said. "But who gets the goody bag?"

Dad smirked. "Well, I would get the goody bag if there was only one goody bag. But everyone who attends with me will also get a goody bag."

"Sweet," Brandon said. "I'm in if Sadie's in."

"I'm in," Sadie said.

✳ ✳ ✳

Saturday morning dawned with cloudless skies that transformed the cold morning to another temperate day. Jason rode in the car with Dad, Brandon, Kyle, and Della. They arrived at Poppy's Corn to discover part of the parking lot sequestered by ropes and covered with tents. Dad parked the car on the street.

"Ohmygosh." Della squealed. "Baby goats." She pointed at a pen and hurried to unhook her seat belt. "Baby goats, baby goats, baby goats."

"What are you trying to say, Dell?" Jason grinned and got out of the car along with her.

"I'll be with the baby goats." Della hopped the curb and ran.

"Hey," Dad called. "Stay with—what about the pop—"

Della was out of earshot. "Well, I guess she'll be fine over there for a while," Dad said mostly to himself.

"She's good, Dad," Jason said. "She made it through the craziness at the League, so she can fend for herself with a few baby goats."

Dad laughed. "Good point."

Near the goats was a mini-carousel, a ride-on train, and a bouncy castle for kids. Closer to the Poppy's storefront was a tented area with picnic tables, and "Free Samples" signs hanging off each side. On one section of the sidewalk, a DJ flanked by tower speakers played upbeat pop songs, and closer to the street was a food truck with its grill fired up and already cooking. A chalkboard sign said: "Enjoy that sweet, sweet Poppy's Corn with some tasty Bar-B-Q." The savory scent of smoked meat wafted through the air.

Kyle inhaled. "I could stay here all day."

"I know how you love a good bouncy house." Jason side-stepped to avoid a punch from Kyle.

"Hey," Brandon said. "Don't knock a good bouncy house. Those were my favorite when I was short enough to get in."

"I remember," Jason said. "I'm pretty sure you cried the first time they stopped you."

"Yeah, but it was a manly cry." Brandon flexed his biceps.

"Let's head inside," Dad said.

They entered the store. Jason's olfactory senses soaked in the sweet scents of caramel, cinnamon, and cherry, popcorn, nuts, and cheese. The walls were painted light blue, the floors were a glossy brown, and a tall, red-headed woman wearing a navy-blue apron stood near the checkout counter.

She glanced up and smiled. "Zachary." She walked over and gave Dad a hug.

Brandon arched one brow and nudged Jason.

"Hi, Poppy," Dad said. "Everything looks great."

"Thanks to you and your hard work," she said.

"No, no." Dad waved his hands. "The account team did all the hard work." He smiled. "I had the easy part."

"We make a good team." She turned to where Jason stood with Brandon and Kyle. "And I'm so glad I get to meet the three of you." She held her hand out to Jason. "Jason, I presume? I'm Poppy. Poppy Johnson, but you can call me Poppy."

Jason shook her hand. "Uh, yeah. Hi."

She also introduced herself to Kyle, and then to Brandon. "I've heard lots of good things about each of you."

Brandon nudged Jason again, and Jason pushed him back.

"And I'm glad you could come by today. Help yourselves to samples outside, and—" She hurried behind the counter and returned with four blue backpacks with the Poppy's Corn logo. "Here are your goody bags."

The weight surprised Jason. "Thanks."

"You're welcome," she said. "You'll find popcorn, a water bottle, a T-shirt, and a mug, all with the logo. And there are two gift cards in the front pocket: one for here, and one for the barbecue truck outside."

"Nice," Kyle said. "I love this goody bag."

She laughed. "Glad to hear it." She looked at Zachary. "Do you want to take the goody bags for the rest of your party?"

"Sure," Dad said.

She handed him four more bags.

"Thank you," Dad said. "This is very generous of you."

"Not at all," Poppy said. "I couldn't have done all of this without you." She gazed around the store. "Are we still going to dinner soon to celebrate?"

"Absolutely. I'll call you."

"I'm looking forward to it," she said. "I hope you all enjoy yourselves. I'll be outside later so I'm sure I'll see you again."

After they exited the store, Brandon held Jason to a slower pace and let Dad get farther away. Brandon leaned close. "I think you're getting a new mom," he whispered.

"Whatever." But Jason did wonder how well Dad knew Poppy. He watched Dad and Kyle head to the food truck.

"Hey." Sadie waved and walked over. "Did you meet Poppy?"

"You know her, too?" Jason asked.

Brandon handed Sadie a goody bag while she relayed the story about the dojo and the grocery store. "Did you guys like her?" she asked.

"Not as much as Jason's dad likes her," Brandon said.

Jason took a breath but before he could comment, Colette walked up. "Good morning." She hugged Jason. "Lena is with Della and the baby goats. You have to see them. We could even do a goat yoga class."

"Ooh, I've been wanting to try goat yoga," Sadie said. "There are also carnival games set up on the far side of the yoga tent. Games now, yoga later?"

"I'm up for games now," Brandon said, "but not that sure about yoga later. Jason and I might need to spend time at the food truck while you two get downward-goaty."

Jason, Colette, Sadie, and Brandon headed to the games. They played water gun horse racing, tried their hands at knocking down bottles with baseballs, and threw darts at balloons to pop them for prizes. Because they arrived earlier than the general public, there was no waiting in lines or paying for games.

"I'm digging being a VIP," Brandon said. "When does the party open to the rest of the town?"

"Noon." Sadie checked the time on her phone. "Thirty minutes from now." She looked at Colette. "We'd better get to the goats before there's a wait to see them."

"First, we all have to do the strength tester." Brandon pointed to a twenty-foot high tower with lines of measurement and a bell at the top. A rubber mallet was poised in a stand next to the target at the bottom.

"I'm in." Colette headed toward the contraption and everyone followed. "Does anyone care if I go first?"

"Have at it," Jason said.

Colette picked up the mallet, took a deep breath and swung. The dinger rose about eleven feet and dropped back down.

Brandon took a turn and sent the dinger a few inches past Colette's. "No way. This has to be rigged."

"Nah," Jason said. "Let me show you how it's done." He swung the mallet, and the dinger traveled close to where it had stopped for Brandon. It *thunked* back to the bottom. "Okay, you're right. It's rigged." He handed the mallet to Sadie. "I mean, as much as I've been working out, there's no way I only got it—"

Bong!

Sadie blew on the head of the mallet as if it were smoking. She grinned. "Not rigged."

"That's my girl," Brandon said.

"So not fair," Jason said. "You kind of cheated."

"How is using my own strength to ring the bell cheating?" Sadie returned the mallet to its stand.

"Because it's . . . you're . . ." Jason searched for a reasonable explanation why Sadie's performance could be discounted. "Okay, it's not cheating. I'm just jealous. You're awesome." He high-fived her.

"Thank you," Sadie said. "And you and Brandon better get something to eat so you can build up your strength."

"Very funny," Jason said. "We'll see you both later."

Jason and Brandon walked to the food truck and found Kyle sitting at a picnic table with two plates of food.

"You're still eating?" Jason asked.

"Not still." Kyle licked his fingers. "Again. This barbecue is amazing."

Brandon gestured toward the second plate. "Is Nessa meeting you here?"

"Nah," Kyle said. "This is all mine. Nessa's visiting her grandparents this weekend."

"Where's Dad?" Jason asked.

Kyle tipped his head toward Poppy's Corn. "He said he had to talk to her about something."

Brandon elbowed Jason. "One new mom, coming up."

"Huh?" Kyle wiped sauce off his cheek with his hand.

"Brandon thinks Dad has a thing for Poppy," Jason said.

"Oh, that. Right." Kyle bit into a rib.

"You mean, you knew Dad had a thing for Poppy?"

"Yeah," Kyle said. "He's been hanging out with her. Coffee meetings, dinner meetings, weekend meetings. There have been a lot of meetings."

"She's who he's been going to see?" Jason thought back about the recent times Dad had "something to do" but hadn't said he was working.

"Yeah." Kyle dropped a bone on his plate and picked up another rib. "And I've heard him talking to her on the phone. Doesn't sound like work talk."

Jason didn't like the idea of anyone joining their family, at least not anytime soon. But at least Dad had someone he liked. As long as she was nice. Jason would be sure to keep an eye on Poppy Johnson to make sure she was nice. His stomach growled.

"Let's eat," Jason said to Brandon. A couple of minutes later, Jason was working his way through a plate of pork, chicken, coleslaw, potato salad, and a slice of white bread. The crowds grew thicker around them and lines formed at each of the attractions.

"VIP time is over," Brandon said.

"Yep," Jason said. "Anything else you want to do?"

"Popcorn."

"Definitely." Jason finished his food, then he and Brandon loaded up on every popcorn flavor. They weaved their way through the crowd to find Sadie and Colette headed their direction. Sadie waved them toward a patch of grass that separated the parking lot from the street.

Jason plopped down on the winter-beige grass next to Colette. "I am stuffed."

"You and me both." Brandon set his goody bag to the side and noticed Sadie and Colette didn't have theirs. "Where are your bags?"

"We put ours in the car." Sadie tilted her face to the sun and closed her eyes.

"Smart," Brandon said.

Sadie took a deep breath and blew it out. "I have to say, it feels good to just hang out and relax. This has been fun today."

"I like the people watching," Colette said. "Oh, there's Ms. Bauer with her wife." She waved at the algebra teacher.

Sadie opened her eyes and waved as well. "And Coach Martel."

Sheriff Gunderson walked by with his family and said hello, and a moment later Jerry Templeman strolled by and waved. Jason wondered about Mr. Templeman's memory but didn't bring the subject up to the rest of the group.

Jason noticed Derek looking their direction but he turned away as soon as Jason caught his eye. *He's probably trying to find a way to talk to Colette.*

Colette held her hand above her eyes to block the sun. "Is that your uncle and Connor?"

Jason looked in the direction she indicated and saw Uncle Alexander steadily pushing through the crowd with Connor at his side. "Yeah. I'm glad they're back." He stood, megaphoned his mouth and yelled Uncle Alexander's name.

Uncle Alexander's head bobbed as he looked for the source of the sound, then homed in on Jason and headed toward them.

"Sadie," said a voice from behind.

Jason turned to see Elly. She wore baggy black pants and a turquoise sweater she'd borrowed from Grandma Lena. Her dark hair hung in a loose ponytail.

Sadie sat up. "Uh, hi. What are you doing here?"

"I wanted to see you, to talk to you," she said. "I hoped I might find you here. Mind if I sit?"

Sadie shrugged and her mom sat on the grass beside her.

"Should we go?" Brandon asked.

"No," Sadie said. "Everyone please stay."

Jason glanced toward Uncle Alexander and saw he'd stopped to have a conversation with the sheriff. Jason sat down again next to Colette.

"Listen," Elly said. "I've been thinking a lot, and I realize I've overreacted about everything. I've been too pushy, too controlling, and I need to step aside and trust that you are in good hands, smart hands. I know Connor would never let anything happen to you, and I see everyone else in your life cares about you and loves you, too. I should have realized it from the very beginning." She tucked a piece of Sadie's hair behind her ears. "I mean, look at you. You're smart and talented, and you're handling every new power you receive with impressive skill. I'm proud of you."

"Uh, thanks," Sadie said.

Elly closed her eyes for a moment. "This is a strange situation for all of us, your friends included." She smiled at them. "And I made it worse by not respecting your life and family and friends who were all here before me. I'm so sorry I didn't realize all of this sooner."

"I . . . uh . . . thanks for saying that." Sadie gazed at her mom's face.

"If you'll give me another chance," Elly stroked Sadie's arm, "I promise I'll be here for you, to help you if you need me, to support you if you need me, and I won't push. Okay?"

"Okay," Sadie said. "Thanks."

"Hug?" Elly asked.

Sadie embraced her mom.

"I do love you, sweetheart."

"Thanks, uh . . . thanks," Sadie said.

Uncle Alexander walked up with Connor. "Hello, everyone," Uncle Alexander said.

Jason stood and gave him a hug. "Glad you're back, Uncle A."

Sadie hugged Connor. "Yeah, we missed you. Did everything go well with your trip?"

"Good in some ways," Connor glanced at Uncle Alexander, "but not as well as we would have liked."

"We need to talk to all of you, Elly included." Uncle Alexander focused on Elly.

"I'll go get Dad and we can meet you back at your place," Jason said. "We were about ready to go, anyway."

"No need," Uncle Alexander said. "It's best if we talk sooner than later. But I would like a little privacy. Let's go around to the back of the building where there aren't any crowds."

"Okay." Jason took Colette's hand and followed Uncle Alexander.

Uncle Alexander turned the corner and continued for another forty feet until they were well away from where anyone might wander by the end of the building. On their left was a cinder block wall about twelve feet high, and to the right was the back of the building with employee-only entrances to the stores. Uncle Alexander stopped, and a broad-shouldered man with ruddy brown hair wearing green khaki pants with a blue peacoat stepped out from behind a dumpster. Even with clothes on he looked like he could easily win a bodybuilding competition.

Heat radiated from Jason's pocket. He released Colette's hand and grabbed the Lex coin. It glowed red.

"Hey, Uncle A—"

A woman with cropped black hair, wearing a black leather jacket and pants appeared behind them and stood next to Connor.

Jason dropped the coin in his pocket and ignited his powers, his arms engulfed in blue and purple bolts.

"I don't think we need that, Jason," Uncle Alexander said, "but be ready, just in case."

"The coin is red." Jason moved out to the side where he had a clear line of sight to both the man and woman.

"I'm not surprised," Uncle Alexander said. "It seems you were right."

"What's going on?" Sadie asked.

"Everyone, please move away from Elly," Uncle Alexander said.

Jason's gut twisted.

Elly's expression morphed to shock. "What? Why?"

Sadie looked from her mom to Uncle Alexander.

Brandon took her hand. "C'mon." He led her to where Colette was now standing, closer to the building and behind Jason. Connor remained in his spot next to the black-haired woman, blocking an easy exit from the area.

Uncle Alexander nodded to the man who then reached behind the dumpster and revealed a tranquilizer gun. He handed it to Uncle Alexander.

"Connor and I were called to an urgent meeting," Uncle Alexander said, "one that I'd very much hoped would have had a different outcome. We spent many hours reviewing data and scans, trying to find some anomaly, some reason the data presented to us was incorrect." He shook his head while he stared at Elly. "But it wasn't."

"What are you talking about?" Elly's eyes were wide, her voice screechy.

Connor's face flushed. "You betrayed us." His lips flattened.

Sadie gasped.

"I didn't," Elly said. "I couldn't. I don't even know what you're talking about."

"A signal was sent to Garrison Devine," Uncle Alexander said. "It originated from my home. The League intercepted it, and I was accused of sending it."

Muscles in Jason's back cinched at the memory of the car waiting to take Uncle Alexander. He squeezed his fists. "Why would they even think that about you?"

"Because of the tear in the Rampart," he said. "They suspected I had leveraged it to bypass the cloak somehow and send a signal. But through questioning, and with additional analysis, they cleared me." His eyes stayed fixed on Elly. "But you, Elly, were not."

Sadie flung a hand over her mouth and muffled a cry.

Uncle Alexander gestured to the man and woman. "Our friends are here to take you into custody."

"No," Elly said. "I did nothing. This is a mistake."

The man and woman moved in.

"I didn't," Elly yelled. "I wouldn't do that to Sadie."

The man and woman grabbed Elly's arms. She struggled to wrench free. "I wouldn't hurt her."

Uncle Alexander raised the tranquilizer gun. "Please, Elly, don't make this worse."

"But you're wrong." She jerked one arm free but the man latched onto her again. "Don't do this."

Sadie took one step forward. "Did you help them find us? That night of the car accident?" She took another step. Her voice boomed. "Are you the reason my dad is dead?"

"No!" Elly's eyes were crazed, wild. A shimmer started around her.

Uncle Alexander aimed. "Elly. Don't."

The shimmer brightened. She yanked her arms free.

"Stop her, Alexander," Connor yelled.

Uncle Alexander fired.

Elly's body morphed as the dart hit. The right side of her body transformed. She staggered forward, her mouth stretched open as if mid-roar, then she fell to the ground unconscious, half-human, half-Yowie.

"Get her secured," Uncle Alexander said.

The man and woman moved in. Uncle Alexander tapped something on his phone. A minute later a silver van drove up, they loaded Elly into the vehicle and hooked her up to monitors. "Her vitals are sketchy," said the black-haired woman. "We need to get her stable before heading back to the League."

Uncle Alexander nodded and the silver van drove away with Sadie's mom.

TWENTY-THREE

Captured

"Where are they taking her?" Sadie asked, the pitch of her voice fighting between anger and alarm.

"To my lab," Uncle Alexander. "Once she's stable, they'll transport her to League headquarters to stand trial."

Sadie's emotions broiled. "But how? How did she—"

"We'll tell you everything," Uncle Alexander said, "but first we need to get someplace safe. We're too exposed outside. Everyone head to Jason's house and we'll discuss next steps. Time is of the essence."

The weight Sadie had set aside knowing the cloak had her hidden while she prepared to defend her Clan now walloped into her.

She wasn't ready.

She. Wasn't. Ready.

"C'mon," Brandon said. "We'll go find Lena and get out of here."

"I'll grab Dad and Kyle," Jason said. "You and Grandma Lena take Della, too. Okay?"

Brandon nodded.

Less than thirty minutes later, everyone had gathered in Jason's living room. Shay sat on the couch next to Sadie.

"So, how?" Sadie asked. "How did Elly send something about me to Garrison Devine? Is the cloak gone?" Her breath felt short, almost absent.

"The cloak remains in place," Connor said. "But she found a loophole in the protection. The cloak will disallow any information about Sadie to be sent from Salton, but Elly was clever. All she sent was a signal as to her own location. No reason for the cloak to stop such a communication. Plus, the cloak has a trust factor built-in which is the reason Alexander and I are able to leave Salton but retain the information that you are here. Your mom, being your mom, and with no questionable history, qualified for the trust factor as well."

"It seems dumb you guys can remember because what if someone, like, captured you and tortured you to get info about Sadie?" Kyle asked.

"The cloak would not allow us to reveal it," Uncle Alexander said.

"Maybe all moms need to be taken off of trust factor lists," Jason said.

"Ahem," Lena said. "Please don't make generalizations."

"Sorry." Jason shook his head. "I didn't mean you." He looked at Sadie. "Or Mamo."

Colette raised her hand. "But wait—if Elly only sent a signal giving her location, Sadie could still be safe."

"I believe the assumption made by Devine's people would be that where there is Sadie's mother, there may also be Sadie," Uncle Alexander said.

Sadie closed her eyes a moment and decided she didn't have time to talk about what had gone wrong. "What do I do now?"

"We," Connor emphasized the word, "have been discussing that exact topic. While the signal to Devine's people was only Elly's location, we must presume you have been compromised. We suspect the only reason no one has shown up yet is because they believed like we did, that Elly was dead. They are likely taking time to verify the signal was valid."

"But it was almost a week ago when the League told you about it," Jason said. "How long will it take Devine's people to verify the signal?"

"We have to assume they've already achieved that objective." Uncle Alexander ran one hand through his hair. "We have to take offensive action."

"How do you know Devine's followers aren't already here?" Colette asked, inching closer to Jason.

"There's no one new in town except Poppy Johnson," Uncle Alexander said, "and she's been here for a couple of months, since before the signal was sent. Plus, the League investigated her background and cleared her."

"And I sense no new Yowie energy in the area either." Connor directed his attention toward Sadie. "Have you sensed anything? Has there been any indication your own ability to recognize Yowie energy has initiated?"

"No," she said. "Nothing seems different." Sadie's mind raced and she forced the next words from her mouth. "Given what's happened, this means I run, leave Salton, right?"

Connor pressed his mouth closed and nodded. "Both of us go. As soon as possible."

"No way," Brandon said. "It's better if we all stay together. Jason and Uncle Alexander, they can help fight off the bad guys."

"We don't know how many of Garrison's loyalists will present themselves," Connor said. "We can't defend against what we don't know. If we leave, we have a better chance at protecting Sadie and Salton."

"I don't need protecting," Sadie said. Shay snuggled close, resting her head-on Sadie's thigh. Sadie's heart clenched at the idea of leaving town, leaving Shay, leaving nearly everyone she loved.

"Of course you don't, my dear. I didn't mean protection in its most basic definition," Connor said. "I meant you, and all of us, need a competitive advantage and relocating is the best way to give us that advantage."

Sadie shuddered inside at the fact that people she cared about were in horrible danger because of her. She sat up, resolute. "Let's go then." Shay's ears perked.

"The League is sending a team to take you to a safe house," Uncle Alexander said. "They'll arrive overnight, and Billy and Divi, the two who took Elly into custody, will stay with us until then. It gives you and Connor some time to pull your things together."

"And Brandon," Connor said.

"Right." Uncle Alexander said.

Brandon's brows scrunched. "Huh? I mean, I want to go with Sadie, but my parents will flip out if I'm not in Salton the next time they visit."

"Actually, your parents insisted you come along," Connor said. "They are the team that's coming for us."

"Excuse me?" Brandon scooted forward.

"It's a long-ish story," Lena said, "one best told by your parents when you talk to them. But the short version is that your parents are part of an elite team within the League who handle covert operations, secret missions and so forth."

"They are . . . my parents are . . ." Brandon shut his eyes and shook his head. "Are you sure you have the right parents? Gwen and Joseph Shaw? They're archeologists. You must be mixing them up with someone else."

A small smile came to Lena's face. "No mix up."

Confusion crossed Brandon's face, but he stayed quiet. A tiny comfort soothed Sadie knowing she wouldn't be leaving Brandon behind.

She stood. She couldn't suppress the building pressure if she didn't get up and give it space. "I guess that's it then," she said, trying to sound bold. "I'll go home and pack." But pack what? Clothes? Pictures? How much could she bring? How much should she bring? What about Nessa? What about everyone? She stroked Shay's head and looked at Uncle Alexander. "Will I ever be back here?"

He cocked his head to the side. "I hope so, but there's no knowing when," he said softly.

A tightness dragged like claws through Sadie's chest. "Will I at least see everyone again before we leave? I'm not ready—" She swallowed hard. "I'm not ready to say goodbye right now."

"We'll make sure of it," Connor said. "Because I'm not ready either."

* * *

A black sedan was parked in front of the house when Sadie arrived home. Divi was in the driver's seat. Sadie assumed

Billy must be positioned somewhere else, like in the backyard, or maybe he was in hiding. Divi stepped out of the car and followed them as Lena pulled into the garage.

Divi introduced herself to Sadie, Lena, and Colette. "We have more personnel arriving from the League. They will be strategically positioned to maximize the protective perimeter. We'll remain in place until Sadie is safely out of Salton."

"Thank you," Lena said. "Has Elly been transported to League headquarters?"

"No," Divi said. "Her condition is unstable. She's returned to human form and is being held in a confined space while the medical team treats her. League members are also guarding the prisoner."

A tangle of feelings slithered through Sadie. Part of her felt bad Elly was hurting, but another part didn't care if she suffered.

"I hope she's better soon so you can get her out of here." Sadie forced aside a sense of loss.

An engine rumbled down the street. Divi spun and placed her hand on a weapon attached at her waist. A mail truck came into view and stopped at the foot of the driveway. Mr. Templeman waved.

"That's just Mr. Templeman," Sadie said to Divi. "He's fine."

Mr. Templeman got out of his vehicle and walked up the driveway. He nodded at Divi, then addressed Lena. "I'm glad you're home. I have a package in the back of my truck that needs a signature, and it's kind of heavy. I much prefer when I can leave those kinds of packages the first time rather than keep lugging them around with me." He chuckled. "Or I should say my back prefers I don't lug them around anymore than necessary."

He handed a scanner to Lena for her to sign. "I'm glad we were here, too," she said. "But I thought you had the day off. I saw you at the celebration."

"That's the usual plan on Saturdays, but another driver got sick and the boss called and asked if I'd finish his shift." Mr. Templeman tucked the stylus into the machine after Lena signed. "Since we'd already had a bit of fun this morning, the wife said she was okay with me earning a little overtime, so here I am." He looked at Sadie. "Mind helping me carry the box up the driveway?"

"No problem," Sadie said following Mr. Templeman to the back of his truck. Divi walked with them. Lena and Colette headed into the house.

"Wait right here," he said as he climbed into the truck. "The hatch door is locked and I need to open it from inside."

Divi scanned the area and remained on alert. A few seconds later, the grumble and screech of the door rolling up filled Sadie's ears. Pain pierced her neck and her vision blurred. Her balance faltered. She grabbed the corner of the truck.

Mr. Templeman leaped over Sadie and landed on Divi. Punches flew. Limbs twisted. Divi wailed.

Splotches of black smeared Sadie's vision. She sank to the ground.

A fur-covered arm jerked her up and tossed her into the truck.

Shadow grew thick as the hatch door slammed.

Sadie lay on her stomach, tried to focus, tried to push herself up but fog washed through and jellied her legs. She fell onto her side. Mr. Templeman's bloody body lay next to her.

Everything went black.

TWENTY-FOUR

Devine

Everyone rushed to Sadie's house after receiving Grandma Lena's call about Sadie's abduction.

"We have to do something." Brandon paced. "We have to find her."

"The League is on high alert," Uncle Alexander said. "All hands are searching for Sadie as we speak."

"And we should be out there with them," Brandon said. "We can find that asshat Templeman."

"I noticed something was wrong with him." Jason relayed the story about Mr. Templeman seeming off and not remembering Jason's name.

"Oh, God." Connor's color drained from his face. "That probably wasn't Jerry Templeman."

"One of Devine's people?" Uncle Alexander asked.

"Worse," Connor said. "There's only one Yowie who can shift to the likeness of any person they choose."

"Devine himself," Uncle Alexander said.

Connor nodded. "This is terrible. I never expected he'd come here himself. He makes others do his dirty work. The bounty on Sadie's head was for someone to bring her to him." He paused. "If Garrison Devine has Sadie—" A gasp cut off his voice.

"Is she dead?" Brandon's eyes were wide. Panicked.

"No, no." Connor paced the room. "He wants her powers. He wants to take the Calling." He swallowed. "Garrison needs her alive for that."

"And *how* does he do that?" Grandma Lena asked. "What does he need to do to make that happen?"

"Uh, he needs time." Connor pushed his hands through his hair. "And he needs to drain her." His gaze flicked across the faces of everyone in the room. "Like a blood transfusion. He needs her blood inside his veins."

Jason's insides oozed with nausea. "I should have gone with her. I shouldn't have left her alone."

"I can say the same for all of us," Uncle Alexander said. "But we thought Sadie was protected. We had League personnel in place at her home, and let's not forget that Sadie is no wilting flower."

"Yeah, but—"

"No buts, Jason," Grandma Lena said. "We have no time for assigning blame. We must help Sadie."

"But how?" Colette asked. "We have no idea where she is."

"And why didn't you sense Devine was in town?" Jason asked Connor.

"He's powerful," Connor said. "He must be able to conceal his Yowie energy, something he's not been able to do before."

"Which may explain why he is the only Yowie here," Uncle Alexander said. "He can hide in plain sight."

"Seems like a bunch of guessing to me." Jason crossed his arms. "We need a plan. Now."

The front door opened and Jason's dad walked in. "I dropped Della at her friend's house. On the way here I passed an accident with a mail truck so I stopped. It was Jerry's truck."

A flood of foreboding swept through Jason.

"Did they find Sadie?" Kyle asked.

"No," Dad said. "But they found Jerry in the back. He'd been beaten to death."

Colette gasped.

"So, Devine transferred himself and Sadie to another vehicle." Uncle Alexander stared at the floor as if he were eyeing a diagram. "Where did he take her?"

"We have no idea what type of vehicle they're in, or which direction they're going," Connor said. "This is an impossible situation."

Uncle Alexander looked up. "Perhaps not. What about the Calling?"

"Sadie will lose it all to Garrison," Connor said.

"No, not that." Uncle Alexander pulled his laptop out of his bag. "The Calling Compendium—it said something about a risk to the candidate."

Connor's eyes widened. "Yes, yes. When the candidate is at risk, the influx of the powers from the Calling will increase exponentially to better enable the candidate to defend themselves."

"Which means every minute that passes, Sadie gets stronger? More powerful?" Brandon asked.

"Yes," Uncle Alexander said.

"And that also means Devine will want to transfer her powers to himself sooner rather than later," Grandma Lena said, "before she becomes strong enough to defeat him."

"So, he's still in Salton, or at least near Salton," Jason said. Shay sat next to his leg.

"I believe so." Uncle Alexander pinched the bridge of his nose. "At least, I hope so."

"Let's say they are still in town." Brandon shrugged. "What do we do? Can Finn and Shay track Sadie?"

Shay alerted at the mention of her name.

Uncle Alexander shook his head. "Devine and Sadie drove away. The dogs are able to follow the scent of the truck, but that doesn't give us any new information since the truck was abandoned."

Connor dragged his hands down his face. "There is one thing that might work if she'll help us."

"Sadie's mom . . ." Brandon dropped to a seat on the arm of the couch. "She has that connection."

"Like she'd help us." Jason almost yelled the words. "She's why Sadie's in trouble in the first place."

"I'd like to talk to her," Connor said. "See if she feels any regret. Or perhaps I can appeal to her motherly instinct, her sense of family."

"What sense of family?" Jason backhanded the air.

"Son," Dad said. "I get why you're upset with her—"

"Because Sadie could die and it's Elly's fault," Jason said. "Yeah, it's obvious why I'm upset with her."

"She might be our only hope of finding Sadie in time," Uncle Alexander said.

"But wouldn't we have to let her out to follow her homing beacon or whatever she has that's connected to

THE FORGE OF BONDS

Sadie?" Jason said. "What if Elly gets away and Sadie still dies? What about that?"

Colette covered her face with her hands. Kyle put his arm around her shoulder.

"It's take a chance with Elly or cross our fingers and hope Sadie receives enough of the Calling to fight her way out on her own before it's too late." Uncle Alexander clasped his hands behind his back and fixed his eyes on Jason. "What do you think we should do?"

Jason's lips pursed. His muscles tensed. "Fine. Connor should talk to Elly." He faced Connor. "But I'm going with you and I'm not letting her out of my sight, not for a second." He grabbed onto the coin in his pocket.

"Wait." Colette's brow furrowed, and she walked over to Jason. "The day you talked to Mr. Templeman, who you thought was Mr. Templeman, and he was behaving strangely." She paused a moment. "Wasn't that the same day you met Elly for the first time?"

Jason ran the memory through his mind. He had met Elly. And he had almost bumped into Mr. Templeman on the way out the door. "Yeah, that was the same day."

"So the coin . . ." Colette said.

"The coin was warning me about fake Mr. Templeman?" One corner of Jason's mouth ticked up. "But Elly sent the signal so the coin could have been freaking out about both of them. That's why it got hot." He looked at Uncle Alexander. "Elly for sure sent the signal, right?"

He nodded. "Except, by the time you met her, Garrison Devine was already here. That is if we do believe the Jerry Templeman you encountered that day was Devine."

"Which means Elly sent the signal at *least* a day or two before then," Connor added. "Would the coin alert on something that had already happened, where it was too late for Jason to resolve?"

"We're still learning about the Lex coin," Uncle Alexander said to Connor. "But we have no reason not to trust its judgment."

"Let's give it another test," Connor said. "Or rather, let's give Elly another test and see what the coin says when we go talk to her now. Fingers crossed it changes in her presence and gives us a green light to trust her."

✳ ✳ ✳

Jason, Shay, and Connor went with Uncle Alexander to see Elly. They walked into Uncle Alexander's house from the garage. Finn rushed to them and whined, then dashed away with Shay.

"Is it me, or did Finn just signal that something's up?" Jason asked.

"It seems quiet enough," Connor said.

"Elly is being held downstairs, so I wouldn't expect any activity up here," Uncle Alexander said, keeping his voice low. "They're keeping her restrained and sedated for transport tomorrow morning. We'll ask the doctor to wake her." He peered out of the kitchen into the living room. "But yes, Finn seems to be signaling that something is wrong. Be ready."

Finn and Shay sat at the closet-elevator door. Finn scratched, wanting to be let in.

Uncle Alexander opened the elevator and stepped inside with the dogs. Jason and Connor followed. The doors closed, the elevator lowered, and the doors opened to another quiet scene. The lights were off.

Hairs on Jason's neck spiked as did Shay's hackles.

Connor and Uncle Alexander stood taller, alert.

Jason activated his powers.

Uncle Alexander bolted from the elevator, flipped on a light, and they all rushed into the lab.

A doctor lay unconscious on the floor.

Unlatched straps dangled from the bed.

A bloody scalpel sat on a nearby tray with more blood soaked into the sheets.

Elly was gone.

Glass shattered from down the hall.

"I've got this. You help the doc." Jason raced toward the noise. He spotted a woman's leg as it kicked off a chair and pulled up through the broken basement window. "Elly," Jason yelled. He scrambled to set the chair upright, jump up, and lift himself out of the window, careful to avoid shards of glass still mounted in the window's frame.

He stood, scanned the area, and spied Elly with another person running in front of her about to scale a wooden fence. Jason yelled her name. He ignited his powers and sprinted toward her.

He could stop her. He could finish her. He could kill her for what she did to Sadie.

Jason set his jaw and punched the idea aside.

He would bring her back. He would make her help them.

Jason aimed.

Elly activated her invisibility.

He fired where she'd been and hit no one. Jason charged forward looking for a track, a sign, any indication of where she was or where she was going. He looked over the fence. He looked beyond the fence.

But Elly and her accomplice had escaped.

✳ ✳ ✳

Back in the lab a few minutes later, Jason handed the doctor an ice pack for the lump on his head.

"What happened?" Uncle Alexander asked.

"Your nephew, Jason," the doctor said. "He buzzed in and said you'd sent him to get something from the prisoner."

Uncle Alexander pointed at Jason. "This is my nephew."

"Oh . . ." The doctor shook his head. "A different kid came to the door. But he knew you, Alexander, and he knew to say his name was Jason. He even knew the prisoner's name. I had no reason not to believe him."

"Why are you here alone?" Connor asked.

"It was all hands on deck after the abduction," the doctor said. "The prisoner was both sedated and restrained so it seemed reasonable to send everyone else after the kidnapper."

"Elly must have been under-sedated," Connor said. "It could be Sadie's recent supercharge to Elly's healing helped Elly rapidly process the drug from her system."

"That doesn't matter now," Jason said. He racked his brain about who he had seen with her, who could have shown up at Uncle Alexander's. Figuring it out might help them find Elly, and find Sadie. The person he saw had seemed familiar. "Did Garrison Devine come here? Posing as me?"

"If that were the case, he would have looked like you, too," Connor said.

"Then who?" The realization slammed into Jason's mind. "Derek. It was Derek."

Uncle Alexander was taken aback. "How could it be him?"

"I saw Derek watching us today at the grand opening," Jason said. "He's been following us around, trying to get close to Colette. He probably followed us behind the building."

"But why would he come—" Uncle Alexander stopped himself. "He saw Elly start shifting to Yowie. He knows who she is."

"And he decided to bust her out," Jason said. "Just like he did when Ash held her hostage at the barn."

"He's a pain in our ass." Connor crossed his arms. "But he's a clever little miscreant, I'll give him that."

"What about the blood?" Jason gestured to the stained sheets. "Did he cut her? Or someone else?" He glanced around the room wondering for a half-second if they'd missed another body.

Uncle Alexander walked over and examined the bed. He bent close to the sheets and scanned them from bottom to top. He eyed the scalpel in the tray. "Hold on." He picked up a long pair of tweezers, flicked the scalpel aside, and lifted something out of the tray that looked like a grain of rice. "What do we have here?"

Connor stepped forward and peered at the tiny item. "A GPS tracker?" He snapped his fingers. "That must be how she notified Devine of her whereabouts."

"Why remove it now?" Uncle Alexander twisted his wrist to see all sides of the tracker. "And why hasn't the League intercepted a signal before this week? She's been living nearby for a few months at least."

"If it's a Yowie tracker, it could work like your Yowie energy thing," Jason said. "The tracker didn't send a signal because, if Elly didn't know who she was, then the tracker didn't know what signal to send."

Connor's eyebrows raised. "You're a clever young man yourself, Jason. I think you're right."

"Then the signal from the tracker is automatic," Uncle Alexander said. "She didn't purposely send anything."

"Doesn't mean she didn't realize what was happening," Jason said. "The bad guys showed up and caused the car accident that killed Sadie's dad, but Elly survived. And the bad guys have shown up in Salton, and Elly's gotten away again. She probably had Derek cut the tracker out because we knew she'd sent a signal and was afraid the League would track her, too."

"A definite possibility," Uncle Alexander said.

"What's more pressing now is that, since Elly has escaped," Connor quashed a shake in his voice, "we've lost our chance at finding Sadie."

"Maybe not," Jason said.

"What are you suggesting?" Uncle Alexander asked.

"Colette," he said. "Derek likes Colette." He hated saying the words aloud. "If he's with Elly, maybe Colette can get him to tell her where they are."

"At the very least, we can verify Derek's phone is on, and perhaps the League can track the signal." Uncle Alexander took his own phone from his pocket and contacted the League of Governors.

✳ ✳ ✳

Sadie's head throbbed. A glare of light burned through her eyelids. She squinted and blinked her eyes open to see mint-colored cinderblock walls and a nearby counter lined with beakers and microscopes. She was in Ms. Feinstein's biology classroom.

"There's our little princess."

Sadie jerked at the sound of the voice. She tried to sit up, to get away, but she was strapped to a long table. It bounced on the floor beneath her. Something clicked into place around her head.

A white-bearded face with matching white hair loomed over Sadie and smiled. "How is our 'chosen one' doing, hmm?" The man used air quotes around the words "chosen one." "I'd say it's nice to meet you, Sadie Callahan, but it's really not. Though it *is* nice to know I have found you, trapped you, and now I will finally stop you from taking everything away from me." He sneered and released a one-syllable laugh.

Sadie's skin chilled. "You're Garrison Devine."

"I suppose you want praise for figuring out the obvious," he scoffed.

The memory of Mr. Templeman lying in the mail truck streaked through her mind. "Please don't hurt anyone else."

He *tsked.* "Besides you? That's up to everyone else. As long as Connor and the rest of your friends stay out of my way, they'll be fine. At least for now." He tilted his head. "Unless you're talking about your friend Ash? I'm afraid it's too late for him."

"What did you do to Ash?" Sadie braced herself but Devine didn't offer details.

"You should be careful about who you associate with," Devine said. "Though I suppose I should be thankful for Ash or I might not have found you."

Sadie started to shake her head but something rigid minimized her range. "I barely know him. He's not my friend."

"I believe you," he said. "Not that it matters." Devine walked to the counter. Metal clanged against metal as he moved things Sadie couldn't see. "My people found Ash because he was offering to sell a Yowie hunt on the dark web. And do you know where he offered this Yowie hunt?" Devine turned around and faced Sadie. He was holding a syringe with a long needle attached. "Right here in Salton."

Sadie pulled against her restraints and felt a slight give in the fabric.

"My people apprehended him and his father," Devine said. "No one selling the death of a Yowie goes unpunished."

"What . . . is Ash okay?"

"Hmm . . . depends on how you define 'okay.'" Devine swabbed alcohol over a vein in Sadie's arm. "He's alive, so I guess there's that. And he's paying for his crimes against the Yowie."

Sadie's stomach tightened but she couldn't think about Ash. She needed to figure out how to escape. Invisibility wouldn't help her while she was strapped to the table. Her strength seemed weak, but she felt it getting stronger. Should she shift to Yowie? Did she have a chance against Garrison Devine?

"How does your head feel?" Devine asked. "A headache I'm guessing, given the amount of drug I used to take you down. I might have overdone it." He wagged his finger. "Also, I wouldn't struggle too much if you know what's good for you. For both of us, really."

Fresh anxiety oozed through her. "Why?"

"Because," he pressed a finger into her forehead, removed a brace, and turned her head slightly right. Pain zinged into her skin and he returned her head to center. "Razors. A fun little contraption I rigged to ensure you don't go Yowie on me. You shift, you receive death by a thousand, well, in this case there are only about twenty, razors. But twenty of my razors is plenty to slice off the back of your skull."

Sadie closed her eyes and tried to think.

"There's no getting out of this." He sunk a needle into her arm. "Thanks to our dear Elly, and bad boy Ash, you and I will be together forever."

"Elly is not 'dear' to me," Sadie seethed.

"I hardly think she deserves such disdain from her own daughter." Devine removed the syringe to reveal a thin tube with a clamp attached to the needle. "You're going a bit over the top with the whole teenagers-with-attitude act, don't you think?"

"Thanks to her, I'm strapped to a table with razors around my brain. So no, I'm not over the top." Sadie closed one fist. Fabric rent slightly under her pressure.

He smiled. "But your dear old mom knew not what she did."

Sadie gritted her teeth. "She sent you a signal."

"Actually, I sent me a signal." He rolled up one sleeve of the white shirt he wore. "When my team chased down your parents like prey, I'd given them orders to implant your parents with tracking devices, just in case they shifted and somehow escaped. Both trackers were active during the attack but soon went dark, so I believed your parents to be dead. How wrong I was." He jabbed a needle in a vein on his arm like he'd done to Sadie. "When we received the signal from Elly's tracker not too long ago, I dismissed it as an error. But when we discovered Ash and his advertisement for a Yowie hunt in Salton, the same location whence came your mother's tracking signal, well, that piqued my interest."

"They didn't give me a tracker?"

"You were too small, too low inside the car to get a clear shot," he said. "Plus, you were a baby. Hardly a threat."

Wooden legs screeched against the floor as Devine dragged Ms. Feinstein's desk closer to Sadie. "Your mail delivery person—Jerry? He made an excellent cover, allowing me to explore the area for a few days undetected. Until he started telling people about time he'd lost."

Poor Mr. Templeman. Sadie wished she could have kept him out of this, wished she could have saved him. "Where's everyone else?" Sadie asked.

"My team you mean?" He smirked. "I came here only to see if Elly was alive. If she was, and if she led me to you, then all the better. But I had zero reasons to fear your sickly mother. And Connor's well beyond his prime. He's more likely to scurry off into the woods like a scared rabbit than take a chance with me. As for you?" He spread his arms wide. "We both know how that turned out."

New pain intensified in Sadie's head and spread down her spine, and her legs. She grimaced and held her breath for a moment.

Devine gaped at the ceiling. "Do spare me your tears. As the Calling's candidate, you must have a little more courage than some pathetic teenager." He'd read Sadie's expression as an oncoming cry.

The pain receded and Sadie glared. "I won't be crying over you."

"Thank god. This process will take long enough without you sniveling in my ear the whole time."

"What process?" Sadie eyed the tubes as Devine moved closer.

"The transfer of powers from you to me, your blood with mine," he said.

"But blood types, what if we don't match?" Sadie latched onto a reason to make Devine stop. "You could die."

"Hardly," Devine said. "I've had the power of the Calling for a long time. There's very little that can kill me now."

"Something can," Sadie said. "And something will."

He laughed. "Hoping for your Rampart Guard friends to barge in and save the day?" he asked. "Guard bolts are like mosquito bites to me. Besides, no one will find us in the school during the weekend, tucked away so cozily in the biology room." He connected more tubes, then twisted a valve. Blood flowed out of Sadie's arm and tracked toward a machine connecting her to Devine. "Might as well get comfy." He laid down on the desk.

Sadie concentrated on where the needle entered her arm. She healed the spot and stopped the flow of blood.

Devine sat up and frowned. "Don't make me do this the hard way." He yanked the needle out of her arm. "Or I'll just cut your throat and be done with it." He growled the words.

Before Sadie could respond, the door at the front of the biology room ripped open and Elly, in Yowie form, barreled at Garrison Devine.

More pain wrenched through Sadie.

Elly slammed Devine into the wall.

Breath returned to Sadie's lungs. She strained against her bindings.

Devine shifted. His Yowie form was huge, about eighteen inches taller than Elly, black fur, yellow eyes, hands like laptops with fingers. He walloped Elly in the ribs.

Elly jumped to her feet and jammed into Devine, shoving him into the hall.

Sadie flexed her arms attempting to tear her bindings.

"Stop," a voice whispered in her ear. "I've got this."

Derek moved into Sadie's line of sight.

Sadie sucked in a breath. "Get out of here, Derek. Now."

"Not before I help you." Derek's fingers flew over the buckles on the straps that held Sadie's arms and legs.

Glass shattered in the hallway.

Derek released the contraption of razors and tossed it aside.

Yowie roars bellowed outside the door.

Sadie leaped off the table. "Thank you." She pointed Derek toward the door at the back of the room. "Now run. Get out of here." Sadie turned, her body tingled, and she shifted to Yowie. She rushed into the hallway to help her mother.

Devine had Elly pinned on the ground, his hands around her throat.

Sadie charged. Broken glass pierced her feet. She dove into Devine's side and knocked him off her mother, crashing with a clang into a bank of lockers.

Devine roared and threw Sadie off. She scrambled to her feet, her height nearly matching his. He started toward her until movement near Elly caught his attention. Derek was with her, trying to help her stand, trying to stabilize her as she staggered taller.

Rage engulfed Devine's face. He marched toward Derek.

Sadie rushed to stop him.

Devine swung his huge arm into Derek's torso and launched him down the hallway. A crack sounded when Derek's head hit the floor.

Elly roared and sank her teeth into Devine's shoulder. He grabbed fur on the top of her head and yanked her back. Chunks of furry flesh tore away as Elly fell.

Sadie sprang and side-kicked Devine sending him sliding through the cafeteria doors. She started in after him when another wave of pain flooded her senses, her nerves, her lungs. She dropped to her knees.

A second later he had her in his grasp. He flung her body across the lunchroom. She slammed into tables, banged into chairs, then skidded on her back to a stop near the far wall. Her head throbbed. Blood ran into one eye.

His feet pounded toward her.

She scrambled up and activated her invisibility.

He stopped.

She scurried sideways.

"I can still hear you." He hurled a metal chair.

Sadie ducked and held her breath. *Wait—he's talking, while in his Yowie form.* Sadie didn't know it was even possible to speak while Yowie, other than with grunts and growls.

Devine walked toward her. "Even invisible, you can't escape me."

Sadie calmed her heart and crawled on all fours, weaving through tables, building distance.

Devine continued forward. Sadie moved behind him.

"How long do you think you can keep this up?" he asked, looking toward a wall where he thought Sadie stood.

"You're inexperienced, you're low on energy, you don't have what it takes to sustain invisibility. Not now, and not ever once I'm done with you."

Sadie scanned the cafeteria for weapons.

Chairs. Tables. Plastic trays. All of them could work against her. But what would work against Garrison Devine?

The doors to the cafeteria opened and Elly stumbled in.

No, no, no. Sadie hurried toward her.

Elly braced herself on the wall and roared. She limped toward Devine, one foot jutting out at an odd angle. Her hand smeared blood in its wake.

Devine sneered and stormed toward her.

Sadie raced to beat him to Elly. She circled her arms around Elly's waist.

Devine yelled and swung his arm.

Sadie pulled Elly back and immediately she disappeared in Sadie's arms.

Devine's punch passed through, connecting with nothing. His eyes widened.

Sadie stifled a gasp. She dragged Elly away silently with no mass to cause friction or sound. She tucked Elly behind the serving counter and whispered for her to stay there and stay quiet.

Sadie glanced up to see Devine eying the floor and heading her direction. *But how?* She examined her limbs. Blood oozed from her feet. She jumped up and ran.

Elly's Yowie form reappeared seconds after Sadie released her hold but Devine paid no attention. He was hunting Sadie.

Sadie flung lunch tables and chairs. They bounced off Devine like rubber balls on hard pavement.

She ran faster.

He closed distance.

She scrambled over shelving.

He swiped but found nothing to grab. "What the hell?" He roared and chased faster.

She ducked under a checkout counter but he followed bloody splats right to her.

He pawed where she'd been seconds before but missed. "Give it up. This is useless," he yelled.

She ran and willed her feet to heal. The bleeding stopped. Her footprints no longer revealed her location.

But she didn't have the fighting strength to defeat Devine one-on-one.

She needed an advantage.

She slammed him with another table but it barely registered against his body. He batted it away and rushed forward.

Sadie dodged and scanned the room again.

Her mom lay unconscious.

Devine was only feet away from Sadie.

A fire extinguisher hung on the far wall.

Fresh adrenaline flooded her body. The extinguisher had the weight and heft she needed. It could give her a chance.

She started toward it. Tingling in her body diminished.

No, no, no. Don't quit on me now.

She ran as hard as she could. She had to get that fire extinguisher. She had to make it a weapon.

The shag of her fur materialized.

Pain racked Sadie as he hit her from the side. She flew and slammed into a trophy cabinet. Glass and metal and ribbons rained around her. Blood filled her mouth.

Devine grabbed the back of her neck and banged her head onto the cabinet's ledge. "Enough."

Dizziness swathed her, but Sadie swept Devine's legs from under him. She jumped and made another push to get to the extinguisher.

Devine grabbed her arms, wrenching them behind her.

She launched from her thighs. His grip released as he flew upward. He crashed onto a lunch table that buckled under his weight, then he bounded to his feet.

Sadie met him head-on.

He backhanded her, but she dodged most of the impact and rammed him skyward.

He landed, recovered, and came at her again. No weaker, no slower.

She made another dash for the extinguisher. She yanked it from the wall.

Her head jerked back and shards of pain shot through her side. The metal leg of a chair jutted from her rib cage. The extinguisher clanged onto the floor.

He slammed her into the wall.

Her lungs shrunk in her chest but she flung him off.

He came at her again and pinned her in a corner.

Sadie clawed at his arms.

He punched her down.

She gasped for air and spun him around.

"Sadie!" Uncle Alexander yelled. Blue bolts hit the wall next to her.

"Don't," she heard Jason say. "You could hit her."

"We have to do something," Uncle Alexander said.

Finn and Shay raced over and chomped their fangs into Devine's calves. He howled and swatted. They released and dodged his blow.

THE FORGE OF BONDS

Sadie tumbled sideways and Devine was on her again. He jammed on the metal rod.

Through blackening pain, she sucked in a breath. She couldn't see the dogs. She couldn't see anything but Devine's enraged face.

"Jason," she yelled, then sucked in another lung full of air. "Skeet!" She exploded power from her legs and rocketed Devine upward.

The room flared with a turquoise glow. A fireball of purple and blue bolts blazed into Devine, veering him sideways like a pinball off a bumper. He smacked high on the far end of the lunchroom wall and slid down hard, unconscious, maybe dead, one arm detached and flopping next to him.

Sadie collapsed on the floor. Her eyes blurred. Jason and the dogs hurried to her side. Shay licked her face and whimpered.

"My mom," she wheezed. "And Derek."

"Connor's with your mom," Jason said. "And my dad is helping Derek."

"The dogs?" she asked.

"Both fine. Shay's upset you're hurt." His eyes skittered across Sadie's injuries. "What should I do?"

Uncle Alexander came over and knelt next to her. "Should we take out the rod?"

Sadie nodded.

"No," Jason said. "On television shows, the doctors always say it's worse to take things out unless they're at a hospital."

"Sadie's different," Uncle Alexander said. "Hold her still."

Jason folded himself over Sadie's broad shoulders and Uncle Alexander gripped the metal rod protruding from her side. "Ready?"

He didn't wait for an answer. He wrenched the bar from Sadie's body.

Shock jolted through her as if Uncle Alexander had zapped her himself. But seconds later the pain receded, her breath returned, and the cut on her lip sealed, no longer spilling blood into her mouth.

"Are you okay?" Jason asked. He scrunched his eyes and held them shut for a moment.

"Yeah." Sadie nodded and sat up slowly. "But how are you?"

"Just dizzy for a second," he said. "I'm good."

"You're certain?" Uncle Alexander asked, his face concerned.

"Positive," Jason said.

"Okay." Sadie glanced at her fur-covered body. "I'm going to need some clothes before I shift back to human."

"Hold on." Jason dashed off and returned a minute later with Salton High sweatpants and a sweatshirt. "I gave Connor some for Elly, too."

"Did you steal those?" Uncle Alexander asked with a disappointed expression.

"Given how the school looks right now," Jason said, "stolen sweatpants is the last thing we should be worrying about."

"Fair point." Uncle Alexander helped Sadie to her feet.

"Will the League be able to restore everything before Monday?" Sadie asked.

"Yes," Uncle Alexander said. "In fact, they've already begun the work in the biology room, and another team is on their way to collect Devine's body."

"He's dead?" Sadie asked.

Uncle Alexander nodded. "No pulse. Heavy blood loss."

Sadie was surprised only a small sense of relief soothed her anxiety about the Calling and Garrison Devine.

Jason gawked up at her.

"What?" she asked.

"It's just, the fact that you can talk when you're all," he flicked his hand up and down, "furry and Yowie and everything. It's kind of freaky. But cool freaky."

"I thought the same thing when he talked." She gestured to where Devine's body was laying.

But Garrison Devine was gone. Only his Yowie arm remained.

TWENTY-FIVE

Run

Sadie shifted to human, rushed to her mom's side, and gathered her in her arms. She wiped blood from Elly's eyes.

Connor reached across Elly and squeezed Sadie's shoulder. "Thank God, you're okay."

"I'm glad you all got here when you did," Sadie patted Elly's face. "Can you hear me?"

Elly didn't respond.

"After what you just went through, I'm not sure you'll have enough energy to heal her," Connor said.

"I have to try." Sadie closed her eyes and focused on Elly's body, focused on Elly's wounds. Warmth caressed Sadie's skin. She sensed light flowing from herself to her mother and sent it searching for injuries needing repair.

"Whoa," Connor said.

Sadie opened her eyes to see an aura of white enveloping her mom, sinking into her skin. Ripples of light undulated around her. Sadie pointed at her mother's obvious injury where her foot appeared like it had been attached backward. "Please realign her foot with her ankle" she said to Connor.

"But the pain, it will be tremendous," he said.

"No, it's okay."

Connor bit his bottom lip for a second then placed both of his hands on Elly's wonky appendage. "You're sure?"

"Yes," Sadie said. "Just turn it until it points the right direction."

Connor grimaced and turned Elly's foot. It slid into place. Elly didn't flinch.

"Is she in a coma?" he asked.

"Just a healing sedative," Sadie said. "She'll be okay."

Jason's dad ran into the lunchroom. "Sadie. Derek needs you."

She leaped up. "Stay with my mom." Connor nodded and Sadie ran into the hallway.

A League doctor knelt next to Derek. "He's in bad shape. He has internal bleeding, and I'm worried about brain trauma. We need to get him to a hospital, but it's dangerous to move him."

Sadie grasped one of Derek's hands, the same one she'd healed when he'd cut it open in school. She laid her other hand on his forehead and closed her eyes. She envisioned white light flooding his body. She directed the warmth to travel through him, to search for damage, to hem gashes, repair holes, rebuild tissues. A moment later, her light faded and she looked at the doctor.

The doctor checked Derek's vital signs. "Better," she said. "We can safely transport him."

"Good," Sadie said. "I can't be sure I found everything."

"We'll take it from here," the doctor said.

Divi stepped out of the biology room. "Ms. Callahan? I believe these belong to you." Divi extended her hand and dropped Sadie's hawk's eye pendant and the charm bracelet into Sadie's open palm. The chains were broken but all the pieces and parts were present.

"Thank you!" Sadie embraced her.

"Oh, uh, you're welcome," Divi said, barely hugging back. "Happy to assist."

Sadie released her. "Any sign of Garrison Devine?"

"Nothing," Divi said. "But the amount of blood loss was significant so he can't have gone far. We won't give up searching."

"Sadie." Jason walked down the hall with Uncle Alexander.

Divi excused herself and returned to the biology room.

"Ready to go?" Jason asked. "There's nothing else we can do here."

"My mom—" She gestured toward the lunchroom.

"They're loading her now to take her back to my place," Uncle Alexander said.

More League personnel scurried by and lifted Derek onto a gurney. "What about him?" Sadie asked.

"They're taking him to the hospital," Uncle Alexander said.

"And his memory?" Jason asked. "What about that?"

"He needs to get stronger first," Sadie said. "But Ash isn't . . . well, he isn't necessarily a problem anymore." She relayed what she'd heard from Devine. "If he was telling the truth about Ash, and Derek still needs his memory wiped, Ash won't be here to trigger any memories."

Uncle Alexander's face fell. "I don't know why Devine would lie about having Ash, and it does explain why the League hasn't been able to find him. But no kid deserves the kind of punishment doled out under Devine's rule."

"Can we get him out of there somehow?" Jason asked.

"I'll talk to Connor about it," Uncle Alexander said. "But given how things are being run, it will be tough to free Ash."

"I hope we can help him," Jason said.

Uncle Alexander nodded. "I'll let you know."

Jason turned to Sadie. "Hold on. What do you mean *if* Derek still needs his memory wiped?"

"He helped me," Sadie said. "And he's saved Elly . . . my mom . . . more than once. Maybe it's okay he remembers everything."

"No, no way." Jason shook his head. "Not Derek."

"We'll discuss that topic with Connor." Uncle Alexander directed them toward the exit.

"No discussion." Jason followed his uncle. "Derek cannot be in on everything."

"He's already in on everything," Sadie said. "I say we let him keep being in on everything."

"Not gonna happen. Connor has to see it my way." Jason pushed on the exit door and the three of them stepped out into the waning dusk of day.

✳ ✳ ✳

Jason sat in Uncle Alexander's living room with Colette, Uncle Alexander, Connor, and Grandma Lena, all waiting for word on Elly. Dad and Kyle had gone to pick up Della and head home. The dogs snoozed on their beds near the fireplace.

"I'd like to have a chat with Elly, once she's strong enough," Connor said, "but I sense it won't be a problem to let Derek keep his memories of all that's happened."

Jason groaned and he slouched into Uncle Alexander's couch.

"In fact," Connor continued, "given that Elly's relationship with Derek has been a highlight of his life as of late, it may be kind of us to leave him with his memories, if we trust he will keep them close."

"Yes," Colette said. "That would be the kind thing to do."

Jason crossed his arms. "I totally disagree."

"We'll follow your lead, Connor." Uncle Alexander widened his eyes at Jason.

"Of course," Connor added, "this is all dependent on whether any of this is resolved before we have to leave."

A tightness constricted Jason's chest. "Do you still have to go?"

"I'm afraid so," Connor said. "Garrison is out there. He's injured now, but he'll recover. We're sitting ducks here. If he doesn't leave Salton while he heals, the cloak has no opportunity to erase his knowledge of Sadie being here. And even if he leaves, well, given his power has grown stronger than we knew, we can't trust that the cloak can override his will to remember."

"But Sadie got a bunch of new powers today," Jason said. "Doesn't that mean she's ready?"

"Her powers increased exponentially." Connor took a deep breath. "Her healing is unmatched, as is her strength, and the fact that her invisibility extends to the pseudo-elimination of her mass, *and* the mass of someone she's in contact with, well . . ." He blubbered nonsense words while he searched for what to say. "It's beyond measure. I can't even begin to categorize it. More work needs to be done to understand her limitations. Time will tell."

"Sadie is outstanding," Grandma Lena said. "Even without powers. But we'll miss both of you a great deal." A sad smile came to her face.

"And us, you," Connor said.

The closet elevator opened and Sadie stepped out with Brandon.

"How is Elly?" Grandma Lena asked.

"She's good," Sadie said. "Sore. And tired. But good."

"Even her foot looks normal." Brandon thumbed at Sadie. "She tried to tell me Elly's foot pointed south when it should have been pointed north, but I don't believe it. She doesn't even have a scratch."

Sadie playfully smacked him on the arm. "She also wanted everyone to know she asked Derek to cut the tracker out of her back. She's afraid he's in trouble. I told her not to worry about it."

"What happens to Elly now?" Colette asked.

"If it's okay with Connor," Sadie said, "she should come with us. I mean, if she wants to. We have to ask her first."

Connor smiled. "I think that's a wonderful idea."

"Oh, and before I forget . . ." Sadie moved to sit near Colette. She held out her hands. "May I try again with your arm?"

"Uh, sure." Colette settled her long-injured arm in Sadie's hands.

Sadie closed her eyes. A white glow lit in her palms. It brightened and flowed around and into Colette's arm.

"Oh my gosh." Colette swallowed. "Oh my gosh," she said again, her eyes blinking rapidly.

A moment later, the light receded and Sadie opened her eyes. "How is it?"

Colette bent her arm and sucked in a breath when her range of motion proved normal. She straightened her arm with the same result. "Oh my gosh." She skimmed her fingers across the skin around her elbow searching for the gnarl of misfit bone that had limited her before. "It's gone. You fixed it." She stared in wonder at Sadie and her eyes filled with tears. "You fixed it. Thank you." She threw her arms around Sadie's neck.

"You're welcome," Sadie said. "And I will miss you so much."

"Me you, too," Colette said.

"Oh, stop now," Grandma Lena said with a whimper in her voice. "You have me on the edge of an ugly cry, and no one needs to see that."

Jason fought his own body's determination to conjure tears. "We can still text. And talk online. We'll share pictures and stuff."

"We can't," Connor murmured. "Hopefully, that will change. But for now, we need to go dark until we understand how best to proceed."

Jason's spirits sank. It was hard enough to have to say goodbye to Sadie and Brandon, but that he couldn't talk to them? Couldn't text them? Wouldn't know if they were okay? He looked at Sadie. "Promise to change that, as soon as you can." Jason bit down hard to block a threatening cry. "You have to."

"I promise," Sadie said. "I promise." Her eyes watered.

Brandon's phone vibrated and he checked the screen. "My parents will be here in two hours and we leave at dawn." He sniffed and returned his phone to his pocket.

Jason's lungs felt like spent balloons.

This was it.

This was the end.

In only a few hours' time, Sadie and Brandon would be gone.

✳ ✳ ✳

Before leaving Uncle Alexander's house, Sadie talked to Elly about joining them on the road, away from Salton. Elly was overjoyed at the invitation but the League doctor, not yet assured of Sadie's healing powers, didn't want Elly to travel so soon. Instead, the League would later arrange a rendezvous.

Connor and Elly also discussed Derek and decided to keep his memory intact, much to Jason's disappointment.

Colette sat on Sadie's bed, watching her pack. "I hate this," Colette said. "I'm not sure I can deal."

"I know what you mean." Sadie sat on the bed next to her. "But it won't be forever."

"Still, just the fact that you're all leaving, so fast." Colette swept a rogue tear from her cheek.

"I won't let it go on too long," Sadie said. "I can't. Telling myself I only have to be gone a short time, just long enough to do whatever I need to do to stop Devine is the only way I'm holding it together right now."

"I hope you kick his ass so hard it blows gas out his earholes." Colette crossed her arms.

Sadie did a double-take. "Ha!" She half-laughed. "I hope so, too."

"And soon," Colette said.

"Absolutely."

Colette paused a moment. "What do I tell Nessa?"

Sadie sighed. "I guess I'm going with the soap opera story."

"About your mom being found in the woods with amnesia?"

"Close," Sadie said. "I'll write a note for you to give her, telling her a woman with amnesia, who might be my mom, has been found in . . ." Sadie thought for a moment. "Let's say New York, and I've had to rush to her side to see if it's her."

"And then what?" Colette asked. "She'll text you. She'll want to call you."

"And I won't be able to answer her." Sadie sighed. "I'm hoping she'll be so preoccupied with Kyle she won't miss me that much."

"That might work for a little while," Colette said.

"Maybe it will be long enough that we'll be at a point where we can use . . . what are they called . . . burner phones to contact all of you."

"And she'll want to know why you've changed your phone number," Colette said. "She's not stupid."

Sadie threw up her hands. "I know. It's not a perfect plan, but it's the best one I can come up with right now."

"Yeah, sorry." Colette shook her head. "I'm not thinking clearly. It's a good enough plan, and I'll do what I can to keep her focused on something besides you. Perhaps it will help me keep my mind off you, too. And Brandon and Connor."

Sadie hugged Colette hard. "This is all so sucky."

"Or . . ." Colette pulled back and patted her legs. "This is all fantastic. We need to look at the upside. You were victorious in your battle with Garrison Devine, an achievement you were questioning not too long ago. And you have amazing powers. And you have elite forces from the League backing you up. And you have all of us here cheering you on. And you are going to kick his ass so hard it blows gas out of his earholes." Colette crossed her arms. "All positive and successful and fantastic things. Right?"

"Right," Sadie said. "Thinking positive."

Colette hugged her again and hung out with Sadie for a little while longer, then excused herself when signs of sleep overwhelmed her.

Sadie finished packing, including a framed picture of her and Mamo, another of her with Finn and Shay, one with Jason, and another one of Colette, Lena, and Nessa. Sadie wrapped her broken necklace and bracelet in one of Mamo's scarves and tucked them in her bag. She left the note to Nessa on her desk next to a note for Lena, another one for Colette, and a note for Jason.

She switched off her light and went to sleep for the last time in Salton.

TWENTY-SIX
Changes

It was still dark when Jason got up to go with Brandon to Sadie's house so he could say goodbye, but Brandon was already gone. He rushed to Sadie's and found Grandma Lena in the kitchen with Colette. Grandma Lena was filling the coffeemaker with water. Colette sat at the table, her legs folded in front of her, and her toes hanging off the edge of the seat.

"They're already gone?" Jason asked.

Grandma Lena nodded. "I guess they got an earlier start on things."

"She left you this." Colette slid a note across the table.

Jason sat and opened it.

Hey, Jason —

So, this sucks, doesn't it? I mean, we haven't known each other that long, but it feels like we've been friends forever and I'm not sure how I'll manage without seeing you every day, or at least knowing you're not too far away. But I guess I'll figure that out.

"I'm always here if you need me," Jason thought to himself.

I know you're always there if I need you. And knowing that does make this a tiny bit easier. Not easy. No way is this easy. But easier.

I won't get too sappy because you don't like sappy, but thank you for everything. You are such a great friend, a best friend. And wow, we ~~made~~ make an amazing team, Sound Dog. :)

I'm always "here" (wherever that may be) for you, too. Hope to see you really, really soon.

> *Love,*
> *Sadie*

Jason reread the note three times, then folded it, put it back in its envelope, and tucked the envelope in his back pocket. "This sucks big time."

"Yeah, it does," Colette said.

Grandma Lena started the coffeemaker but didn't speak.

"What do we do now?" Jason asked.

"We go on," Grandma Lena said. "We think positive thoughts, assure ourselves they are safe, and we go on."

"Should we move out of Sadie's house and back to yours now that it's empty?" Colette asked.

"No," Grandma Lena said. "I'd like us to be here where we can take care of the beehives and keep Sadie's home ready and welcoming when she's able to return."

"If she ever comes home," Jason said.

"She will." Grandma Lena took a deep breath. "When it's time, Sadie will come home to Salton."

❋ ❋ ❋

Monday slogged by without Sadie in school, the only highlight being how often Jason found himself surprised when he entered a space marked by destruction two days ago now appearing pristine and intact.

At the end of the day, he and Colette emptied the contents of Sadie's locker into a cardboard box.

"You should move over here, out of your locker and into this one," Jason said. "I mean, if you want to."

"Good idea." Colette shut the locker door. "I'll switch everything tomorrow."

"Cool." Jason put on his backpack and picked up the box. They headed toward the exit.

"You haven't changed your mind, have you?" Colette asked. "About visiting Derek in the hospital?"

"No changing my mind. I'm in."

Uncle Alexander waved to them from his truck in front of the school. Jason set the box of Sadie's stuff on one side of the back seat and he sat on the other. Colette rode up front.

"I'm glad you both agreed to come along," Uncle Alexander said as he pulled into the flow of traffic. "We have some interesting news for Derek, and given who else is meeting us there, I figured it would be good to have Colette along."

"Just Colette?" Jason asked.

"You, too," Uncle Alexander said. "Though you have to be nice. And supportive."

"He helped save Sadie," Jason said. "For that, I can be both nice and supportive." He paused. "As long as he's not a jerk."

Colette turned and huffed.

"Okay, okay." Jason held up his hands. "I'm nice and supportive no matter what."

A few minutes later, Uncle Alexander parked and the three of them walked into the hospital to find Sheriff Gunderson waiting with Ms. Bauer, the algebra teacher from Salton High.

"Thanks for coming, Colette," Sheriff Gunderson said. "I understand you're one of Derek's closer friends, and given the news we're about to deliver, we thought it would be nice for him to have at least one of his peers there to listen, maybe help him digest things."

Colette's brows furrowed. "Oh no, has something bad happened?"

"No, nothing like that," the sheriff said. "But it still might take some time for Derek to process." He gestured to the algebra teacher. "Ms. Bauer is here to help out as well."

"Okay . . ." Colette looked at Ms. Bauer, then Jason, then back at the sheriff.

"No point in belaboring things here," the sheriff said. "Let's go see Derek."

After asking Derek's permission, they all filed into his room.

Derek sat up and seemed to be a million times better than the last time Jason had seen him. He had a bandage on the back of his head but otherwise appeared uninjured.

"What's going on?" Derek asked.

"We're all sorry about your fall, Derek," the sheriff said. "It's a good thing Alexander, eh, Mr. Fallon, found you at the bottom of those boulders when he did."

A fall. So that's the story Uncle A gave.

Derek's eyes flicked to Uncle Alexander, then to Jason and Colette. "Yeah, it's really good."

"I have more news," the sheriff continued, "good news."

Derek waited.

"When the hospital entered your name into their system, some interesting information came to light." The sheriff removed his hat and scratched the top of his head. "It seems your dad set you up with a trust fund, one that is paying for health insurance for you, among other things. We learned your step-mom was listed as the executor of the trust fund, and it paid money to her every month for your care and well-being."

Colette inhaled a quick breath.

"Well, knowing what I do about your step-mother, information that I'm not at liberty to divulge here, we discovered evidence that your step-mother was skimming additional money, money she was not entitled to, from your trust fund." The sheriff nodded once. "She's been arrested and she won't be getting out of any charges this time."

Derek's mouth dropped open. "But . . . so what does that mean?"

"Well, it means several things." The sheriff continued. "First off, you still have plenty of money in your trust fund to cover basic living expenses and probably pay for college, if that's something you're considering. And second, you own your house and property free and clear."

Derek's eyes saucered.

"But as a minor, you can't live there alone. Not to mention the fact that work needs to be done to make that place livable again." The sheriff shook his head. "I was shocked to see how run down it's become since your dad passed on. I'm sorry you were living like that."

"I . . . I didn't . . ." Derek shrugged.

"Not a reflection on you," the sheriff said. "I just meant I'm sorry the woman your dad trusted to take care of you did not fulfill his wishes, and I'm sorry we didn't learn this earlier so we could have taken action. But that's neither here nor there. What matters now is making sure you're well taken care of going forward."

Derek mouthed the air like he was searching for a word.

"Do you know Ms. Bauer?" the sheriff asked.

"Yeah." Derek lifted two fingers off his blanket and waved. "Sure."

"She has something to say to you." The sheriff gestured for Ms. Bauer to go ahead.

"I've been talking to the sheriff about what's happening with you, and I bet this is all a lot to absorb," Ms. Bauer said.

Derek nodded.

"But you're a good student, Derek, one I've enjoyed having in class."

Surprise skipped through Jason. He'd seen Derek get sent to the principal's office more than once and assumed all teachers found him annoying.

"And we—my wife and I—understand you need a guardian, and a place to stay while the courts sort everything out," Ms. Bauer continued, "and we want to invite you to move in with us. You'll still have an attorney, and we'll stay in close contact with them, and with the sheriff, and whoever else you might need on your side." She glanced at Colette and Jason. "But we thought it would be nice to make sure you could stay in Salton and stay at Salton High."

"Uh . . . I . . ." Derek blinked hard and scanned everyone's faces. "I don't know." He looked at Colette.

"I think it's a wonderful idea," she said. "You're free of that awful woman, and you don't have to go into foster care. Seems like a win-win."

"What about my step-mom's husband?" Derek asked the sheriff.

"He has no legal claim on anything," the sheriff said. "Even if he reappears in Salton with Ash, they're both out of luck."

"So, that's it? They're all out of my life?"

"That's right." The sheriff put on his hat.

Derek fell back on his pillows, then popped back up and faced Ms. Bauer. "And I can really come and live with you? For real?"

"Yes," she said. "As soon as you're ready to leave the hospital, we have a room waiting for you."

"Okay," he said. "I mean, thanks. Uh, yeah, thanks."

Jason had never seen this side of Derek Goodman. He was being polite. He was almost smiling.

"Then it's settled. We'll put the paperwork in motion and take care of everything." Sheriff Gunderson squeezed Derek's shoulder. "You just focus on getting better, okay?"

"Yeah, okay." Derek turned his attention to Jason, Colette, and Uncle Alexander. "And thank you for everything. I mean . . . just thank you, all of you, for everything."

"You're welcome, Derek." Uncle Alexander stepped forward and shook Derek's hand. "You need anything else, you call us." He tipped his head toward Jason and Colette.

"I will," Derek said.

At that moment, Derek Goodman didn't seem so bad.

✳ ✳ ✳

One week to the day since Sadie's and Brandon's pre-dawn departure, and with zero news from them since they'd left, it was time to celebrate Kyle's sixteenth birthday. Grandma Lena and Colette joined them for the festivities along with Uncle Alexander, Nessa, and Poppy Johnson. Elly had already been transported by the League to connect with Sadie somewhere unknown.

Everyone gathered in the living room to watch Kyle open presents. Shay sat at his feet and eyed his every move hoping he'd unwrap something edible. Finn watched from the couch.

Kyle started with a card from Poppy and found a gift card for the barbecue food truck. "Sweet," he said, holding the card above his head. "I love that barbecue. Thanks."

"You're welcome," Poppy said. "The owner mentioned you were their number one customer during the grand opening."

"If I had a car," Kyle said, cocking his head toward Dad, "I would go buy us all barbecue right now."

"If you had your driver's license," Dad said, cocking his head back at Kyle, "I might let you borrow my car to go buy us all barbecue."

"I'll totally pass my test tomorrow." Kyle picked up a small package wrapped in blue and gold paper. "No problem."

"We'll see," Dad said.

Nessa pointed at the package. "That one's from me."

Kyle tore off the paper and opened the box to find another gift card for the barbecue truck. "No way. This is awesome." He gave Nessa a quick kiss on the cheek.

Jason felt his face flush.

"How did you know?" Kyle asked Nessa.

"You kind of haven't stopped talking about their food," she said. "Even now, we're talking about their food." She laughed.

Kyle opened presents from Uncle Alexander, Colette and Grandma Lena, then he opened a gift from Jason and Della. It was another gift card to the barbecue food truck.

"I wanted to get you a goat yoga class," Della said. "But Jason thought you'd like this better."

"Because, dude, you might be in love with that barbecue," Jason said. "Nessa should be worried."

She laughed and threw a wadded-up napkin at Jason.

"It's great barbecue," Kyle said.

"We know," said Jason, Nessa, and Colette at the same time.

Kyle saved the biggest gift for last. It was a large box, about three feet by three feet, wrapped in mismatched papers and stuck with mismatched bows. Kyle read the tag: "To Kyle, love Dad."

Dad leaned back and crossed his arms, a grin on his face.

Kyle ripped off the paper and popped the tape holding the box closed. Inside was another wrapped package. Kyle opened that box and found yet another wrapped package. He opened it, and another box, and another, and another one after that. Spent wrapping paper surrounded him in festive waves of color.

"How many packages are there?" Kyle asked as he tore open one more.

"Just keep going," Dad said, still smiling.

Finally, Kyle found a small, gold foil box, too tiny to hold another package. He removed the lid. A scroll of paper lay inside, tied with green ribbon. He uncurled the message and read it aloud: "Go look in the driveway."

Glee glommed onto Kyle's face and he leaped up. He ran to the front door, whooping as he went.

Dad stood and followed along with everyone else.

Kyle dashed outside and stopped hard at the edge of the driveway.

Jason hurried to stand next to him. The smile had dropped from Kyle's face.

"Here are the keys." Dad beamed and held a key fob in front of Kyle.

Kyle's hand raised and grasped onto the fob. "It's a . . . it's a . . ."

"It's a Prius," Dad said. "You said you wanted something reliable, with a solid history, and when Ms. Feinstein mentioned she was selling her Prius, I realized it was the perfect car for you."

"Wait." Kyle turned toward Dad. "This is a teacher's car?"

"*Was* a teacher's car, yes." Dad crossed his arms. "She provided all her maintenance records, and I verified she has taken excellent care of this car. It has a solid history."

"A Mustang, Dad," Kyle said. "I meant a solid history like a Mustang. And reliable because they've been around, like, forever."

Jason pressed his lips tight to suppress a laugh. Colette bumped his shoulder.

"A Mustang? I'm buying myself a Mustang before I buy you a Mustang," Dad said.

"But a Prius?" Kyle's posture sagged.

Dad held out his hand. "If you don't want it—"

"No, no." Kyle straightened and pulled the key fob close to his chest. "I want it. And I love it. It's awesome. I love my Prius."

"I'm glad to hear it because it came with a bumper sticker."

Jason followed Kyle around to the back of the car. An "I love my Prius" sticker decorated the bumper.

"This car is so you," Jason said. "I bet Nessa likes you even more now that you own a Prius."

Kyle punched Jason in the arm.

"I like him no matter what car he drives." Nessa rubbed Kyle's back, and he smiled.

"Thanks, Dad, for real." Kyle walked over and gave him a hug. "This is awesome."

"You're welcome. Should we take it out for a spin?" Before Kyle could answer, Dad's phone buzzed. He checked the screen. "Huh."

"What is it?" Jason asked.

Uncle Alexander's phone buzzed a second later. He stared at the screen, then looked at Jason's dad. "Should we take this seriously?"

"I think so," Dad said. "My father isn't one to joke about something like this."

"What is it?" Jason asked again.

Dad glanced up. "Your grandfather is moving back to the United States."

"GQ?" Kyle scrunched his brow. "I thought he never wanted to move back here."

"He's found a project that's interesting enough to motivate his return," Dad said.

"Whatever it is, it's cool he'll be living here," Jason said. "We can hang out with him, show him stuff to do in Salton. He could rent Grandma Lena's house." He turned her direction. "Right, Grandma Lena?"

"That could work," she said.

"He won't be living in Salton," Dad said. "He's been asked to open a North America headquarters of the League of Governors in Boulder, Colorado."

Jason put his hands in his pockets. The Lex coin lay cool to his touch. "Boulder's not that far. Especially compared to Europe. We can visit him."

"If we accept what he's proposing, he'll be closer than you think." Dad seemed to be reading the message on his phone again.

"What do you mean?" Jason asked.

"Your grandfather wants to talk to us about helping him run the new location," Dad said without looking up.

"Us as in . . ." Kyle waved his hand in front of Dad's face signaling him to keep talking.

"Me, your uncle," Dad said, "and Grandma Lena."

Grandma Lena shrugged but said nothing. Jason suspected she was in the loop before Dad and Uncle Alexander.

"Would you work remotely, from Salton?" Poppy asked.

"Based on GQ's note," Uncle Alexander said, "our accepting any of the positions would require a relocation."

"Oh, I see," she said.

Colette grabbed onto Jason's arm.

"But, hey," Dad said clicking off the screen of his phone. "It's just a conversation. I doubt the League could offer enough of a deal to attract my interest and make it worth the hassle of moving again."

"I agree," Uncle Alexander said. "It's unlikely to happen."

Grandma Lena smiled and kept her thoughts to herself.

❄ ❄ ❄

That evening, Jason scrolled through websites not really looking for anything, but not really wanting to go to bed either. After Dad's mention earlier in the day of a possible new job and a move to Boulder, Jason's brain wouldn't turn off.

What about Colette? Would she stay with Grandma Lena?

What if Grandma Lena moved?

What about starting at a new school, again? That would suck.

But Jason would be back in Colorado.

And Boulder was cool.

And being near a League headquarters could be cool.

But only if Uncle Alexander moved, too.

And Grandma Lena.

But what about Colette?

And what about Sadie? What if she came home and all of us were gone?

An email dinged into Jason's inbox. The subject line read: "Do you read GQ?"

Jason hovered his mouse over the trashcan to delete the note but a thought poked in his mind. It was a weird coincidence to get an email about reading "GQ" on the same day Dad receives a message from Grandpa Quentin, who liked to be called "GQ," wasn't it?

Jason opened the email.

Hi!

CharmingOne invites you to play Hawk's Quest. Prizes include a trip to Mexico, California, and Australia. But winning won't be easy. You'll be rattled before the game ends. Click the link to play, if you have the heart.

There was no signature, and Jason knew unknown links could mean bad stuff happening to his computer. But then it hit him: charming, Mexico, California, Australia, even the rattle and the heart. These were all things related to Sadie's charm bracelet.

And Hawk's Quest had to be a reference to her necklace, her hawk's eye pendant, didn't it? The message was from Sadie. It had to be.

His heartbeat raced. Jason clicked the link. A second later his screen faded to black.

No, no, no. Please don't be malware. Please don't be malware.

He held his breath.

A few seconds later, a green cursor flashed on the black screen. The cursor moved right. Green characters appeared in its wake: "Jason?"

"Yes," he typed.

"Hi! It's S."

Jason typed as fast as he could. "OMG how are you?"

"Safe. All good. Can't chat long. Too dangerous."

"Okay," Jason replied. "We miss you. Weird without you both here. Connor, too."

"I know how you feel," Sadie wrote. "Hold on. B wants to type."

"Dude—my parents are freaking spies," Brandon said. "Cannot wait to see you again and tell you everything. They're actually kind of cool."

"Sounds like it," Jason said. "Can't wait for stories."

"Soon. Maybe. Or not. We'll keep trying."

"The sooner the better," Jason typed.

"Turning keyboard back over to S."

There was a brief pause.

"S again. Have to sign off. But wanted to say Boulder might be a good idea."

"How did you know?" Jason asked.

"Spies." :)

"Right," Jason said. "Okay. Good to know. Didn't want to bail and have you wonder where we were."

"We're in loop," she said. "Always know where you are."

Comfort blanketed Jason. "Nice."

"Love you all. Kiss the dogs. Will be in touch when we can. Bye."

The green cursor blinked out and Jason's screen returned.

He shut off his computer, climbed into bed next to Shay and kissed her on top of the head. "What do you think about moving to Boulder?"

She opened one eye, winked at Jason, then blew her breath out through her jowls and went back to sleep.

"I like the way you think, Shay."

THE END

Reviews are greatly appreciated and they help other readers discover books they would enjoy. It would mean the world to Wendy if you took a minute to write a review of *The Forge of Bonds*.

ACKNOWLEDGEMENTS

Sitting alone at a computer and writing a story is easy. Writing a *good* story, however, is hard. And it can't be done alone, at least not by me. There are many people who contribute to my writing, both directly and indirectly, and I adore each and every one of them.

My first thank you must go to those who are most overworked by me — my critique group:

- Terri Spesock—she is the master of the correct use of lay / laid / lie (a superpower, if you ask me), and she improves my vocabulary
- Judy Logan—she knows the perfect balance of cheerleading mixed with critiquing
- Kim Byrne—she's a guru for me in both writing and living life in the best way
- And Marco's Coal-Fired Pizza who has hosted us since we formed our band of merry wordsmiths in late 2012. Marco's, we'll follow you and your pizza through as many name changes as it takes (though we're glad you're back to "Marco's.") :)

Thank you to friend, fellow author, and firefighter, Chuck Harrelson, who helped with firefighting-related facts in this novel. If something isn't right in my detail, it's my fault. Chuck knows his stuff and generously let me pester him for his knowledge.

Kudos and praise to this team of experts whose skills and services I treasure:

- Developmental editor, the Noveldoctor, Steve Parolini
- Interior designer, Novelninjutsu, Ali Cross
- Cover designer at Novak Illustration, Steven Novak
- Copy editor, Susan Brooks
- Voice talent and narrator, Brian Callanan
- Advance readers near and far — you keep me honest, focused, and authentic in bringing the story out of my head and onto the page

To my family and friends who understand when I scurry into my writing cave for weeks on end, hardly seen or heard from until an objective is achieved—thank you. Thank you for supporting me, for not pressuring me, for letting me feed this passion that both drains me and fills me up.

A big shout out to Rocky Mountain Fiction Writers. I love the organization, I love the people in the organization, and I love how we believe in each other. A rising tide lifts all boats.

Another shout out to Pikes Peak Writers and the first writing conference I ever attended. PPW is a first-rate group of first-rate people I'd see more if geography allowed.

Thank you to Shea the wonder dog, the mighty dog, the pup who tries to be brave even when she's a bit unnerved. Shea sticks by my side whether I'm in my writing cave, binge-watching a favorite show, or catching some Zs. You make me smile every day, probably every hour. You bring joy, joy, and more joy.

And most of all, thank you to the readers of my stories — it thrills me that you're here! I love telling these stories, but knowing there are readers who appreciate what I'm creating brings me happiness I can't really describe. You rock, you're awesome, you are the BEST.

ABOUT THE AUTHOR

International bestselling author **Wendy Terrien** received her first library card at age two, and a few years later started writing her own stories.

Her debut novel, *The Rampart Guards* (February 2016), earned a Kirkus starred review and was named to Kirkus Reviews' Best Books of 2016. Next in her series are Jason's book two – *The League of Governors* (August 2017), and Sadie's book two – *The Clan Calling* (August 2017), both award winners. Book three in the series (and the fourth physical book) is *The Forge of Bonds* (February 2020).

Wendy graduated from the University of Utah (go Utes!) and relocated to Colorado where she completed her MBA at the University of Denver. She focused her marketing expertise on the financial and technology industries until a career coach stepped in and reminded Wendy of her passion for writing. Inspired, Wendy leaped and began attending writers' conferences, workshops, and retreats, and the storytelling hasn't stopped since.

She is on the board of Rocky Mountain Fiction Writers, and is a member of Pikes Peak Writers, the Colorado Authors' League, and the Author's Guild.

Wendy lives in the Denver area with her husband, Kevin, and their dog, Shea. She's team dark chocolate, a fan of technology, and believes every dose of nature nurtures the soul. Wendy is also committed to promoting pet adoption from rescues or shelters. If you're in Colorado, you may even spot her "Adopt a Shelter Pet" license plates.

Twitter: twitter.com/wendyterrien
Facebook: facebook.com/wendyterrien
Instagram: Instagram.com/wendyterrien

CPSIA information can be obtained
at www.ICGtesting.com
Printed in the USA
LVHW011636290121
677805LV00001BA/41

9 780998 336954